TIES THAT BIND

JUDITH PELLA
TRACIE PETERSON

THORNDIKE PRESS

An imprint of Thomson Gale, a part of The Thomson Corporation

THOMSON

GALE

Detroit • New York • San Francisco • New Haven, Conn. • Waterville, Maine • London

THOMSON

™

GALE

LIBRARY OF CONGRESS CATALOGING-IN-PUBLICATION DATA

Pella, Judith.
    Ties that bind / by Judith Pella and Tracie Peterson. — Large print ed.
      p. cm. — (Ribbons west series ; 3) (Thorndike Press large print Christian historical fiction)
    ISBN 0-7862-8916-3 (hardcover : alk. paper) 1. Women journalists — Fiction. 2. Railroad stories. 3. Large type books. I. Peterson, Tracie. II. Title.
PS3566.E415T54 2006
813'.54—dc22
                                       2006024972

U.S. Hardcover:
ISBN 13: 978-0-7862-8916-5
ISBN 10: 0-7862-8916-3

Published in 2006 by arrangement with Bethany House Publishers.

Printed in the United States of America on permanent paper
10 9 8 7 6 5 4 3 2 1

CONTENTS

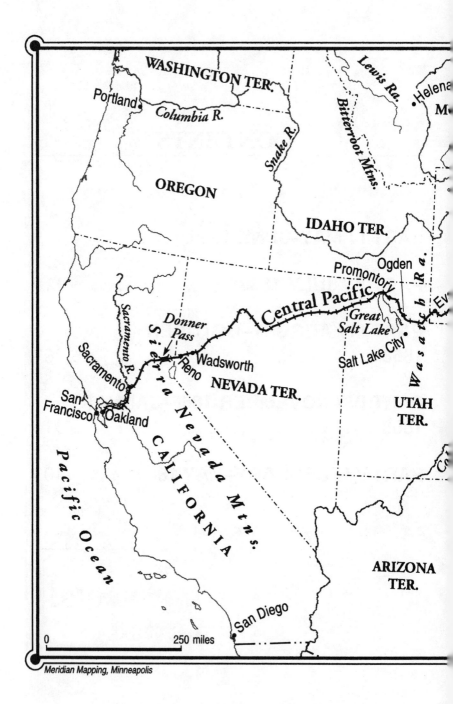

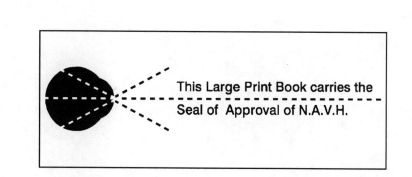

This Large Print Book carries the
Seal of Approval of N.A.V.H.

TIES THAT BIND

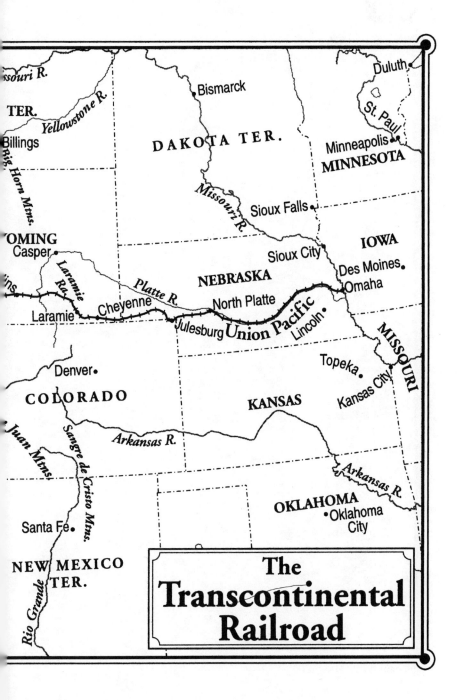

The
**Transcontinental
Railroad**

■ ■ ■ ■

PART I
MAY–JUNE 1868

■ ■ ■ ■

ONE

SACRAMENTO

Jordana Baldwin stared at the letter in her hand. The posted date alone left her feeling rather despondent. Three years had passed since she'd come west to California, and in those three years she had nearly perished from boredom. Now, as if rising like a ghostly specter from the pages of her mother's newsy letter, Jordana's former life seemed to be slowly slipping away.

Her baby sister was in love, their mother wrote. The young man in question was the youngest son of a prominent stockbroker there in New York, and while Amelia was nearly fifteen years old, Jordana felt it impossible to consider that time had moved so quickly.

Feeling the need to be about something else, Jordana quickly scanned the rest of the letter, with a promise to herself to read it more carefully later. The family appeared to be doing well and fine. She marveled that

11

her mother loved New York City enough to remain there. The Civil War had driven the family north from their Baltimore home, but now that the conflict was over and the states were once again united, Jordana had assumed James and Carolina Baldwin would take their remaining family and return home. But not only had her mother loved New York, her father found he had a real flair for the business deals born and bred in this rapidly growing city. Her mother had once written that while they had traveled abroad and seen a great deal of the world, there appeared no more exciting a town than New York City.

It seemed strange that Jordana couldn't remember it with such enthusiasm. Had it really been only six years since she herself was enrolled in the Deighton School for Young Women, suffering the boredom of the city her mother now called the most exciting in the world?

"Perhaps I just don't fit in anywhere," Jordana muttered and folded the letter. Maybe she would feel more like reading it later. She went to her dresser and pulled out the top drawer. There she absentmindedly placed the letter, then glanced up to catch her reflection in the mirror.

At twenty-two, Jordana had grown into a

handsome woman. She knew this to be the case because she was told it quite often. As for herself, she felt her face was a little too thin, her cheekbones a little too high, and her eyes a little too unusual. Surrounded by dark, sooty lashes, her brown eyes reflected tiny amber specks that were instantly noticeable. The glints of gold had always been there, but it seemed as she'd grown older, they were somehow more pronounced. Charlie Crocker, a good friend of the family and the man in charge of moving forward the actual building of the Central Pacific Railroad, said that it looked as if her eyes had been sprinkled with the same coveted gold dust that robbed his railroad of a proper labor force. Even now the memory made Jordana smile. Not so much for the compliment Charlie had given her, but for the memory of Charlie himself. He was a fun-loving but hardworking soul, who was completely devoted to his family and the railroad. And somewhere along the way, he had also devoted himself to Jordana's extended family.

"Charlie would think me a ninny for brooding," Jordana told herself in hopes of bolstering her spirits. "No one is keeping me here."

And perhaps that was what bothered her

the most. Nothing was keeping her in Sacramento. Nothing but routine, and that certainly wasn't enough to merit continuing in the feelings she had grown weary of courting.

"I need a change," she told her reflection. "And I need one soon."

She thought of the three, almost four, years since she'd left the Nebraska plains to come west with her brother Brenton. They came to be with their sister Victoria and her husband, Kiernan O'Connor, and they came to bring Kiernan's sister Caitlan. Now Caitlan and Brenton were married, quite happily, and Brenton busied himself with the photography business he loved. Sometimes Jordana helped him, but for the most part, Caitlan assisted Brenton, and she seemed for all purposes to love photography as much as her husband did. That left Jordana to help Victoria around the house and with the laundry service her sister had helped to start some years ago. Now that money was no longer a real worry for Victoria and Kiernan, however, Kiernan had insisted Victoria give the laboring tasks of washerwoman over to hirelings. At first Victoria had protested and the words had grown quite heated and angry between the two. But then, after a time, Victoria had suddenly changed. It seemed she realized her husband's suggestion would afford her a way to help some of the less fortunate in their community. One thing led to another, and soon Victoria found herself in charge of a force of twenty workers whose laundry services were being used by people all over the Sacramento community. They had even moved the facility to a storefront downtown.

But in spite of all of this, Jordana knew a growing restlessness inside her that would not be quenched. She had written copious, lengthy letters home — letters describing her exploits upon the plains and the wonder at seeing the territories beyond the Mississippi. She had shared these thoughts primarily with her mother, because she knew Carolina had always longed to explore the world and learn all that could be learned. But she also shared these thoughts because she was afraid of losing them in a wash of indifference and monotony.

Surprisingly, Jordana found this creative outlet led her to something infinitely more satisfying. Her father had shared one of her long letters with a friend who just happened to be an editor at the *New York Tribune.* The man instantly latched on to the missive, pleading for the right to reprint it in his newspaper. He ranted and raved about the popularity of such stories, how the public was hungry for adventure and knowledge of the West. And so the column of J. Baldwin was born, and Jordana found herself writing a regular series of stories about the American frontier. Unfortunately, her memories were fading, and more and more she relied on stories from her good friend Captain Rich O'Brian, a cavalry officer now stationed in Nebraska.

Thinking of Rich brought a second smile. He had been so good to continue their correspondence. Jordana eagerly awaited each of his letters, always relishing his tales of army life, needing to feel herself drawn into what she could not otherwise participate in.

"This is ridiculous," she whispered, the smile fading. "Nothing is keeping me here. I don't have to stay." She frowned, wondering why she had said the words aloud. Was she trying to convince herself that they were true?

"Jordana? Are you in there?" her sister Victoria called.

Jordana sighed and opened the bedroom door with a deliberate slowness that was uncharacteristic. "I'm here."

"You didn't come down for breakfast," Victoria spoke, her dark-eyed gaze quickly taking in Jordana's petite frame. "You aren't

16

sick, are you?"

"In a sense I think I am," Jordana admitted. "I'm sick of living in one spot. I'm sick of life passing me by with nothing ever happening to me, and I'm sick of myself."

Victoria smiled. "Sounds to me like you need a change of pace."

Jordana nodded. "I was thinking much the same thing. I hope you understand that it has nothing to do with you or Kiernan. You've both been so good to let me live with you these last few years. It seems silly to talk of being bored with my life when Kiernan has been gracious enough to take me out on the Central Pacific's line so I could write about it. It's even more senseless when I think of all the places I've gone with Brenton and Caitlan as they've photographed various developments in the railroad and the communities that have sprung up as a result." She moved across the room and plopped down on her bed, pale pink muslin swirling around her feet as her skirt ballooned out softly.

"I'm twenty-two years old," she said rather mournfully.

Victoria came to sit beside her. "I've known for some time that you would leave us. I've even mentioned it to Brenton in order to prepare him for such a plan."

17

Jordana looked at her older sister in surprise. "You did? But how could you know? You're so content to live here, to keep house and busy yourself in working with the laundry and the Chinese. How could you understand so well what I'm feeling when we're nothing alike?"

Victoria reached out and took hold of Jordana's hand. "We may not be alike, but you are the very image of our mother. I remember quite well her love of travel and the restlessness that seemed to haunt her when she stayed in one place too long. Why, as much as she loves the house she now lives in, she wrote me not long ago of her desire to journey south and spend time in Baltimore and Washington."

"It's the wanderlust we inherited from our grandfather Joseph," Jordana answered, then added, "At least, that's what Mother calls it."

Victoria nodded. "I only ask that you think through carefully what you will do. Have a plan and let people know something of it. Be accountable to someone for the sake of safety, if nothing else. I know you long to venture out into the wilds of the frontier, but it might be wise to assemble a force of traveling companions to accompany you."

"But that's part of the problem," Jordana protested. "I don't want to be tied down to a group of people, especially strangers, who will tell me once again what convention says I must and must not do. I want the freedom to move about on my own. I have my own money now that I've passed twenty-one, and Father and Mother are both quite understanding of my needs. They don't always approve of my plans, but they recognize the need." She paused and studied Victoria. Her sister was a great beauty with ebony hair and eyes that seemed nearly as dark. She was the kind of woman that men, and even women, noticed, but beyond her physical beauty there was a generosity of spirit and a tenderness of heart that put Jordana quite at ease.

"You understand that need too," Jordana continued. "I can see it in your expression and in the fact that you would work to prepare our brother, who no doubt will be the voice of opposition."

"I think he and Kiernan will both worry and fret about the idea of your going off on your own. That's why I suggested a traveling companion. Someone who could act as a sort of protector." Victoria paused, growing thoughtful. "What about someone like that captain you write to all the time? You said he had plans to get out of the army. In fact, if I remember correctly, he should already be mustered out."

"You think it would be more acceptable for me, as a single woman, to travel through the wilderness with Rich O'Brian rather than alone? Won't people talk about the inappropriateness of that?"

Victoria laughed. "Won't they talk anyway? I do not question your virtue or your motives, Jordana. I know you well enough to know that you would not have bothered to correspond for so many years with this man had he not shown clear signs of being a proper gentleman. Still, if it really bothers you, maybe you could find a lady or two who would also like to accompany you. Maybe you could hire a maid as a traveling companion."

"You know how poorly I get along with other women. I'm always too outspoken or too outrageous in my thinking. I mention my thoughts on matters of politics and find myself scorned for worrying my pretty head over such matters. Remember the scene at the Hopkins' house when we were all so formally assembled? All I said was that gerrymandering was only going to lead us into another civil war, and you would have thought I'd suggested we all run naked in the streets."

Victoria giggled. "No one had any idea what the word meant, much less want to hear that there was any possibility of further war. Most of the women out here find it rather comforting to be removed from the rest of the United States. And while the idea of the transcontinental railroad reaching completion suggests profit for every state in the union, some would just as soon see the separation continue."

"They're all simpletons!" Jordana declared.

Victoria shook her head and gave Jordana's hand a squeeze. "It doesn't make them simpletons to be content in their lives, any more than it makes you wanton and crazed to desire the right to wander at will across the territories. Don't condemn what another sees as perfection, just because it doesn't fit your ideals. You want that respect from them, so be the first to give it when considering their position."

With a sigh, Jordana knew her sister was right. She had a short temper when it came to realizing her goals were disregarded by so many. "I'm just mean-spirited."

"No, you're not," Victoria reassured. "You're young and you have a heart for adventure. You have financial backing, which not many can boast, and you are intelligent and skilled at learning new things. You are the perfect candidate for the life you desire. I'm just asking you to keep in touch — to help those of us who are not quite so brave to keep from fretting about your well-being."

"Not quite so brave?" Jordana said with a hint of amusement. "You came to this place when it could hardly boast one woman to every hundred men. You traipsed about from mining camp to mining camp, faithfully remaining at your husband's side even when it cost you your health. Please don't imply to me that you are not just as brave, for I will not believe it."

Victoria released her sister's hand and stood. With a knowing glance, she replied, "Our bravery is perhaps one of those things best judged by others. In honesty, I did what I had to do, not because I was brave, but rather because I was committed to the man I loved."

"Well, perhaps the motives were different, but the accomplishment was the same nevertheless," Jordana said. She smiled at her sister and stood to hug her. "I will consider all that you've said. Maybe I'll even write to Rich and see what he thinks, although I'm sure he would probably think it a nuisance to follow me about. He surely has his own goals and aspirations."

"Perhaps," Victoria answered, "but maybe they could somehow be molded to include your plans. At least for a short time."

Jordana considered the matter and realized that of all the people she knew, the idea of having Rich for company was one that actually seemed appealing. Rich knew where to draw the line and how to keep to his place of being nothing more than a friend to Jordana. He didn't write to her with flowery words of love and adoration; instead he told her about his horse named Faithful and of the men he commanded. He wrote her line after line about Indian attacks and other conflicts. Maybe Victoria was right. Maybe Rich could somehow be persuaded to consider coming under her hire. People would talk, but then again, they would no matter what path she chose. God knew her heart — surely that would be enough to concern herself with.

"Thank you for understanding," Jordana said softly to her sister. "It seems I've underestimated your wisdom."

Victoria moved to the door, then glanced over her shoulder. "God has great things planned for you, Jordana. I just know it."

With that she opened the door and quietly

disappeared down the hall. Jordana stared after her for a moment, then muttered, "Well, if He does, I sure wish He'd clue me in on the plan."

TWO

"Caitlan!" Brenton called out to his wife. "Come quick, I have news!"

It wasn't often that Caitlan's husband entered the house bellowing her name. Brenton Baldwin was normally a quiet, sedate man. In a world where men most generally seemed to be given over to yips and yells, no matter the occasion, Brenton maintained himself in a rather reserved manner. This hadn't been the only thing to attract Caitlan to her husband, but it was one of the reasons she found him unique. Most of the men she had known growing up had been hulking, brawny Irishmen with easily ignited tempers and opinions on every subject. She had despaired of ever finding a soul mate, a man who could really reach inside to see the quickly kindled passion of her heart. But then she had come to America, and Brenton and his sister Jordana had met her at the dock, and instantly she had known, here was a man to love.

"Now, with yarself hollerin' like a fishmonger, I can only be imaginin' ya've got good news." She hurried from the kitchen, wiping the dishwater from her hands as she went.

Her husband had inherited money shortly before their marriage, but both he and Caitlan preferred a simple, unspoiled life. Other women of means might hire their dishes washed, and that was fine by Caitlan, but she'd rather be responsible for her own things. They also lived in a modest two-story home not far from her brother and sister-in-law.

"I do have good news," Brenton declared. "The very best. Charlie has hired me to photograph a stretch of the Central Pacific. I might even be hired on permanently to document the route as it continues."

"I'm not surprised." Caitlan put her hands to her hips. "Ya've been naggin' the man night and day." She grinned at her husband and reached up to touch his handsome face. " 'Tis a good thing yar a persistent man, Mr. Baldwin."

"Otherwise I wouldn't have managed to marry you, Mrs. Baldwin," he said, covering her hand with his own. "You are a priceless gem, my love. I can't imagine my successes meaning anything without you."

Caitlan felt her cheeks grow hot at the compliment. How this man could stir her blood. When he lowered his lips to kiss her, Caitlan melted against him and sighed.

"So how shall we celebrate?" Brenton murmured as he ended the kiss.

"I'm sure ya'll be thinkin' up something," Caitlan replied, not at all in a hurry to pull away from her husband's embrace.

"Why don't you go upstairs and put on that lovely green gown you wore to church on Sunday? Do up your hair and I'll take you to supper. We shall make a night of it, in fact," Brenton told her. "I shall show you off to everyone. We'll dine and then go to the presentation being given at the church. I believe there is a new organ master performing Handel."

Caitlan sighed and smiled. "I'll try not to keep ya waitin'."

She hurried upstairs, portraying an enthusiasm she didn't feel. She would do this to please him, but she would have been just as happy to remain at home for the evening. She felt out of place in society circles, and while she tried hard to fit in by watching the other women and mimicking their actions of grace and elegance, Caitlan could not shed the heritage that so thoroughly followed her. Not that she wanted to. She was a poor Irishman's daughter. There was no sin in that, although some would say otherwise.

She'd caught the glances of women who obviously held themselves as better than Caitlan. She'd spoken with them at church in the briefest greetings, passing their scrutiny in murmured replies and veiled looks of disapproval. Her husband was a Baldwin. A family of great importance and influence. Her mother-in-law was an Adams. An even greater family of influence. And now she herself bore the title of Mrs. Brenton Baldwin, and with it came a heavy mantle of responsibility. She was expected to be seen and to conduct herself in a proper manner. But not just this, it was a matter of what "they," the women of proper society, considered acceptable.

She'd once spoken to Kiernan about it, but he wasn't much help. He had experienced much the same, but nevertheless had no solutions except for her to always remember that her husband thought her a woman of worth. That did not lessen the sting of rejection from the wives of men with whom Brenton so easily rubbed shoulders. Men seemed to be far more accepting in social matters. Men might traipse about in

28

muddy boots drinking out of tin cups in the finest of homes were it not for women declaring that such things were barbaric and uncivilized. Women were the ones to set the tone of civility. Women put finery on tables, flowers in vases, and exquisite carpets on the floors. Women took houses and made them homes, offering feminine influence over all that they touched. Even their men.

Women of society knew the proper way to set a table and the appropriate discussions to be allowed in their parlors. These grande dames of etiquette could also sight a fraud a mile away. They knew when a young lady had not been born to such graces. And Caitlan had definitely not been born to anything even remotely related to grace.

She sighed and untied the strings to her apron. She would be tolerated because of who Brenton was. But she would never be quite good enough to be accepted into any inner circle of society. Should Brenton die tomorrow, God forbid, she would be nothing more than a disgusting Irish widow — albeit a rich one.

Shedding her clothes, she sat down at her vanity and unwound the braided coil of cinnamon-colored hair. With long, determined strokes of her hairbrush she tried to work out her worries and frustrations. She didn't want Brenton to be unhappy, and if she showed the slightest bit of displeasure, she knew he would immediately sense it. He was so good about such things, and while it served him proudly to be so sensitive to the needs of others, it also served her poorly. Caitlan never felt she could quite be honest with him about some of her feelings. She loved him so fiercely that it nearly took her breath away. How could she willingly make him unhappy or fretful?

Brenton whistled and scanned the newspaper as he waited for Caitlan to return. Life in the West had been grand and glorious for him. Oh, there had been those moments when he had been dealt some rather harsh blows, but overall, he had become a very contented man. He could boast a beautiful wife, money in the bank, and a profession of honor and interest. He felt a strong bond of kinship with his family, and he knew the peace of God in his soul. What more could a man ask?

Children would be nice, he mused. They would no doubt come in time. Of course, his sister Victoria had not yet managed to bear children. He knew this to be a deeply felt heartache for his sister. She had a great deal of love to give, and he had seen her gentleness while dealing with other women's children. She would make a good mother, yet she had no sign of that becoming a reality. Adoption had been discussed more than once, and both had agreed that after Kiernan finished his work with the transcontinental railroad and established himself with a job of permanency there in Sacramento, they would adopt several children.

Brenton knew Victoria wished it might come sooner. The transcontinental railroad wasn't planned to be finished for several years, maybe even as much as another decade. By then Victoria would be forty years old or older. The prime of her youth would be past, and most of her friends would be looking to their children's weddings and grandchildren's births.

He felt a deep, abiding sorrow for Victoria. Sometimes he wished he could turn off his feelings. Like at times when Caitlan felt unwelcome or incapable of dealing with the refined women of Sacramento's better homes. He knew she felt awkward. He could see in her eyes whenever they arrived for a dinner or party that Caitlan felt her place was around back with the rest of the servants.

If only he could keep her from her self-destructive thoughts. If only he could convince her that the time would soon be upon them that such issues were unimportant. But in truth, he knew the status of a person's birth would probably always matter in one way or another.

"Yar lookin' mighty deep in thought, Mr. Baldwin," Caitlan said as she reached the last step. "Surely the news isn't all bad."

Brenton looked up and felt robbed of breath. How beautiful she was!

Caitlan smiled in that soft, sweet way he had come to love. "So do I meet with yar approval?"

"Without a doubt, my sweet wife. You are the loveliest woman in the city, and I shall be proud to show you off." He moved forward, discarding the newspaper. Reaching out, he grasped hold of her hand. "Not that I wouldn't be proud of you if you were dressed in nothing but rags."

He felt her relax a bit, sensed that she understood his sincerity. Somehow, someway, he hoped to find a place for them where she would understand the role of importance she had in his life.

Loud banging on the front door startled both Baldwins. Brenton's brow immediately furrowed and Caitlan's eyes widened. "Whatever could that be about?" She stared uneasily at her husband.

"I don't know." That banging could hardly indicate someone upon a social call. He opened the door to find a gangly youth of fifteen or sixteen. "Mr. Baldwin, sir. You've got to come quick! Your picture-takin' shop is on fire!"

THREE

By the time Brenton arrived, there was nothing to be done but to watch his shop burn. A large crowd had gathered, and the spirit of revelry among them was a sickening contrast to the destructive tongues of flame consuming Brenton's life. Some of those gathered were talking and pointing, appearing to size up the situation in regard to other nearby businesses. But still others stood by chatting with neighbors and trying to keep a sudden abundance of children from getting too close to the blaze.

The fire brigade had come to try to contain the fire, and in fact seemed to be doing a decent job, but there was no hope for Baldwin Photography. The chemicals necessary for the business of taking and developing pictures had obviously allowed the place to go up rather quickly. Someone in the crowd mentioned it being good that Brenton's shop and the three in the same building sat apart from an adjacent massive block-long stretch of stores. Otherwise, all of Sacramento might go ablaze. When someone finally recognized him as the owner of one of the burning stores, he was inundated with a mixture of sympathetic comments.

"Quite a bit of bad luck there, Baldwin."

"Saw it burnin' from clean across the park."

"Never saw anything go up so fast in my life."

Brenton watched the flames engulf the businesses, scarcely hearing the voices. Stunned by the scene, he thought of all the photographs he'd taken and put on display within the studio. He'd mounted his pictures with a great deal of pride, knowing they were good, feeling confident they would draw new business. There were pictures of vast prairies and the people who struggled to farm them. Pictures of the snow-capped Rockies, majestic and regal in the fading light of sunset. And, of course, a variety of portraits to prove his mettle where photographing people was concerned. And now . . . they were gone. With exception to the photographs he had on the walls of his home, it was all gone. The pictures, the camera, the chemicals, the glass plates. Gone.

"Caitlan came and told us," his brother-in-law said softly, coming up next to him. " 'Tis a sorry day for us all."

Brenton looked at Kiernan O'Connor and shook his head. "I can't believe it. I'm watching it happen, but I still can't believe it."

Kiernan laid a hand on Brenton's shoulder. "Do they know what happened? What caused the fire?"

"If they do, no one is telling me," Brenton replied.

"And for sure, they may not be knowin'," Kiernan said, his tone sympathetic. "Why don't ya come on back to the house? Caitlan's waitin' there to hear the news, as are yar sisters."

Brenton shook his head. "How can I tell them that my entire world has just gone up in flames?"

" 'Tis scarcely yar whole world, man. Ya still have yar health and yar wife. This could be yar home yar watchin' burn, with yar loved ones still inside."

"Don't you understand?" Brenton stared in disbelief at Kiernan. "I realize that, but my pictures are — were an important part of me. They *were* me." He lowered his head and stared at the rivulets of water now draining away from the burning building and eddying around his feet. The fire brigade had done their job. They'd saved the rest of Sacramento from destruction. Pity, Brenton thought, that they couldn't save me from such a fate as well.

Deep in the grip of his melancholy thoughts, he turned to his brother-in-law. "Go home, Kiernan. I'm going for a walk. Tell Caitlan to stay with you tonight because I don't know when I'll be home."

"Brenton —"

"I mean it, Kiernan. I just need to be alone."

Kiernan watched Brenton leave the scene in defeat. His usually ramrod-straight back was now stooped over in grief. He would not suffer this loss easily.

Deciding to let the younger man go his own way, Kiernan hurried back home to let the women know what had happened. No doubt they would all be beside themselves in wonder and worry. That is, if they were even still remaining at the house as he had instructed them to do. Each of the women alone were quite industrious and opinionated, but when you put all three together — well, it was just best to stand back and clear the road. They had a way about them that would brook no nonsense when their minds were made up.

And sure enough. He no sooner rounded the corner than he caught sight of the ladies making their way down the cobblestone walkway.

"Hold up now, ladies," he called. "Yar not gonna be goin' down to the fire. 'Tis nearly over anyway. They're just givin' it extra water to make sure it's truly out. There's nothin' there but charred wood and ashy water."

"Where's Brenton?" Caitlan asked, hurrying past the others to greet her brother. "Is he all right? Is the shop completely destroyed?"

"Aye, the shop is gone," Kiernan admitted, meeting his sister's mournful expression. "Yar husband took himself off for a few moments alone. In fact, he told me to have ya stay with us tonight. He has business to attend to."

Caitlan shook her head. "I want to help him. I want to be there for him."

"I know ya do," he said sympathetically. "But now is not the time. Ya got to let the man have some time to hisself."

"What caused the fire?" Jordana asked.

Kiernan shrugged. "I'm sure I'm not

knowin', but I do know this night air is hardly good for yarselves. Come on with ya, now."

"Do you truly think it's a good idea to let Brenton go out there by himself?" Victoria asked, her concern evident.

"He's suffered a great loss. He'll be needin' some time alone now." Kiernan held out his arms as if to usher them all back to the house.

"I can't be just stayin' here, not knowin' if he's all right," Caitlan said, pulling aside from the walkway. "I want to go find him. Did he say where he'd be?"

Her worried tone touched Kiernan's heart. Here was the little sister he'd only really come to know in the last three years. She'd been but a wee one when he'd left Ireland for America, and in all his years of absence, she had grown to be nothing more than a memory. The last three years had changed all of that, however, and with each passing day, Kiernan saw more and more of their mother in Caitlan.

"Ya'll do him more good if ya leave him be," he insisted.

Caitlan said nothing more. Moonlight shone down from overhead and cast her in a milky glow. The sorrow she felt was quite clear to them all.

"Come along," Victoria said, taking up her husband's initiative. "Let's put on a pot and have tea. We can think better once we've settled ourselves." Victoria reached out to take hold of Caitlan's arm.

"I don't want to feel better until I know Brenton is safe." Caitlan's stubborn nature was no more evident than at this moment. She was no baby sister now, but a woman, strong and good. She jerked away from her sister-in-law. "I can't be stayin' here. I have to be to home."

Kiernan understood his sister's determination. "Come on with ya, then. Have some tea and then I'll drive ya home."

Caitlan looked at him for a moment as if to verify the truth in his words. "I'll only be stayin' for a few minutes," she replied. "Then whether ya drive me or I walk, I'm going home."

Kiernan nodded. "Ya have me word."

Half an hour later, Kiernan helped Caitlan down from the carriage in front of her little house. "Yar sure ya want to stay here by yarself? What if Brenton stays out all night? Ya'll not even have a maid to keep ya company. I could go bring Jordana back here to sit with ya."

Caitlan shook her head. "I'll be fine on me own. Ya know me husband. He is a private man. I know he needs this time to hisself, but when he does come home I want to be here to comfort him."

Kiernan nodded. "I understand. Let me see ya inside."

Caitlan allowed him to help her to the steps of her home. She paused at the door and hesitated a moment before opening it. "Yar sure he'll be all right?" For a brief instant, she was his little sister again, lost and afraid.

Kiernan looked into her mournful eyes and hugged her close. "He's got a level head, yar husband. I'm thinkin' he'll find his way home just fine. I'll be prayin' and ya'd do well to do the same. This is a terrible burden for him to bear. His picture takin' was very important to him."

" 'Twas *everything* to him," Caitlan emphasized, pulling away. She opened the door, letting a warm glow of light flood through the portal. "Looks like I left the lamp burnin'," she said.

"Ya'll have to be more careful or you'll be burnin' down the house," Kiernan replied. "And comin' on the heels of the other, I'm not sure any of us would be takin' the news too well."

She gave her brother a quick hug. "Thank

41

ya for carin' so much for us. Ya do our folks proud."

Kiernan felt his face warm at the compliment. "Ya do them proud yarself." He turned to go, then pausing on the bottom step, called back, "Don't be gettin' any fool notions of goin' out to look for yar husband. He'll come home in due time."

"I'll wait for him here," she promised.

Kiernan smiled to himself. "Ya see that ya do."

Back at home, Kiernan found himself having to contend with not only his wife's worried questions but Jordana's concerns as well. And of the two, he'd take dealing with his wife any day. Victoria could work up a steam and get herself all worried and tuckered over a matter, but Jordana Baldwin was more of a spitfire than most men would care to take on. Frankly, he was surprised to come home and find Jordana still there. Knowing her persistent and adventurous nature, it would befit her personality to be out combing the streets of Sacramento looking along every pier and alleyway for her brother. Then once found, he could just imagine her bullying or even cajoling her brother until he left off with his sufferings and followed her back home.

"I hate just sitting here, Kiernan. Are you

sure we shouldn't be out there looking for him? What if something happens to him?"

"He's a grown man, Jordana. Would you go interferin' in his needs? A man can't always be sharin' his heart with his women-folk. Sometimes it's just too much to bear and better given over to God than put off on the people he loves."

Jordana looked at him oddly for a moment, then lifted her gaze to the ceiling. "Men! You are all a strange breed."

Kiernan laughed, lightening the mood. "And ya think women are any different? Yar the most curious, confusin' creatures to walk the face of the earth. Why, look at yarself. Yar of an age to be settlin' down and raisin' a family, but that's not enough for yarself. Ya have money and a family who loves ya, yet the restlessness in yar heart threatens to strip ya of all happiness. Still, there are those times when ya dress in yar finest and go to church or the opera house or one of the society balls and ya look for all intents and purposes to be a lady of such regal upbringin' that I would believe ya to be royalty if I didn't know ya better."

Jordana smiled. "I guess I'm just multifaceted."

"Well said," Victoria interjected. "Honestly, Kiernan, she's no different than I was when you met me. I had a spirit for adventure as well. I wouldn't be here if I hadn't wanted to taste that adventure. We Baldwins have a determined character. I believe our mother and father raised us to be that way."

"Then be countin' Brenton to be raised the same way and be givin' him the chance he needs to set hisself to rights."

The women glanced at each other with a rather chagrined expression. "He's right, you know," Victoria told her sister. "We never really do give Brenton much credit for knowing how to take care of himself."

Jordana nodded. "He's just so kindhearted and easygoing that I always worry someone will take advantage of him and hurt him."

"He's a good man," Kiernan told her earnestly. "He'll not be puttin' hisself in danger and riskin' what's left to him. He'll be gettin' over this, but I'm thinkin' it's gonna take time and patience on our part."

For the first time since Caitlan brought the news, Kiernan sensed a bit of peace returning to the house. The two sisters seemed to notably relax, and the tension gradually eased from their faces as they appeared to accept his suggestions.

As the clock chimed the hour of ten, Jordana gave him a weak smile and sighed. "I

44

guess I'll go on up to bed. You'll let me know if you hear anything?"

"Of course I will," Kiernan replied. "Ya'll soon see for yarself. Brenton will be fine."

Brenton eased the front door of his house open and stepped inside. A misty rain had begun to fall, leaving him wet and chilled. This only added to his otherwise defeated emotions.

"Ya'll catch yar death," Caitlan whispered from the front parlor door. She stood in her nightgown, a light blue shawl wrapped around her shoulders, her long auburn hair hanging down to her waist.

"It's all gone," he managed to say.

Caitlan nodded. "I know."

"All those years of work. All the equipment. Gone." He shook his head and pulled the gold wire-rimmed glasses from his face. Rubbing his sore eyes, he didn't know that Caitlan had crossed the space between them until she took hold of his hand.

"I've got hot water on the stove. I think ya should have a hot bath and get right into bed. Ya won't want to be catchin' a chill. We can talk about all of this in the mornin' if ya'd like."

He looked at her and saw the sympathy in her expression. Nodding, he let her help him shrug out of the damp coat. The wetness did nothing to hide the obvious odor of smoke. Painfully, it only served to bring the vision of his dreams going up in flames once again to his mind. Discouragement and sorrow permeated his soul, and with deep shame he felt tears come to his eyes. It was not the first time he'd succumbed to tears that night, and he hated that now he should break down in front of Caitlan.

But before he could respond or otherwise hide his emotions, Caitlan reached up and touched a tear as it slid down his cheek. Her own eyes filled with tears, but she held his gaze and continued to stroke his cheek.

"I'm so glad yar home safe," she whispered. "Yar all I desire in the world, and if I lost ya now, I'm not entirely sure I could go on."

Brenton pulled her into his arms and held her tight. "I'm sorry if I worried you," he whispered against her ear. He felt his strength return. She gave him hope and filled him with new purpose. It wouldn't change the past nor take back the fire, but it would help with facing the future.

"I love ya, husband," she said, her accent thick with emotion.

Brenton stroked her hair and breathed deeply of Caitlan's sweetness. She'd bathed in rosewater and he loved the way the aroma lingered in her hair. It was such a vast contrast to the bitter, stinging smoke he'd inhaled at the scene of the fire.

"I do love you, Caitlan," he finally whispered. He could only pray that their love would be strong enough to sustain him when he had to return and face what was left of his shop.

FOUR

Weeks passed, leaving Jordana deeply worried about Brenton and Caitlan. They had kept almost entirely to themselves, refusing to come to Sunday dinner or to sit together with the rest of the family for Sunday morning services. And when Jordana visited them they welcomed her with great reserve. It so infuriated Jordana that she'd finally voiced her opinion of Brenton's withdrawal.

Caitlan had assured Jordana that time would help to set things right, but Jordana couldn't help being concerned. All of her life she had felt partially responsible for seeing to her brother's well-being. It hardly mattered that she was younger and that he was now a man. When their parents had left them in school in New York to venture to Russia some years ago, Jordana had felt herself just as responsible to see to Brenton as he had been to her.

Now Jordana felt misplaced and helpless.

Brenton didn't need her. He was clinging, and rightfully so, to Caitlan. To say that he appeared to be discouraged would be like suggesting that the Pacific was nothing more than a watering hole. Brenton rarely spoke about what had happened and whenever pressed to discuss details he had later learned about the fire, or what he would do to replace his equipment, Brenton would only shrug.

Jordana tried not to be jealous of her sister-in-law. Caitlan came as a pillar of strength to bolster and encourage her husband, and for this Jordana was grateful. But at the same time, the incident only served to leave Jordana feeling even more out of sorts than she had to begin with. Three years of living in Sacramento — three years of tagging along with one married sibling or the other — had taken a toll on her. Now in the midst of adversity, she wasn't really needed. In fact, when she came to visit and speak to Caitlan and Brenton, she felt like an intruder.

With June in full bloom, the family finally had a glimmer of hope. Sunday morning found Brenton and Caitlan in what had become the family pew at church. They were hardly the animated, lively couple they had once been, but both nodded and smiled, and afterward they promised to be at Victoria's for the traditional Sunday dinner.

Jordana hugged her brother as they stood outside in the churchyard. "I've missed you," she whispered. They pulled away and he gave her a thoughtful nod.

"I know, and I'm sorry. I needed to do this my way."

Jordana knew he was right, but the words seemed to sever yet another strand that tied her to Brenton. He didn't need her. Not in the way he once had. It truly was time to move on.

Helping Victoria set the china for their Sunday dinner, Jordana wondered what the day would bring. Having Brenton and Caitlan back in their lives would bring them a certain amount of joy, but there would no doubt still be times of testing.

"You're awfully quiet," Victoria said, arranging flowers for the table.

"I guess I'm a bit worried about how things will go today."

"I'm sure Brenton will be more like himself." Victoria placed the vase of flowers between two candelabra. Her countenance boasted a radiance that suggested her absolute contentment.

"I hope so." As Jordana set an extra plate

where Charlie Crocker would sit she commented, "I'm glad you invited Charlie. He always seems to liven things up."

"Well, with Mrs. Crocker off visiting friends in San Francisco, it only seemed right. Kiernan does so enjoy his company."

"You'd think he'd want to get away from his boss whenever time permitted," Jordana said with a smile.

"Kiernan sees Charlie as a sort of mentor. They even came back together from the front of the line this week. They rode in Charlie's private office car. It's quite nice — almost as if you were riding in a man's private study. Nothing as elaborate as the private cars we rode in back east when Mama and Papa took us on trips, but very nice nevertheless."

"I hope Charlie can somehow help Brenton," Jordana murmured absentmindedly. She glanced at the door as if sensing her brother's nearness. "I think I hear them."

She went to open the door and found Caitlan and Brenton coming up the walk. "They're here!" she announced to Victoria.

"Good. Kiernan and Charlie ought to be here any minute and then we can sit down to dinner."

"Hello, Brenton — Caitlan." Jordana caught her brother's glance and felt a flicker of hope. He actually smiled.

"Good afternoon to you, Jordana," he called and took hold of Caitlan's arm. Together they climbed the broad-based steps and joined Jordana at the door. "Something sure smells good."

"Victoria has prepared enough food for an army. That new cook she has working for her doesn't quite know how to master our sister's recipes, so Victoria spent half the afternoon showing her exactly what to do."

"Nothing is quite so pleasant as Sunday dinner with the relatives," Brenton said with a grin.

"What has you in such a good mood?" Jordana asked, fearful she'd cause him to slip back into his moodiness with the comment, but curious nonetheless.

"My dear wife has told me what a bear I've been," Brenton said rather formally.

"Well, I told you that days ago," Jordana replied. "I believe I called you that and a few other choice names." Her smile broadened when she saw that he had taken her teasing in a good-natured fashion.

"Indeed you did, and they were well deserved."

"Ho there, Baldwin!" Charlie Crocker called out as he climbed down from the O'Connor carriage. Kiernan drove the conveyance around to the carriage house even as Charlie made his way up the walk. "I had hoped to talk to you today. The Central Pacific is on the move and we need your help."

Jordana saw Brenton's expression change in an instant. She worried that somehow Charlie would single-handedly send her brother back into his bleak depression.

"What is it you need from me?" Brenton asked, brow knit.

Jordana could sense the struggle in his tone.

"Well, that's one of the reasons I'm here." Charlie's heavy frame caused the steps to groan slightly as he mounted to the porch. "Suppose we go inside and discuss the matter with a drink."

Jordana shared a quick, worried look with Caitlan, then stepped aside to let Charlie and Brenton come into the house. It seemed only natural to follow Charlie Crocker's imposing figure. He emanated a huge amount of energy, like a charging bull, Jordana thought. He was boisterous, tough, at times even crude, but Jordana believed that his heart was at least as big as his two-hundred-sixty-five-pound girth, as evidenced by his many kindnesses toward Kiernan and Victoria. And now toward

Brenton? Jordana hoped that was his intention. For now she also remembered Charlie could be rather tactless, speaking what he thought but at times not thinking at all about what he said.

"I hope Charlie knows what he's doing," Jordana whispered to Caitlan. "I was just starting to see some hope of Brenton returning to his old self."

"Don't I know it!" Caitlan's own tension was clear. "I ain't never seen a man spend half so much time in prayer as me husband has lately. Unless of course it was a man of the cloth."

"You don't suppose Brenton is about to change professions, do you?" Jordana let a half-joking, half-serious grin bend her lips.

"I'd be acceptin' that just fine," Caitlan replied, "if it meant he'd stop being so sad."

Jordana nodded. "We both would."

They followed the men to the parlor where Victoria was already serving large glasses of iced tea, which was all the rage these days in the homes of Sacramento during the summer. Jordana had to admit to liking it herself. She took up a glass just as Charlie launched into a story about troubles in the mountains.

"We built several miles of snow sheds last year." Charlie paused and had a lusty gulp of tea, seeming to enjoy it almost as much as the whiskey he preferred. "These were stretches of framework covering the tracks and offering protection from the snow. This way, no crew needed to waste time out on the line clearing tracks from ten- or twenty-foot drifts, and the trains were protected from falling debris."

Kiernan came in about this time and Victoria handed him a glass. "I see yar already tellin' them yar plan," he said. "And on a Sunday!"

"That I am," Charlie admitted. "I think the good Lord would honor my enthusiasm for the plan. I told Mr. Baldwin I'd need his help, but I haven't told him why."

"That's true, and let's just say, we're all quite curious, so please continue," Jordana interjected.

Charlie laughed and nodded. "Well, a good portion of the sheds were lost to us in avalanches. We couldn't keep the land above the shed cleared, and instead of passing over the track and shed as we had hoped, the snow collected on the slopes above and then destroyed everything in its wake as it plunged down the side of the mountain."

"So what will you do now?" Brenton asked.

"Well, we're already doing it, and that's

where you come in. I know you've lost your photographic equipment, but I need you to come ahead as we planned and take pictures anyway. I have some equipment you can use until you reorder and receive things from back east. It's not the good stuff like you had, but I obtained it from a man desperate to head into the gold mines and make his fortune."

"I suppose I could look it over," Brenton said.

Jordana found herself exhaling rather loudly. She hadn't realized she was holding her breath. She felt a surge of hope as Brenton continued.

"I know you spoke of the importance of the sheds and that you wanted me to help you with a historical record of the line, but what do you have in mind now?"

"Much the same," Charlie replied. "We're going to need to make changes as we repair the snow sheds. We figure to put a line of retaining walls up the mountainside. This will block the snows and prevent slides."

"It's bound to snow as much as before." Jordana tried to picture Charlie's plan in her mind. "Won't the snow just avalanche again and destroy the walls as it did the sheds?"

"We don't see it that way. First off, we

plan to build them so that when the snow builds to a certain point, it can just go over the top and down — much like a dam holding back water. Then we're going to rebuild the sheds to have an angled roof to match the mountain's slope."

"So that if the snow goes over the wall, it will proceed down the mountain and over the sheds as though there were no structures in the way at all," Jordana murmured.

"Exactly so," Charlie agreed. "I want Brenton to come and keep a photographic journal for us, and we'll see to it that his new equipment catches up to him wherever he is along the line." At this, all eyes turned to Brenton.

"My wife tells me I've been idle too long," Brenton said aloud. "I suppose it wouldn't hurt to try. But as for new equipment, well, I've not ordered any."

"What?" Jordana exclaimed before anyone else could speak. "Why not?"

Brenton looked first at Caitlan and then Jordana. "Because I wasn't sure I would go back into photography."

"Not go back? But that's been your dream — your life," Jordana said in disbelief. "How could you not go back?"

Brenton smiled wanly. "I don't know, but it has been a consideration."

"Well, consider it later," Charlie declared. "I need you with me on the line. I want to hire you on to help us document the rest of the route. At the slow rate the Union Pacific has set, we'll build all the way to the eastern Utah territories before they come anywhere near to meeting our track front. I want pictures of it all, and so do Hopkins, Huntington, Stanford, and my brother the judge."

Charlie had just named the most important people on the Central Pacific's board. If they wanted this, Jordana had little doubt it would be done. Now it was just a matter of getting Brenton to agree to help.

"I suppose I could give it a try," Brenton finally said. "Caitlan can come along and help me. You too, Jordana. If you want to," he said, seeming to extend the offer as a gift of peace. "You could surely find plenty to write about for those New York papers."

Jordana smiled broadly. "When do we leave?"

Charlie laughed heartily. "If I weren't married, Miss Baldwin, I think I'd be seeking you out to court. You're a woman after my own heart. See a thing and get it done — that's my motto."

Jordana nodded enthusiastically. "Mine too."

"Well, if that's all settled," Victoria said, beaming her guests a smile, "I would like to suggest a toast." She lifted her glass high. "Here's to the future of the Central Pacific — may you double the line this summer and add hundreds of miles in addition to the original plan."

"Here, here!" Charlie declared, starting to put the glass to his lips.

"And," Victoria said, before anyone could drink, "to my own family, which is about to add another member."

They all looked at her in stunned silence.

"What do you mean?" Jordana asked, glancing from Victoria to Caitlan. Surely Brenton and Caitlan weren't expecting a child. But if not them . . .

"I'm going to have a baby," Victoria announced.

Jordana gasped. "Oh, Victoria, are you sure?"

But Victoria was hardly listening, for Kiernan had caught her in his arms, spilling tea and ice all over the parlor rug. He swung her in a circle, his face nearly as radiant with joy as Victoria's.

"I guess she's sure enough," Brenton said, lifting his glass again. "To the new arrival."

Jordana lifted her glass as well. "To the next generation of Baldwins and

59

O'Connors!" Sipping her tea, she felt nothing but pure joy for her older sister. After waiting a lifetime to make this announcement, Victoria was finally going to have the baby she'd dreamed of.

FIVE

Jordana thought the front of the track should more appropriately be called the "end of the line," for it was here that the supplies were stacked and waiting and the track ended amidst a stretch of graded wilderness. Writing her thoughts on the scene, she paced along the area where men were arranging gravel and ties for the acceptance of rails.

Trying to ignore the whistles and catcalls from the Irish and Welsh workers, Jordana moved among the men with a straight back and professional demeanor. Many of the men knew her, and she realized their rather ribald attention was good-natured, but still it irked her. She wore a simple skirt of navy serge and a sleek navy-and-gold vest that lay snug over a crisp white blouse. Her hair had been bound up and pinned securely to keep it from interfering in her tasks, and atop this she had secured a functional straw bonnet.

Leaving Brenton behind to photograph the snow sheds near Donner Pass, Jordana had accompanied Charlie Crocker to the front near the Truckee River in Nevada. Her purpose and mission was to arrange an in-depth story of what it was like to build the Central Pacific Railroad. Brenton had wanted her to remain with him and had argued with her long and hard about risking her reputation and well-being. Charlie saved the day by suggesting he would be responsible for Jordana and keep the men in line. He also promised to accompany Jordana as she gathered her interviews with the men. With this settled, Brenton surrendered.

But even with Charlie's help, Jordana found her task quite frustrating. The men were far more interested in asking her to dine with them or join them for a drink in town than to tell her their thoughts on building the transcontinental railroad. She persisted, however, probing first one and then another. Her pencil and paper were ever ready to jot down an interesting aspect of the taxing physical labor.

Little by little, Jordana managed to ascertain a bit of information. It was never exactly what she wanted or hoped for, but it was a start. After that it became her creative job to turn her bits and pieces of news into a story worthy of reading. She knew it would be gobbled up with great enthusiasm back east, but frustration edged this victory. There was so much more to be told. The intricate lives of the railroad workers held many mysteries. But she was only a woman, and in most cases, she was simply not welcome to pry into such secrets.

But Jordana continued in a relentless manner and from time to time found herself rewarded. Just the day before she'd managed to get some of the tunnel workers farther back on the line to talk to her about their native homes. Some of the men were originally from mining towns in Wales. Collis Huntington had managed to bring them away from their homes and families to work for the Central Pacific Railroad, attracting them with the promise of good pay and better conditions. The men were good at their jobs, as Jordana soon learned. Rather than playing blindly at the use of explosive materials, they were well trained in the dangers. Many were missing fingers or bore some other scar from their mishaps, but all seemed devoted to their tasks, and to Jordana's great surprise, many of them were musically talented. Often in the evenings, these burly Welshmen would entertain the other men with a mixture of songs that included everything from bawdy tales of feisty women to church hymns taught them by Methodist missionaries. It was a wonder to be sure.

Many of the Irish and Welsh complained because of Crocker's rule against liquor. No alcoholic beverages were allowed on the building site, and while that didn't stop the men from riding or walking into the nearest town after work concluded on Saturday, it did manage to keep the work area freed up from the problems associated with drinking. Of course, Blue Mondays had to be dealt with and often slowed production considerably as the men battled hangovers. It was enough to make Charlie consider forbidding the men to drink at all while under his employ, but Jordana doubted he'd go through with the thought. There were precious few laborers as it was. If he forbade the Saturday and Sunday excursions into town, the men would riot or simply walk off the job never to return.

At one point, Charlie took Jordana to the place where her brother-in-law was supervising the building of a particularly tricky trestle bridge. Here Jordana actually felt welcome.

When the Irishmen learned that she was kin to Kiernan, they treated her as one of the family. It was here that she finally managed to get some of the more intimate details she desired for her newspaper stories. She listened to them talk about their lives, noting a hint of sorrow and longing in their voices as they spoke of the green hills of home. Some, like Kiernan, had been in America since the 1840s when the potato crops had failed, leaving them destitute and starving. Others had come at the appeal and call of those who had gone before them. All of the men seemed to hold a deep respect for Kiernan O'Connor, who, while brooking no nonsense or fighting from his men, also understood that differences were bound to occur.

Jordana studied her notes from the encounter with Kiernan's men and wished she could have as much luck with the other railroad workers. Especially the Chinese.

The Chinese, or "Crocker's Pets" as they were often called, were a most unusual people to be sure. Jordana had experienced working with Chinese women back in Sacramento. Victoria hired them almost exclusively to help in her laundry business. Victoria had a deep concern for their welfare and despised the prejudicial manner in which they were generally treated by others.

Charlie Crocker, seeing that it was impossible to keep the size of the workforce he needed for the Central Pacific's ever growing line, decided to bring in Chinese to help. At first he brought only a few, less than one hundred. They were to do only the simplest and most menial tasks. This usually involved hauling basket loads of rock and debris from tunnel sites. Later, however, once they'd proven themselves to be more durable than originally believed, Charlie put them to work doing just about everything. Now the Central Pacific simply would not be making progress without this massive force of thousands.

Jordana had tried many times to speak with these workers, but they would have nothing to do with her. Hindered by the language barrier, there was also a type of gender stigma that was worse than any Jordana had experienced with men of her own race. The Chinese men seemed to feel it most inappropriate for a female to address them with questions about their positions, families, or homeland. Jordana did her best to include them in her stories anyway. After all, they had rapidly outnumbered the other men working for the Central Pacific.

Charlie tried to help her as best he could. He told her about their peculiar diet and how he had to bring in specialized foods for them — rice, bamboo shoots, seaweed, oysters, cuttlefish, and exotic finned fish. Jordana paid close attention to the Chinese men as they worked to prepare their meals, amazed that their food almost always came dry, requiring the addition of water. They cooked most everything in peanut oil and drank tea almost exclusively.

To Jordana's quick eye, she noted that the Chinese were rarely ill and wondered if it had more to do with their diet or the fact that they were wont to taking warm baths on a daily basis. Not only this, but they kept their clothes and sleeping quarters regularly washed. They were a remarkable people as far as Jordana was concerned. She only wished that she could influence some or all to talk to her through their translator. But even the translator wanted little to do with her.

"Having any luck?" Charlie asked.

He had startled Jordana out of her deep thought, nearly causing her to jump down from the rock on which she'd taken up residence. It was quite evident that she was once again studying the Chinese workers, for all of the Irish and Welsh were farther down the line. "No, I'm afraid not. I do wish they weren't so difficult."

"Well, I can't say they're difficult," Charlie said, leaning back against the rock. "They are hard workers. I never have to call them twice to work. They labor steadily and work until the job is done or the hours are over. They don't sit around fussing and feuding over imagined wrongs, and they aren't given to drinking whiskey. A man could hardly ask for better than that in a worker. A few would run off for the gold-fields now and then, but nowhere near the numbers of white workers. They are a very intelligent people who realize a steady paycheck is more valuable than the promise of a gold vein they might never find."

Jordana smiled and nodded. "I wanted to thank you for getting me that sample of food. I've never tasted anything quite so good. Pork has never been one of my favorites, but the way they fixed that together with the salted cabbage and vegetables was quite delicious. If only I could get some of the recipes for my stories."

"I'll see what I can do. Maybe if I approach them and request it for you —"

"Maybe if I dress in dungarees and cut my hair they'll talk to me themselves," Jordana interjected wryly. Then a smile crossed her face. "Why not?" she murmured.

"I don't like what I think you're thinking," Charlie said, eyeing her suspiciously.

"I've cut my hair before, and frankly, if I plan to venture off on my own, dressing as a man just might suit my needs better than traveling as a woman. I mean, think about it. You've seen the attention I've received from the men on the line."

"Exactly! You go putting on breeches and you're sure to cause a riot."

"Well, I didn't mean to do it here, where everyone knows me. But maybe I could go back to where they're working on the sheds or anywhere else where the Chinese are working on the line. Didn't you say you were going to start grading in Utah just to get a jump on things?"

"Oh, no you don't! Your brother would boil me in oil for going along with such a plan. If you're so all-fired interested in snooping around, why not do it for me in a proper manner and keep your fancy dresses?"

"What do you mean?" Jordana leaned forward, her curiosity and interest evident.

"I mean, there's a lot of strange things going on along the line. We've suffered minor bouts of sabotage, but something tells me we're just seeing the beginning of a trend. The government is paying by the mile, and the Union Pacific doesn't want to see us accomplish any more than what they deem to be our fair share. Which isn't much. I need someone to go nose around the Union Pacific folks and see what plans are afoot. If someone is thinking to waylay us, I'd like to know it."

"What makes you think I could do anything to help your plan?" Jordana was hardly able to contain the excitement she felt at the idea of such an adventure.

Charlie grinned. "You made good friends back in Omaha. Many of those men are now out there on the line itself. They're plotting and planning just like me. I'm going to return to Sacramento shortly, and your brother-in-law, as well as other men I trust, will be left here along the line to supervise the building. Getting some firsthand knowledge of what's being discussed along the UP might very well mean the difference between keeping my men alive or seeing them buried."

Jordana bit at her lip and considered his words for a moment. "Do you honestly think you're up against something so monumental and deadly? I mean, I thought both sides wanted to see this railroad completed.

Even the political arenas back east see this as a factor to knit our wartorn nation together again. My father said that men of power are constantly considering the benefits and how they might play a part once the line is in place."

"Yes, but there are equally powerful men along the line who wish to see one or the other side set back or stopped altogether. You have no idea the rumors I've heard. We've had enough trouble without anyone stirring up problems or spying out our weaknesses, but now I think the whole scheme of things may well turn ugly. Collis Huntington thinks so too. He wrote to me with reason to believe that the Union Pacific had plans for sending someone out here to spy on our accomplishments. I'm afraid that when they see our progress, they might well strive to put an end to it."

"Do you have proof of that?" Jordana probed. "I mean, I could write about this entire issue and bring it to the foreground."

"No," Charlie said quickly. "I don't want to expose this, at least not just yet. If there are spies afoot and trouble is planned, I'd like to get to the folks in charge. In the meanwhile, I'd simply like to keep everyone alive and the railroad prospering."

"I'm still not sure I understand how I

could help." Jordana tucked her pencil and paper into her skirt pocket and looked to Charlie for an explanation.

"My thought is that you could go back to Omaha to start. Mingle with some of the folks you were friends with before coming out here. Talk to them about what's happening along the line. See if you can't weasel out any information on plans to slow down the Central Pacific."

"What makes you think they'd talk to me — a mere woman?"

Charlie took off his hat and scratched his head. "Well, they might not at that. I'd consider asking your brother, but it was hard enough just to convince him to photograph the snow sheds. Maybe once you got involved, he would jump in too. Then I could have pictures as well as words."

"I don't know," Jordana began. She leaned back against the warm rock and lifted her face to the sun. "I mean, I've worked at this for a while. I know how difficult it is to get anyone to take me seriously. I think I'd probably have better luck if I posed as a man. I could cut my hair, buy me a suit, even some fake whiskers, and then move about the line. I could tell them I was a reporter for the *New York Tribune*, maybe even pass myself off as Brenton's younger brother."

"Wouldn't they recognize you?" Charlie asked.

Jordana shrugged. "I have no way of knowing. It has been three years, almost four. I've changed quite a bit."

"Well, we could think on it a bit. Maybe talk to Brenton and Kiernan and get their thoughts on it."

"Neither one is going to want me to go," Jordana replied, jumping up off the rock. She dusted off her skirts and said, "They expect me to be a prim-and-proper lady. Brenton would love nothing more than for me to go back to New York and bide my time with our parents until I found some decent man to settle down with." At the mention of a decent man, Jordana stopped. Rich O'Brian was just such a man, and he was mustering out of the army, in fact should already be rid of their authority. He knew a great deal about the Union Pacific as he had acted as guard and companion to many of the survey teams and board members. Perhaps he could tell her if something was going on.

". . . but otherwise I'd feel kind of funny about it," Charlie concluded.

Jordana shook her head, realizing she'd

73

been lost in her thoughts of Rich. "I'm sorry, what did you say?"

Charlie looked at her rather curiously. "I said it would only be right to talk to Brenton and Kiernan about it. I'm not saying I'd rescind the offer if they disapprove, but I would feel kind of funny about sending you out there without even discussing it with them. They'd need to know what you were up to and where you were."

"Why?" Jordana replied angrily, her hands on her hips. "I'm a grown woman. They aren't my bosses. Just because I've stayed on with Kiernan and Victoria doesn't mean I take my orders from Kiernan. I'm tired of being told what to do and where to go. If you want me to work for you, I will. But I'd rather it stay between the two of us unless it honestly requires someone else knowing about it. Besides, if someone is involved with planning sabotage, the fewer people involved the better. You don't know but what you have a traitor amidst your current workers."

"That's true enough," Charlie replied. "Well, how do you propose to explain it to your family?"

"I'll simply tell them the truth. I'm gathering materials for my newspaper stories, and I'm going to meet up with an old friend."

"An old friend?"

Jordana nodded. "Yes. They'll know all about him."

"Him? You mean you have a male acquaintance waiting for you in Nebraska?"

Laughing, Jordana replied, "Not in the sense that you probably imagine. Captain O'Brian is a good friend, nothing more. He's due to leave the army and then his plans are uncertain. He might very well be able to help me obtain the very information you're seeking."

"Or he could be a part of the problem," Charlie said. "You have to be careful who you trust, Jordana."

"I trust Captain O'Brian implicitly. He's saved me from trouble more than once, and I know he'd do nothing to harm me." The thought of Rich caused her cheeks to grow warm. "My," Jordana said, touching her hand to her cheek, "it's grown rather warm out here."

Six

Rich O'Brian rolled over in bed and noted the strong shaft of light coming into the room from beneath the heavy green shades. He couldn't remember the last time he'd slept past sunrise. Stretching his arms above his head, Rich forced himself to get out of bed. Taking up the pocket watch from his dresser, he nearly yelled out loud.

"Eleven o'clock!"

He was supposed to meet with the Union Pacific officers at eleven-thirty. That didn't leave a whole lot of time to waste. To be in Omaha for this meeting, he'd ridden nearly all night from Kansas City, where he had been looking into some job prospects. Arriving at four in the morning, he had fallen onto his hotel bed fully clothed and had slept, apparently very soundly. He wasn't certain what had awakened him.

Hurriedly he grabbed up his shaving gear and, rather than wait for the water to heat, shaved with a thin lather of soap and cold water. With his face stinging from the experience, he quickly found a clean shirt, one of two he'd purchased in Kansas City. He hadn't wanted to be at the mercy of the growing populace of unscrupulous con men flooding Omaha these days. Rich knew con games and underhanded deals were plaguing all the new towns along the Union Pacific, but especially Omaha. The little town had simply grown too big for its britches.

Pulling on his boots, Rich noted they could have used a good coating of boot black. No time for that, he thought, realizing only too well how quickly the time was getting away from him.

The last bit of effort he gave his appearance was to pull on a new navy broadcloth coat. After wearing his captain's uniform for nearly a decade, these civilian duds felt foreign. For the first moment since making his decision to leave the army, Rich seriously wondered if he'd done the right thing.

With a sigh, he slicked down his black hair, meeting his steely eyed expression in the mirror. Never look back, he told himself mentally. What was done was done. The past could not haunt him if he refused delivery on the memories.

Ten minutes later he stood in the offices of the Union Pacific. Across the desk from where Rich stood, a grave-looking General Dodge offered a cautious welcome. "Captain O'Brian."

"Just Mr. O'Brian now," Rich corrected.

General Grenville Dodge, chief engineer for the Union Pacific Railroad, was, at thirty-seven, only a few years older than Rich. But the man held himself with such an air of dignity and command that one seemed naturally to fall under his authority. Dodge had distinguished himself during the war both by his talent at quickly rebuilding railroads and bridges destroyed by the Confederacy and by his valor in battle, during which he was twice wounded. Near the war's end, he was assigned to fight the Plains Indians, where he again displayed a strong determination and vigor or, in the opinion of some, a savage ruthlessness in his dealings with them. When Washington ordered him to cease his Indian campaigns in deference to recently concluded treaties, he responded by leaving the army and taking up his present job with the Union Pacific. He attacked railroad work as everything else, with energy and determination.

"Ah yes, of course, I see you decided to leave the army. Have a seat." Dodge motioned briskly, as if he had little patience for interruption, toward a chair opposite his desk. "Oh, and forgive my poor manners in my abruptness. I'm beating a path to Salt Lake City as soon as we're done here and there isn't much time to waste."

Rich nodded and did as he was instructed. "The message said this was urgent."

"And indeed it is," Dodge said. "As you well know, last year nearly spelled disaster for the Union Pacific. The Indian conflicts alone threatened to bring us to our knees. Troubles with the Arapaho, Cheyenne, and Sioux have cost us the lives of many good men. Not only this, but we fought a constant battle to keep the Indians from tearing up the track nearly as fast as we could lay it. Now there are some five thousand men along the line, and it is still not enough — and may never be enough."

"I don't entirely understand," Rich replied.

"We've been having some difficulties along the line that I believe have nothing to do with the Indians. I believe there are men out there who would just as soon see us fail at this mission."

"For what purpose?" Rich questioned incisively. "The railroad stands to benefit everyone."

"Some more than others," Dodge declared. "To put it bluntly, we believe the Central Pacific may well have sent in spies to relay information back to their superiors in California."

Rich nodded. "And how would this present a problem for you? The development of the line is fairly well-known. The eastern newspapers have reported on it. Durant and his New York friends seem to keep the entire world apprised of every inch of track laid. Congress gets a neat and orderly report in order to see the funding continued. I don't know what the CP could hope to gain by sending spies."

"It's more than this," Dodge said, lowering his voice. "I believe some of the mishaps befalling us, and being blamed on the Indians, are indeed actions paid for and provoked by men of seemingly good standing."

"You are speaking of sabotage?" Rich spoke the question with an edge of uneasiness in his gut. He'd hoped the end of the war would have brought a halt to such activities.

"I can't say this for certain, but some of the incidents are just too coincidental for my liking. I need a way to know for sure what's going on." Dodge leaned back in his chair, his gaze focusing intently on Rich. "I feel confident from my sources that it's just a matter of getting the right man into the throes of things. And I believe you're that man."

"The right man for ferreting out who's responsible for plotting mayhem against the UP?" Rich also leaned forward, his own gaze steely and mixed with suspicion. "Why me?"

"You know the territory, O'Brian. You are good friends with many of the men involved in building the railroad and guarding it. You will have little trouble moving in and around the various building sites. If there's a troublemaker in the bunch, I feel certain you'll be able to smell him out."

Rich still felt a bit surprised at this new turn of events. "And what would I do with him once I found him?"

"Bring him to me for prosecution. Bring his entire entourage. I don't care how high up this thing goes, I won't see the line destroyed any further. Neither will I see us waste the government's money for rebuilding when we haven't done everything in our power to keep the destruction from happening." Dodge lowered his voice. "O'Brian, your superiors tell me you are entirely loyal to the UP. I've known you long enough to feel comfortable in accepting that as gospel. Will you take this job and help us see this line put through? We stand ready to pay you quite handsomely."

Rich rubbed his chin thoughtfully. "I am not opposed to good honest work, especially when paid handsomely. But you still haven't addressed the issue of how you will incorporate me onto the scene. I mean, won't it look awkward to have me suddenly appearing along the line?"

Dodge nodded. "We have that figured out as well. As I said, I'm just now trying to get to Salt Lake City. I've taken a leave of absence from the House of Representatives — never really wanted to be there in the first place," he muttered rather absentmindedly. Seeming to realize he'd strayed from the issue, he straightened. With brows knit together and eyes narrowed, he stated, "The fact is, we have it planned to utilize you as a courier. You'll be sent up and down the line as needed, but you'll also have the freedom to move about and linger where you will. If anyone questions your actions, you will tell them that you are on the business of General Dodge, and if they have further questions, they may take it up with me. My thought is that the only man who will overly protest your presence is going to be the man who is afraid of being revealed."

Rich nodded. The plan sounded feasible, and beneficial, for that matter. He had mustered out of the army without any real purpose or direction. He had inquired into a few jobs, but none had appealed to his sense of adventure. He'd thought constantly of Jordana Baldwin. They had shared an enthusiastic correspondence over the last few years, and Rich found it a growing interest to seek her out. The idea of spending time with Jordana and seeing if they might not find a way to share a future together was one that had startled him at first in view of his avowed disinterest in marriage. He simply could not marry with his past rising up like a brooding storm on the horizon. He couldn't expect Jordana to understand, although there was a part of his heart that thought she just might if he could find the courage to share these things with her.

"Will you do it?" Dodge prompted, breaking through Rich's thoughts.

"Yes," Rich answered without wavering. "I believe I would like to give it a try."

Dodge nodded. "I've written up all the particulars." He reached into the desk and pulled out a packet of papers. "You'll find a list of names and people who are working on the UP and the various locations for which they serve. My first order of business will be to have you accompany me as far as North Platte. From there I'll continue to Salt Lake and you will stay on and learn what you can."

"Why start there?" Rich asked.

"As you probably remember," Dodge answered, "our most vicious Indian attacks have come from within a hundred-mile radius of that town."

Rich remembered only too well. He'd been a part of the troops defending the workers, not only as they originally put the track down, but then later when they were sent out to repair or augment the line. The Indians had been a constant threat in the lives of the UP workers. Vivid images of heinous massacres with wounded men left to die on the Nebraska plains came to Rich's memory. It was something he'd worked hard to exorcise from his mind. He'd even written to Jordana about it — not in any real detail, of course. But he'd written her with as much information as he felt she could handle. She was a strong woman, and he greatly admired her for her vigor of living life to the fullest. Had she been a man, Rich would have been given over to calling her his truest comrade. He would have seen her in the role of Jonathan to his David, or vice versa. But because she was a woman, Rich thought of her in an infinitely different manner. One he had promised her he wouldn't think of her as — a soul mate, a lifelong mate, a wife.

Grateful that he still held his gaze to the papers Dodge had just bestowed upon him, Rich dismissed the thoughts and nodded as he scanned the list. There were many familiar names on the page before him.

"I don't see Sam Reed listed here," Rich commented.

"Sam headed out to Salt Lake about four weeks ago. Somehow we have to break the news to Brigham Young that we won't be building through to Salt Lake after all. It's just not a feasible route."

"Where will you go instead?"

"Ogden, most likely. We need to handle the matter very carefully, however, or I'm afraid Young will pull his support of the UP and give himself over to aiding the Central Pacific."

"Sir, please don't misunderstand me," Rich began slowly, "but why are we divided in this matter? Haven't we learned anything from war? If we see this railroad as the one mechanism to unite the country and bring settlement and prosperity to the West, then shouldn't we be working *with* the Central Pacific instead of against her?"

"O'Brian, I know what you're trying to say and I agree. The end result should be one that uniformly brings about positive construction and migration throughout the United States of America. However, at this point — and I even regret to say that this is true — it's all an issue of money. We have to build and complete the track in order to get support from the government and entice investors for the future. It's more than just laying the track, it's settling the towns along the way. It's who will settle those towns, and how they will benefit the Union Pacific more than how they will benefit the country as a whole."

"I'm sorry to hear that." Rich rubbed a finger across his mustache, deeply sensing he was going from one war into another. "You might as well know, I have good friends working with the Central Pacific. I don't see how it would interfere with my job, though, as I know them to be honorable people who would never consider sabotaging the Union Pacific or participating in anything that could bring about bodily harm to any person. But they are my friends, and I share correspondences with them and have told them from time to time what the Union Pacific's progress is about. I never felt I was betraying confidences, because as I mentioned before, the progress was neatly written on the lines of eastern newspapers and spouted from the pulpits of politicians up and down the eastern seaboard. If you think this is a problem, you should dismiss the idea of hiring me, because I won't be giving up my friendships for any man's cause."

Dodge smiled. "If anything, it makes me only more certain that you are the man for the job. Your honesty is noteworthy and your loyalty to your friends impressive. Perhaps, if they are the honorable people you claim them to be, they might even prove to be an asset to you in this mission."

"I won't lie to them or use them," Rich declared. "However, if there is a way for them to help, I'm sure they would do it in a heartbeat rather than see more blood spilled."

"Good. Then gather your things and bring your horse. We'll take the train to North Platte, but after that you may find it easier to move about on horseback. You'll have an unlimited pass for travel on the train and papers that will allow you to take whatever freight you want — your horse and tack, or anything else that seems necessary. You'll also be given an account to draw upon for expenses. This will be available to you through any of the depots. Simply present your credentials and the matter will be taken care of."

Rich grinned. "You'll have everyone wanting to be a courier."

Dodge raised a brow and shrugged. "But not everyone would want the task of being a spy."

SEVEN

North Platte was known to every man along the Union Pacific as "Sin City." If something underhanded or otherwise perverse was desired, it could be found in North Platte. But then again, there were a dozen such settlements along the line. Known as "Hell-on-Wheels" towns for the way they were birthed from the very tracks that put them on the map, they very often resembled the biblical cities of Sodom and Gomorrah.

Rich bid Dodge farewell and made his way back to the freight car, where he claimed his gear and horse. Faithful, the gelding that had accompanied him for the last eight years, appeared surprisingly undaunted by the trip. Not so the baggage man, who'd put up a complete rebellion when Rich had approached him about bringing the horse. The car wasn't equipped for such things, the man declared, but General Dodge himself had intervened and simply told the man to make it so.

Now the man stood almost as white as a ghost, clearly unnerved by the entire experience, as Rich checked the horse over for any damage.

"Looks like you both fared well enough," Rich finally said. He tossed the man a coin and touched the brim of his new felt hat. "For your trouble."

The man recovered from his apparent fright quickly enough to snatch the coin from the air. He smiled at the sight of the money. "Thank you, sir. No trouble, sir."

At this he quickly disappeared inside the car, causing Rich to grin. No doubt the man wanted to get away before Rich could suggest some other fool scheme. Leading Faithful at his side, Rich moved away from the depot and into the dusty streets of North Platte. He sized up the small town, noting the throngs of activity along the main street. It was nearly evening, and it was quite clear that people were preparing for the activities of the night to come. A freighter stood impatiently waiting to be paid for the whiskey his hired help was even now carrying inside a nearby saloon. Several women of questionable virtue lounged around the door, cooing and calling to the men who passed by.

"We're gonna have fun tonight," one called to Rich. "Wouldn't you like to come and spend the night dancin' with me?"

"Hey, mister, ya want to get in on a profitable game?" a filth-ridden man questioned from his side. The man had appeared out of thin air.

"No, thanks," Rich replied and moved off down the street. The sooner he could get to his business, the sooner he could leave town.

The paper in his hand gave an address in the better part of town, or so he was told. Glancing around, he wondered quite dubiously if there really was a better part of town. With little more than sketchy directions and the name Baxter Montego, the paper was pretty useless. Baxter Montego wasn't a name familiar to Rich, but Dodge had assured him the man had been privy to a great many of the Union Pacific's secrets. The man apparently worked to promote additional construction in the area for both the railroad and the town. Dodge had suggested Rich start his investigation first with Montego, then glean information and names from their conversations and use the information to help in his search for saboteurs. And all the while, Rich would continue to pose as a courier for the railroad's upper echelon.

Continuing to lead Faithful rather than ride him, Rich passed by grocers, mercantile stores, banks, and saloons. Many of the "buildings" were nothing more than tents, but several rather substantial structures were either in place or being constructed. The town apparently felt it had staying power with the Union Pacific track so close at hand.

Asking directions from a white-aproned store clerk, Rich finally located the two-story home of Baxter Montego. It wasn't much to look at. The box-styled structure was stark in its whitewash. There were no shutters at the windows or pediments to crown the single, centered door. Just clapboard and windowpanes and the slight show of a chimney peering over the back side. The ground around the house was just as barren, as though the house had recently been built and the land had had no time to recover from the intrusion. Behind the house and to the side stood a small barnlike structure, which appeared to act as a carriage house.

Tethering Faithful to the hitching post at the end of the dirt walkway, Rich made his way to the house. He had no idea what to expect. Dodge hadn't given him much information on Montego. The general had, in fact, admitted that he really didn't know Montego. The man was a friend of Thomas Durant, and because of his relationship to the current vice-president of the Union Pacific Railroad, Montego had earned a position of respect.

Rich knocked on the door and waited anxiously for what would be his first encounter with Montego. Soldiering had given him the ability to act authoritatively and gave him some flair for scouting out the enemy, but spying in this capacity was something entirely new. He carried papers from Dodge for Montego, a good way to get Rich in the door, but ferreting out information after that would depend on Rich's own wits. He was to deliver the information and await answers on some of the questions Dodge posed. It seemed a good way to keep Rich in Montego's presence and give him a chance to examine Montego's character.

The door opened to reveal a beautiful dark-haired woman. Rich ascertained that she could not be much past her twentieth birthday, if that, and she was clearly one of the most exotic women he'd ever seen.

She cocked her head coyly and tilted her chin upward. The pose seemed to be to her advantage, as though she'd practiced it many times and knew the effect it had on men. "May I help you?"

Rich cleared his throat. "Uh, yes, ma'am. I'm here on business from General Dodge. I'm to meet with Mr. Montego."

She smiled and lowered her lashes. Her voice was smooth and honey sweet. "Mr. Montego is my father. He's just stepped out, but I expect him back shortly. Won't you come inside and wait for him?"

Rich nodded and snatched the felt hat from his head. "Thank you, ma'am. I'd be obliged."

She swept back away from the door, her long peach-colored skirts following after her in a wave of color. "Would you care for tea or coffee?" she offered.

Rich shook his head. "No, please don't go to any trouble. A glass of water would be just fine. I'm afraid the train was not all that accommodating on matters of keeping the grit and ash from inside the car."

"Oh, I can well imagine, Mister . . ." she drew out the final word, then stared at him expectantly. "I'm afraid I don't recall your name."

"I'm afraid I was rather remiss in delivering it," Rich admitted. "The name is O'Brian. Richard O'Brian."

"Ah," she said and smiled in a most enticing manner. "And I am Isabella Montego."

The name fit her well. He thought her obvious Spanish heritage had played itself out nicely in her elegantly coiled ebony hair and tanned skin. Her dark brows were arched delicately over even darker eyes — eyes that seemed to watch him with such intensity he almost found himself blushing.

She instructed him to take a seat in the simple parlor. "I will return in a moment with your refreshment."

Rich nodded and marveled at her graceful retreat from the room. Women were a mystery to him. How they ever managed to move about in such an agile and flowing manner while confined by yards and yards of material was beyond him. Realizing he was missing an opportunity to snoop, Rich pushed such concerns aside and glanced around the room for anything that might imply Montego's involvement in something less than beneficial for the Union Pacific. It was hard to imagine that a friend of someone like Durant would want to do anything but make money by the railroad. That was, after all, the biggest goal Rich could see Durant involved with. Money appeared to mean a great deal to the former medical doctor turned investor.

The room held no secrets, Rich decided.

Or if it did, he didn't know what to look for. Contemplating this, he took his seat only moments before Isabella Montego returned with a silver tray bearing a glass of water and a linen napkin.

"I'm sorry, but my maid is in town shopping for our supper."

"I'm the one to apologize," Rich offered. "I didn't mean to put you out. I only just arrived in town, and my instructions were to come here directly."

"How marvelous," Isabella replied. "Then I know my father shall insist you stay with us while you're here in North Platte. This house, though sparsely furnished, is far better than anything you'll find at the hotel or boardinghouse in town."

"Thank you, but I couldn't impose," Rich replied, taking a long, welcomed drink as he wondered about a woman who would so enthusiastically invite a stranger to stay in her home.

"I assure you," Isabella said, her expression most inviting, "it is no imposition. We have just come to the area. My father travels between here and Laramie, where we own a good portion of land and work with the local people to bring in settlers. With my father's responsibilities for the Union Pacific, he is quite often traveling, and I

96

sometimes accompany him. For this reason, he had this house built for us. Now we have a place in both towns."

"I suppose that makes a good deal of sense," Rich said, smiling. "But I'm a stranger and I can't imagine your father being at ease with my spending the night."

Just then the door burst open and a tall dark-headed man entered with a dramatic flair. "This godforsaken country will be the death of me, Isabella. Come and help me with my things."

Instantly Rich and Isabella were on their feet.

"Father, we have company," Isabella replied before going to her father's side. "This is Mr. O'Brian. General Dodge has sent him. I was just telling him he should stay with us tonight rather than take a room with the rowdies in town."

Montego's gaze sized up Rich before he turned to his daughter. "How very kind of you. You are so like your mother." She smiled sweetly and kissed him on the cheek before taking his satchel and hat and setting them on a hall tree. "If my daughter is extending you invitations to stay, perhaps you should state what business you have with me."

Rich produced a packet of papers from an

inside pocket. "General Dodge has sent this correspondence with the instruction that I am to await your answer."

"I heard Dodge was in town. Where is he now?" Montego asked, stepping forward to take the papers.

"He found it most urgent to go ahead to Salt Lake City."

"Ah, those pesky Mormons."

"I beg your pardon?" Rich questioned.

"The Mormons are counting on the UP to come through Salt Lake, but that isn't going to happen. They'll no doubt raise quite a stink, and why not? Salt Lake is the biggest town between Omaha and Sacramento, at least in accordance with the proposed transcontinental line. Rightfully the railroad should probably consider their desires, but Ogden makes more sense. It's a more direct route, especially if they decide for sure to go north around the Great Salt Lake." He paused as if to contemplate something of great importance, then added, "And if you think this country is godforsaken, you should see that area. Alkali flats and vast barren salt beds. It's hardly going to attract anyone to settle there, and on that you may quote me."

Rich smiled and tried to remain polite. "I don't particularly think this country to be forsaken by God. Perhaps your own home-land is more charmingly put together, but I find a bit to hold my attention most every-where I go."

Montego looked at him for a moment and nodded. "I suppose some folks feel that way. No doubt there will be someone who is charmed by the Salt Lake desert regions. But not me. I find it no better in Laramie, where I hold property. The surrounding mountains are a pleasant diversion, but they are nothing more than that. And the winters out here are unbearable. I can't imagine how the Indians survive it, much less live to cause us so much grief." He pulled a cigar from his pocket and extended it to Rich. "Smoke?"

"No, thanks," Rich replied and waited for the man to clip the end of the cigar. Isabella brought him a lamp, and while Montego lit the cigar, Rich questioned him rather non-chalantly. "I understand you are good friends with Thomas Durant. Are you then originally from New York?"

Montego straightened and drew on the cigar for a moment. "I hail from Con-necticut originally," he finally replied. "My family settled there from Spain at the turn of the century. Montegos have been there ever since. It's quite lovely back east. Have you been there?"

"Connecticut? No, sir," Rich replied. "I haven't had that pleasure."

Montego nodded as if he'd expected such an answer. "Well, take my word, Mr. O'Brian, it's a little bit of heaven on earth." Montego then turned to his daughter. "I expected supper to be ready, but the air bears no indication that this is true."

Isabella nodded. "Melina went some time ago to shop for our supper. She's not returned."

"You don't suppose some manner of harm has befallen the girl, do you?" Montego questioned.

To Rich's surprise, Isabella merely shrugged, as though it were of no real concern to her either way. "I could go look for her, if you give me a description," Rich offered.

"Nonsense," Montego replied. "I'm sure the girl will return as soon as she can."

"Unless she's run off with our money," Isabella replied.

Rich studied the beautiful woman for a moment, finding her far less appealing in her lack of concern for her absent maid.

The sound of the back door being opened caused all heads to turn toward the hall. "There, you see," Montego replied, "she has returned. Isabella, why don't you go and instruct her to prepare food enough to include Mr. O'Brian?"

"Of course, Father," she replied, all hint of harshness now gone from her voice.

"Mr. O'Brian, please have a seat and we'll get right down to business." Montego motioned to the chair Rich had earlier occupied.

Rich complied, all the while watching the man with great interest. Dodge said no one was to be overlooked in considering the Union Pacific's safety, and Montego was no exception. He remained silently observant as the man leafed through the papers Dodge had provided. He looked to be in his late forties, but certainly no older. His dark hair bore no sign of gray, and his frame suggested a healthy man who was still in the prime of life.

"Yes, yes," Montego said, nodding at the papers. "I can provide answers to the general's questions, but it will take me a few days. I'll need access to several accounts in order to give him accurate figures. Can you stay?"

"Yes, sir," Rich replied. "I have, in fact, been instructed to do just that."

"Marvelous!"

"What is marvelous, Father?" Isabella asked as she returned to the room.

"Mr. O'Brian has just consented to stay with us for a few days."

"Then he'll be able to attend our party next week," Isabella declared with a smile.

Rich nodded and returned her smile. "What's the occasion?"

"My birthday. A small soiree with friends, but there is to be music and dancing." As Isabella spoke she leaned down to position a pillow behind her father's back.

As she did so Rich couldn't help noticing an ample display of her womanly attributes. Quickly looking away, Rich cleared his throat nervously. "I should probably see to my horse."

"We have a small stable in back," Isabella offered, straightening. "I could show you. Father's carriage man should be out there to assist you." Again she flashed Rich a smile and gave him a look that suggested she knew very well what she'd just displayed for him.

Rich picked up his hat and stood once again. "I'm sure I can find the way by myself. I wouldn't want you to take in too much night air." Her expression changed to a bit of a pout, and Rich decided that was the perfect moment to make his exit. "If you'll both excuse me. I should only be a few moments."

He slipped quickly from the house, feeling for some odd reason as if he'd just escaped a fate worse than death. The woman was clearly flirting with him, and while he had been given ample attention from women in the past, Isabella Montego looked at him as though she had already formulated a plan for what she would do with him.

Shuddering, Rich took up the reins to Faithful and clicked his tongue. "Come on, boy. Let's see to a proper rest for you." Glancing up at the house and spying Isabella Montego watching him from the window, Rich gave serious thought to making his bed with Faithful. He didn't know exactly what the woman had in mind for him, but he could tell it was probably only going to spell trouble for his assignment.

EIGHT

Jordana found traveling as a woman a benefit at times, but it greatly hampered her work as a reporter. When it came to speaking with railroad workers, she was clearly dismissed as a frivolous distraction. Supervisors refused to take her request for interviews seriously, and even when she presented copies of her stories as credentials, they scoffed and put her from the camp, declaring that building the railroad wasn't any garden party.

By the time she'd reached Salt Lake City, Jordana had decided enough was enough. Searching throughout the growing community, she finally managed to purchase clothing for herself. She determined to cut her own hair very short and play a man's game as a man.

Hidden inside her hotel room, Jordana took up the scissors she'd purchased and began cutting her dark tresses. Layer after layer fell to the floor, and in less than five minutes she was both pleased and shocked to see the effect of her actions.

"I look rather like Brenton when he was young," she said to her reflection.

She studied the image a moment longer. The result was shocking, for her cut was far shorter even than when she'd been forced to cut off her hair to escape the bushwhacker. She still remained obviously feminine, but having struck on a brilliant idea while shopping for clothes, Jordana reached into her handbag and pulled out a pair of silver wire-rimmed glasses. Putting them on, Jordana felt pleased with the way they altered her appearance and gave her a more masculine air. She decided against using the fake theatrical mustache she had purchased, because the harshness of the elements out on the rail line might too easily dislodge it. Best to keep things as simple as possible.

Her new clothes helped tremendously in establishing her disguise. The brown tweed jacket and gabardine trousers were sturdy and comfortable. It felt both strange and wonderful to wear the trousers. Why hadn't women thought of this earlier? Before she put on her linen shirt, she wrapped her bodice snugly with a long strip of cheesecloth in order to smooth out and conceal her bosom.

With a bit of brilliantine slicked on her hair and a natty tweed cap, Jordana felt certain she had adequately camouflaged her womanly identity. True, she looked more like a boy of eighteen than a man, but that should fit well with her plan of passing as Brenton's younger brother.

An hour later she proved to herself she had done just that. Doing her best to imitate her brother's lengthy stride, Jordana made her way to dinner. If exposed or questioned as a fraud, she would simply make up some excuse. Perhaps she could convince people she was involved in the theater and this was nothing more than a costume. She wondered silently if the highly religious Mormon community would find her actions such an abomination that they'd instantly jail her if her game were revealed.

But nothing happened. At the restaurant, she was seated and waited upon with nothing more than the perfunctory nods given most men. Then later, after dinner, she walked down the street with little concern or care for her appearance, completely confident that for all intents and purposes, she was thought to be a man.

Back in her room for the night, she started a journal of her experiences. She carved the initials "J.B." onto the leather cover. Mostly the journal would be the insights and adventures of Joe Baldwin, but she would also comment on what it felt like to move about in a man's world.

The next day she packed her things into a carpetbag, leaving out all her feminine apparel, which she would drop off at a mission in town. She could not risk the contents of her bags exposing her. If she should require a dress, she would purchase things as needed. She then went to wire Charlie Crocker about the changes. Standing before the telegraph operator, she considered her words carefully.

Charlie, my sister Jordana sends her best. Proceeding east. Will be in touch. Joe Baldwin.

She pushed the paper at the man, paid the requested amount, and waited until he'd actually keyed out the message before turning to go. Picking up her bag, she startled when the telegraph operator called out.

"Hey, mister, you want to wait for a reply?"

She turned around and forced herself not to smile. "Nah," she said in as deep a voice as she could muster. "Got a stage to catch."

The man nodded and Jordana hurried out the front door, afraid that if she lingered she might be required to further converse with the man.

As she traveled, her disguise proved to be a great success. Aboard the stage there were no masculine glances considering her every curve. She could simply sit back, tip her hat over her eyes, and doze without concern of someone trying to take liberties. Days later she managed to catch a produce freighter that was heading out to the front of the line where the UP was rumored to have created its own traveling town just east of Rawlins Springs.

Amazed at the freight cars, some with tents and crates stacked atop, Jordana found herself ushered into the world of the Union Pacific Railroad. The desolation of the land here was still far more appealing than what Jordana had left behind in Utah. At least here, sage covered the ground in a gray-green pattern that broke the monotony of the high desert plains. Rolling hills and occasional flat-topped mesas could be seen holding vigil over the camp, but otherwise the land was nondescript at first glance. However, Jordana knew the deception of this. First glances seldom gave her the information she needed. Leaving her bags,

Jordana started to amble off in the direction of a small rock ledge.

"Hold up there, young man. I need to know your business. If you're lookin' for work," the older man said, eyeing Jordana rather skeptically, "then you need to head up to that front car. The office is up there."

"I'm not here for a job," Jordana told him, trying to sound confident of her task. "I'm writing a story for the newspaper."

"What paper?" the man asked with the raise of a brow.

"The *New York Tribune,* sir."

"Ah, I thought you looked like a city fella. Well, you'll need to be talking to the bosses. Head on up to the front."

Jordana nodded and followed the rocky grade to where the boxcars stood one after another like an idle wooden serpent. Climbing the steps up to the platform, Jordana took a deep breath before knocking on the already open door.

"Yeah?" A short, wiry man who looked to be in his late forties appeared at the door.

Producing her credentials, Jordana explained, "I'm Joe Baldwin, and I'm writing stories about the railroad for the *New York Tribune.*" She found immediate approval in the man's expression. Newspaper stories meant publicity, and publicity equaled public interest. Public interest meant more investors, and that produced dollars for the UP cause.

"Mr. Baldwin," the redheaded man said, "glad to have you with us." He shook her hand with such a tight grip that Jordana was sure he'd broken it. She was glad she had thought to wear gloves in case her blunt-cut nails weren't enough to disguise her small, girlish hands.

"Good to be here, sir," she replied low and throaty.

"What kind of story are you lookin' to write?"

"I've been doing a regular series for the newspaper," she told him honestly. "The stories have varied from focuses on the wilderness and settlements beyond the Mississippi to the railroad. I come from a railroading family, and I'd like to see folks back east take a big interest in the transcontinental railroad."

"I think the boss'll cotton to you just fine," the man replied. "You stay here while I go fetch him up."

Jordana nodded, and once the man had gone, she glanced around the room, mentally comparing it to what she'd seen on the Central Pacific. Part of the boxcar had been turned into an office with a crude partition put in place, no doubt to divide the rest of the car off for private quarters. The office itself was dirty and lacked any charm whatsoever. Papers were strewn about the two desks, and a table set against one wall was covered with surveyor maps. Edging over to take a look at the plans, Jordana nearly jumped out of her skin when she heard heavy boots on the platform outside the door.

"Baldwin, is it?" a bearded man bellowed as he entered. Another man followed close behind the first.

"The name's Casement. Jack Casement, and this is my brother Dan. I understand you're writing stories for the paper."

"Yes, sir."

"What kind of stories are you writing?"

Jordana produced samples from a satchel and handed them to the man. "As I explained to your assistant, I've written stories to excite people about the West. I've written about the railroad because it's in my blood." She used the phrase she'd heard her father use many times over. It had a masculine ring to it, she decided.

Casement looked at the articles, then at Jordana. "Who is your family?"

"My father is James Baldwin. Perhaps you've heard of him."

"Yes indeed," the man replied.

Jordana tried to speak as she imagined Brenton might have responded. "My father helped me to get this job, and he is currently in New York." Jordana pressed on confidently. "My editor wishes to see stories on the development of the railroad, as well as episodes in the lives of men out here working the line. I would like to stay with you for a short time and gather material for my work." She fixed her gaze on the man's face and hoped she looked bold and determined.

"I think we can accommodate you, Mr. Baldwin. We have six sleeping cars for the workers. I can put you in there with the other men and you're sure to get your gut full of their bragging."

Jordana's stomach clenched. She couldn't very well maintain her identity and share a boxcar with a hundred other men. "If you don't mind, sir, I can just sleep outside under the stars. I have a tent." She silently praised herself for thinking to buy camping gear. "Most of my gear is outside with the produce freighter," she added nervously when she noted that Jack appeared to be looking for proof of her statement. "I sometimes stay up late into the night to write my stories, and I wouldn't want to cause the men to lose sleep just because I was about my work."

Jack nodded, but it was Dan who replied, "Set up your tent just the other side of the mess car. You can bed down there in privacy and have the place to write up your stories, and still be close enough to the action that I doubt you'll ever go in want of good conversation."

Jack agreed. "That would work well. We're up before sunrise around here and out on the line at first light. You're welcome to eat with the men, and I'll see that someone gives you a proper tour of the place after you're settled. There's a telegraph office in the rear car, so if you need to send a wire it's no problem. I'll be wiring General Dodge later today, and I'll let him know you're with us and see if there are any other instructions for you. Do you plan to stay with us for long?"

"I'll be moving back and forth along the line," Jordana replied. "I might only be able to stay a day or two for now, but in time I'll return for more information."

"Well, it's good to have you, no matter. Oh, and if you need clothes washed, the laundry's in the third car back. If you don't want to use our facilities, there're some women staying down by the river. You can get your shirts laundered for a fair price and get just about any other comfort you desire for a fair price as well." He snorted and laughed as if he'd just told some great joke.

Jordana refused to let herself be embarrassed. She wasn't stupid. She knew full well, or at least imagined she knew, what railroad men did with the bevy of camp followers when time and money permitted moments of pleasure. Charlie had tried to shield her from this aspect of the railroad, but she had chided him soundly, reminding him she was no longer a child. Maybe she'd go down and have a talk with some of those washerwomen and see what possessed them to give themselves over to that particular trade. It might make for a fascinating side story. Then again, it might prove too risqué to even be considered for print.

With the Casement brothers at her side, she reclaimed her gear and paid the freighter for allowing her to ride along. Jack called to a couple of men who were lounging in the shade of the mess car.

"Eberson and Myers will show you around," Jack told Jordana as they waited for the men to join them. "Men, this is Mr. Baldwin. I want you to give him a tour of the grounds and introduce him to some of the men. Take him out on the line and answer his questions regarding our work here. When it's your shift, take him with you and show him how it's done firsthand. You can even let him get his hands dirty, if he wants to give railroad work a try. Oh, and fellas, talk nice to the man — he's with the newspaper."

Jordana looked at the two ruffians, not exactly sure she wanted to be left alone with them. The first man was hardly taller than she was, but the stench of body odor and the line of tobacco juice that had made a permanent stain on the side of his mouth almost made Jordana sick to her stomach. The second man was tall, probably over six feet. His broad shoulder frame and thickly muscled arms suggested to Jordana that this man was no stranger to hard work.

"Name's Eberson," the big man told her, extending a hand in welcome. "Most folks call me Eb."

"Good to meet you, Eb," Jordana replied, hoping she sounded friendly.

"So yar a newspaper feller, eh?" the other man said, taking a moment to spit before continuing. "I'm Sam Myers, but most folks just call me Pup."

Jordana nodded. "Well, you can just call me Joe," she replied.

"Well, Joe, let's see to gettin' you settled in. There's a lot of sunlight left and the work sure ain't back here at the dinner car," Eb said, grabbing up her things with one hand. He hoisted them over his shoulder as though they weighed nothing at all. "We can put you over there," he said, slapping her on the back with his free hand.

Somehow Jordana managed to stay on her feet, but just barely. The powerful blow had caught her off guard, and while she knew the man was just giving her a friendly nudge in the right direction, she began wondering how she was going to be able to endure the days to come.

Pup laughed and then spit a long brown stream. "I need to take care of business first," he said and wandered off toward some bushes at the back of the dining car.

"What?" Jordana said, turning to see what the man was doing. She didn't look long, however, as the man was clearly working to unfasten his trousers. Men! she thought. Had they no manners? Did they not constantly offend one another with all their crudity? She willed herself not to turn red by focusing on her other companion.

"How'd you get a job like this?" Eb asked her. "You ain't much more than a boy. You ain't even shavin' yet."

116

Jordana swallowed hard and nodded. "I will be soon enough." Her tone was as defensive as a boy's might be at such a comment. "My father is an important man, however, and he got me this job. He thought it might help to grow me up."

Eb nodded. "Couldn't hurt. Maybe put some meat on those bones of yours. Can you shoot?" he asked, abruptly changing the subject.

Jordana nodded. "Pretty well."

"Good," the man replied.

Jordana frowned. "Why do you say that?"

Eb shrugged. "We get attacked now and then. Indians don't much like us tearing up the land. We ain't that far out of Rawlins, but we're far enough from civilization to keep an eye open."

By this time Pup was returning, and Jordana felt her cheeks grow hot in spite of herself. Her embarrassment along with a vivid memory of Rich describing some of the Indian attacks on the line caused Jordana to turn away. Pretending to cough, she straightened to see Pup and Eb staring at her oddly.

"What's the matter?" she asked gruffly, fearful of the answer.

"You ain't a lunger, are ya?" Pup asked.

"A lunger?" Jordana asked, looking from

117

man to man. "You mean consumptive?" She chuckled at the worried look on their faces. Perhaps they thought she was contagious. "Nah," she replied, trying her hardest to sound earthy and casual. "I swallowed a bug and about a pound of dust getting here. Just trying to spit some of it back out."

They grinned, apparently satisfied with her response. "Bugs around here get big enough to shoot," Eb told her with a laugh. "You'll get used to 'em soon enough."

But Jordana wasn't sure she'd ever get used to anything. Her back still ached from where Eb had slapped her, and she found their open crudity to be in sharp contrast with the exposure she'd had to these workers as a woman. It was amazing how differently they responded to her as a man.

Watching as Eb went to work on her tent and Pup stood scratching himself in a rather disgusting manner, Jordana could only glance heavenward and pray for strength.

■ ■ ■ ■

PART II
JULY 1868

■ ■ ■ ■

NINE

Brenton looked at Charlie Crocker and shook his head. "I can't believe you promoted her going."

Charlie looked sheepish. "I figured since she planned to go anyway, it might be a good way to get some information. It also forces her to keep in touch. Besides, I got a wire. She's due to meet up with me in Reno next week. You can come along as well and talk to her then."

Brenton shook his head. The thought that Charlie Crocker had orchestrated his sister's activity of spying on the Union Pacific was more than he wanted to think about just now. "If she gets hurt —"

"I know . . . I know. It's not that I didn't think about that myself. But like I said, she was determined to go one way or the other. I would have preferred you go with her, but I figured you'd want to stick close to Sacramento until your supplies came in. Maybe she'll hook up with that friend of yours. I told her it might be wise to have someone along. Someone she could trust, however. Do you suppose that Captain O'Brian is trustworthy? He might well be working against us, you know."

"I certainly don't know him as well as Jordana does, but I figure him to be all right. He's been honorable toward our family in many ways. I doubt he's a double-crosser."

"Still, he probably wouldn't see working against the Central Pacific to be the same as double-crossing Jordana and you."

"I suppose you're right," Brenton agreed. "I just don't know what to tell you, Charlie. I know these problems and troubles aren't going away."

Charlie rubbed his chin. "You can say that again. It's been one problem after another. If it's not a matter of supplies being delayed or sidetracked along the way, we're having to fight our own folks over which city deserves to have the railroad run through it."

"Are you still hearing protests from Carson City?" Brenton questioned.

"Yes and then some. Their own newspaper ran articles suggesting that the Central Pacific was seeking to move the capital to Reno. Like I have time to worry over where they put their capital. I'm trying to build a railroad, nothing more. I'm moving ahead at the fastest possible speed, using the best methods and men I can lay my hands on. Why, already the original estimates of many years till completion of the railroad have been shattered. We could have this thing together in less than a year. How can people have the audacity to accuse me of playing at politics?"

"What about the issues in Utah? Have you cleared the way to grade and lay track?"

"We filed a proposal with the secretary of the interior. I proposed a route from Humboldt Wells, Nevada, to Monument Point in the northwest corner of the Great Salt Lake. Later, so I'll file to bring the tracks all the way to Echo Summit."

"Where exactly is that?" asked Brenton.

"About seventy miles east of Ogden."

Brenton shook his head. "The Union Pacific will never tolerate that. They aren't going to be happy if you are allowed to build outside of Nevada. If you want to avoid conflict, Charlie, I'd say you're going about . it all wrong."

"I'm going about it in a manner that will benefit the CP. We're just as entitled to build this road as they are. The Union Pacific has dillydallied around and that is hardly my fault. They've finally managed to lay their track across the barren plains of the Midwest and now sit poking about somewhere west of Laramie. They've already arranged grading and track work with Brigham Young, although once that man learns there are few if any reasonable plans to bring the rail through Salt Lake City, General Dodge and his men may find they have a war on their hands instead of a railroad."

"And you send my sister into the middle of this as a spy?" Brenton commented dryly. "Charlie, I don't know what ever possessed you."

"She's very persuasive," Charlie admitted. "She had me convinced that she could take care of herself."

"I'll bet she did," Brenton replied. It was time to get back to work, and getting up from the table, Brenton glanced around Charlie's elaborate railcar office. "You've got it pretty nice here, Charlie. All the comforts of home." He could only hope that Jordana was finding herself just as comfortable. He glanced at the older man, and realizing that berating him further would do no good, he took up his hat and headed to the door. "You'll let me know the first chance you hear something from her?"

"Of course," Charlie replied. "The very

minute I know something, I'll send word to you."

"I guess we just have to wait, then, until Jordana deems it safe enough to check in."

"They're having a big party in Laramie," Jack Casement told Jordana as she dined with Eb and Pup in the mess car. "I've been told to bring you. It's some sort of gathering with all the big men on the UP."

Jordana shook her head. "Why would I be invited?"

"They want to meet you. Apparently some of them know your father and have read your stories."

"I'm not really much for parties," said Jordana honestly, "but I suppose I could go and report the matter."

"You take life too serious, Joe," Eb said. "Besides, there's gonna be women at this here party. Maybe you'll find yourself a western-styled sweetheart."

Jordana wanted nothing more than to be left alone, but seeing that this wasn't about to happen, she replied, "Well, now, there's a thought."

Pup grinned and elbowed Eb. "A good woman and free whiskey will get their attention every time."

"A free woman and good whiskey, don't

ya mean?" Eb countered. "I'll bet those UP velvet coats won't waste decent drink on us."

"I heard there was gonna be free whiskey," Pup replied. "And that's what I'm countin' on."

"Who said you were invited?" Casement demanded. "This is a party for the bosses. Why, it's even rumored that the Republican candidate for president will be there."

"General Grant?" Jordana questioned with disbelief. "Why would he come all this way?" She wondered if there might be something afoot that would spell trouble for the Central Pacific.

Casement shrugged. "He's good friends with Dodge. He ain't gonna be the only brass there. Dodge's good friends General Sherman and Sheridan are also coming."

"Sounds like a party to honor the heroes of the Civil War," Jordana muttered, now more certain than ever that the gathering couldn't be good for the CP. "I suppose a fellow would have to be daft to miss out on something like that. I'll go," she declared, pushing her plate back.

A train whistle blew loud and long, but it didn't keep Jordana from hearing Pup's and Eb's disgruntled complaints about being left behind.

"Sorry, fellows," she said, getting to her feet. "I promise to get all the interesting facts and tell you about it when I get back."

Laramie was a youthful town with a bevy of tent dwellings and a few permanent ones. The town itself had been nothing more than a trading post in the shadow of nearby Fort Sanders until the railroad had come through. Now Laramie held great promise to becoming one of the next great cities of the West.

The party, Jordana learned, was to be held in celebration of the Union Pacific and its progress. Durant would be there, as would many of the other important names associated with the UP. Joe Baldwin would be there as well, and hopefully, the occasion would give the Central Pacific some much needed information.

They were met at the depot by uniformed soldiers. The party, it appeared, was set to take place inside the fort. Considered to be safer there than in Laramie's wild surrounds, Jordana found herself feeling only slightly more at ease. The thought of appearing in this gathering of men, pretending to be one of them, made her especially nervous. Perhaps this time she finally had gotten in way over her head. Her mother had always chided her about leaping before she looked.

Still, considering how she would handle matters if she were found out, Jordana didn't realize they'd reached the fort until someone called out for the procession to halt. She glanced up, observing an exchange between soldiers and immediately thought of Rich. How he would laugh if he could see her now. He would probably howl at the thought of her posing as a man. She would have to write to him and explain the situation, at least in part. She didn't feel that it would be right to share all of Charlie's concerns, but there certainly couldn't be harm in asking Rich if he knew anything about the rumors of sabotage.

Thinking of Rich made Jordana feel a sudden loneliness. She missed his letters and hoped that Victoria was minding them carefully for her until she returned to California. She had determined to go as far as Omaha, or to take as long as the end of August, whichever came first. If she waited much later in the year, it would be difficult to get back to Sacramento. The Sierra Nevada were unpredictable with their snows, and even with the Central Pacific in place and several miles into Nevada, travel would be harrowing at times. Problems with avalanches and destroyed snow sheds were evidence of this. Of course, if the party proved productive, she might well find herself traveling back to give Charlie the information he so badly needed to keep his railroad in competition with the UP.

They were quickly ushered inside the mess hall, where the party was already under way. The large room had been decorated with garlands and flags and red, white, and blue bunting. The army band had just assembled and was tuning up for a promising evening of music. Jordana quickly scanned the room, noting both uniformed officers and civilian officials. Sparsely coloring the collection of men were stylishly clad ladies. Each woman, even the oldest and most plainly dressed, had more than her share of attention. The sight of these women being so openly spoiled and pampered caused Jordana to feel strange. She would normally be among their number. She could easily remember occasions back in California when she herself had been the object of such attention.

Chiding herself for being silly, Jordana allowed Casement to make introductions to several people before he slipped away into the crowd to talk to someone across the room.

"So you're the Baldwin son who is writing

stories about our railroad," a man declared.

Jordana peered up into the face of a man who looked oddly familiar. "I plead guilty as charged," she replied in a low, sure voice.

The man laughed. "Durant, Thomas Durant," he said and extended his hand. "I'm the man who had the vision for this line."

Jordana thought him rather pompous and said, "May I quote you on that?"

Durant chuckled. "Most assuredly, although there are others who would deny it. General Dodge, for one, thinks I haven't got the line's best interests in mind, but I am more than fixed on my point of concern. The Union Pacific must be built, and it must succeed, and it cannot be held back for any reason. If we dally, that nonsensical Central Pacific Railroad will eat our profits alive."

"Nonsensical railroad?" Jordana raised her voice to be heard over the band, which had struck up loud introductory notes. They were calling the first dance, but Jordana wanted to hear more from Durant. Perhaps the idea of sabotage came from the highest level. "I've been out along the Central Pacific," she said, hoping this might put him at ease. "I would hardly call their effort nonsensical."

Durant eyed her sharply. "I've read much

of what you've written about that bumbling line. They can't keep laborers or entice investors. I'll probably have to rebuild the entire line when we finally reach their efforts."

Jordana wanted badly to comment that Durant would find the CP line in perfect order and probably closer than he wanted to believe, but she held her comments, choosing a different line of questioning instead.

"I understand the Union Pacific is making progress in Utah. Are you willing to speak on the details, sir?"

Durant nodded. "It's no secret we have a contract with the Mormon leader Brigham Young. There are already four thousand men at work blasting out the approaches to the longest tunnel on the UP line."

"Where will that be?" Jordana hoped to remember all the details of the conversation.

"Echo Canyon," Durant told her, then turned to welcome another gentleman. "Ah, Mr. Baldwin, have you met Baxter Montego?"

Jordana looked up to meet the dark-eyed man's expression. "No, I haven't yet had the honor."

"Mr. Baldwin," Montego said with a nod.

"Our young friend here," Durant told Montego, "is writing a newspaper story for the *Tribune*."

"The *Tribune?*" Montego asked.

"The *New York Tribune*," Durant explained. "He is one of the Baltimore Baldwins, the railroading family."

Montego's interest perked up considerably at this. "I am most pleased to meet you, sir." He flashed an oily grin.

Jordana nodded curtly. "The pleasure is mine, sir."

"I was just informing young Baldwin about our progress in Utah," Durant continued. "The Mormons are an easy breed to work with. Such a difference from the hotheaded Irish rowdies."

"How so?" Jordana asked.

"They neither drink nor gamble. They are completely devout in their faith, praying over meals and concluding their day's work with the same. They refuse to work Sundays and spend their time in prayer and worship, but the energy they expend during the week more than makes up for the loss. I would take one of Brigham Young's men any day over an Irishman, and you may quote me on that."

Jordana nodded. "When a man is seeking to please God, he often takes a serious pride

132

in his work that he might not otherwise consider."

"It is not only a desire to please God that causes a man to take pride in his work," Montego countered. "A man must first learn what labors are important to him — beneficial to him. There must be a sense of priority and clear vision of the future."

Jordana eyed him seriously. "And what is your priority for the future, Mr. Montego?"

The mood seemed quite tense for a moment, but then Montego laughed and swept his arm in the direction of a stunning young woman. "My daughter, Isabella, is my priority, Mr. Baldwin. Her future happiness is most important to me. I would seek to have her happily settled with a man of means and conviction." He looked back at Jordana and gave a wry smile before adding, "Perhaps even a man such as yourself."

Jordana struggled to keep from laughing, but just as she thought surely she would burst into unladylike howls, she saw something that took her breath away.

Rich!

When the scarlet-clad Isabella pulled back from the man she had so possessively taken to the dance floor, Jordana could clearly see that her partner was none other than Rich O'Brian.

What is he doing here? she wondered. And what is he doing with *her?*

"She is beautiful, is she not?" Montego said with great pride. "A bit spirited, but in the right way. She would make a good wife to any man, but to the man who wins her heart . . . well . . . there would be no end to the joy and benefit."

Jordana felt fixed to the spot. Staring at the couple, she knew in her heart that Montego figured her to be taken with Isabella. And why not? Dressed as Joe Baldwin, she could hardly claim to be otherwise.

"She is lovely," Jordana finally managed to say. She despised the way the woman leaned into Rich's lead, pressing herself against him in a bold, unsuitable fashion. And Rich! The man was smiling. Laughing and enjoying himself as if . . . as if . . . Jordana bit her lip and turned away. She didn't want to admit what she was sure of. He was enjoying himself. There was no other word for it. He had a beautiful woman in his arms, and she had captured his attention quite thoroughly.

Durant was now speaking to Montego in hushed tones that neatly omitted Jordana from the conversation. It was clear they wished for privacy, and while Jordana knew she should probably try to hear what was being said, she couldn't keep herself from turning back to watch Montego's daughter in the arms of Captain O'Brian. Jordana's Captain O'Brian.

Why do I feel like this? Jordana questioned herself. It isn't like the man can't dance with whomever he pleases. But Jordana had known flirtatious women like Isabella Montego. She could tell, even from this distance, that the woman was up to no good. Never mind that Jordana knew nothing at all about her.

Jordana stood seething in silence. To all appearances, she was a young man captivated by a beautiful woman. And no matter what else happened, she couldn't reveal herself to be otherwise. Still, she fought the urge to rush into the circle of dancers and throw the coy ninny onto her backside. Without thought for what she was doing, Jordana edged a little closer to the circle. Perhaps up close, Isabella Montego was ugly. Maybe Rich was just being nice.

She tried to convince herself that either way it really didn't matter, but she was having no success. The music concluded and the dancers halted to applaud. Isabella possessively gripped Rich's arm as though he might somehow blow away if she were to let go. As they neared the place where Jordana stood, panic ripped through the facade of Joe Baldwin. Quickly, Jordana retraced her steps and forced herself into the conversation with Durant.

"So what is your projection for the completion of the line?" she asked rather breathlessly.

Durant had just opened his mouth to answer when Isabella Montego's honeyed voice called out. "Father, you really should dance. The exercise would do you good. Why, it's even put color into the cheeks of our Mr. O'Brian."

Jordana balled her hands into fists and held them taut at her side.

"Isabella, my dear, you may do the dancing for this family," said Montego.

"I should go," Jordana muttered and started to edge around Durant, but Montego took hold of her shoulder and pulled her back around.

"Don't leave. I wanted to give you a proper introduction to my daughter." Turning to the young woman in question, he added, "Isabella, this is Joe Baldwin. He's a reporter for a newspaper in New York City."

Jordana could feel Rich's shock before turning to meet his stunned expression. Isabella smiled coyly and extended her hand in a fashion that suggested a kiss rather than a shake. Opting for neither, Jordana barely took hold of her hand and bowed over it quickly before letting go.

"I'm so pleased to meet you, Mr. Baldwin," Isabella purred.

"I would be interested to meet you as well," Rich said suddenly.

Jordana forced herself to meet his eyes. She saw a mixture of humor and surprise and maybe even a hint of anger in his expression. She extended her hand. "Joe Baldwin." Her voice squeaked slightly as she spoke.

Rich gripped her hand tightly, refusing to let go. "Baldwin. That name seems familiar. I don't suppose you know a Jordana Baldwin." Still he held her hand. "Or perhaps a Brenton Baldwin?"

Jordana could only stand there as Rich continued to torture her hand in his viselike grip. "They are my . . . ah . . . sister and brother," she finally managed.

He dropped his hold and smiled. "I know them both quite well. You must be one of their younger siblings. But I don't recall them talking about you. Of course, that Jordana was usually up to her neck in some kind of trouble, and Brenton was just as busy following after to put her back in line. She was a twenty-four-hour-a-day project, let me tell you."

Jordana gritted her teeth and fought the urge to slug him. "I'm sure she was spirited in the very best way. I happen to know my sister better than my other siblings, and she is very cautious and considerate, even when being judged to be otherwise. As for me, I've been busy working with my father and the newspaper he so graciously put me in touch with," she finally replied.

Rich grinned. "Now that you mention it, I do recall them talking of a younger brother. That must be you."

"How marvelous," Montego declared. "Then you are all practically old friends."

Isabella appeared intent on pitting the two potential suitors against each other and began to make contrasts immediately. "Why, I wonder if you dance as well as Mr. O'Brian."

"I'm sure that Mr. Baldwin must," Rich countered before Jordana could speak. "He was raised in one of the best families to grace the eastern seaboard."

"How charming," Isabella replied. "I do seem to recall hearing of the Baldwins, Father. Don't you?"

"We're a big family," Jordana replied. "Now, if you'll excuse me."

"But aren't you going to dance with Miss

138

Montego?" Rich pressed.

Isabella struck a questioning pose and smiled in an enticing way. Jordana shook her head. "Perhaps another time. I'm feeling a bit fatigued."

"Well, that's all right," Isabella said, a hint of a pout on her exquisite face. "I'm sure Mr. O'Brian has enough vigor to dance all night."

Jordana couldn't stand the way she clung to Rich, and without thinking of what she was doing, she reached out and took hold of Isabella in a forceful manner. "Maybe just one dance."

As she pulled Isabella through the crowd in a most ungentlemanly manner, Jordana could hear Rich's laughter ring out from behind her. *I will pay him back for this if it's the last thing I do,* she silently vowed.

Thankfully the dance went quickly, and to Jordana's relief, it was a reel that sent her down a line of partners without much time to make small talk or endure bodily contact. When the dance ended, Jordana bid her partner a good evening and quickly ducked out through the crowd as several men came up to vie for Isabella's attention. Reaching a line of buildings, Jordana disappeared into the shadows to regain control of her shattered confidence. The summer sun provided light well into the evening, but now as it faded beyond the horizon, the inevitable night would soon be upon them and Jordana had no idea what to do next.

Forcing her nerves to steady, she tried to imagine how she could deal with Rich and the Montegos. She began to relax and feel her breathing even out as she heard the band strike up another waltz. No doubt she was not even missed in the growing crowd.

Then, just as Jordana turned to walk farther beyond the parade grounds and people, she was stunned to find herself slammed up against the barracks wall. Without having to look up, she knew that Rich had followed her.

"For the love of money, woman! What in the world do you think you're doing?" There could be no doubt of the worry and anger betrayed in his voice.

TEN

"You haven't answered me," Rich said, still gripping the lapels of Jordana's tweed suit. "What are you doing here?"

"Well, I'm not fawning all over that over-exposed siren, like some folks I know," Jordana replied hotly, pushing away from Rich's hold. She was only now getting over the shock of seeing him here. Forcing herself to calm, she added coyly, "I think she has plans for you."

Rich ignored the barb. "Why are you here? Why didn't you answer my letters?" Glancing over his shoulder nervously, he swallowed and put several inches of distance between them.

"I didn't answer your letters because I haven't been home to pick them up. I wrote you and told you I'd probably be traveling for a short time."

"Yeah, but you didn't say you'd be traveling to Laramie."

141

"Well, I didn't know it myself," Jordana replied.

Rich appeared to calm a bit also.

My, but he was handsome. Jordana felt as if she were looking at him for the first time, and in truth, it had been such a long time that she now realized his features had begun to fade in her memory. They stood out in bold relief now — very bold. Jordana liked the way he'd trimmed his mustache and slicked back his hair for the dance. She liked seeing him in civilian clothes as well.

"I guess you got out of the army without any trouble," she commented casually.

Rich eyed her strangely for a moment, then nodded. "I've been out for a few weeks now. I'm working as a courier for the Union Pacific."

Jordana perked up at this. "That's wonderful! You can tell me all about the railroad and what's happening."

"Why?"

"Why?" she repeated. "Because I'm writing stories for the *New York Tribune*. You know very well that I've been doing this for some time."

"Oh, that."

"Rich, you sound like you have something else on your mind," Jordana said, brushing a mosquito off the back of her neck.

"I just can't believe you're standing here dressed like this, and that you've chopped all that beautiful brown hair off again, and that you were dancing with Isabella Montego as if you'd been doing it all your life."

Jordana grinned. "I didn't know you thought my hair was beautiful."

Rich moaned and looked heavenward. "You're treading in dangerous waters, Jordana."

"Joe. You'd better get used to calling me Joe."

"All right, Joe —" He intoned the name through gritted teeth. "Don't you know that the railroad is having enough trouble? There are all sorts of fools out there trying to make money off the various companies involved. There are a passel of underhanded dealings going on, and you're standing smack in the middle of the biggest gathering of Union Pacific officials to date and acting as though it's nothing more than a Sunday school picnic."

"I fail to see why you're so worked up. I've been doing just fine," Jordana replied. "I've been living at the camp just outside of Rawlins, and the men are wonderful. A bit crude, granted, but they're really nice. They even invited me to join them the next time they go to town to celebrate."

"Do you know how men like that *celebrate?*" Rich asked with emphasis.

Jordana grinned. "Eb says it involves women and whiskey. The stronger the better, as he likes them both with a bit of kick."

"Listen to yourself!" Rich exclaimed in complete exasperation.

"I'd advise you to do the same." Jordana looked at him intently, turning suddenly solemn. "Do you really think I'm going to set myself up for exposure? Do you honestly believe me so stupid that I would let them liquor me up and treat me to a night with some washerwoman or saloon girl?"

She was surprised to see, even in the evening light, Rich grow embarrassed by her statements. Looking down at the ground, he asked, "Does your brother know what you're doing?"

Jordana snickered. "I doubt very much that Charlie Crocker had the guts to tell him."

"Charlie Crocker? The same one who's in charge of building the Central Pacific? Why is he involved with what you're doing?"

Jordana didn't like the suspicion in his tone. She realized she was perilously close to betraying her true mission. She was coming to doubt if Rich would understand about her spying for Charlie, and she

144

certainly didn't expect him to approve her plan. No, it was best if she kept him believing she was doing nothing more than writing stories.

Considering her answer carefully, Jordana replied, "Brenton is taking photographs for Charlie Crocker. That's how I get ahold of my brother. It's either that, or I have to send letters through my sister Victoria and then wait for Kiernan to have a chance to find Brenton. Oh, speaking of Victoria, did I tell you she's finally going to have a baby? We're all very happy."

"Jord— Joe, you're changing the subject."

Jordana smiled. "Yes, I am. You are much too serious and worried. I think you should take a rest, Captain O'Brian."

"I'm no longer a captain."

"That's right," Jordana replied, "so I expect that you won't be trying to boss me around anymore."

With a sigh, he shook his head. "I'm not trying to boss you around now. I'm just worried about your well-being. There's been enough trouble on this line, and now with you involved, it's bound to double."

"Well, thank you very much," Jordana responded curtly, turning to go. "And here I thought you'd be happy to see me again."

Rich was immediately at her side. "You

know I'm happy to see you," he muttered low. "I'm just not happy to see you passing yourself off as a boy."

"A man," Jordana corrected. "I'm supposed to be a young man."

"Yeah, sure. I wish you'd reconsider and go home," Rich replied.

Jordana began walking back toward the party. "I am going home. Probably within the next week. I miss my family, don't you know? But I'll be back. There's just too much work to do."

Rich reached out and took hold of her arm. "You're gonna get yourself hurt if you're not careful."

"Are you offering to go with me as my bodyguard?" Jordana said mockingly. She didn't have any idea what she might do if he replied in the affirmative.

"No," he said, shaking his head. "Although I think someone ought to be following you around full time. You know as well as I that every time I've come in contact with you, you've been in one kind of trouble or another."

"Did it ever dawn on you, Mr. O'Brian, that *you* might be the problem? I don't seem to have too much trouble at all until you appear on the scene. Maybe it's your fault."

"Look, I'm just suggesting that you're out

of your league here. You need to be careful." The exasperation in his tone was clear.

She took pity on him, forgetting about her own insecurity earlier. "I promise to be careful, Rich. Don't worry so much. I only knife-fight with my eyes open these days."

She left him standing there, wishing with all her heart she could continue talking with him. There were a million unspoken questions, and the answers were clearly within Rich's grasp. Why did she have to like him so much? Why did she have to care what he thought?

Forcing herself to go back among the crowd milling about the parade grounds, Jordana wondered what Rich would think of her mission. Would he understand? Being a logical man, it would seem he'd view it as most productive. Dangerous, maybe. But definitely productive.

The next morning she traveled back to the railroad camp with Jack Casement. She had no further opportunity to see Rich and decided it was better that way. She had wanted to tell him all about her work for Charlie and enlist his help, but her intuition told her to hold off and say nothing. Something made her most uneasy about the whole situation, and while she couldn't explain it, she felt slightly guilty for not being honest with Rich.

After two more days at the camp, Jordana felt it was definitely time to get back to Charlie. The only problem was, she couldn't very well wire the information without it being clear to the telegraph operator that she was a spy for the Central Pacific. She thought of sending a post, but realized that could take weeks given the problems that always seemed to hound the postal service. She decided to keep to their previous arrangement to meet in Reno. How to get there was another problem. Then her problem resolved itself when the same freighters she'd ridden into camp with reappeared with their weekly shipment of produce. Hitching a ride back to town was no problem at all, and from there it would be a simple matter of taking the stage. If seats were available.

Word was rumored to her that Charlie had moved into the Utah Territory in order to press forward a claim he'd made for the Central Pacific. Jordana hoped this was the case and arranged with the stage driver to leave her off if they should find this to be true, but there was never any sign of the man and his railroad, so Jordana traveled, as originally planned, to Reno.

Where only weeks ago there had been

little more than a watering hole, Reno was now a city fully grown. Over two hundred crude structures stood as witness to the boom that had been brought about by the arrival of the Central Pacific. With a deep sense of amazement, Jordana stepped off the stage into a world she couldn't even begin to recognize.

Tasting the dirt in her mouth and realizing that her clothes and body were just about as dirty as they could possibly be, Jordana desired nothing more than to find a bath. The stage had stopped not far from one of the newly arranged hotels, but Jordana felt an uneasiness at taking up residence there. A group of rather rough-looking fellows stood outside the place calling out and harassing passing travelers. At one point, Jordana watched as one man stuck out his leg and tripped a young suit-clad man. Jordana could only imagine what they might do to her.

Mustering up her courage, Jordana picked up her bags and headed down the street in the opposite direction. The stage driver had told her of a more respectable boarding-house several blocks away, and Jordana figured this would be far more to her liking. But before she could get that far, Jordana was nearly run over by a crush of people.

Momentarily expecting to be in the midst of a full-blown fistfight, Jordana instead found herself surrounded by giggling young ladies who couldn't have been much older than herself.

Dressed in delicately patterned gowns with their hair hanging in curls from high atop their heads, the girls were clearly a part of some more formal celebration. Jordana was surprised by her unwelcome feelings of envy. For the first time in a long while, she actually missed her feminine clothing. She even missed the companionship of other women. The girls giggled and chattered, all the while moving off toward what appeared to be a church. It was only then that Jordana realized one of the young women wore a veil atop her artfully styled hair. The revelation explained the entire matter. They were a wedding party making their way to church.

Jordana tried not to be overcome with feelings of sadness. There was no reason to feel so out of sorts, but looking down at her dusty attire and manly design, she felt a longing to once again be a lady. And why not? she reasoned. After all, that's what I am.

But then the hard realization of the task before her set in. She had a job to do — a job that could not be done in ruffles and petticoats. She had to continue the pretense of being Joe Baldwin. With a sigh, she continued down the road. Maybe she was crazy. Maybe she had missed God's plan for her life and had instead chosen one that was taking her ever farther away from His will for her. She wished she could talk to Rich about the entire matter, but she knew what his counsel would be. He didn't understand why she was doing these things. And with good reason. Jordana wasn't entirely sure she herself understood, so how could Rich possibly know?

ELEVEN

Jordana had a brief meeting in Reno with Crocker, imparting what little she had learned thus far about the Central Pacific's competitors. She also had a visit with Brenton and Caitlan. It was wonderful seeing them again and just being with family. Yet she always felt their — well, mostly Brenton's — disapproval of her activities. She hated his being upset with her, and she hated causing him to worry, thus she decided to remain in the Reno area for a time, where Brenton and Caitlan had taken up temporary residence as they photographed the progress of the railroad.

Jordana devoted much of her time to the work of the Central Pacific, and it wasn't long before her days began to follow a predictable routine. Every camp was very nearly the same. The horses and mules needed to help with hauling the supplies were staked out at the edge of the camp, the carts and wagons positioned to neatly wall them into a compact circle. Mule skinners and blacksmiths were available to see to the animals' needs, and with the first shrill whistle at dawn until the end of work at sunset, these men and their animals were vital to the building of the line.

The men worked well together, having learned the smoothest path of least resistance. The graders and bridge builders were set out ahead of the main track layers. They were responsible for the preparation work necessary to bring the line forward. Jordana, maintaining her persona of Joe Baldwin, mingled among the men, listening to their tales and collecting information as she went. As Joe Baldwin, no one was overly concerned at her presence. Charlie had made it clear that Joe was to be allowed access to the camps.

As was the routine, a supply train would arrive just before dawn. With little ceremony, iron plates, ties, spikes, and rails were unloaded, along with an assortment of hardware and telegraph poles. As the railroad was built, new telegraph lines were installed to provide instant communication for the workers on the line.

Once the train was emptied, the workmen could draw from the supplies throughout the day. Ties were carried along on wagons; rails were more readily moved on low flatcars. These were, in truth, little more than frames on wheels drawn by the horses or mules over the already positioned tracks. Weighing in excess of 560 pounds each, these steel ribbons were meticulously pounded into position through the seemingly inexhaustible efforts of the Irish and Chinese workers.

Taking tea with several Chinese workers one afternoon, Jordana found the tables turned on her. Instead of asking the men questions and listening to their broken English answers, she was the focus of their interest.

"You plenty small for a man," one man told her. "You know how to fight?"

Jordana shook her head. "Can't say that I do." She couldn't imagine where this line of questioning would lead.

"You need learn way to fight," another man, this one younger and more talkative than the others, stated. He stood and motioned to Jordana to do the same. "You take off coat. I teach you."

Jordana smiled and shook her head. "That's all right. We don't need to worry about it. I carry a small pistol in my satchel."

"What if can't get gun? Look here, you do

this," the older of the three ordered. "You not big. You not like other men."

If they only knew, Jordana thought to herself. Standing up with great reluctance, Jordana shrugged out of her coat. She wasn't at all sure where this would end up, but she saw no other way to deal with the situation.

"You need to be fast," the man told her. He reached out with lightning-quick reflexes and took hold of Jordana's wrist. Before she realized what was happening, the man had somehow flipped her over onto her backside.

The three Chinese laughed heartily at her stunned reaction. Staring up at the man who had deemed himself her teacher, Jordana could only join them in laughing.

"You not fast enough, Preacher."

"Preacher" was the nickname some of the Irish had given her, and the name had stuck. Refusing to join the men for nightly brawls or sojourns into the saloons, Jordana chose instead to remain in camp quietly reading the only book she had in her possession at the time — her Bible. One of the men, seeing her interest in Scripture and lack of vices, deemed her to be the camp preacher, and that was the beginning of a new identity. Now even the Chinese had taken it up.

Dusting off her backside, Jordana got up

slowly. "Well, you've proven your point," she said, meeting the sinewy man's knowing nod. He was hardly taller than she. "I guess it wouldn't hurt to learn a little bit. Especially if you can teach me to do what you just did."

The man grinned. "I show you plenty, Preacher."

Jordana could not say her weeks in the Reno area were a complete waste. Just what she learned from her Chinese friends was invaluable, and she had a feeling these Oriental fighting methods they called "jujitsu" might well save her life someday. She tried to ignore her growing restlessness, and when Charlie approached her about going to North Platte to check out some rumors he'd heard about a new rail-laying technique the UP had developed, she turned him down. Her relationship with Brenton seemed to be improving, and she simply was reluctant to do anything that might harm it.

However, this seemed an especially futile endeavor one day when she returned home to the little rented house she shared with Brenton and Caitlan. She was covered with dust and grit from crawling about in a tunnel to get the true feel of the Welsh workers' experience.

"You look awful," Brenton had told Jordana with a grimace. "I can't believe you continue to do this to yourself."

"You should have seen me two hours ago!" she laughed as she shrugged out of her ruined jacket, which she hung on a peg next to Brenton's clean woolen coat.

"Jordana, you cannot keep venturing about as a man. One of these days someone is going to find out."

"Yar brother's right," Caitlan put in. "Ya'll end up getting yarself killed."

"I'll be fine." Jordana sat in a chair and began tugging off her mud-caked boots. "I know how to stay out of trouble."

"Since when?" Brenton snorted.

With one boot gripped in her hand, Jordana lifted narrow, defensive eyes toward her brother. "I have an important job to do. And this is the best way to do it." Her tone brooked no argument.

But that didn't stop Brenton. "Charlie can find someone else to do his spying — preferably a real man!"

"I wish you would stop this, Brenton. I'm tired of your constantly standing in my way. I have a peace about what I am doing."

"Do you have a peace about defying our parents?" he rejoined sharply. "They would never condone your behavior."

"I seriously doubt that," Jordana responded confidently. "They have never stood in the way of us fulfilling our dreams. I admit dressing as a man isn't exactly my dream, but it is the most expedient way to achieve it. I did in fact write Mother and Father about Joe Baldwin, and though they were a little shocked, they only told me to be careful." She smiled inwardly as she recalled that letter from her mother, who had adjured her to take care of herself and her new "son" Joe.

"Brenton," Jordana went on, "your support means a lot to me, but I cannot build my life entirely upon it. I wish you could accept me as I am, but I will be who I am regardless."

Brenton gazed at her long and hard, making Jordana feel uncomfortable beneath his close scrutiny. But she held her ground.

Finally, with a heavy sigh, he replied, "I see I have no say in your life. I just thought you might care about my feelings on the matter." With that he turned to leave the room.

"Brenton, I —"

But he hurried out the door before she could finish. No more was said on the matter when he returned, and the next day, Jordana accepted Charlie's assignment to go to North Platte. It seemed best for now to put some space between herself and Brenton. She hated hurting him, yet she truly believed she had been right in telling him she could not always fashion her life to suit him. She prayed they could one day come to terms with these issues. She prayed it would be one day soon.

"There's been nothing but trouble since that newspaper fellow was here," Dodge told Rich O'Brian. "I'm not sure if it's coincidence or merely the fact that more information has been put out there for public consumption, but we're now facing yet another matter of sabotage."

"What has happened?" Rich knew full well Jordana couldn't have been to blame.

"Explosive materials have gone missing," Dodge replied. "There have been other supplies missing as well, but this is the most worrisome."

Rich nodded. "I can understand why."

"Worst of all, the supplies were stolen from here in Laramie. Taken from right under our noses on the night of that big party at the fort."

Rich considered his encounter with Jordana and knew beyond doubt that she'd had nothing to do with it. Jordana had departed from Laramie fairly suddenly after they met, but he was almost certain her departure had more to do with him and his displeasure in her than in the Union Pacific. "I spent time with Baldwin," he finally said. "I don't think he's at all interested in sabotage."

"Have you heard anything suspicious? Seen anything?" Dodge questioned sharply. "Have your travels not rendered you even one possibility as far as who is responsible for this interference? Perhaps Baldwin is in cahoots with someone else. Someone who does the dirty work after Baldwin learns all the answers."

Rich didn't feel at all comfortable in explaining Jordana's appearance, and so he kept the matter to himself. "There are always suspicious things going on. Most have a logical explanation once a fellow checks it out in full, but I really have nothing solid to offer you. I can say this, however. I know Joe Baldwin. He's a good man and his family has invested in the Union Pacific as well as the Central Pacific. I don't think we have to worry about him being a problem."

"You're certain?"

Rich nodded. "I feel very confident that Mr. Baldwin will not present a problem for the UP. He isn't the enemy."

Dodge considered Rich's words for a moment. "Very well, then. We still need to find out who *is* our enemy."

Rich had already been considering this matter quite thoroughly. "What do you know about Montego's involvement in land development around here?"

"Not a great deal. I know there was some previous scandal regarding land being sold for exorbitant prices. There was also some controversy about the construction of the line. Apparently some of the parties involved were thought to be estimating outrageous prices. I'm not sure what the outcome has been or if there has been any solution. Durant seemed unconcerned, and I'm uncertain as to what part Montego has played. Do you have some reason to believe Montego is a problem?"

"I'm not sure. It's more a hunch than any certain knowledge. I'm uneasy when I'm around the man."

"His daughter seems to have a definite interest in you," Dodge said with a wry smile. "Perhaps as a confirmed bachelor you find her presence to be your undoing."

Rich shook his head. "I don't think so, sir, but Isabella Montego may well be a part of the problem. She seems quite interested in the business dealings of the Union Pacific."

"Most unusual for a woman," Dodge agreed.

"Perhaps not as unusual as it used to be," Rich replied, thinking of Jordana.

"Well, either way," Dodge continued, "we need to find the source of our trouble. In the wrong hands, those explosives will prove to be deadly."

Rich nodded. The man was of course right, and it was his job to find out the truth on the matter.

TWELVE

Moving from Laramie to North Platte, the last person in the world Rich had expected to run into was Jordana Baldwin. But to his surprise this was exactly whom he encountered stepping from the train on that hot afternoon.

Dressed in a new tan suit and possessively carrying her bags, Jordana looked for all the world to be a young man of no more than eighteen or nineteen. Rich had come to the depot in order to speak to the station manager about the management and security of UP supplies when he spied Jordana bounding down the steps of the passenger car.

Without thought as to how it would appear, Rich quickly bid the station manager good day and went after Jordana. He felt his pulse quicken at the thought of being with her again. She had very nearly haunted his dreams at night, and he wondered for a moment if she were actually here or if he had somehow conjured her in his mind.

"What are you doing in North Platte?" he asked in a low voice as he caught up to her. Reaching out to touch her, Rich assured himself she was very real.

Jordana turned and offered him a heartening smile. Perhaps she had put their last encounter behind her. "Just the man I'd hoped to find," she said.

He narrowed his eyes. "Why me? What's going on? And why are you still in trousers?"

Jordana grinned and looked around her, then whispered, " 'Cause I'd raise quite a scandal if I took them off."

"You know what I mean," he fairly growled, forgetting his joyful moments before upon seeing her. "I don't know why you aren't back home with your brother."

"Because Reno's not home," Jordana replied.

It seemed to him her words had even surprised her. He thought she looked rather sad, too, or regretful, and he might have told her so had it not been suddenly imperative to get her out of the middle of the street.

"Comin' through!" a voice called out from behind them, and Rich barely had time to pull Jordana to one side of the road before the teamster swung his wagon around the corner.

"Let's go someplace where we can talk," Rich said.

"I'm starving!" Jordana declared. "How about we go someplace to eat? I'm so empty my ribs are ticklin' my backbone."

Rich stopped dead in his tracks and gaped at her. "Listen to yourself. You sound like anything but a lady."

She grinned at him in that manner that went straight to his heart. "I'm not supposed to be a lady," she whispered. "Just in case you've forgotten."

"No, but I think you have." Rich grabbed her arm and nudged her in the direction of a building across the road. "We can eat over there. The food's a bit greasy, but the coffee's good and strong."

"Sounds fine by me. After eating railroad food, I think I can stomach just about anything."

Rich shook his head. "I can't believe I'm hearing you talk like this. Here, give me your gear."

Jordana looked up at him, her warm brown eyes melting his heart into a pool of liquid. "Don't you think that would look a little odd? One man carrying another man's baggage?"

Rich rolled his gaze heavenward. "Fine. Have it your way."

After they ordered thick beefsteaks and bread, Jordana turned to Rich and smiled. She was enjoying herself, and for some reason, that irritated Rich all the more. "I read all your letters and figured I'd answer them in person. Besides, I needed more information for my stories. So that is why I'm here. How about you? Why are you still here? I was only hoping against the odds you might still be in town, since your last letter was postmarked from here over two weeks ago."

"The Union Pacific sends me where they will. I've been back and forth from one place to another over the last two weeks. You just happened to catch me here. Actually, I'm waiting for some papers from Baxter Montego. You remember him, don't you? He's the man who was considering marrying you off to his daughter."

"I remember his daughter was the one exposing an unnatural amount of her no doubt best attributes and clinging to you like you were a life ring and she was about to drown."

"Why, Joe, you sound jealous," Rich teased.

Jordana's face flushed and she stiffened

and looked away. Surprised by her reaction, Rich wondered if he hadn't hit upon the truth. Was it possible that she was jealous of Isabella? And if so, what exactly was she jealous of?

"Well, anyway, my work is all along the line and then some," Rich explained. "But I still don't understand why you are here."

"I've told you before," Jordana countered. "I'm writing stories for the newspaper. The stories have been a tremendous success. I've even received a raise. They're paying me top dollar for my work. You don't understand, but people back east are hungry to know what's going on out here in the West. They need to see it for themselves, and because it's so difficult to put pictures out there for them, I create pictures for them in words."

"But what about the dangers? You are constantly putting yourself in a place where someone can and will take advantage of you."

Jordana merely shrugged, tired of defending this worn argument. Deliberately, she picked up her cup and tossed back nearly all of the thick black coffee as though it were milk.

Rich shook his head. "I suppose you can handle your liquor just as well."

Jordana laughed. "You know I'm a teetotaler. The guys at the camps call me Preacher, on account I don't drink or smoke or play cards or visit the ladies in town."

Rich waited to respond until the waitress, a heavyset matronly woman, deposited their steaks and bread on the table.

"If you gents need anything else, just give me a holler. We've got some good pie today. Made fresh-like with new berries instead of preserves."

"We'll consider it," Rich told her, then turned his attention back to Jordana. "Look, the truth of the matter is, I don't like thinking about you sleeping out there by yourself, traipsing all over the country without someone to protect you from harm. It just doesn't make good sense."

"Let's say grace," Jordana murmured, then bowed her head. She prayed quickly and quietly over the food, then began to dig in almost immediately after issuing the "amen."

Rich watched her attack the meal with great gusto for several moments before continuing. "Did you hear what I said? It isn't safe for you to be out there."

"Does it make good sense for *you* to travel alone?" Jordana countered.

"No, in fact, it's just as dangerous in some ways," Rich admitted. He ran a hand through his dark hair in exasperation. "But this is different. You are, whether you dress and act the part, a lady, and sooner or later someone may very well take advantage of that fact. I haven't been able to think of much else since I knew what you were up to. You just have to listen to me."

"Rich, you worry too much," Jordana said. Then grinning, she leaned forward. "I wonder why you worry so much."

"That's easy," he replied, without concern as to how it might sound. "I don't want to see you hurt."

"Are you sure there isn't something more?" She seemed to be pushing him for some inner truth.

"Because I don't have many friends," Rich answered, knowing that it was far more than that. "I'd like to see the ones I have remain alive. And unhurt."

Jordana chuckled, then began hacking away again at the steak. "Admit it, Captain, you care about me because . . ." She stopped in midsentence. The expression on her face suggested a sudden epiphany. She put down her knife and, with the teasing very clearly absent from her voice, said, "Please tell me you don't care about me for the reason I think you do."

Rich grew uneasy and picked up his own

knife and fork. "I'm not about to propose, if that's what has you worried. I care because we're friends and I enjoy what we have together. I'd hate to lose that. If nothing else, you amuse me."

Jordana stared hard at him for a moment, then nodded. "I can live with that."

They ate in silence for several minutes until Rich could regain control of his thoughts. Jordana was clearly sensing in him something that he was rapidly realizing he couldn't deny. He hated to think of her out there among other men, because, frankly, he would just as soon keep her to himself. But how could he tell her that? He'd made a promise to be nothing more than friends. He'd assured her that men and women could be friends without becoming romantically linked. Finally Rich decided to put forth an idea. He'd thought about it for a long time, and given Dodge's concern that Jordana might be inadvertently passing information back to the wrong people, he figured it was a plan that could benefit them both.

"What if you stuck close to me?" he asked suddenly.

"What are you talking about?"

He settled back in his chair and rubbed his chin thoughtfully. "I have an idea that just might help us both."

"Well, I'm listening."

"I am moving along the UP line on a daily basis. Sometimes I have to linger in one town or another while I await information to take on to the next town. You could travel with me, get the information for your stories, and talk to all the people you need to talk to. Then you could write your stories, and at the same time I would be at peace knowing that nothing bad was happening to you."

"How in the world would you ever get your bosses to approve something like that?"

"Why would they care, so long as you weren't dictating the stops? I mean, if you would agree to travel with me at my pace, I don't see why they would concern themselves with the matter. After all, didn't you tell me they'd given you a free pass on the UP?"

"Yes," Jordana replied. "They did. They like the idea of their progress being reported back east. And the stories have in fact generated new investors."

"So why do you suppose they would have a problem if you were traveling under my care? If nothing else, they would also see it as my keeping you from sticking your nose in where it didn't belong."

"And where might that be?"

Rich had begun working the steak over once again. "There's always trouble for any business venture. You know there have been problems for the Union Pacific. We've had more than our share of Indian attacks and murders. We've had to endure sabotage and destruction of the line, whole sections of rails torn up, and telegraph wires destroyed. We can't be lending ourselves over to someone who might either purposefully or inadvertently give the wrong information to the right person."

"Are you accusing me of trying to cause harm to the Union Pacific?" Her tone was quite indignant. "Do you not realize the harm that has been done to the Central Pacific? Harm that clearly bears the markings of the Union Pacific's desire to see the line halted in Nevada or at least slowed to a crawl so that the UP can gain better footing and mileage?"

Rich hadn't expected this kind of answer. It did nothing to put his mind at ease and everything to set his nerves on edge. "Jord— Joe, talk like that around here can get you killed. And it's exactly the reason I think you need protection. You're already suspect to many folks."

"I'm working for the newspaper. The

proof is there for anyone who desires to see it," she said, throwing down her napkin. "I don't have to take this."

She got up and stormed out of the room, leaving Rich no choice but to follow after her. Throwing down some coins, he took up the things she'd left behind in her hurry and caught up to her halfway down the block.

"I don't know why you're acting this way," he said, tossing her things on the ground in front of her.

Nearly stumbling over the bag and rolled-up tent and bedding, Jordana stopped and looked at Rich with great solemnity. "I have family involved with both sides of this railroad. I would love nothing more than to see it completed and done so in a timely and beneficial manner for both sides. I despise the politics of it and wish men weren't such ninnies."

Rich saw the misery in her expression, and his heart went out to her. "Look, I'm not accusing you. I just want to keep you from harm. I don't want your reputation damaged."

"And my living on the trail with you would do less to damage my reputation?"

Rich felt a deep pang of emotion. How could he explain? He had lost his heart to her — just as he'd promised he wouldn't. He wanted nothing more than to be with her, to express his love for her, to have her love him in return. Why did this have to be so hard?

"Look, Rich," Jordana said, picking up her things. "I know you've made a valid offer. I like the idea of having the companionship of someone I trust, and perhaps if I remain in this costume, no one will be the wiser but us." She straightened and smiled. "And since I know how you feel, I can trust that my reputation will remain completely safe. But if we're to spend time together, you've got to stop worrying about whether I can take care of myself and whether or not my motives are pure. I'm not going to do anything to hurt either side of this venture."

Rich wanted to shake her and tell her that it had nothing to do with the harm she might cause. He worried about her getting hurt. He couldn't bear to see the woman he loved brought to harm. Perhaps he should speak honestly with her. Maybe he should just tell her how he felt. In fact, his heart demanded it, but his head told him to hold back. Jordana would run like a frightened rabbit if he declared that his feelings for her were more than friendship and brotherly concern. And, in truth, his feelings had him pretty frightened as well. Swallowing his emotions, he nodded.

"So we're agreed? You'll stay with me?" he prompted.

"For a time," she replied. "But I won't tolerate your treating me like a child, or worse, some fragile china doll."

Rich shook his head. "I have no intention of treating you like a child, and I will allow you free rein in your activities — within reason, of course." However, he looked away as he spoke, for fear his eyes might betray him if he gazed into her face.

At least she would be safe. He could keep an eye on her whereabouts and know that if anything should go wrong, he'd be nearby to set things right. Now he'd just have to convince Dodge that his logic was sound. He'd have to explain that he wanted only to relieve Dodge's suspicions. Jordana wasn't the problem, of this he was sure. But some-one else was responsible for the disappear-ance of the nitroglycerin and other materi-als, and Rich still needed to find out who that person was.

"Well, well. If it isn't Rich O'Brian, the great and glorious cavalryman himself."

Rich glanced up at the voice harshly intruding upon his thoughts. He easily recognized the face of a man he'd not seen in almost ten years. The man had been practically a boy then, but his features were nearly identical, except now they were hardened with age and anger. Staring at this newcomer as if seeing a ghost from his past, Rich found any words of acknowledgment sticking in his throat.

The scowl on the man's face left no doubt that this wasn't to be a joyful reunion. "So tell me, O'Brian. Kill any wives lately?"

Rich heard Jordana's gasp, but that's all he heard before he lunged at the intruder, balled fist smashing into the man's smug face. An instant later, he knew he had done nothing but fan the flames of a painful memory. Rich found little satisfaction in the action. The fact that he'd avenged himself in front of Jordana did not wipe out the accusing words.

Kill any wives lately?

The echo of the horrible accusation was the last conscious thought Rich had as the man's beefy fist plunged up against the side of his head.

THIRTEEN

For the rest of the day Jordana tried desperately to get someone to explain why Rich was now unconscious in a North Platte jail cell. The man who'd accosted Rich on the street turned out to be one of the deputies, and the sheriff seemed unconcerned with Jordana's declaration that the fight had been prompted by him and not by Rich.

"I want to see him," she demanded in her lowest, most authoritative voice. For more than once she was glad to be clad in trousers and a suit coat, knowing full well that no one would have given her the time of day had she swept into the office in a gown and curls.

"He's still out cold," the sheriff declared. "He was probably drunk when this all started."

"He was not drunk! I'd just had dinner with the man. Send for a doctor."

"I ain't wastin' the doc's time," the man

replied. "Men have been sleepin' it off in this jail since it was put together. He's just one more."

"He'll no doubt come around," the ill-tempered ruffian who'd prompted the fight declared.

"I find your treatment of this man intolerable," Jordana raved. Then reaching into her satchel, she produced paper and pencil. "I'd like to write about this for the newspaper back east. Could I please have your names?"

The sheriff paled considerably. "You're that newspaperman I've heard about? The one writing the stories about the West and the railroad?"

"That'd be me," Jordana said with a bit of a drawl to her voice. "I find it fascinating to report on the people of the West. Yourselves included. That a man can simply be walking down the street, minding his own business, and have a sheriff's deputy pick a fight with him — well, that's newsworthy in my book. Especially when the man ends up jailed for defending himself. I think it rather fits the eastern thoughts of the uncivilized West. Perhaps it can serve as a warning to others when considering North Platte as a place to settle down and raise a family."

"Now just wait a minute, mister," the deputy said, stepping forward. He had the same ugly scowl on his face that Jordana had seen him use on Rich.

"I sure hope you don't plan to hit me like you hit him. I'm afraid our size difference would put me at a great disadvantage," Jordana stated, cowering back just a bit for effect.

The man stopped short. "I wasn't plannin' on hittin' anyone. O'Brian hit me first."

"Well, you did insult him and start the entire matter," Jordana replied. Glancing down, she jotted notes. "Now could I have your name?"

"The name is Patrick Worth. Not that it means anything to you. But it means a good deal to that man in the cell," the deputy declared.

"Look," the sheriff interjected, "we don't want trouble."

Jordana nodded. "Neither did we. That man in there is my friend, and I intend to let the world know of his treatment."

"Don't go getting all uppity." With a curse, the sheriff tossed the keys at the deputy. "Worth, go wake him up. I don't care if you have to pour half the Platte River on him. Just get him on his feet."

Grumbling, the deputy did as he was told, and Jordana put her paper and pencil away. "I appreciate your help, Sheriff."

"I intend to get to the bottom of this," the man replied. "And not just for fear of it turning up in your story."

Jordana smiled to herself but said nothing more. In the other room she could hear Rich moan and then shout at his treatment.

"Leave me alone, Worth!"

"Bring him in here," the sheriff called out.

Jordana braced herself for Rich's appearance. His eye had already been blackening when Worth had thrown him over his shoulder and hauled him into jail. No doubt he would look even worse now.

Staggering somewhat, Rich appeared in front of Worth. He was dripping wet from where Worth had obviously poured a bucket of water over him. His face, bruised and blackened, caused Jordana to wince. His right eye was nearly swollen shut. He glanced only briefly at Jordana, and she thought he looked rather regretful to find her there.

"Now I want to know what this is all about," the sheriff demanded.

"Ask him," Rich muttered.

The deputy shrugged. "It's personal."

"Well, it just got *un*personal," the sheriff replied. "After all, it was my jail that you chose to park his carcass in. Now I want to know what's going on."

Both Rich and the man called Worth seemed to squirm uncomfortably. Something was desperately wrong between the two, and she recalled the cryptic words that had passed between them. The man had accused Rich of murdering his wife. Jordana didn't even know that Rich had ever been married, much less widowed. Then again, maybe that wasn't what the man was implying at all. Perhaps Rich had somehow been responsible for killing Worth's wife. Maybe while still with the army, Rich had accidentally killed Mrs. Worth.

The standoff was most uncomfortable, and finally Worth, seeing that his employer meant business, growled and moved across the room, as if he wanted to put some distance between himself and his adversary. "He used to be married to my sister. It's just a family dispute."

The sheriff nodded. "I don't know what caused this ruckus between the two of you, but I don't have the time for this. If it's family trouble, keep it outside of my jail. Pat, you get on back to your business. And you two" — the sheriff jerked his head at Rich and Jordana as he took his seat at a well-weathered desk — "get out of here, and see to it you stay out of trouble. I'd suggest, O'Brian, that you keep clear of my deputy."

Rich looked at the sheriff and then at Jordana. "It won't be a problem unless he makes it one." The anger in his voice was still evident.

Jordana grabbed her luggage and followed Rich out into the street, struggling to shift her things to one shoulder while scrambling to keep up. For a block or more they were silent, but when they neared the hotel where Jordana had told Charlie Crocker she would be staying, she forced Rich to stop.

"I wired ahead to have a room waiting for me here," she said. "Why don't you come inside? We can sit in the lobby and you can tell me what's going on." It was more a suggestion than a question.

"I don't want to talk about it," Rich said without even looking at her.

Jordana maneuvered around to stand directly in front of her friend. "Rich, this doesn't make any sense. The man is your brother-in-law and obviously there is some trouble between you. Why not just tell me about it, and maybe together we can come to some positive conclusion."

"No!" he said between clenched teeth. "I can't talk about it."

"Can't or won't?" Jordana asked angrily.

At this, Rich finally met her gaze. "Will you just let it be?"

She knew it was probably not a good time to goad him, but at the same time she was hurt that he'd never shared this part of himself with her. He had been married and never mentioned it? And now, even more troublesome were Worth's accusations about Rich killing his wife. How could Rich claim to be her friend and still keep such important matters from her?

"Don't I have a right to know what's going on?" She tried to keep the hurt from her tone but not very successfully.

"No, you don't," he replied flatly. "It has nothing to do with you." His swollen eye narrowed even more, and the fixed, steely expression did nothing to mask the pain he so clearly felt.

"Maybe it should have something to do with me," Jordana replied. She felt certain that it would be better if they got this out here and now. Perhaps if Rich could talk about the problem, he would be able to free himself of the obviously painful memories. "We've been friends for a long time now. Don't you trust me?" she asked softly.

"It isn't a matter of trust, Jordana," he said, barely remembering to drop his voice as he spoke her name. "It's a matter of privacy. I'm not ready to share this with you, so please, stay out of it."

Jordana could not keep from feeling wounded by his words. Shifting her things once again, she pushed past him. "Fine. I have a reservation here. I'm going to get my room and then I'll be about my work. Don't bother to follow me. I'm not ready to share this part of my life with you, so all bets are off."

"You're being childish," he said, taking hold of her arm.

Jordana fought to keep the tears from her eyes. "Leave me alone." She pulled away, leaving him to stand alone outside the hotel. Perhaps she was being childish, but he'd hurt her feelings by so deliberately refusing to talk to her about what had happened. Then it dawned on her. Perhaps it wasn't Rich's refusal to talk so much as Jordana's sudden awareness of his having been married.

Stepping up to the front desk, Jordana arranged for a room and quickly hastened to find some sanctuary in its privacy. The room was nothing to boast about. It held little more than a narrow iron bed and washstand and mirror, but it was a place where Jordana could strip away the facade of being Joe Baldwin and allow herself to rethink the day's events.

Why am I so angry? she wondered as she

dropped her luggage on the floor and gave her hat an angry toss onto the bed. Stalking back and forth at the end of the bed, she pounded her fists against her legs. I won't give in to this. I won't feel anything more for him than friendship. It isn't prudent and it certainly doesn't fit with my current task.

Taking off her outer coat, she hung it on a peg on the back of the door. Dust scattered onto the floor, and seeing how dirty she'd become, Jordana began to pound and shake the coat in a fury of emotion.

"If he doesn't want to share it with me," she muttered, "then let him sit in his silence." She coughed slightly, realizing the mess she'd stirred up.

Going to the window, she pulled up the heavy green shade and raised the window. Sticking her head out for a breath of fresh air, she gazed out onto the street. Soon it would be dark and she'd already been warned that the nightlife of North Platte was not for the weak willed. On the train, the man riding next to her spoke of how he wouldn't wish North Platte on his worst enemy. He spoke of the horrors he'd endured there and how ruthless the people were. Suddenly she found herself wishing that Rich were taking up residence in the room next to hers. At least then she'd know where to find him. Now, however, she had no idea where he might have gone.

A light knock on the door, followed by the announcement of a message, sent Jordana in a rush to learn the contents. Perhaps Rich felt bad for the way he'd treated her and wanted to apologize. Perhaps not.

"I'm Joe Baldwin," she said as she met the curious gaze of a young woman.

"I have a telegram for you, Mr. Baldwin. We're real sorry for not giving it to you when you first came. A man brought it before you registered. My ma had it in the back room, so my pa, the one who signed you in, he didn't know nothin' about it."

Jordana nodded. "That's all right. I understand." She handed the girl a coin from her vest pocket and took the telegram. "Thank you," she murmured and closed the door on the girl's continued open stare.

Jordana scanned the contents of the letter and smiled. It was from Charlie in a strange cryptic code they had worked out some time before. It was agreed that messages would only come when absolutely necessary, and apparently Charlie had deemed this matter to be of utmost importance. Apparently Leland Stanford was overnighting in North Platte after a meeting back east with Collis Huntington. Charlie referred to him as Mr.

186

Addison, a family friend, while Huntington was simply called Mr. H. Jordana was to meet Stanford at a nearby boardinghouse at exactly five o'clock.

Jordana hoped she'd recognize the man, because for certain, he wouldn't recognize her. They had met before, but Jordana had been introduced as the sister-in-law of Kiernan O'Connor. She wondered if he would find her costume change too much of an assault on his sense of propriety. Then, too, she wondered if Stanford might be trying to conceal his appearance. He was quite well-known in certain circles. If the UP folks spotted him in town, they might very well accuse him of spying. Still, as the governor of California, he had business that entailed more than the Central Pacific and could perhaps convince them that his dealings back east had nothing at all to do with UP and CP developments.

Glancing at the pocket watch she kept, Jordana realized there was little time to reach Stanford by the suggested hour. Hurriedly, she caught sight of her reflection in the mirror over the washbasin and decided it would have to do. She looked the part of the road-weary traveler, to be sure.

Hurrying downstairs while pulling on her coat, Jordana paused at the front desk only long enough to ask where she might find the Meredith Manor Boarding House.

With less than five minutes to make the journey from one end of town to the other, Jordana found her pace quickened and her determination fixed. She paid no attention to the enticing calls offering everything from gambling to drink to a comfortable bed. She felt only a pang of regret when she happened across a sign that read "Turkish Steam Baths." At this point, she'd have loved any kind of bath, but in her state of disguise, public bathing wasn't an option for certain.

At the wrought-iron gate of the Meredith Manor, Jordana paused for a moment to catch her breath. She could clearly make out the form of Leland Stanford as he sat smoking a cigar and enjoying the afternoon from the manor's wraparound porch. Several men were standing not far from him, and together they appeared to be sharing casual conversation.

Jordana hoped that Stanford would understand when she introduced herself. She had no way of knowing if Charlie had mentioned her costume to Stanford. Steadying her hand, Jordana opened the gate and made her way to the porch.

"Mr. Addison?"

"I'm Addison," Leland Stanford replied, sitting up to take note of the young man calling his name. "You must be Joe Baldwin."

"That I am, sir."

"Your brother is a good friend," he said, reaching out to shake Jordana's extended hand. "Gentlemen," he said, getting to his feet, "I hope you'll excuse me. I've a message to deliver to this young man, and I'm sure he'd like to hear about his family."

The men murmured their understanding, and Jordana readily followed Stanford to the far end of the porch. After casually glancing around them to ensure privacy, Stanford smiled.

"Crocker told me you were going about in trousers. I just had to see it for myself."

Jordana laughed softly. "I wasn't sure but what you might burst out in laughter upon seeing me. Charlie did."

Stanford nodded. "It's just most unusual to see a young woman dressed as you are. But I must say, you play the part well."

"Thank you. But what is it that has Charlie sending you to meet up with me?" Jordana questioned.

"Charlie's had more trouble on the line. This time he's had to halt along the way to play diplomat to the Shoshone Indians.

Supplies have disappeared from time to time, and it seems there have been shots taken at the track builders. A couple of the Chinese were injured. Nothing serious, but enough of a problem to halt the line temporarily."

"Why were the Shoshone at odds with the railroad?"

"Apparently," Stanford said, lowering his voice even more, "they don't like the Chinese, and they didn't like Charlie tearing up the lower Truckee River."

"Did Charlie manage to calm them down?"

Stanford smiled. "You know Charlie. He arranged a peace treaty by announcing that he was a big chief, too, and wasn't about to stand by while his people were killed. The Shoshone chief sat down with him and together they agreed upon a treaty. Charlie told him the penalty for breaking the pact was death."

"What arrangement did he make?" Jordana asked, wondering just how this information was pertinent to her position.

"The Shoshone will ride free in first-class cars, that is as soon as we have them up and running through that area, but they have to stop shooting at the builders and leave the supplies alone."

"It sounds like Charlie settled the affair amicably. I guess I don't understand what it has to do with me."

Stanford's brow knit together earnestly. "At one point, Charlie asked the chief to return the supplies that were missing, but the man said he'd already sold them to another group of white men."

Jordana felt a cold chill go down her spine. "Did Charlie ask the chief where these men could be found?"

"He tried, but the chief seemed to realize that he had said too much and pretended not to understand. They finished signing their treaty, and Charlie said the chief quickly took up his copy and disappeared with his men."

"And Charlie thinks I might be able to find out if the Union Pacific had something to do with this?"

"They're about the only ones who could use the supplies, unless of course they were merely destroyed. Charlie's hopeful that evidence might be produced. If it can be proven, Huntington wants to take it before Congress and demand that the Union Pacific be forced to compensate the Central Pacific, and that they be forced to halt their line in Utah and give that over to the CP to continue building."

"Surely he doesn't think the Union Pacific will ever go along with that," Jordana replied. "They're already enraged that Charlie would dare to put men in Utah to survey, much less to actually build. They aren't going to just walk away and let Charlie and the CP have Utah."

"Well, if you can find the evidence we need, it just might sway Congress to see things our way. You'll have to be quick about it, however. Now that the treaty has been signed, Charlie isn't sure who these men will get to do their dirty work next."

Jordana nodded. "I'll do what I can. I suppose this takes precedence over my original assignment."

"Yes, proceed on this immediately."

"How will I get word to Charlie? If I send a wire, I could expose myself as a spy. The post will take longer than what Charlie will want to wait."

"If you learn something, you'll have to come back to where we're building and deliver it in person. Charlie plans to be at the forefront of the activity, but he's set up a base of supplies in Wadsworth. With the line ever closing, it's nearly as quick for you to come to us as to work it any other way."

Jordana nodded. "All right. If I learn anything important, I'll take the UP to the

192

front and hire a stage from there."

"Good. I knew we could count on you. I leave in the morning for home, but if you should need anything, just let me know."

"I will," she promised. "Oh, by the way, would you mind taking this back to my brother?" she asked, producing a folded piece of paper. "It's a letter. I didn't have time to post it. He's worried about me, and I try to keep him posted whenever I can. I doubt it will set his mind at ease, but it's all I can offer him right now."

"Consider it done," Stanford told her. "And, Joe, Charlie suggests you continue to downplay the success of the CP in your newspaper stories. Perhaps if the Union Pacific doesn't feel it's such a threat, they'll become careless and expose themselves without giving us over to a lot of extra work. And whatever you do, don't mention Charlie putting men to work in Utah."

"Very well," Jordana replied. "I'll write instead of the woes that have befallen the Central Pacific with missing supplies and Indian conflicts."

Stanford nodded. "That's just the thing. And the entire truth as well!"

Fourteen

Hidden in the alleyway across from the Meredith Manor Boarding House, Rich watched as Jordana talked intently with a gentleman who, by the look of his attire, was of some means. Rich thought he recognized the man but was uncertain. Why was Jordana here, and who was this man? Obviously they had something of great importance to discuss, for they'd had their heads together for over ten minutes. He had thought of walking by and pretending to just happen upon them but figured it would look too suspicious.

She had been so angry and hurt when they had parted in the street. He had gone back into the hotel lobby and was debating whether to seek her out when she'd made a mad dash back out into the street, giving him little chance to declare himself. Following her had been easy, but now he wondered if it had been at all prudent. He questioned his own motives, telling himself that he merely did not want her loose on the rowdy streets of North Platte without some protection. But why not call out to her and reveal his presence? He didn't know. Perhaps he was just afraid to face her. He should never have kept from her that part of his life that had included his wife, and now that it had come out into the open, he should not continue to cling to his secret. They were friends — close friends, he hoped. It was wrong to treat Jordana so.

It was also wrong to stand in the shadows spying on her. But just as Rich had determined to let the incident slide and walk away, he saw her give her companion a piece of paper. Dodge's concerns about Jordana being in the business of sabotaging the Union Pacific came back to haunt him. Had she managed to get herself caught up in some form of mischief? Had her brother-in-law, a man whom Rich knew worked for the Central Pacific, convinced Jordana to aid them in the destruction of the UP's ambitious progress?

Ducking into the shadows, Rich waited until Jordana was headed back down the street before following after her at a leisurely pace. He didn't know quite what he would say to her or how he would ever be able to find out about her dealings with the man at the boardinghouse. Perhaps, he thought, he should abandon the idea of following Jordana back to the hotel and instead go see to the identity of the man.

Torn between keeping Jordana under his protection and accepting that she was fully capable of taking care of herself, Rich finally decided to go back to Meredith Manor. After all, the man was still on the porch enjoying his cigar. Surely Rich could think of something to say that might shed some light on the man's identity.

The iron gate moaned in protest as Rich pushed it open. He paid no attention to closing it behind him, but instead strode up the walkway as if he too were in residence in this very boardinghouse.

"Good evening," he said as he mounted the steps.

"Good evening," the impeccably dressed stranger replied.

"Looks like rain," Rich offered.

"I suppose it does," the man answered. "I hope it stops by morning. I shall be traveling and I would hate to endure closed windows and stuffy temperatures."

"Ah, so you'll be taking the train?"

"Yes. I have business in the West."

"Seems like everyone does these days,"

Rich said, smiling. "By the way, I'm Mr. Rich." It was the best name he could come up with on the spot. "I've just come to see if there's an available room."

"Addison's the name," the stranger replied, "and I don't think you'll find anything available. As I understand it, the last room was let to me."

Rich nodded. "Well then, I suppose I'll make my way back to town. Seems a bit rowdy, but a fellow can't always expect a quiet night's sleep."

"No, I suppose not," the man said with a smile.

Rich retraced his steps and made his way straight to the hotel where Jordana had taken a room. Inquiring as to the whereabouts of her room, Rich made his way up the stairs and down the hall. He paused for a moment at the door, wondering if this was the wisest thing to do. She might very well slam the door in his face.

Deciding he would present her with an apology, Rich knocked and waited for Jordana to open the door.

"Who is it?" she asked in a low voice.

"It's me, Rich."

She opened the door and looked at him with surprise. "I didn't expect to see you again. I figured I'd made you about as mad as a wet hen and you were probably halfway to Laramie."

He grinned. "I kind of figured the same thing about you."

She smiled, and, encouraged, he continued. "Actually, I figured we could have supper together. Maybe talk about our plans for the days to come."

Jordana shook her head. "I think I'd better just go to bed."

"You have to eat," Rich pressed. "Look, the hotel has a fine dining room. Let me buy you a meal and apologize properly."

"You're making an apology?" she asked in disbelief.

"I have been known to do that from time to time," he answered.

"I didn't figure you'd ever admit to being wrong."

He shook his head. "I never said anything about being wrong. I simply wanted to apologize. I was about to come after you before, but you shot straight past me and raced off down the street."

She appeared to pale at this. "Supper would be fine," she said abruptly and stepped into the hall. Pulling the door closed behind her and locking it, she looked up at Rich as if expecting him to lead the way.

Realizing that he'd somehow unnerved her, Rich motioned toward the stairs and allowed her to go first. He followed after her, wondering how to tactfully question her regarding her actions with Addison. He decided that nonchalance was probably the best bet.

"Like I said, I came after you, but then I saw you'd met up with some friend down at the Meredith Manor. I didn't want to be rude, so I waited until you were done."

Jordana bit at her lower lip and kept her gaze focused on the stairs. "Mr. Addison is a family friend from California. I was surprised to find him here in Nebraska."

Rich felt a bit of relief in her statement. At least she hadn't tried to lie to him about meeting the man. "Did you have a nice visit?"

"Yes," Jordana replied, offering nothing else.

Rich pointed the way to the dining room and waited until a young woman seated them at a nearby table before continuing. "Did he bring you news of home? Is your family doing well?"

"They're all fine," Jordana replied. "I gave him a letter for Brenton. I penned it on the train. I was hoping to explain why this job is so important to me. I hate not having his

199

support. I don't suppose my letter will matter, but I thought I would give it a try, nevertheless."

Rich felt all of his remaining worries fade. She hadn't tried to conceal the fact that she'd given the man a paper. And now it all made completely good sense. She was merely writing to her brother, and with Addison headed home in the morning, it would prove to be the quickest way to get the letter to Brenton. But just as his relief was restoring his good nature, Jordana spoke again.

"Look, Rich, I don't think it's going to work out for us to be together. I've thought about this today, and after talking to Addison and hearing that there're all sorts of activities going on in Utah and Nevada, activities that would make for good story material, I'm afraid I'm going to have to leave North Platte in the morning."

Rich fought to keep his wits about him. He didn't want to let her get away, and he still felt the need to prove to Dodge that she wasn't a threat. "Are you just saying this because you're angry at me? I am sorry for the way I acted."

"I'm sure you are," Jordana said earnestly. "I'm sorry too. I was just worried about what had happened with the Worth fellow, and I wasn't at all sure why, when we'd been telling each other so much over our years of correspondence, you all of a sudden became so closemouthed."

"Even so, that's no reason to put aside our ideas of working together. Just think how much happier it would make Brenton to know you were under my protection."

"I don't need your protection," Jordana replied defensively. "I was only seeking your companionship. And before I learned of the activities in the West, it seemed like an acceptable thing to stick around here with you and then travel wherever the courier business might lead you. But now it's different."

"Well, it doesn't need to be," Rich replied. "I'm sure to have work that requires my presence in Utah or even farther. General Dodge even told me that I might be used to deliver the new congressional papers regarding the discussion of where the two railroads will meet. If that's the case, I'll be going to California or wherever else they might need me."

Jordana appeared to consider this for a moment. "It seems rather odd that they would send their courier that far. Why not just have the information sent by post?"

"Probably because of all the problems we've experienced. They won't want to trust that information to just anyone."

"I suppose not," Jordana replied, not sounding completely convinced.

"So will you just humor me and wait until the day after tomorrow?" Rich asked, a gentle entreaty in his tone. "I'm sure I can have my traveling orders by then and know exactly what's needed of me. I promise, if I can't journey with you west, I won't put up a fuss about you going on alone."

She smiled at this. "Very well. But I hope that sooner or later you'll learn to trust me."

He gave a start at this. "What makes you think I don't trust you? Didn't I tell you earlier that I wanted to clear your name from being associated with anything to do with the trouble along the line?"

"I wasn't talking about that," Jordana said soberly. "I was referring to your encounter earlier in the day. You know, you really should have put ice on that eye of yours. It looks positively awful."

Rich touched his eye gingerly. "It's still pretty sore, but I think some of the swelling has lessened."

"Perhaps a drop from your miraculous blue bottle will help," she taunted good-naturedly. When he chuckled in response, she added more earnestly, "Still, you don't trust me enough to tell me the truth about what happened."

He looked at her briefly, then turned away. "It's not a matter of trust, Jordana. It's an issue of pain."

The following morning, Rich made his way to the railroad depot, where he hoped to get a wire off to General Dodge. It was imperative to keep the general apprised of his plans, and now that he'd promised to take Jordana west, he needed to ensure that Dodge would stand by his plans.

The westbound train was just loading, and amidst the bustle of passengers and baggage, Rich made his way to the telegraph office. He did as he'd done on several other occasions. Presenting a letter to the operator, Rich waited until the man had read the contents, then dismissed the operator to handle the telegraph himself. Tapping out the message, he sent the wire to Dodge. When he'd completed the transmission and indicated that he would not be on hand to await a reply, Rich called the telegraph operator back to his job and made his way out onto the depot platform.

He hadn't taken two steps before Jack Casement caught up to him. "O'Brian, you takin' the morning westbound?"

"No, I just came to send the general a

wire. How about you?"

"I'm here for some supplies. They're supposed to arrive this morning or this afternoon, and I'm to accompany them on to the front."

Rich nodded. "Are we still making good progress?"

"For the most part. We've had a few Indian scares, but with the increase of army personnel, I think we'll see a decrease in that problem. You still keepin' time with that Montego beauty?"

Rich shook his head. "No, not that I ever was in the first place. I left the Montegos in Laramie."

"Well, I'll be," Casement said suddenly.

Rich looked at the man and found his gaze fixed on one of the train passengers. It proved to be none other than Jordana's Mr. Addison. "What is it?"

"That man," Casement said in a low voice. "Do you know who that is?"

Rich decided to play dumb. "Not really. Who is it?"

"That's none other than Leland Stanford, the governor of California and one of the Big Four on the Central Pacific's board."

Rich felt a sickening feeling settle over him. "Are you sure?"

"I'd bet my last dollar on it. I met the man

once before. He looks like he's trying to keep a low profile. I wonder if he's been here spying on us. You know this could spell trouble for the line."

Rich nodded. "Yes, I'm sure that's a possibility." He'd lost all enthusiasm for the conversation. If that man were truly Stanford, then Jordana had lied to him and so had the man in question. That the man had lied meant only that he was up to no good in Rich's book. For some reason he didn't want anyone to know he was in North Platte. But for Jordana to lie — well, that was an entirely different matter. Suddenly Dodge's concerns about Joe Baldwin didn't seem quite so unfounded.

■ ■ ■ ■

PART III
AUGUST–OCTOBER
1868

■ ■ ■ ■

FIFTEEN

Jordana sat moodily by the window, watching as the train pulled out of the North Platte station and headed down the track. Rich had gone to talk to the conductor at the other end of the car, leaving Jordana to contemplate their travels together. The small passenger car was the only one on this particular train, with the rest devoted to freight. They were carrying supplies west — supplies for the various settlements along the rail, as well as supplies for the building of the Union Pacific Railroad.

Jordana tried not to worry over what Rich was up to or how he might end up figuring into her investigation. She didn't like feeling so hemmed in, and in truth, had never before thought of travel with Rich as anything but fun. But this wasn't fun. They were on edge for unspoken reasons. Perhaps it was because they were both so intent on their duties. Jordana knew she owed it to

Charlie to find out who was causing problems for the Central Pacific, but she also cared about Rich, and her feelings for him would not be set aside. And the wall caused by his secret ate away at her heart in a most distressing way.

Staring absentmindedly upward, Jordana noted the overhead racks that lined the top of the passenger car above the windows. There, a supply of rifles and ammunition awaited any need the passengers might have. The Union Pacific had been carrying extra firearms this way for some time now, and Jordana knew there had arisen more than one occasion requiring their use.

She thought it a decent precaution, but for all the times she'd ridden back and forth on the UP line, she'd never seen any real need for it. Once, she recalled, when traveling from Cheyenne to North Platte, she had witnessed a group of Indians gathered on a ridge in the distance. They had watched the train with seeming indifference, then rode hard in the opposite direction as if to put distance between the past and the future. Jordana felt sorry for the Indians who inhabited the plains. As much as she supported the railroad, it was true it would forever change the lives of these natives. No change came easily, especially when it was forced upon people, such as the government was doing to the Indians. It should be no surprise that they would fight back. She'd heard of their raids and their savage attacks, but she'd also read accounts of peaceful tribes being attacked without provocation by white soldiers bent on revenge. Surely not all Indians were bad, just as all white men were not without feeling for their plight.

"You seem awfully deep in thought," Rich said, sliding into the seat beside her.

"I was just thinking about the Indians and the railroad. How strange it must be to have spent your entire life out here, and all of a sudden you find this great iron beast tearing through the stillness of the countryside. I remember my mother speaking of seeing her first train. Some people likened it to a monster. Women fainted and children cried. It appeared to be both the beginning of something wonderful and the end of the world. I'm sure the tribes out here feel much the same."

Rich nodded. "I wouldn't be surprised. Still, it doesn't give them license to attack and kill our men just because they don't like progress."

"I don't suppose compromise is easy to reach in such cases. Especially given the feelings of most whites that the Indian has no right to any of this land or its benefits."

"I don't think it's exactly fair to lump all whites into the same way of thinking. There have been a great many men who have advocated leaving the plains to the Indians. There were all manner of arrangements to keep whites east of the Mississippi and let the Indians have everything between there and the Rockies. But folks got greedy and adventurous and inventive. They saw a different future and a vast expanse of promising territory."

"And the Indian had no part in that," Jordana replied softly. "I know it's a dichotomy. I can reason it for myself. What part can they possibly play in white society? Just look at the freedmen in this country. They are struggling, in some ways worse now than when they were slaves. They are often turned away from jobs, they are allowed only the poorest of housing, and they are still being refused schooling in many areas. My mother wrote me of this, so I know it must be true," she said with great conviction. "And they speak English. Some can even read and write. They dress appropriately when they are well-enough off to have proper clothing, and still they are denied the rights white people take for granted.

Where does that leave the Indians, who for the most part cannot speak English and dress in ways that we often find scandalously offensive?"

"Your concerns are reasonable, but consider this as well," Rich replied. "Most of the tribes I've dealt with want little to do with the whites. They aren't asking to be a part of our society. They are asking to be left alone."

"And so why is that a problem?" Jordana asked quite seriously. "Why can't they just be allowed to go their own way?"

"And where do you suggest they go? Do we give them the choicest land or the worst? Do we allow them to dictate which areas are acceptable to them, especially when the place is already overrun with white settlers who have paid out money for their land and its improvements?"

"I don't know," Jordana replied, turning her attention back out the window.

"And neither does anyone else." Rich sighed wearily. "Oh, they think they do, and unfortunately, most of the reserves given the Indians are far from the best of lands. Then when drought strikes and the game goes to better pastures, the Indians follow after for food and, lo and behold, find themselves incarcerated for violating their peace treaties with the whites. It's a situation that appears to have no easy answers."

The train moved along at a decent pace, lulling Jordana into a drowsy state with its rhythmic rocking. She noted that many other passengers, what few there were, had already fallen asleep, their heads nodding up and down as the train progressed down the line. Perhaps it was this gentle sense of security that caused the next few moments to be so startling in contrast.

Without warning, Jordana found herself slammed against the seat in front of her and then her entire world quite literally turned upside down as the train jerked and lurched, seeming to fly into the air and take leave of the tracks. She heard herself scream for Rich in a voice as detached as the train was from its tracks. Then debris crashed down upon her and time stood still as the train slid in sickening thuds against the prairie. In the midst of it all, gunshots blasted above the clash of metal against metal. Although Jordana's senses were rather dulled as she finally came to a stop under a crush of broken seats, rifles, and bodies, she could not mistake the blood-chilling yells that filled the air.

They were under attack. The Indians must have somehow derailed the train and were now gathering to finish them off. Jordana fearfully remembered Rich writing of previous raids — of no one being left alive to tell the tale.

"Jordana!" Rich called to her, forgetting that she was supposed to be Joe Baldwin.

She grimaced at the weight of something metallic against her legs and pushed to free herself. "I'm here," she called out.

Then, just as she knew he would, Rich somehow appeared and pulled her free from the wreckage. Their gazes locked, and for a moment Jordana was certain she saw evidence of something more than friendship. In fact, for the briefest instant, she thought he might very well kiss her. And furthermore, she would have accepted it quite willingly.

"You'll have to put your shooting skills to the test," he told her, reaching down in the mess to pull up a rifle. He tossed it aside, muttering something about the barrel being bent, then took up another one. "Here, use this." He handed her the rifle, then went in search of ammunition.

Other passengers were gathering their wits and also responding. Some of the men were already returning fire, while the few women passengers were seeking to gather the UP rifles and ammunition amidst the sound of bullets and death cries.

Rich turned to Jordana. "I want to get up to the engine and see if the engineer and fireman are okay. The passengers have some cover afforded them from the car, but the men up front won't have anything but the open cab. Hopefully, they have been thrown clear from that. I can present some cover for them and, if they're alive, get them back in here with the others."

Because the car had come to rest on its side, most of the defenders were having to climb up the seats to reach the only available windows. Popping up to fire out of what was now the top of the car, Jordana felt sure these defenders were little more than sitting ducks awaiting execution. As Rich jerked around and half walked, half crawled down the aisle of the mangled passenger car, Jordana followed.

Rich managed to pull the door open and let it slam back against the wall with a dull thud. A bullet ricocheted past him as he stuck his head out the opening, causing him to pull back quickly. He slammed up against Jordana, nearly knocking the breath from her.

"Sorry," he murmured, touching her cheek for the briefest moment. "Get back into the car, Jordana."

But his eyes were on the front of the train, and he did not notice that she didn't move. The tender car had spilled over, as had the engine. Rich and Jordana could see the smoke still streaming out from up ahead. Hideous screams could also be heard, and Jordana felt certain that the Indians were probably torturing the engineer and fireman.

"Don't go out there," she told Rich, reaching out to take hold of his arm. "You'll get killed."

"I have to try to save them," he said. "You stay here with the others and keep firing at the Indians. That will give me cover. Everyone is going to have to do their part or we aren't going to get out of this alive."

He started out the door, but still Jordana held on to him. "Please, Rich. Please be careful." She knew her emotions could be easily read, but she no longer cared. The idea of Rich getting himself killed and not knowing that she would be devastated by it made it imperative for her to speak her mind. "I don't know what I'd do without you," she murmured a bit lamely. This really wasn't the time to speak of her feelings for this man, even if she could have put them into words.

He smiled. "Back in North Platte you

couldn't wait to be rid of me. Now you don't want me to go." He gave her hand a squeeze while freeing her hold on his coat. "I'll be back. Don't you worry about that. Just keep yourself alive."

Jordana nodded. There was nothing else to say or do. She was needed elsewhere, just as he was. Wasting more time with words probably wasn't going to benefit either one of them, so she turned back into the car.

Rich edged his way along the tender car, taking cover wherever he could. He fired off several rounds as the Indians moved ever closer to the track. Bullets zipped around him, ringing out as they glanced off the iron of the engine and tender. He vaguely noted that there were more bullets flying than arrows, and even from his distance, he saw several of the attackers were carrying good-quality rifles. But these thoughts were quickly obliterated by the screams of some tormented soul, which could still be heard just beyond his sight. He had to try to reach the man and do whatever he could to save him.

Pressing as tightly as he could to the now exposed iron trucks and axles, Rich managed to inch around to the engine. However, what he found once he reached that point was a sight that, though he had feared it, he could have never been prepared for. There on the toppled engineer's platform, the fireman was slowly being roasted alive — pinned tightly against the red-hot firebox.

"Help me!" the man cried out over and over. "For the love of God . . . help me." His screams tore at Rich's heart, but there seemed no way to answer the man's pleas without burning to death himself.

Just then, the man seemed to sense Rich's presence. He looked over, his pain-wracked eyes meeting Rich's. "Please," he cried mournfully. "Have pity."

Rich couldn't have torn himself away from the man's agonized expression if he'd wanted to. Forgetting all good sense, Rich tore at the iron bar that trapped the man. He tugged and pulled at the thing, his leather gloves scorching at the heat, but it was wedged in as tightly as if it had been meant to be there. Flames from the box began licking up at him. The heat from them singed Rich's hair, and he had to jump back to keep from being burned as well.

The man screamed as his clothes caught fire.

"Oh, God," Rich prayed, "I am so sorry."

Just then an Indian galloped toward the engine, seeming to have caught sight of the helpless figures on the platform. The warrior fired toward Rich, who returned fire. Just as flames fully engulfed the man, Rich heard more close rifle fire, but this time not directed at him. Racing toward the engine aback his pony, the painted warrior flew off the horse in attack. Rich's attention was drawn to the engineer, who lay not fifteen feet away from the engine. The engineer had tried to shoot, but his gun appeared to be empty. The brave now had the man by the hair and, taking his knife in hand, let out a bloodcurdling yell. Without any further hesitation, Rich leveled his gun and shot the Indian, who was threatening to scalp the poor engineer. The engineer flattened himself against the Nebraska prairie ground, appearing determined to stay alive in the only manner left him. Rich wished fervently he could reach the man and was about to inch his way out to him when the fireman gave up one last scream and succumbed to the fire.

Falling back against the iron wall, Rich couldn't tear his gaze from the burned body of the fireman. The man's charred arm was extended toward Rich as if attempting one last plea for mercy. It was a sight Rich would not soon forget.

Within a matter of minutes the attack was

over. Apparently having tired of their game, the remaining warriors headed their ponies off across the prairie amidst the persistent gunfire from the UP passengers.

Rich hadn't noticed the presence of anyone else until a hand touched his shoulder. The engineer had come to join Rich, tears in his eyes. "He was like a son to me," he said, nodding toward the burning firebox. "He was a fine man. I wouldn't have seen anyone die a death like that."

His tone wasn't accusing, but Rich took it as such. Somehow all the times he had rescued others, saving lives of settlers and travelers while he was in the army, paled in the glaring light of this horrible failure. He knew he was being unfairly hard on himself, but he could feel no other way, especially when he closed his eyes and still saw the pleading hand of the man reaching out futilely to him.

Angry and confused, Rich left the engineer to mourn and went in search of Jordana. She was already crawling through the door when he reached the passenger car, and without worrying about the appearance, they embraced and held each other tightly for a moment.

"I'm so glad you're alive," he whispered, wishing he could kiss her lips and run his fingers through her short hair.

"I was so afraid," she said. "Not for me but for you. I was just sure you'd end up getting yourself shot."

He pulled away and regained his composure. "You don't have much confidence in me, do you?"

Jordana frowned. "Of course I do. Do you suppose I would have let you go out of that car alone if I didn't think you capable of defending yourself? What happened? Did you find the engineer?"

"Yes," Rich replied, unable to hide the emotion he felt. Tormented by the face of the fireman, he said, "Just don't go up there, Jordana. Don't go to the engine."

He left her standing there and stalked off down the track to the freight cars. He'd arranged for Faithful to ride in the third car from the last, and now it was clear that even these cars had managed to derail in the accident.

It wasn't easy to pry open the boxcar, and once he had, Rich could see from the flood of sunlight into the pit below that Faithful had suffered most grievously. The horse lay on its side, pinned to the side of the car by a wooden shaft. Whinnying softly, it seemed the horse pleaded with the same doleful look of the fireman for Rich to help relieve his misery.

"Oh, Faithful, you deserved a whole lot better than this," Rich said, tears coming to his eyes. Taking out his revolver, Rich knew what had to be done. "I'm sorry, boy. I'm so sorry."

He fired two shots and watched as Faithful drew his last breath. If only he'd been able to do at least that for the dying fireman. Without caring who saw or what they might think, Rich sat down atop the overturned freight car and let his tears fall. His mother had once said it was only a strong man who could allow himself to cry from time to time. He'd only shed tears on one other occasion, and that was when Peggy had died.

God, I so wanted to help that man, Rich prayed silently. *I hate it when I am helpless like that.*

Had Rich's grief not been so deep, he might have smiled at his foolish words. He was not infallible, but he believed in a God who was — a God who certainly had the life of that fireman in His care. And Rich knew in his heart that God would have provided a means to help the man if it had been in His will. Rich did not pretend to understand the workings of God's will, but he did trust God with all his heart. And that was as much as a man could be expected to do.

My helplessness only proves, he prayed once more, *that I've got to trust you above all things. I have to believe that you had this situation in your hand from the beginning.*

Sixteen

The dark-headed man squatted beside the campfire and smiled. "Your work was quite good. Of course, it would've been better had you been able to kill the passengers and pillage the freight for yourself, but nevertheless, I commend you."

The painted face of the warrior never changed in expression. "Have you brought our pay?"

"Certainly. There are three wagons down in the ravine. I expect you to unload them so that my men can be about their business. There's a good quantity of meat, blankets, flour, sugar, and everything else you requested."

"Good," the Indian replied, getting to his feet. "We'll go now."

"Don't forget our agreement about the bridge over Lodge Pole Creek."

The man nodded. "It will be done."

Satisfied with the Indian's response, the

dark-haired man nodded and also stood. Extending his hand, he offered his thanks. "It may not make much sense to you as to why these things are helpful, but I thank you nevertheless. It is to benefit both our peoples."

The brave said nothing and, refusing to shake the man's hand, ventured instead down the side of the rocky path and into the ravine.

The man smiled to himself with a sense of great satisfaction. It was all too simple to get people to do your dirty work for you. There wasn't a man who couldn't be bought by one means or another. Pulling a cigar from his pocket, he took out an ornate snipper and clipped the end.

"Child's play, really," he said, rather pleased with himself.

Jordana had somehow managed to sleep the last fifty miles into Wadsworth. It was a fitful sleep, fraught with images of Indians and wounded soldiers. She was taken back in time to when she and Brenton had been attacked while venturing out with a survey party for the Union Pacific. Tossing and turning, she replayed the attack in her mind, feeling the urgency and fear mount in her like a great volcano about to erupt. The scene of her dream then changed and she found herself with Rich weeks earlier. They were overturning, only this time they seemed to roll and roll and never come to a stop. Somewhere in the midst of the destruction she could see Rich as he was crushed beneath the weight of the train car. With a start, Jordana jerked upright in her seat and would have jumped to her feet but for Rich's steadying hand. The only other stage passenger, an elderly man, glanced up for a moment before going back to sleep.

"Nightmare?" Rich asked.

She pulled off her spectacles and rubbed her eyes. "Yes." She yawned, feeling more tired than when she'd first fallen asleep. She hadn't had a decent night's sleep since the train derailment nearly two weeks ago. She had tried to keep herself distracted by gathering material for the newspaper while accompanying Rich on his courier runs. But her nightmares proved she had been only marginally successful.

"You know, if you'd quit this foolishness and stay home with your brother, you wouldn't have to worry about coming to harm." He spoke more casually than urgently, as if he were merely doing his duty in making the suggestion, with little hope of its being heeded.

"I'm not worried about coming to harm," she lied. "I'm just overly tired. My mother always said nightmares were more a by-product of having too little sleep than of actual events."

"But fear keeps you from resting properly," Rich countered.

"Sometimes joy does the same," Jordana mused, then fell silent. Ever since their intimate encounter with death and destruction, she'd been completely confused by her feelings for the man at her side. Rich was more important to her than she'd ever allowed any man to be, save for her father and brothers. The turmoil it caused her heart and soul was nearly more than she could deal with. Had she fallen in love with him? Was this what true love was all about?

Her nights were consumed with scenes of Rich lying dead. She often woke up crying his name over and over, sobbing against her tightly hugged pillow, desperately sorrowing that she had lost something deeply important.

The stage began to slow, and a quick glance out the open window revealed they were nearly upon civilization again. The town of Wadsworth lay just ahead, and with it, Jordana knew she would have to face Charlie with what little information she'd managed to gather. He wouldn't be very satisfied with her report. She doubted seriously that he would be impressed by the numerous Indian attacks rendered against the Union Pacific. Nor would he like what she had to ask in regard to the possibility that their own people might have had something to do with the destruction and delays facing the UP. He wouldn't understand her concern, because the Central Pacific was all he cared about. He wouldn't worry over whether Rich met with harm while serving as a courier on the UP, because Charlie would no doubt see Rich as the enemy. It was a no-win situation.

"Will Brenton be here?" Rich asked casually.

"I have no idea," Jordana replied. "I wired him and told him when to expect us. I'm hoping he and Caitlan will both be here or nearby. Since he's photographing the progress of the CP, I'm figuring he'll be somewhere close."

"You've been awfully quiet these last few days. Are you worried about coming home?"

"It isn't home," Jordana muttered, forcing herself to look at him. His face seemed to grow more handsome every day. He had tanned in the summer sun and his ebony hair curled slightly at the nape of his neck.

It seemed to beckon her touch, as did his straight, firm jaw, now peppered with a two-days' growth of beard from his inability to shave properly while on the stage.

"You've mentioned that before. Where do you consider home?" he asked, his blue eyes boring holes in her soul.

Jordana looked away and shook her head. "I don't have a home, and I don't need one. I'm a free spirit and I'm happy to be about my own business. I like coming and going at will and having no one to answer to." She wondered if it sounded to Rich as though she were trying to convince herself, for that was what it felt like inside her heart.

"Wadsworth!" the driver yelled from his seat overhead.

"Well, I guess we've arrived," Rich said.

They stepped from the stage looking very much like two businessmen bent on duty — Rich in his navy blue serge suit, topped with a black felt hat, which gave him a most distinguished look in spite of his stubble of beard, and Jordana in her lightweight tan broadcloth. They appeared as associates, and that was fine by Jordana. She felt the utmost confidence in Rich O'Brian. There was no possible way that he could be responsible for the problems on the Central Pacific line. It wasn't like Rich to deal in an underhanded manner. At least that was how Jordana saw it.

"Baldwin!"

Jordana looked up and found Charlie Crocker making his way to where she stood, his substantial figure easily parting a way through the small crowd.

"Mr. Crocker," she replied, then turned to Rich. "May I present Mr. O'Brian? He's a courier with the Union Pacific, and he's brought you some important documents."

Charlie eyed Rich suspiciously, then nodded. "Let's take this to my office."

They walked from the stage drop to the depot, which was even now under construction. Charlie had his private car sidetracked, and it was from here that he dictated the movements of the Central Pacific.

He ushered them on board and, once inside the opulent car, offered them chairs and cold refreshments. An ancient-looking Mexican man clad in the uniform of a servant offered a tray of beverages to them.

"I have just about anything you could want," Charlie told them. "My man has iced tea, but we could have something else if you prefer something stronger. Except for you, Joe. I promised your brother I wouldn't further corrupt you with hard drink."

Jordana laughed and tossed her straw

skimmer to the overhead bin. "I don't like hard drink and you well know it. Iced tea is fine for me."

"For me as well," Rich replied.

"Not another teetotaler?" Charlie intoned with some surprise.

"I like to keep my head clear, especially when I'm working," Rich answered, meeting Charlie's engulfing scrutiny.

Jordana watched as Charlie looked Rich up and down before motioning to the servant. "Very well. We shall drink tea. I also have fresh fruit and cheese and some little sandwiches fixed up by my wife."

"So you finally brought Mrs. Crocker to the front," Jordana said with a smile. "Good for you. I'm sure your wife suffered great loneliness without you in Sacramento. It's not good to be alone all the time." She instantly regretted her words. She prayed no one would read anything into them and suggest that she somehow needed similar companionship.

"She hates it out here, save for being with me," Charlie replied. "And frankly, she's not entirely happy with me. I've become quite a bear — not at all my jovial self these days." He took the offered tea and waited until Jordana and Rich did likewise before continuing. "I'm afraid the railroad business has not given me overmuch to be cheerful about."

"Is the line not going well?" Jordana asked.

"It's gone most miserably." Charlie rubbed his beard, which Jordana had always thought resembled a goat's tuft, especially in that there was no mustache to balance it. "There are delays at every turn. We constantly find ourselves deficient in one area of supplies or another. If I have ties to lay and graded road on which to lay them, then I'm without rails to top them with."

"I had no idea things were so bad," Jordana said, completely surprised by this news, and even more so at his candor before a stranger. "I shall have to write it up for the newspaper. What seems to be causing the problems?" She decided to play along. Perhaps he merely intended on painting a grim picture to this UP man before him.

"Supplies aren't coming as regularly as they used to. It's more difficult to get materials in, and when we get them, they often disappear. There's a great deal of mischief afoot, and sometimes it's quite destructive."

"We know that feeling well," Rich replied. "I know Jordana wired you about being delayed in Laramie, but I also know she did not speak of the reason." Jordana said nothing as Rich continued. "The fact is, our train was derailed in Nebraska, and after assessing the damage to the line, we were picked up by another train and taken on to Laramie, where I was to meet with General Dodge."

"A good man, Dodge. I can't say that I've ever had reason to dislike him."

"He is a good man, and a fair one," Rich said.

Jordana sipped at her tea and let the two men talk. It was easier that way. She felt completely at ease in their presence, but at the same time she battled her heart over Rich. Something would have to give and give soon. Perhaps it would simply be that she would have to bid Rich good-bye and take herself off away from him. She couldn't have him coming between her and the life she desired. And sadly enough, she felt certain she couldn't have both.

She refocused her attention in time to see Rich pull out a stack of papers from a leather satchel. These were papers given him by Dodge. Papers, he'd told her, responding to issues of the UP's efforts to survey the line and exactly where they felt it would be most advantageous to bring the railroad lines together. Some of the information had come from Washington and the lengthy discussions offered among Congress and the representatives of both lines. Some was pure conjecture on the part of the Union Pacific officials, and some were General Dodge's personal choices.

"It seems wise that we consider the groundwork already laid by our companies," Rich said, handing the papers to Crocker. "There are those who would pit us against each other for the purpose of financial gain, but others seem far more concerned with simply building a functional railroad that ties the country together from coast to coast."

"And which are you a party to, Mr. O'Brian?"

Jordana smiled to herself. Rich would not be intimidated by Charlie Crocker, of that she was certain. She liked that about Rich. Liked his strength in dealing with other men, especially crafty men like Charlie. She admired his ability to see right through their ploys to practically read their minds. Then a thought struck her. What if he could read my mind? Why should it be so hard for him to second-guess her thoughts when he's so obviously good at it with other people? The very idea put Jordana in a cold sweat.

Rich seemed to consider Charlie's question for a moment, then took a long drink before answering. "I am on the Lord's side," he said rather simply.

Charlie laughed. "I wasn't sure the good Lord had an interest in this railroad. Seems to me, He quite often forgets those of us who are out there laboring in the middle of nowhere to build it. Maybe you could explain yourself."

"I could," Rich replied. "I'm not a man of politics. It was one of the things that drove me out of the army. I despise petty games, especially ones that bring harm to other human beings and their property. I consider my faith an issue of the utmost importance in whatever task I adopt. If I am working as unto God, instead of the Union Pacific or the army, then I am serving the best interests of all."

"I see."

"No, I'm not entirely sure you do. I know you're wondering how I fit into this and whether I'm a risk to your precious line." Rich set down his glass and leveled a steady gaze at Crocker. "I know you're probably thinking Jordana ten kinds of fool for trusting me, but the truth is, I have no one's agenda in mind. I'm doing my job the best I can and just happen to be in the employment of the Union Pacific. But being so employed does not mean I intend to perform any service that will bring about harm for either side. Now, if you don't mind, I'm exhausted. I'd like to find a room, have a bath, and sleep for about ten hours."

Charlie laughed. "You've brought us an interesting character here, Jordana."

"Yes, he's quite the character," she said, catching Rich's glance. "Is my brother Brenton in town, Charlie?"

"Indeed he is. He and Caitlan are staying in some rooms on the back side of the railroad station. Since their work here is just a temporary situation, I couldn't see them having to rent out a house or live in a tent. They have the comforts of home, however. I've seen to that. There's even a small makeshift kitchen for Caitlan to cook meals in. And my, but that woman can cook!"

"Good. Then we'll make our way there. I have the same desires as Rich." She felt her cheeks grow hot as she suddenly realized the implication of her words. She averted her eyes from both men. And they mercifully let her comment pass.

"You're more than welcome to stay with them or with the missus and me," Charlie declared. "Or if you like, there's a fine hotel already in business, even though, like the depot, there's still some construction going on."

"That's all right. I'm sure my brother and Caitlan will expect me to stay with them, and they will also want to see Rich. We all owe Captain O'Brian our lives from adventures past. We'll have a great deal to reminisce about."

"You'll find Brenton and Caitlan just across the way. They're on the opposite side from where all the building is going on. Still, I can't imagine that it's very peaceful there. You may find it quite impossible to sleep."

"I doubt anything could make it impossible to sleep," Rich said. A shrill train whistle filled the air, causing them all to take note. "Even that."

The three of them stepped from Charlie's car and made their way across the dirt and gravel just in time to see the train from Reno halt outside the Wadsworth station. Jordana suppressed a yawn and forced herself to walk straight and tall. She could hardly wait for Caitlan to mother her, as she was certain to do. For once, the idea sounded so inviting that Jordana very nearly ran to the depot.

But just as they crossed the tracks and came up to the building itself, Jordana halted in midstep to see Isabella Montego and her father step off the train.

"What are they doing here?" she muttered.

Rich looked up and also caught sight of them. He shrugged. "It's a free country, Jordana."

She elbowed him. "Joe. Call me, Joe."

He grinned. "Sorry, I forgot myself. You aren't going to go courting her, are you?" he teased. "Did you know, Mr. Crocker, that Joe here is quite the ladies' man? He can dance up a storm when need be."

Jordana elbowed him more sharply. "Don't listen to him, Charlie. He's delirious from lack of sleep."

Charlie laughed at the exchange, then questioned, "Who are those people?"

Jordana answered first. "Baxter and Isabella Montego. They own a lot of land in the Laramie and Cheyenne area. I guess they own some in North Platte too. They're from back east originally, but they've got their teeth sunk in deep and tight with the Union Pacific. I've even had it suggested that Montego is involved in bid rigging where construction of the railroad is concerned."

Rich looked at her oddly. "How in the world would you know all of that?"

Jordana felt rather smug in his surprise. "I'm a good reporter, Mr. O'Brian, and in order to be a good reporter, you must first be good at gathering information. I talk to folks and they talk to me. You'd be surprised just how eager people are to share what they know."

Rich said nothing more. He didn't get a chance to, for in the next moment, the Montegos had spotted them and were making their way over to where the trio watched at the edge of the station.

"Why, Mr. O'Brian and Mr. Baldwin, what a pleasant surprise!" Isabella Montego purred in her usual manner. "I just about despaired of ever again seeing anyone I knew."

"Our friends on the coast are limited to only a handful," Baxter Montego replied before extending his hand to Rich and then Jordana. "Good to see old friends again."

Jordana wanted to comment that she would hardly consider herself a friend, much less an old one, but instead turned to introduce Charlie. "Mr. Montego, Miss Montego, may I introduce Charles Crocker?"

"Mr. Crocker. I've heard a great deal of good about you. You seem to be the champion of all Californians. Building your railroad through the seemingly impenetrable wall of the Sierra Nevada, and now you face

240

the barren Great Desert."

"I must say you have me at a disadvantage," Charlie replied.

"We've just come from San Francisco," Montego continued, "where they sing your praises night and day."

"Yes, well, if not mine, then someone else's," Charlie said rather modestly.

"And, Mr. O'Brian, Mr. Baldwin, what in the world brings you to Wadsworth?"

Jordana felt Rich tense as Isabella moved closer. "We have missed your company while we were away. But now that we are headed back to Laramie, I do hope you'll not be far behind us. Perhaps you could even accompany us."

"I have business here," Rich said curtly.

Isabella smiled in her seductive way and took up her parasol to shield herself from the growing heat of the day. "Then, perhaps we can take a meal together while we're in town. I'm certain my father would love to hear about all the events on the Union Pacific. Why, we heard there was a terrible derailment not long ago. Several people died, as we understand."

"It was not far from Ogallala, as I understand it," Baxter Montego stated thoughtfully. "The rails were pried up and lashed to a stack of ties with telegraph wire, making it impossible to send for help by wire."

"Yes," Rich replied. "Mr. Baldwin and I were on that very train."

Isabella put her hand to her throat. "No! How simply terrible. You must tell us all about it over dinner. Would you care to join us as well, Mr. Baldwin?"

"No, thank you," Jordana replied. "I want nothing more than a hot bath and soft bed. My brother and sister-in-law live here, and their home is my destination at this moment."

"Mine too," Rich threw in. "I'm afraid dinner will have to wait."

The Montegos seemed none too happy to let them go, but after Rich promised to meet with them later, father and daughter made their way in the opposite direction while Charlie led Jordana and Rich to the back of the depot.

"Funny about their having heard of the derailment so quickly," Jordana said absentmindedly. "Especially if they were in San Francisco. I guess the West is being more open about what happens along the Union Pacific. Then again, maybe they merely reported it out here to show the problems being suffered in the East. You know, that whole rivalry thing. Still, that the Montegos would have heard about it in such detail seems rather odd."

Rich was already frowning, and this statement did nothing for his mood. "I wondered at that myself," he muttered. "I think we'd do well to keep our concerns to ourselves, however."

Jordana nodded, feeling a chill course through her. What had before seemed merely curious to her now seemed ominous, and obviously Rich felt the same way.

SEVENTEEN

Brenton marveled over his sister in her masculine fashions as if seeing her for the first time in this manner. It pleased Jordana to no end that he thought her to have quite perfected her pretense. His admiration meant the world to her. Brenton still held that special place in her heart that would never be filled by anyone else. To feel his agitation or disapproval of her actions was always most troublesome. Even if she had the gumption to continue with her plans in spite of him, it still caused Jordana some guilt. To travel with Brenton's blessing was always preferred to traveling without it.

"How much longer can ya be stayin' with us?" Caitlan asked Rich and Jordana. "These last two days with ya have been wonderful, but just not enough."

"I'm not sure how long I'll be here," Jordana replied, finishing off a bowl of beef stew. "I want to get down to the front. Charlie's all worked up about the fact that some five hundred Chinese workers have disappeared off the line. Apparently someone has been telling the workers all manner of elaborate tales, and the Chinese left in fear of something bad happening to them. Rumor has it that the Paiute told the Chinese, whom they have no fondness for, that the Nevada and Utah deserts were full of snakes so big they could eat a man whole. Charlie found half his workforce gone before first light. They didn't want to go farther into the desert and find themselves eaten alive."

"There are always stories of one sort or another," Brenton commented. "Mark my words, you'll have more legends and fables coming out of the building of this railroad than anything else in our history. Years from now, people will probably believe that the railroad was built by magic fairies and such. The stories simply run rampant."

"But that's marvelous," Jordana declared. "A wonderful new angle for my articles. I shall call it 'The Myth and Mystique of the Transcontinental Railroad.' "

"Unfortunately rumors and stories have a way of getting people hurt," Rich stated, pushing back from the table. "And as for how long I can stay on, it won't be long. I figured if Jordana wanted more stories on the UP, she'd accompany me back to our route."

"Well, I do wish ya'd stay on with us for a spell. I miss conversin' with ya," Caitlan said with a smile. "Oh, and Jordana, I had a letter from Victoria. Seems she's doing quite well. She says the baby is kickin' up a storm, and Kiernan is forcing the issue of a job in Sacramento."

"I wondered if I might see him," Jordana said thoughtfully. "I fully expected to find him at the front of the tracks."

"Not anymore," Brenton told his sister. "Kiernan is ever the concerned husband and father-to-be. I think he knows exactly what this baby means to both of them, and he doesn't want to risk anything happening to Victoria."

A knock at the door sent Caitlan to admit Charlie Crocker. Jordana had thought to question him about his Chinese problem just then, but his mood was quite black.

"Jordana, I want to talk to you," he said ominously, then glanced at O'Brian and added, "alone."

Jordana thought his reaction rather strange but nodded. "Why don't we take a walk on the line? You can tell me about your Chinese problem, and I can tell you about my plans."

She followed Crocker outside, feeling

246

Rich's narrow gaze follow her the entire way. But why should he care if she talked with Charlie? Why should he scowl so at the idea of her speaking to Charlie in private?

"Jordana, we have troubles aplenty," Charlie said when they were well away from the house. "I hate to say this, but since your Mr. O'Brian has come among us, things have gone wrong. I had someone trail after him these last couple of days since you've come to town and it doesn't look good. He's met with those Montego folks a couple of times, and he's always snooping around where he shouldn't be. I'm more certain than ever that he's spying for the Union Pacific. And not only that, but sabotaging us as well."

"That's not fair!" Jordana countered in quick defense of her friend. "Of course he's working for the Union Pacific, probably keeping his eyes open for the details of our progress, but Rich wouldn't see us harmed. He isn't like that, Charlie. You don't know him like I do."

"Well, one of my supervisors saw him down on the line in the middle of the night last night. They said it was O'Brian sure as anything. He was messing around one of the supply sheds. My man confronted him, spoke to him for a few moments, then saw

247

him head back here. This morning, however, that same supervisor found the shed broken into, along with six others along the line."

"Rich would never —"

"I'm telling you, Jordana, my man saw him there," Charlie replied, his face reddening in anger. "It's bad enough my workers are running from dangers both imagined and real. What have you told O'Brian? Does he know what you were sent to do for us?"

"No," Jordana admitted.

"Why not?" Charlie asked pointedly. "I thought you trusted him."

"I do," Jordana protested. "I just don't think he would understand."

"Perhaps he would understand only too well."

Just then a man came racing down the track from the depot. "Charlie! Charlie! There's been an explosion! Some of that old nitro went unnoticed, and when one of the men disturbed it, it went up just like that!" The man snapped his fingers for emphasis.

Charlie looked at Jordana with a grave expression. "Get him out of here. Whatever you have to do. He's not going to be allowed to keep this line from progressing."

Jordana felt consumed with guilt and pain as she watched Charlie walk away. She'd had no idea that Rich had gone to spend time with the Montegos, and neither did she realize he'd been out on midnight forages along the CP's supply lines. Biting her lip, she searched in her mind how she could deal with this matter without completely accusing Rich of what Charlie suggested.

Sitting down on an upturned crate by the construction site of the new depot, Jordana tried to think. The sounds of hammering and the shouts of workers, along with the smell of sawdust and sweat, should have been distracting, but instead, they were rather soothing in their mundane way. Jordana's thoughts soon turned to prayer. She had sorely neglected her prayers of late, and while she had read her Bible religiously on the line, she had fallen away from the practice since coming back to Crocker.

God, I just can't believe Rich would do this thing. He knows you and claims to care about your Word. Surely he wouldn't jeopardize the lives of people on the Central Pacific just because he works for the Union Pacific. With a heavy heart she contemplated the issue, realizing that there was a great deal she didn't know about Rich O'Brian. Perhaps he wasn't the man she thought he was. After all, letters written over time and distance did not prove a man's character. Perhaps he was a consummate actor and he had her fooled along with everybody else.

"I thought you were meeting with Crocker," Rich said, drawing Jordana out of her prayer rather quickly.

"What are you doing here?" she asked more sharply than she'd intended.

Rich looked at her oddly. "What's wrong?"

"I might ask you the same thing," Jordana replied.

"Nothing's wrong with me. I just came out to see when you intend to head up the line."

"Why?" She got up and watched his expression change at her sudden coolness.

"Jordana, you want to tell me what's going on here?"

"Charlie saw you conferring with the Montegos."

Rich laughed. "Is that what this is about? You jealous that Isabella is more interested in me than you?" he taunted.

Jordana took out a handkerchief and wiped her brow. Even though it was nearly September, the hot desert sun was enough to make a man or woman wish for the cooler air of the mountains. Trying hard to think of a congenial way to accuse Rich of spying, Jordana gave up at the sheer futility of it.

"Charlie wants you off the line. He thinks you're spying for the Union Pacific."

"And what do you think?" Rich asked seriously.

The question struck through to her heart. "What I think doesn't matter," Jordana replied, turning away. "You have to go."

"No one can make me leave if I don't want to."

Jordana turned back to face him. "You were at the supply sheds last night, and now they've been vandalized and robbed. Eyewitnesses placed you there. Are you going to deny it?"

"No. I'm not denying that I was there last night," Rich replied. "I went for a walk. Nothing more."

"That's easy enough to say."

"So you do think I'm spying. You think I'm collecting information to create problems for the Central Pacific. Is that it?"

"Your actions are suspicious."

"And yours aren't?" Rich retorted. "I mean, it's rather convenient that you run about the country on the pretense of writing stories. You may collect all the details and information you desire, and no one is to question your work."

"How dare you!" Jordana exclaimed indignantly, momentarily forgetting she was doing just that. "My stories speak for themselves."

"I don't remember you writing an article telling how Leland Stanford met up with you in North Platte. Or how shortly after that, the UP suffered two derailments and several other attacks. One of which included burning a bridge down and forcing the work to be redone."

Jordana felt light-headed. How did he know about Stanford? She met Rich's eyes and knew that she couldn't defend herself on that issue. "I was on one of those derailed trains, as you well know. I would never do anything to risk human life."

"But you don't deny that your Mr. Addison was none other than one of the Central Pacific's Big Four."

"No," she said softly. "I don't deny that. Mr. Stanford asked to keep his identity unknown. He didn't want to be answering a lot of questions as to why he was in North Platte."

"And why was he there?"

Jordana balled her fists and hit them against her legs. "None of your business. I don't know why you should care. You know very well that I want this railroad completed. My parents stand to benefit from it. Frankly, I stand to benefit from it as my father has invested in both sides. So don't you dare stand there and accuse me. I thought you were my friend."

"I thought you were my friend," Rich countered, "but instead you talk for ten minutes to Charlie Crocker and suddenly I'm the enemy."

"Things have gone wrong since you've been here. Charlie's suspicious."

"Charlie doesn't appear to be the only one," he growled and stomped off in the direction of the depot.

Jordana wanted to call after him but held her tongue. Instead, she turned to walk away in the opposite direction, knowing that Rich had every right in the world to accuse her. She was a spy for the Central Pacific. But not for the reasons he believed. Now she had insulted him and left him without a feeling of trust between them. What had she done? How could she possibly hope to make this right?

When Jordana returned to Brenton and Caitlan's, the sun had already set and heavy storm clouds were threatening on the horizon, turning the twilight ominous in shades of gray and green. She walked into the place where her brother and sister-in-law had taken up residence, only to find them quite animated. Their excitement was clearly in contrast to her own black mood.

"What's going on?" she asked.

"We're off to Utah to photograph some of the territory for Charlie," Brenton told her. "He wants some pictures before cold weather sets into the mountains and makes the work too difficult to continue."

"We're leavin' in the mornin'," Caitlan announced. "Charlie's provided us a wagon and supplies. Isn't that excitin'?"

"Yes, it is," Jordana replied, casting a glance around for Rich.

"He's gone, if you're looking for Rich," Brenton said, sobering considerably. "I don't know what happened between the two of you, but he came back here muttering and fussing. I could hear your name from time to time, but other than that, he packed his bags, thanked us for the hospitality, and left."

"Did he say where he was going?" Jordana was not at all certain what she would do even if she knew.

"No," Brenton said, shaking his head. "He didn't offer and I didn't ask. He didn't seem to be in the mood for questions."

"No, I don't imagine." Jordana sat down despondently.

"So since yar at odds with the good captain," Caitlan suddenly said, "why don't ya come with us? Ya can get yar stories about the railroad legends, and we can have a good visit."

Jordana considered it for a moment. "I don't know if that would work out for Charlie or not."

"I can't see why not," Brenton replied. "It's not like he owns you."

Jordana thought of what Charlie's accusations had cost her. "No, it certainly isn't."

"We should be back before it gets too cold," Brenton offered. "We hope to be back in Sacramento before Victoria has the baby."

"Well there's plenty of time for that. She's not even due until February," Jordana said, contemplating the situation. "Utah, eh?"

"Utah and maybe more. Charlie said, if the mood strikes us and the weather is good, he'd like to see what the land looks like around the border. He's thinking that if he gets enough workers, he just might push out fast and furious and meet the UP before they can even build their line that far."

Rich would no doubt go back and tell General Dodge all about the accusations and problems he'd endured in Wadsworth. She hated him believing her capable of spying for the benefit of hurting other people. If she had to confess what she'd been doing, then she would, but she didn't want

Rich to go on believing the worst of her. Perhaps if she let some time pass, she might be able to talk some sense into him and get to the bottom of their loyalties.

"I'll do it," she finally told her brother. "I'd like to spend time with the two of you."

Two weeks later Jordana found herself on the sandy alkali landscape of the front tracks. They had passed Carson Sink and Humboldt Lake and were headed up the Humboldt River past the Trinity Mountains. Here she met with Charlie's supervisors and men and discussed the building of the line. Again she followed Charlie's orders and played down their success when she wrote her stories for the paper, but in fact the line was progressing quite nicely. It was even believed they could possibly be to the Utah border by the end of the year. Of course, it was Charlie who believed it, but that man had a way of making things happen. Jordana marveled that not long ago estimations of completion of the line had run to years, as many as ten. Now it looked quite possible the lines could meet in less than a year.

Discipline was good among the workers, and morale was not too bad either. The liquor had been cut off from the Irish workers, and without a nearby town of any real means, they were forced to spend their evenings sitting around camp, telling stories and playing cards.

The Chinese had caused quite a stir, Jordana learned, when it was found that an opium den had been improvised along the track grading. Forty or more Chinese workers had turned to the pleasures of that particular vice, and like Jesus clearing out the temple of the money changers, the supervisor for the line had gone into the den and cleaned it out. Firsthand witnesses told Jordana of how the "bossy man" had taken the pipes and opium, scattering the occupants and owners of the materials from the site in a matter of moments.

"What do you suppose the effects of opium are?" Jordana asked one evening while Brenton considered his latest photographs.

"I've seen the effects firsthand," he replied. "The men are good for nothing but lying about. Their minds see things that are not there, and they appear to suffer from severe vertigo. They have no real sense of balance or the ability to steady themselves. The opium somehow works against their equilibrium. It's worse than alcohol."

Jordana found it quite fascinating to be

back where the real progress of the line was being made. The workers no longer minded her appearance or her questions. She was discreet in her observations, as was her brother, and the men appreciated her interest. Her stories made them out to be American heroes, and who wouldn't want to be thought of in that manner? Those who could read passed her copies of the stories along to those who couldn't by sharing the tales around their campfires late into the evening. Jordana almost felt that she could reveal herself to be a woman at this point, and they still would have accepted her presence in their lives. But that feeling wasn't strong enough to make her change from her facade of Joe Baldwin. She couldn't risk the possibility that they would reject her and thus put an end to her livelihood.

The next morning, Joe, or Preacher, as many now called her, was up and moving along the line before dawn. There was a sense of the sacred that came right before the workers set out on their various duties. As the men ate their morning meal and grumbled about the work ahead of them, Jordana walked along the graded ground and contemplated the road to come. The future was right here. Everything about her world would change once this line was complete.

Then her thoughts went to Rich and his anger at her. She had written to him twice but had received no word back. Not that she really expected an answer. She had disappointed him with her accusations, and she had been unable to give him the answers he needed to relieve his own worries.

Gazing off across the valley, Jordana shivered at the chill breeze that cut across the river. Perhaps it was better this way, she told herself. She couldn't very well expect Rich to understand her feelings toward him when she didn't understand them herself. The constant worry that she'd fallen in love with the man gave her enough heartache without having to consider what he might think of her once he knew the truth about her work for Crocker.

The train's whistle blasted in a long signal that the workday was about to commence. Jordana looked toward the pale pink horizon and wondered what the day might bring. Silently, she prayed for guidance and understanding, and then she added a prayer for Rich. She couldn't bear not knowing if he were dead or alive. She couldn't stand the thought of him having come to harm, or worse, to have chosen the company of Isabella Montego, in light of his separation from Jordana's company.

"Let's get to work!" the supervisor called out. "You men get over here and help unload these rails. Put your backs to it, lads. We've a railroad to build."

Jordana glanced toward the front of the track where twenty some men worked together to lay the next set of rails. No one man could boast the building of this railroad and neither could just one company. Perhaps that was the next story she would cover in her articles for the *Tribune*. Perhaps she would chide both sides for their childish games of intrigue and destruction.

Shaking her head, Jordana made her way back to the front. She ignored the curses of the workers and smiled at the good-natured teasing they gave one another.

"My mother could lift that rail better than you boys," one yelled.

"Maybe your mother could come to work for the Central Pacific!"

"She's already got a job with the Union Pacific, and that's why they're beatin' the pants off of us!"

Laughter filled the morning air as the men continued unloading and arranging their supplies. Charlie had long ago worked them into a routine, and now it was second nature. The supply train came, and within a matter of minutes the men had swarmed the cars and cleared them of materials. The train then backed away and down the track and soon another would come and another, until there were enough supplies at the head of the track to progress for several miles. They were averaging as much as six miles of track a day, and at this rate, Jordana knew it would be no time at all until they reached Charlie's predicted goal of Utah by the new year.

EIGHTEEN

"Joe Baldwin has to go," Baxter Montego said to the gathering of men in his home. "There has been nothing but trouble for me since his appearance on the line. With him out there snooping around and keeping company with O'Brian, I've had trouble getting things done. That fool's story about the Indians' attack on the UP caused Congress to agree to more troops on the line. That in turn is causing me considerable complications."

Isabella glided into the room, a tray bearing brandy and glasses in her hands. "Now, Father, don't work yourself up. I'm sure we can think of something."

"I've already thought of something," her father replied. "That's why I've called you all here this evening."

Isabella placed the tray on the tea cart and began to pour the brandy. "What plan have you come up with?" She was not one to be shy about speaking her mind, even in the presence of her father's male guests.

"We need to rid ourselves of the good Mr. Baldwin. I know his family is powerful, but so is ours. And you, my friends, are at the core of that power," Montego said, smiling as he accepted a snifter of amber liquid from his daughter. "We are not ruffians as some might suppose. We are civilized men who work in civilized means whenever possible. However, this situation calls for a most uncivilized plan."

"You gonna use the Arapaho?" one of the older gentlemen questioned.

"I believe they might serve our purpose quite well. Or perhaps the Sioux or Pawnee. It doesn't really matter. One Indian is pretty much like another, and all have their price." He grimaced. "Well, perhaps not all, but most. I haven't yet found a single tribe that can't boast at least one corrupt man."

"So what is the plan?" someone asked.

Montego smiled. "Since Joe Baldwin is so concerned about the Indians and why they are raiding the railroad, I suggest we put him in the company of those very people. Perhaps he need not be killed. After all, he is a very public figure, but on the other hand, think of how sweetly that might work to our advantage."

"But, Father, if the land is not safe to settle and well-known citizens are disappearing in Indian attacks, will that not hurt your desire to build up cities and sell land?"

Montego considered his daughter for a moment. She was both intelligent and beautiful, and it had served them well. "My plan is to see people settle the lands and cities that are most advantageous to me. Let the world believe Nebraska to be the very heart of hell itself, but let them love Laramie, Rawlins Springs, and Green River. Let them rush here to settle the territory where I own great parcels of land. Let them, seeing the peaceful protection afforded them, come in droves to purchase what we in this room will offer to sell.

"The Indian attacks are all taking place in Nebraska at this point. That has been my direction, and perhaps now is the time to turn our attention elsewhere. I simply utilized a problem that was already in existence — the Indians were already at odds with the railroad when I came into the picture," Montego said, sampling the brandy. "Land sales are good, and the outrageous prices I'm making for building houses and businesses is enough to allow all of us to live out our old age in style. However, if Joe Baldwin has his way, writing as he does about our towns as though they were the very modern re-creation of Sodom and Gomorrah, detailing the deadliness of merely walking down the street unescorted or the high percentage of crime per capita, no one will settle our towns, and, gentlemen, we will be left holding a great deal of useless property."

"Sounds like we need to get right to this, then," someone called out, only to be followed by a unison call of affirmation.

Montego smiled. "Well, then, we are in agreement." He lifted his brandy and smiled. "To our success," he said with a glance at his daughter's smug expression.

"To success," she murmured, lifting her own glass.

October in Utah was proving to be an uncomfortable matter. Cold weather had set in rather early, even in the valleys, and the Baldwins found it greatly interfered with the business of photography.

"I think we might as well give it up and go home," Brenton said after trying for the third time to photograph a stretch of land not far from the territorial border. "The lens keeps fogging, and the coating on the glass is drying quicker than I can take the pictures."

265

Jordana nodded. "I suppose you're right. This cold isn't going to let up, at least not in the way you would probably benefit."

"I'd still like to get pictures from Echo Canyon Tunnel. I'm sure Charlie would like to see those."

Jordana nodded and pulled on a warm woolen coat she'd managed to purchase in Ogden. "I'm sure the photographs you took of the route Charlie intends to propose to Congress will help more than a picture of the Echo Tunnel. Charlie feels quite confident that if your photographs accompany his surveyors' information, Congress will have no choice but to approve his route for the completion of the transcontinental."

"The line is a sound one, in my estimation," Brenton said, packing his equipment into a large leather case. "As long as the line follows that low pass through the Ombe Mountains, I think the Central Pacific will have it quite good. That puts them eventually on a twenty-five-mile flat stretch along the northern edge of the Great Salt Lake's Spring Bay. And for as ugly as that area is, it doesn't look like it will be all that difficult to work."

Jordana smiled her agreement as Caitlan appeared from inside the wagon. "Feeling better?" she asked her sister-in-law, who had taken to the wagon earlier in the day with a stomach complaint.

"Only marginally." Caitlan did look pale.

"It's probably just something you ate," Brenton said offhandedly. He hoisted the case into its place at the back of the wagon, then helped his wife down.

Caitlan laughed and shook her head. "I'm thinkin' it's nothing six or seven months won't cure."

Jordana giggled, having been Caitlan's confidante since she'd first suspected her pregnancy. "I think you shall have to draw him a picture, Caitlan."

Brenton looked at Jordana oddly, then realization dawned on him and he reached out for his wife. "A baby?"

She laughed and nodded. "Yes, Mr. Baldwin. A baby."

Brenton let out a loud whoop and lifted Caitlan into the air but just as quickly set her back on her feet with apologies for his rough treatment.

"I'm no porcelain doll, Brenton," Caitlan assured.

"Well . . . uh . . ." Brenton looked just as pale as his wife.

Caitlan smiled and gave a whoop of her own, causing Brenton to grin. With a shrug, he grabbed her hand, and the two, with Jordana chiming in, continued whooping and dancing. All at once, theirs weren't the only shouts to be heard. These new yells, however, were not ones of pleasure, but rather they were hostile and intent on harm.

Jordana was first on her feet. She grabbed up a rifle and began to run to the front of the wagon. "Indians!" she called out over her shoulder.

By then Brenton and Caitlan had rifles and, using the wagon as cover, were returning fire. But there were too many, and soon the little party would be overwhelmed. The only thing Jordana could think to do was to somehow divide the attackers.

Jordana freed her mount, then shouted to her brother. "I'm going to try to draw them off."

And before anyone could respond, she swung herself up on her horse's bare back with nothing more than the animal's mane to assist her. Looking over her shoulder, she saw three braves bearing down on the camp. She fired at these men, and it was only then that Brenton realized what she was up to.

"Jordana!" he yelled.

But there was no time for him to berate her foolhardiness. He had to keep shooting. And Jordana had no time to worry about his displeasure. When they discussed it later, as she was certain they would, he would have to realize that it was especially imperative that he remain with Caitlan to protect her and their unborn child.

Jordana urged the horse forward and, with a powerful kick, felt every muscle of the beast leap into action beneath her. She hadn't ridden bareback in years, but now was no time for worrying about it. Firing off in the direction of the newest line of attackers, Jordana counted another five men bearing down on their camp.

Hearing shots behind her, Jordana could only pray for her family's safety. Glancing around as her horse tried desperately to climb the rocky terrain, Jordana realized that her plan was a success; in fact, it was quite shockingly successful. With the exception of one or two, all of the braves were now following her! A sickening feeling permeated her senses. If they caught her, they would kill her.

Urging the horse and praying at the same time, Jordana crested the butte and found herself face-to-face with another half dozen braves. It appeared to be a hunting party. Knowing her efforts were futile, Jordana didn't even attempt to shoot at the group but, instead, pushed her horse into the direction away from the gathering. Crouching low to the horse's neck, she heard several bullets whistle by her.

Then the shots stopped, and Jordana thought for the briefest moment that she had somehow managed to elude her captors. Just as quickly as the thought came to her, a mounted warrior rose up in her path. The suddenness of his appearance made her mount jerk skittishly, throwing her to the ground. Hitting her head hard against a rock, Jordana fought against the blackening cloud of unconsciousness. Her last image was of an Indian warrior, probably no older than herself, kneeling over her to survey her injuries.

Brenton gathered his wife into his arms and held her as she cried long and hard. The events of the morning were more than either one of them could possibly understand or felt up to considering in any detail. The shock had made them numb and then had rendered them grief stricken in the wake of Jordana's disappearance.

Brenton had watched stunned as the entire party of attackers had gone off in pursuit of his sister. He knew she had not intended for this to happen but rather had simply wanted to break up the war party and give Caitlan and him a better chance.

Only two Indians remained behind, and these had seemed uninterested in anything Brenton and Caitlan had to offer, including their scalps. The two braves had stripped the wagon of what they wanted — blankets, food, rifles — but the photography equipment seemed of no interest, and since the chemicals were inedible, they simply tossed them to the ground. Brenton had been amazed that the entire wagon hadn't erupted into flames.

Within moments these Indians also left in the direction of Jordana's path of departure. They neither acknowledged Brenton's and Caitlan's existence, nor concerned themselves with the wagon's horses.

"Oh, Brenton, what are we to do?" Caitlan said in tears.

Brenton shook his head. "I'm not sure. I don't know what to think."

"Do you think Jordana got away?"

Again he shook his head. "I don't know. I need to round up our horses and go look for her."

Caitlan nodded vigorously. "Aye. That's what we should do."

"Not we, *me.*" His firm tone was edged with fear.

"But I don't want ya to be goin' alone, and neither do I want to be left here all by meself," Caitlan replied. "I'll stay where ya tell me to, but don't leave me here."

How could he best protect her? What if he should make the wrong choice? "All right. We can come back for the wagon."

He took the spare saddles from the wagon, and in minutes two animals were ready. They searched for several hours, and the only thing Brenton could find was Jordana's discarded hat. What grieved him the most was the wet blood he found smeared at the rim. Swallowing hard, he searched the horizon from the butte and tried to see where the Indians might have taken her. But there was no sign of life out there. The barren land revealed nothing, and the growing cold of the wind seemed to indicate that the weather was soon to turn quite harsh.

Glancing at Caitlan, Brenton felt he had once again failed Jordana. He was unsuited for this harsh land and its dangers. Unsuited to keep his family safe while venturing out to do nothing more difficult than take photographs of the landscape.

Heavy clouds had been gathering since early morning, and now a light rain began to fall, chilling Brenton to the bone. Jordana was out there somewhere — she, too, was no doubt cold and wet — and bleeding, he reminded himself.

With a cry that reached clear down into his gut, Brenton bellowed out her name against the angry Utah skies. "Jordana! Jordana!"

The silence deafened him in reply. "I can't do this alone," he said, lifting his face to the heavens. "I know nothing about how to go finding her. I don't know what to do."

Rich. The name came to him like a whisper of hope. Rich O'Brian not only knew Jordana and cared deeply about her, but he knew this land. He had been a soldier, and he also knew about tracking and Indians. Rich was the answer!

"We have to get to town!" Brenton cried, and with renewed hope spurred his mount into a gallop. "We have to find Rich." Caitlan raced after him.

Jordana awakened to hear the murmur of voices somewhere near. She struggled to understand the words, feeling certain she recognized one of the voices. Charlie? she wondered, then shook her aching head. No, it didn't really sound like him.

Forcing her body to comply with her desires, she rolled to her belly and crawled toward the sound of the voices. She was lying on the ground but in some sort of enclosure. Although her vision was blurry, she could make out a crack of flickering orangish light through some sort of a door. What had happened to her? Why did her head hurt so much? Had she gotten sick back in Wadsworth?

Her eyes adjusted somewhat to the dim lighting of the room, and as she began to focus on the objects around her, Jordana felt as though she must be in a dream. Smells she had never known before assaulted her senses. What had happened to her? Where was she?

Laughter broke through her thoughts. She had heard that laughter before. Where? She edged closer toward the light until she came up against something rather soft: the walls of the room — or rather the tent. A leather flap seemed to be the only closure between her and the outside world. Carefully lifting it, she peered out but fell back as a sharp pain shot through her head. The pain nearly blinded her, but not before she could make out the figure of a white man and several Indian braves outside, seated around a campfire.

Panting hard and struggling to sit up, Jordana could no longer take the pain. She eased back to the mat on which she'd been placed. The voices came to her, muffled but clear enough to distinguish.

"We took the man just as you said. We left the others unharmed."

"Good, good. No sense in everyone getting into an uproar. You'll find your price is even now being unloaded from my wagons."

Jordana fought to stay conscious, anxious to know what this meeting was about. What man was he talking about? Should she scream and let the man know that she was being held captive? Perhaps he could help to rescue her. He obviously seemed to be friends with this particular tribe of Indians.

"Are you interested in another job?"

"Against the railroad?" came the reply.

"Yes."

"I will speak to my people. If it is to our benefit, then I will consider it."

Jordana could not tell who was speaking because the two speakers both used excellent English. Yet she was certain by the clothing that only one of the men was white. Before she could consider further, the voices grew muffled and the words became slurred and unrecognizable. It was only then that Jordana realized she was about to pass out again.

Just then the flap opened and the orange light of the fire made eerie shadows dance about the tent. She struggled to clear her head but pretended to remain unconscious.

She didn't know why, but instinct told her this was for the best.

"There he is," the Indian said. "Is this your man? Your Mr. Baldwin?"

"That's the little troublemaker," the other man replied. "Do with him what you will. Just don't let the body be found."

"The signs promise a bad winter. My people are preparing to leave for better ground. Perhaps we will take him with us to help with the move. Your job must come soon or we will not be here to help you."

"The sooner the better, as far as I'm concerned. Just keep Baldwin out of my hair."

Jordana felt a cold sensation settle on her body. When the flap was once again in place, she shuddered and realized that whoever the man was, it was he who had caused her to be captured by the Indians. Then the other words of his conversation came back to haunt her.

"Are you interested in another job?"

The man was hiring the Indians to work against the Union Pacific. Perhaps even the Central Pacific. Yielding to the blackness, Jordana closed her eyes. If only she could somehow let Rich know about the deception. If only she could remember whose voice it was that she'd just heard. She had tried to see the man through her narrowly opened eyes, but the light had been too dim. Perhaps she could somehow learn his identity from the Indians. That was, if they let her live long enough to ask questions.

NINETEEN

When Jordana next awakened, she found herself lying warm and snug beneath a pile of furs. She shifted her weight to roll over and the fur fell away from her shoulder. The air was quite cold and caused her to shiver. Then realization dawned on her. She wasn't wearing her clothes. Feeling along the lines of her body, Jordana realized that she wasn't wearing any clothes at all.

Startled, she opened her eyes and focused on the room. An old Indian woman sat not two feet away from her. She watched Jordana with curious eyes and spoke in halted English.

"You no move. You hurt."

Jordana reached up to her head and felt a sticky concoction. Pulling her hand away, she wasn't at all sure what the substance was, but it appeared to be some kind of poultice.

"Where am I?" she asked, her voice croaking from disuse.

The old woman shrugged. "You rest."

"I need clothes." Jordana clutched the fur tight to her breast. "Where are my clothes?" She motioned to her body, then to the woman's layered outfit of buckskin.

"You no man. You woman," the woman replied matter-of-factly.

Jordana nodded. "Yes, I am a woman."

The old woman grunted and went to the far side of what Jordana now recognized as an Indian tepee. The woman brought a bundle of clothes and thrust them at Jordana. "These for woman."

Jordana smiled. "Thank you." She realized quickly that she wasn't about to get her old clothes back, and being in no position to make demands, she simply smiled and accepted the woman's offering.

After the woman left, Jordana struggled against a blinding headache to put on the mismatched outfit. The clothes, apparently those taken in a raid on white settlers, were mostly too big. Pulling on a cotton chemise, Jordana laughed as it fell down to her ankles. The design was fairly straight and didn't allow for a great deal of movement, so Jordana tore a slit up each side to give her more mobility. Next, she pulled on a well-worn calico dress that had apparently suited a much heavier woman. The length wasn't so bad, but the width of the waistline left Jordana's petite frame swimming within the garment.

The old woman returned, and seeing the way the clothing fit, or rather did not fit, she went again to the far side of the room and rummaged amidst a collection of goods before bringing back a leather belt.

Jordana smiled and again thanked the woman as she pulled the belt around her waist and caught up the bulk of the material with it. Then she turned and asked the old woman if she could help button up the back. The woman didn't appear to understand until Jordana turned and pointed to her back.

Grunting, the old woman did up the buttons, then pointed to the closed flap. "You rest plenty. Now you come."

Jordana nodded and followed. There seemed no other choice.

Stepping outside the relative warmth of the tepee, Jordana shivered as her bare feet touched the snowy ground.

"May I have my boots back?" she asked the old woman.

By now a group of other women and children had formed just beyond Jordana. They pointed at her as they talked amongst themselves.

The old woman didn't understand, so Jordana raised her skirts and showed the old woman her bare feet. Nodding in understanding, she then ducked back into the tepee. When she returned she held up a pair of pounded-hide moccasins. Jordana accepted them gratefully and while balancing on one foot and trying to keep her skirts from interfering, she pulled first one moccasin on and then the other. The hides were soft and supple. Jordana relished the protection they afforded.

"These are very nice." She smiled in a friendly manner.

The old woman nodded, then pointed Jordana in the direction she wished her to go. "You go there."

Jordana walked as instructed toward another cluster of tepees. Apparently she was to move to another location, but for what purpose, she had no idea. The gathering of women and children followed after her, chattering in their native tongue, while the old woman padded along beside her in silence. Jordana had no idea what to make of it.

She didn't have long to wonder. Within moments the old woman shoved her toward the largest of three tepees and pushed her through the opening. Jordana came face-to-face with a council of seven men. They sat gathered around a fire, their hardened brown faces no longer bearing the paint of warriors.

Reaching up, Jordana nervously touched the edges of her hair, which had grown down past her ears. She had figured to have Caitlan cut it again before they returned to California but hadn't managed to get around to it. Thinking of this caused her to wonder about her brother and sister-in-law. Were they dead? Were they alive and here, somewhere within this same camp? The thought made her suddenly very courageous.

"Where are my brother and his wife?"

The man at the center of the group looked at her rather harshly. "You will not speak until I give you permission."

It was clearly the voice of the man she'd heard earlier. That refined voice with a knowledge and understanding of proper English. She wondered how and where he had come by such refinement. But curbing her reporter's curiosity, she turned her full attention on him and took a defiant stand. She had always heard from Rich that Indians admired courage. She prayed it was true.

"I'm not going to stand here in silence until I know if my brother is alive and well."

The man fixed her with a steely gaze, then nodded. "Your brother and his woman were left unharmed."

"So you were only there to get me?" Vaguely, the conversation between this man and the white man she had heard earlier came back to her. How long ago had that been? But she had to focus on the immediate conversation.

"Yes," the well-spoken Indian replied.

"Why?"

"That is not important. You are not what you appeared at first. You were thought to be a man, but you are a woman."

Jordana nodded. "Yes, I am."

"Why were you dressed as a man?"

"It's a long story, but suffice it to say, I found myself better protected against harm as a man." She forced her voice to remain even. She had to prove herself strong and courageous. Just then a Bible verse she had memorized as a child came to mind: *"Have not I commanded thee? Be strong and of a good courage; be not afraid, neither be thou dismayed: for the Lord thy God is with thee whithersoever thou goest."* God was with her even here in the middle of this Indian camp. It gave her strength to go on.

"Why am I here?" she asked suddenly.

The man seemed surprised that she should question him on the matter. "You will not question me." The man to his right leaned over and spoke in a low voice. The first man nodded.

"You will stay with us. We are to move to the south and you will come."

"I don't wish to go with you," Jordana replied bravely. "I don't understand why I am here, and I don't understand why I am being held captive."

"It is not important that you understand. Only that you know if you do not do as you are told, you will be punished. We do not seek your harm, but you will not disobey."

Jordana felt that perhaps it would be best not to argue with the man. Instead she nodded.

"It has been suggested that you should become wife to one of our braves."

Jordana felt her resolve give way to fear. Wife? She started to say something, but the old woman began chattering at the man. He in turn grunted out a reply and turned to his council as if to consider what they had to say about the matter.

Oh, God, Jordana prayed, *please help me. This is too much to deal with. Please don't force me to endure such a thing.* The idea of marriage to any man was more than she wanted to consider. Unless, she realized, that man was Rich O'Brian.

The room once again fell silent and Jordana awaited the council's decision. The Indian who was the spokesman and interpreter, if not the leader, eyed her cautiously, and his very demeanor suggested that something had changed.

"My mother tells of a vision she had. A vision of a white woman who brought about destruction upon our people. Our braves will not want you as a wife, but until we decide what to do about you, you will work. You are not to speak with our people. You will sleep alone and you will eat alone."

Jordana found his words a blessing and comfort. As her heart sang out thanksgiving to God, she merely nodded in the direction of the man and his council.

Immediately, the old woman grabbed hold of her and forced her back through the opening and into the cold air. The dusting of snow was even now melting in the warmth of the morning sun, and Jordana prayed fervently that somehow winter might be held off just a few more weeks. At least long enough to give her a chance for escape.

And escape was the uppermost thought on Jordana's mind. When the tribe collected their belongings and broke camp the next morning, Jordana was loaded with heavy packs and forced to march, dragging long lodgepoles behind her. Her hands were somewhat callused from her time spent along the railroad and the lack of care she had given them while posing as a man, but dragging these poles left them blistered and bleeding.

After several days of the long, strenuous routine, Jordana began to grow desperate. She had no idea where she was or where she could go, even if she somehow managed to escape. The movements of the sun indicated they had traveled east and south, but otherwise, Jordana was at a complete loss as to her location.

Days passed into weeks, and the trails chosen by the tribe leadership seemed to take them farther east and south. The mountains to the south rose up as a natural barrier, and already they bore evidence of a crowning of winter snow. The air warmed during the day and gave Jordana hope that perhaps they would not have to endure the miseries of winter, but at night it once again grew bitter and her resolve weakened. It seemed futile to escape only to die in a winter wilderness.

Once during the long hours of the night,

the silence around her threatened to eat her alive. Her heart was completely void of hope, and discouragement set in oppressively. Tears poured from her eyes as she wept silently. No harm had come to her, save the insistence of her taskmasters that she work from sunup to sunset. But also no one spoke to her. No one smiled or shared any sign of comfort. The old woman had seen that she received her warm coat, but otherwise her things had long since disappeared, and the misery of having nothing familiar was almost more than she could bear.

Oh, Father, she cried softly, *please deliver me.* Sitting up in the darkness of her lodging, Jordana tucked her knees up under her chin and began to rock back and forth. She thought of her mother and how if she knew about this ordeal, she must surely be frantic with worry. She thought of the adventure of the matter and tried to keep in mind things she could tell about if she should ever manage to escape. If . . .

The winds howled down through the canyon where they'd taken shelter, and nature's mournful cry did nothing to reassure Jordana's sick heart.

"Where are you, God?" she whispered. "I need you. Please show me that you are still here — that you haven't forgotten me." She thought of Bible stories where David had felt much the same. Cries he had made in the psalms he'd written. Cries of anguish and fear — cries of desertion and loneliness.

That night Jordana heard something move about outside her door. She crept to the opening. There not a foot away stood a pale-colored Indian pony. He looked at her with indifference. Jordana felt her heart begin to race. Would it be possible to take the horse and escape the camp?

She had slept fully clothed with her warm woolen coat tucked under her head as a pillow. Crawling back to her bed, she pulled on her coat and took up one of the blankets she'd been given. She realized escape was foolish, but she feared her despair might kill her just as easily as would the snow and cold. And just the other day, the old woman had mentioned that the men were discussing which one would take the white woman for a wife. It seemed they had lost respect for the old woman's vision.

Believing she had no other choice and that this could well be the answer to her prayers, Jordana stealthily made her way outside. A light snow had begun to fall, and with it the thick clouds overhead blocked out any hope of moonlight.

Fearful that the horse might whinny or protest should she mount him, Jordana took up a piece of rawhide strapping that had bound her lodgepoles and slipped it around the horse's neck in a makeshift lead. As she cautiously led the horse away she saw near the edge of the camp a dark figure crouched near the bushes. She stopped abruptly, but she was in clear sight and had no place to hide. Then she saw it was the old woman. Quietly, Jordana moved forward. The old Indian woman said nothing, merely nodding as Jordana came near. Jordana wanted to speak, but fearing discovery, she only smiled as she led the pony past the woman to the outer edge of the camp and down the trail from whence they'd come. The entire time she expected some alarm to rise, but there was nothing save the intense quiet of the night. Why had the woman helped her? And Jordana was certain now that the pony had not materialized on its own. Had the woman also concocted the story about her vision just to save Jordana? But why? Jordana would never know the answer. She would just remain eternally grateful — if indeed she survived this escape.

When she felt confident that she'd gone far enough, Jordana hiked her skirts up between her legs and pulled herself up onto the horse's back. He remained silent, as if he were as determined as Jordana to escape his life with the Indians. Jordana suspected that the animal's cooperation had more to do with the fact that after weeks among the Indians she had come so to smell like them that the pony could not tell the difference.

Nudging him gently, Jordana thanked God for the beast and prayed silently that she would somehow find her way to safety.

But from the first moment away from the shelter of the canyon, Jordana realized the degree of her folly. She was in unfamiliar territory and the winter weather was closing in on her. The snows thickened on the ground, leaving great tracks behind her. At one point she thought she heard pursuers and got off the horse to wipe out the tracks, but soon it was evident that no one was following, and she remounted and urged the horse forward.

As the wind picked up she no longer had to worry about leaving tracks in the snow. Jordana couldn't even tell what direction she'd come from. For all she knew, she might well be retracing her own steps. The skies lightened marginally as dawn approached, but in turn the storm intensified, and soon she was nearly blinded by the swirling white veil around her.

Desperation drove Jordana forward. There was no thought for anything but escape. No thought for the numbness in her toes and fingers. No thought for the icy crust that had formed on her brows and eyelashes. She pulled the blanket tight around her head and shoulders, but still the wind seemed to whip right through and chill her to the bone.

The pony moved more slowly now, and as the snow grew deeper, Jordana realized she would soon have to take shelter or lose the beast altogether. Twice she dismounted and warmed the poor horse's nostrils with her own breath, breaking away a buildup of ice so that he could breathe more easily. But the efforts were rather futile, and Jordana felt certain that all hope had escaped them.

As night came on, she was no longer able to make sense of her surroundings or even of her own thoughts. She couldn't remember where she was or why she was so cold. She plunged into a waking dreamlike state. Her hold on reality slipped her grasp. Finally, she heard her name being called over and over, and sliding off the pony's back, she let go her hold on the rawhide reins and sank to the ground.

"Jordana," the voice called again.

The Indians had found her.

"Jordana!"

How did the Indian know her name? But it did not matter. All she wanted to do was sleep.

The first thought Jordana had upon opening her eyes was that the wind had somehow stopped blowing. The silence and warmth were a comfort to her, and without concerning herself as to where she was or how she had gotten there, she fell back asleep and let the warmth soothe her into sweet dreams.

The next time she woke, she could hear the wind in the distance, and focusing her eyes, she could see that she was inside a cave, and a fire was blazing cheerily near the opening. Moaning at the stiffness in her limbs as she attempted to sit, Jordana fell back and merely lifted her head. She noticed the pony, along with a much larger mount, standing at the back of the cave. From the shadows near where the animals stood, a man appeared.

Jordana forced herself to remain calm. She would deal with whatever came. The man stepped out of the darkness, and in that moment, Jordana thought her eyes were playing games with her heart.

"Rich?"

"Glad to have you among the living, Jordana," he said casually.

"How? Where?" In shock, she stuttered and, forgetting her aching body, sat bolt upright, shrugging out of the warmth of the blankets he'd obviously placed around her shoulders.

"Just stay put. You'll get cold." He moved toward her as if to force the issue. "And after I had a devil of a time getting you warmed up."

"Where are we?" Jordana asked, looking around her once again.

"I'm not sure. As best as I can figure it, we're somewhere south of Bear River." Rich squatted down beside her. "You gave us all a real scare, you know."

"Yes, well, it wasn't my idea to take up camping with the Indians. How did you find me?"

"Brenton told me what happened —"

"Brenton? Then he's all right?"

Rich nodded. "He and Caitlan are both just fine. Worried half out of their heads, but fine. I alerted all my old army friends to keep their eyes and ears open, and I have been following leads for weeks. Most leads went nowhere, but finally I heard about a band of Sioux that had a white captive. It wasn't the first such rumor I'd heard, but this one seemed promising because the fellow who told me had heard two Indians in town talking about the white woman with shorn hair. The two Sioux weren't about to help me, but I managed to track them some distance before I lost them. That was a day before I found you. I just kept searching in the general area hoping to stumble upon their camp. Instead, I stumbled upon you."

Jordana leaned back against the rock wall and looked at Rich for a moment. The haggard look on his face told her everything else she needed to know. Without a word she reached out and pulled him forward to embrace him. "Thank you, Rich."

Catching him off guard, the gesture sent him tumbling forward, leaving the bulk of his weight atop her covered legs.

Laughing, Jordana apologized as Rich tried to ease himself away without hurting her. "I'm sorry. It's just that it's so good to see you again. I figured you might never want to even talk to me, much less go to this kind of trouble."

Rich scooted next to her and leaned back on his hands. "Just call me a glutton for punishment." He smiled and it warmed her heart.

"So where do we go from here?" Jordana asked, realizing that the statement could very well be taken two ways. She'd leave the direction to Rich.

He watched her very carefully for a moment, his blue eyes giving careful scrutiny to her face. Jordana held her breath, feeling as though he could read her thoughts — know her heart. And then, the moment passed them by and Rich looked away toward the mouth of the cave.

"We wait until it stops snowing and then I get you back to your brother."

Jordana hid her disappointment and squared her shoulders. She thought of the discussion she'd heard with the white man and the Indians and had nearly decided to tell Rich all about it when he moved away and got to his feet.

"I suppose you'll go back to working for Charlie Crocker?" he said, and Jordana could not tell if it was a question or a statement.

"Why do you say that? What makes you think I'm working for Charlie anyway?"

"It was pretty obvious back in Wadsworth. I don't know what you're doing for him, but I have to warn you that the danger and risk to yourself are great."

Jordana knew that fact only too well. "My priority has always been to write stories for the newspaper. The transcontinental railroad is an important issue. Do you know that there are already a dozen other reporters working along the line?"

"Good, then you can give it up," Rich replied. "I would imagine all of those other reporters are men and much more capable of staying out of trouble."

"Rich O'Brian, you are a pigheaded ninny!" Jordana crossed her arms and leaned back against the wall with a great thud. She winced at the pain she'd caused herself, but kept her face turned so that Rich wouldn't know.

"If trying to keep you from getting yourself arrested or killed makes me a ninny, then I'll gladly take the title. Jordana, look at me," he said firmly.

She lifted her face and met his stern expression. "What?"

"I can't let you travel around spying on the Union Pacific for whatever reason you think you might be doing it."

"I'm just trying to keep my interests protected. I want to know what's happening. I have family on the Central Pacific, family who have been endangered more times than I can even know. I don't care about the politics of your precious Union Pacific," she said. "I care about them."

The conversation was clearly over as far

as she was concerned. Closing her eyes, she wondered how she'd gone from hugging Rich in gratitude to wishing fervently she could slug him for doubting her motives. Their forced isolation in this small cave was surely going to prove interesting.

Hours later when darkness left Jordana with little choice but sleep, she found herself pondering whether she should just come clean with Rich. Why not tell him everything? Explain the motives. Explain the reasoning for her choices and duties. She could tell him about the Indians and the encounter she'd overheard. Then another thought came to mind. She could find out who the white man was at the Indian camp and expose him herself. He was harming the Union Pacific and probably the CP as well. She could expose him and bring him to Rich's attention and then maybe she'd be vindicated in Rich's eyes.

She glanced over to where Rich slept fitfully near the fire. He tossed and turned, moaning out unintelligible words and leaving Jordana to wonder at his state of mind. What was it that had him so worried? Was it her doing or his own? He settled a bit, then appeared to sleep more restfully. Jordana shook her head. What was she to do with him?

Twenty

The storm abated, leaving behind a drifting covering of snow. Rich took the opportunity to pack their things and set back on the trail for home. He felt himself withdraw little by little, knowing that Jordana could never hope to understand what he was thinking. Neither would she understand his past and why he had never concerned himself with offering her more than friendship. At least not until now.

Now his head was filled with all kinds of tormenting thoughts. Tormenting, because he was certain he could never make them work into anything productive. He dreamed nightly of Jordana, but inevitably those dreams of hope and love faded into pain and desperation. He would find himself standing over the grave of his young wife — guilt coursing through him with every heartbeat. How could he explain to Jordana when he couldn't explain it to himself?

They were three days on the trail and still no sign of civilization. Jordana appeared unconcerned with this and instead seemed quite preoccupied with her thoughts. Rich would catch her watching him, her looks causing him to wonder if she hadn't released herself from that ban against taking a husband. But even if she had, he couldn't release himself from the past and, therefore, knew he could never offer her anything more than friendship. It was enough to drive him half mad. He wanted her and yet he was afraid, of his past and also of the promise he had made to her long ago about just remaining friends. The promise he could deal with, but his past was a matter that went to the depth of his soul. He feared it could not be changed.

The long hours on the trail, the intensity of worrying over whether the Indians would find them, and the ever changing weather were enough to put Rich and Jordana at odds. No matter what Rich said to her, Jordana seemed to take it wrong. Once he'd had a strange creeping sensation at the nape of his neck, as if he were being watched. He had tried warning Jordana not to ride too far behind him for fear someone might sneak up on them and grab her. But instead of appreciating his concern, she had snapped at him that she was fully capable of taking care of herself. Women! He just didn't understand them.

Gazing up at the clear skies later that night after they had made camp, Rich couldn't bear to think of what might happen once they reached civilization. Jordana would go back to work doing whatever it was she had managed to get herself tangled up in, and Rich had his duties to the Union Pacific. There continued to be problems along the line, although after the bridge-burning at Lodge Pole, their Indian troubles had appeared to calm a bit. It had been at least three weeks since anyone had anything to report in the way of Indian conflicts, and Rich could only hope this signaled the Indians' acceptance of the railroad.

Turning to his side, Rich studied Jordana's sleeping figure. She lay on the other side of their campfire, her face turned toward the warmth of the blaze. She had fallen asleep almost immediately after supper, and Rich worried she might grow ill from her exhaustive ordeal before he found her. He had no way of knowing what the Indians had done to her. She assured him no real harm had come to her and she appeared all right, but he wondered how much of that was her bravado to keep him from worrying.

Her face now in complete rest was almost angelic, and her dark hair curled ever so gently around her cheek and over her brow. He wanted to reach across and touch her, but just as he knew he'd be burned by the flames of their campfire, he knew his heart would be seared by allowing himself any further entanglement with her.

"God, what do I do with myself?" he whispered aloud. Then his prayer went silent as his heart continued to cry out to his Father in heaven.

You know me. You know what I did. I don't deserve to love again. I don't deserve this woman. But I love her, and the thought of spending my life alone — without knowing where she is or what she's doing — is more than I can handle.

He rolled over and tried to find that elusive sleep. But something besides his own private woes nagged at him. Just as had happened earlier on the trail, he had a gnawing feeling in the pit of his stomach. What was it? What was out there?

Jordana was certain she heard movement nearby. Startling awake, she forced herself to lie still. She tried to glance over at Rich's sleeping form without appearing overly conspicuous. Then a twig snapped and she was certain her senses had not played tricks on her. Something or someone was out there.

She opened her mouth to scream a warning, but before any sound could pass from her lips, several gunshots blasted through the still night air. She lurched up, then froze, her gaze fixed on the place where Rich was lying. The gunshots had ripped through the blankets. Through Rich! An intruder had entered their camp and was now standing over Rich, a gun, still smoking, in his hand. Now Jordana did scream. She sat straight up and began screaming hysterically.

The intruder turned toward her, his face twisted and bitter. It was only after Jordana forced herself to look at him that she realized the identity of their attacker. Patrick Worth!

"Are you going to try to kill her as well?" came Rich's voice. And in a moment, his entire figure, like a ghost, stepped out from the covering rocks.

"I . . . uh . . ." Worth stammered, though nothing intelligible came from his lips.

"Rich! You're alive!" Jordana scrambled to her feet. Never had she been so relieved to see anyone in her life. He might have been killed and would have been had Worth had

302

his way. She wanted to jump across the fire and punch Worth in the face. How dare he!

"Patrick, you need to throw down your gun," Rich said in a voice that sounded entirely too calm.

"You deserve to be dead, O'Brian. Dead like my sister. You're scum and you don't have a right to live." Worth continued to grip his gun, though his hand dangled at his side. Both his hands were shaking. "I've been tracking you for weeks now, waiting for the right time. I failed this time, but I ain't giving up."

"I'm sorry you feel that way," Rich replied.

Worth turned to Jordana, as if hoping to enlist support. "He killed my sister as sure as if he put a gun to her head. Dragged her out into the prairie, wouldn't let her come home to her people. Left her there for days and weeks while he went all over the territory trying to settle his land claim. Left her there to die when she caught pneumonia."

Jordana looked at the man, his grief and anger marring his otherwise handsome face. "She died of pneumonia? How does that make Rich a killer?"

Worth turned to eye Rich with great contempt. "He left her alone to fend for herself. The nearest people were at the fort, but it was too far away."

"You don't know the truth of it," Rich said, his own expression heavy with pain. "Now put down the gun. It's time we had a long overdue talk."

Jordana waited impatiently as the men faced off, and Worth finally decided to give up without a fight. Rich took up Worth's weapon and handed it to Jordana, with instructions to shoot him if he moved.

"She's a fair shot," Rich told Worth as both men sat on the ground. "I'd suggest you hear me out."

Worth scowled. "I don't know why you'd expect me to believe anything you say."

"Because it would be the truth," Rich replied. "Unlike the lie I told your mother when Peggy died."

Jordana fingered the revolver cautiously, trying hard to take in all the details of the conversation while ever worried that Worth might try something. Could she really shoot him if he attacked Rich? There was no time to consider the question as Rich continued to tell his story. At least now, she was finally getting some answers to the past and why Rich was so troubled after meeting up with Worth in North Platte.

"Peggy and I married and had a dream of homesteading in the Kansas Territory. We staked a claim and tried to make a go of it.

My claim, however, was disputed. Trouble started up and our lives were threatened. One night, shots were fired into the house, and I knew it was important to get Peggy to safety before I could finally see justice done for us and our home.

"In the meantime, Peggy's family was extremely unhappy with our choice," Rich said, looking at Jordana. He seemed to be explaining himself more to her than to Worth. "They wanted Peggy close to home in Kansas City. They wanted to control her life and mine. Peggy didn't want that any more than I did."

"That's a lie. Ma and Pa only wanted to keep her safe. The prairies weren't safe, what with the Indians and storms. They'd heard of too many folks dying in their own backyards from snakebite if nothing else," Patrick cried out. "They weren't trying to control anyone."

"Peggy grew weary of their badgering. She wrote to her mother saying that if she didn't stop with the harassing letters and ugly things she was saying about me, Peggy would never see any of them again."

"That's a lie, I'm telling you." Worth looked from O'Brian to Jordana as if she somehow had the power to judge the situation.

Mesmerized by the entire scene, Jordana said nothing and instead looked at Rich, hanging on to his words.

"Your mother wrote back telling Peggy that her harsh letter had caused your father to have a stroke. By this time the attacks on our claim had become so threatening that I feared for Peggy's life. I suggested she go home to Kansas City and straighten things out with the family while I in turn would go to the law and try to straighten out our homestead. She reluctantly agreed. She didn't believe your mother. She felt certain her statement about the stroke was merely a ploy to bring Peggy running, and of course later I found out that it was exactly that."

"There's no way my ma would have said such a thing. Our pa was as strong as an ox. Peggy would have known he was healthy, and Ma wouldn't have risked her believing poorly of her."

Rich went to his bedroll and pulled back the bullet-shot blanket. Under it were several large piles of sticks and underbrush arranged to look like Rich's body. His saddlebags had been put in the place of his head and were unharmed because Worth had been aiming at the body. Taking up the bags, Rich opened one side and pulled out a packet of letters. Tossing them to Worth,

306

he said, "The proof is all right there. Every word your mother ever sent to Peggy. Every word of hatred and anger. Read them for yourself."

Jordana could see Patrick's hand trembling as he reached for the packet. "That still doesn't prove anything," Worth muttered. "You still killed her. You left her there on the prairie to die while you went to fight for your precious land."

"No!" Rich said, a little harsher than necessary.

Jordana could tell his anger was piqued by this statement.

"She died trying to get back home to her mother!"

Worth and Jordana both looked at Rich for further explanation.

"She didn't die from pneumonia. I only told your mother that so she wouldn't feel guilty for the truth of it."

"Which was what?" Worth questioned, his face etched with grief.

Rich reached down and drew Worth up by his shirt collar. "Peggy didn't want to leave me. She begged me not to send her home to her family. She didn't believe her father to be ill, but she was worried, nevertheless, that it just might be true. I didn't want her to always wonder, and I sure didn't want her to stay on at the homestead while I tried to settle our claim. I put her on the first stage to Kansas City — against her will." He let go of Patrick and shook his head. "I should have listened to her."

"What happened, Rich?" Jordana asked softly.

He looked at her as if needing the reassurance that he had not somehow alienated her. "The stage overturned and Peggy was killed. So were two other passengers. It didn't happen very far down the line, so they brought her home to me for burial. Cold weather was setting in, and all I could think of was how in the world I was going to make it through a cold winter without Peggy to keep me warm at night. How was I going to wake up in the morning without knowing she would be there, smiling at me in that way she had?" His words grew heavy with emotion. "She was carrying my baby, and we were going to be very happy as soon as we got the land straightened out."

Jordana's eyes stung with tears. Worth seemed to take the news in a stunned state of disbelief.

Rich dropped down by the fire. Clearly he was no longer worried about Worth being any real threat. Perhaps, Jordana thought, he wouldn't care if Worth attacked him again. At least it made clear the reasons for Rich's nightly bad dreams. A man could hardly be expected to bear such a loss and not be haunted by the responsibility and guilt of it all.

"She didn't want to go," Rich said softly. "And I forced her to go. So in that sense, I did kill her." He turned to Worth and looked up. "As much as I was angry at your mother for what she'd done, the threats she'd made, the way she'd badmouthed me, I couldn't bear to throw this in her face. I didn't want her to know that Peggy died while trying to get home to her."

"They never told me any of this," Patrick said, shaking his head. He too slumped as if the energy had been completely drained from his body.

"That's because they never knew. They still don't, even now after all these years," Rich replied. "I wrote and told them she'd died of pneumonia because I couldn't bear the idea of telling them the truth. Oh, don't get me wrong, there was a part of me that wanted very much to hurt your folks. I wanted to rub it in their faces that Peggy was dead because of them."

"Why didn't you?" Worth asked softly.

"Because there was a preacher and his wife who took me under their wing and wouldn't let me go home to an empty claim. Night after night, the man and his wife talked to me about the love of God and how Peggy was in heaven because she had taken Jesus as her Savior during one of their services. I didn't know any of this about Peggy. I didn't know what getting saved was even about. I knew she'd go to church whenever there were services anywhere nearby, but I figured it was more for the company of other women. The preacher helped me to see that it was for much, much more. They talked to me about the love of Christ, about how when He was on the cross dying to save us from our sins, He asked God not to hold it against the people who were killing Him. I figured if Jesus could forgive the people who put Him on the cross, I could find a way to forgive your folks for making my life so miserable and, as a result, causing me to put Peggy on that stage."

"I don't know what to say," Patrick replied, looking from Rich to Jordana.

Jordana gave him a sad smile. "I don't think you need to doubt that this is the truth," she told Patrick. "Rich just risked his life to save me, and we're nothing more than good friends. I don't believe for one minute he would have risked the life of the woman he was so clearly in love with if he hadn't believed it to be for her good."

Rich looked up and met her eyes with an expression of utmost gratitude. She smiled and knew the bond between them was more than friendship, but for the sake of this night, this moment, she would hold her tongue and say nothing more.

"I was wrong to lie to your family, Patrick," Rich said, taking his gaze from Jordana and returning it to Worth. "I should have told them the truth, even though it would have been painful for them to reconcile. I've been haunted by Peggy's death for all these years. I couldn't let go of blaming myself, and why not? I knew you all blamed me as well. It seemed only proper. But now — now I finally feel at peace. The truth is told. The past is dead."

Rich sighed and Jordana wondered if it was so. Could he really put the past behind him so easily?

"I pray you'll forgive my deceit," Rich went on, "but I can't force you to do so. I'll always remember Peggy fondly, but that part of my life is over. I'm going to look forward to the future."

"I'm not sure I know how to forgive, O'Brian," Patrick said.

"Forgiving isn't always easy," Jordana said

softly. "But it is very freeing, and without it, you always have something standing between you and God. That may not seem important now, but take my word, there will come a day and a time when you'll think otherwise."

Worth shook his head. "That's too easy, for me and for Rich," he said, looking hard at Rich. "My sister's still dead. Someone's gotta take the blame. Maybe killing you, Rich, ain't gonna bring her back, but . . . someone's got to pay!" He paused, then his lips twisted ironically. "Guess it'll be me. You can turn me in for trying to kill you."

"I'm not gonna do that, Patrick," Rich said.

"What, then?"

"Just get on your horse and ride away. My punishment for what happened to Peggy will have to be forever watching my back. I just hope you won't be living your entire life trying to get revenge for one terrible mistake."

"I don't want to live that way, but I don't know what else to do." Patrick strode with a heavy step to his horse and stuffed the letters inside his coat before he mounted.

Jordana put her arm around Rich as they watched Worth ride away. They sat in silence for a long while. There seemed little else to say for the moment.

Finally Rich rose. "It's in God's hands now," he said to no one in particular, then he stoked up the fire and made coffee.

■ ■ ■ ■

Part IV
November 1868–
January 1869

■ ■ ■ ■

TWENTY-ONE

After learning from a passing trapper that they were less than a day's ride to Laramie, Rich and Jordana packed up their things and prepared to follow Worth's trail back to town. For some reason they felt no imminent threat from Patrick. Rich said he was basically a decent man and that it would be hard, if not impossible, for him to attempt murder again after having heard the full truth.

Jordana felt glad for the time with Rich. She wanted to explain everything that had happened. She needed to let him in on her work with Charlie and all that she had stumbled across in working on stories for the newspaper. She also wanted to share her heart with him, and if the moment presented itself to her, she would.

"You're still looking pretty worn, Miss Baldwin," Rich said as he helped her up on her pony. "Will you be able to manage bareback?"

"I am pretty worn, Captain." She gave him a lighthearted grin. Just making the decision to open up to him had lifted a burden from her. "But I figure I'll last. And I am getting used to no saddle, but I'll be happy when I can get one." She waited until he went to his own mount, then laughed as the horse gave a skittish dance. "He certainly isn't as mild mannered as Faithful was."

"Not by a long ways," Rich agreed, trying to bring the black gelding under control.

"What do you call this one?" she asked as Rich finally managed to swing up into the saddle, only to suffer the horse's rearing up.

Rich clung to the horn and leaned upward toward the horse's neck. "Troublesome," he declared. "I call this fool horse Troublesome."

Jordana laughed and waited until the horse settled before speaking again. "Rich," she said softly, "there are some things we need to discuss."

He gave his mustache a thoughtful rub and nodded. "I believe you are correct."

"Look, this won't be easy, but please hear me out," Jordana said. "I have been working for Charlie Crocker and the Central Pacific. But not for the reasons of causing destruction on the line. I was speaking truthfully when I said I wanted to see both sides thrive."

"Go on," he encouraged.

"Well, the fact of the matter is, I have some information, and I don't even know how it all figures in. I can't give you a name, because I don't have one, but I know there is trouble afoot, and I want to help put an end to it."

"What are you talking about?"

Jordana bit her lip and shifted her weight. "Shouldn't we head on toward town? It's kind of cold out here."

Rich looked at the icy blue sky and nodded. He nudged Troublesome on down the trail that Worth had taken only a few hours earlier. When the trail widened enough, Jordana soon came up alongside him and continued the conversation with great hesitation.

"I . . . well . . . you see, the thing is . . ." She paused and looked down the trail. How could she possibly explain it all? "Charlie wanted someone to tell him what the UP was planning against the CP. He'd suffered several setbacks and was certain that someone was sneaking around looking to cause trouble for him. He asked me to go see what I could find out. He wouldn't have asked, but I was restless and had already decided to go out and see what I could of the line and write about it for the *Tribune.* Plus, I wanted to see you. He knew I'd be headed to Omaha, or thereabouts, and he knew I'd see plenty of the line."

"So you dressed like a man and came snooping?" Rich said.

She was relieved at the hint of teasing in his tone. "Yes, so to speak. I would never have given Charlie information that would have allowed for him or anyone else to cause harm to the Union Pacific Railroad, however. I just want you to understand that. In fact, I had a great deal of information in my journal that I would never have shared with either side."

"Where is that journal now?"

"The Indians took it from me when they took all my other clothes. I don't have any idea what they did with it. It shouldn't have been of value to them. It was just a small brown leather journal with my initials on it. But that brings me to something else. While I was with the Indians I managed to overhear a conversation between some of the chiefs and a white man."

"A white man?"

"Yes. I saw him, but then again I didn't. I had hit my head when the Indians first attacked us. They took me to their village, and when I woke up, I was alone. I heard voices and crawled to the opening of the tepee and saw a white man, but only for a split second. The pain blinded me and I had to lie back down. But when the man laughed at something, I knew it was a voice I recognized. I just couldn't place it, however."

"What does that have to do with spying for Charlie?"

"Little, but it has to do with spying for you," she said, smiling, "if you want to look at it that way. Apparently, this white man was involved in causing trouble all along the Union Pacific Railroad. He'd been hiring Indians from this particular tribe — maybe others too — and enticing them with the promise of food and blankets and other supplies they needed. I heard him offer more work to this man, and I also heard him acknowledge that he'd paid the Indians to kidnap me."

"What!" Rich pulled back the reins, but his tone of voice had startled the gelding. The horse snorted and did another dance of protest before Rich could bring him under control. "Are you saying that whoever is causing the UP trouble had you taken deliberately?"

"Yes. Not me, of course, but Joe Baldwin.

321

As Joe I must have presented some sort of threat, but I can't see how. Anyway, I wouldn't be surprised at all if that man doesn't have my journal, and if he does, Rich, he has information on both sides of the railroad that could cause all manner of trouble."

"Great," Rich said, shaking his head. "Does it also reveal that you aren't Joe, but Jordana?"

"I did make mention of that, but I am certain that when he was in camp, the Indians hadn't yet found out that I was a woman."

She saw Rich pale and look away. He seemed particularly upset over this statement, and she could only wonder at his reaction. Then it dawned on her that he must have feared for her, wondering how the Indians treated her, realizing that they knew she was a female.

"They didn't hurt me, Rich. Not in the way you're thinking about," Jordana said quickly without waiting for him to question her on the matter. "No one touched me except an old Indian woman. She was some sort of seeker — a prophetess, or so she was considered by her people. She told them she'd had a vision of a young white woman who would bring destruction and harm to the tribe if anyone touched her, and she said I was that woman. After that, they set me to living in a small tepee by myself, and while they forced me to work like a mule, no one hurt me or came anywhere near. They wouldn't even talk to me."

Rich's expression betrayed his relief. "I'm glad you weren't hurt."

They rode in silence for several minutes, and then Rich surprised her completely by making his own confession.

"I'm not just a courier for the Union Pacific. I was hired by Dodge to ferret out the saboteurs who were wreaking havoc with the line. I was to move along the line on the pretense of delivering messages, and in fact, I did take letters and papers with me to prove my position. However, I have been just as guilty as you of snooping around for ulterior motives."

"So Charlie was right?"

"Not in the sense that he thought I had broken into the sheds. That wasn't me. I, just like you, would not have done anything to see people hurt or the line jeopardized."

"I know that, and I don't think I ever really thought otherwise. So now what do we do?" Jordana asked. "Is there a way to work with what we know and catch whoever is at the center of this espionage? The person or persons obviously have no concern about what damage they do to either side."

"And that's what's truly strange about the entire matter." Rich looked for all the world as though a great puzzle had just been laid before him. "I can understand a person finding a reason to cause grief to one side or the other. The government is paying out money on completion of track, and the more track laid, the more notice Congress takes of the company. Perhaps to the benefit of future railroads and additional lines. But to purposefully sabotage both lines — well, that leaves me a bit in the dark."

Jordana nodded with a grin. "Perhaps together we can come at it from both sides and shed some light on the matter."

Rich nodded. "I much prefer working with you than working against you."

Sobering, Jordana said, "I don't like being at odds with you, Rich. I enjoy your company too much." She paused to consider what else she might say but decided against saying anything more, when Rich interrupted her thoughts.

"Thanks for what you did for me back there with Worth. Standing up for me like you did. I know Worth is hurting, but maybe now he can work things out."

"Maybe you can, too," Jordana replied.

Rich seemed to consider her words for several minutes. He rode beside her, staring straight ahead, and when he spoke Jordana knew beyond a doubt that now was not the moment to speak of her heart. "I was pigheaded, just as you've stated on many an occasion. I sent Peggy to her death, and that's something I shall always live with. She was my entire world, and with one act, one very foolish act, I forever destroyed all that mattered."

Jordana knew there were no words to say. Nothing she could tell him would alter the way he felt. For him, at this moment in time, the words he spoke were the truth that troubled his soul. Her silly adoration for him or suggestion that he had been more than admirable in the way he'd handled himself and his wife would never see him changing the way he perceived himself. There was nothing at all to be done.

Well, maybe pray. She smiled. Her mother had always said that prayer was the last resort to which Christians came and the first place they should have checked into. Prayer would make a difference, she had no doubt. She hadn't known how to pray for Rich before, but now she did.

Laramie in all its corruption had changed

very little since the last time Jordana had passed through. The biggest exception this time was that her brother Brenton awaited them at a nearby hotel.

"I thought I'd lost you forever," he said, helping her down from the pony.

"I thought so too," she said, wrapping her arms around his neck. "Are you all right? Did they hurt you?"

"The Indians?" Brenton questioned. "No, they seemed not in the leastwise interested in me or Caitlan."

"Speaking of my expectant sister-in-law, where is she?"

"I sent her on to Sacramento. I figured this part of the world was just too wild. There have been hangings going on left and right and vigilante groups deciding who's to get what kind of justice and when. It's already caused a lot of trouble. Albany County has just been founded and Laramie is assigned as county seat, but it seems more like the center of chaos than of anything productive."

Jordana nodded. "I suppose folks like the Montegos and other upstanding citizens don't stand a chance."

"Probably not." Brenton released Jordana and turned to Rich. "I can't thank you enough for finding her. I want to give you a reward, and please don't be insulted by that. My father and mother would no doubt insist."

"They don't know about this, do they?" Jordana's brow creased. She worried about the effect it might have had on her family.

"No, I didn't tell them. I figured if this crossed over into the new year, then I might have to, but as it is you'll be able to be home for Christmas."

"Home?" Jordana repeated as if speaking a foreign word. "I'm not exactly sure where I'd stake that claim."

Brenton's expression changed to reveal his sadness. "I wish you'd think of it as where those folks who love you reside. I was hoping you'd come back to Sacramento with me. Victoria's baby will be due in February, and then Caitlan will be having a baby next spring. You'll be needed."

Jordana smiled. "I'll think about it." She looked at Rich. "Are you going to telegraph Dodge?"

Rich nodded. "I need to find out where he is. For all I know he may well be right here in Laramie. If I don't see you right away, please don't worry. Leave word where you'll be. Now, if you'll excuse me," Rich said, taking up Troublesome's reins.

"Are you sure you don't want my pony?"

Jordana teased. "He's very calm and even tempered, and his gait is quite smooth."

"And for a young woman who weighs all of one hundred pounds dripping wet, I'm sure he rides quite nicely." Rich hoisted himself into the saddle. "But I think two hundred pounds would be too much to ask of that little guy."

Jordana laughed. "Have it your way. But if I hear about you shooting him —"

"You'll know it was just cause," Rich interjected and nudged Troublesome in the direction of the telegraph station. "I'll send you word."

Brenton put an arm around Jordana, hugging her close, and watched as O'Brian disappeared down the street. "I didn't even have to ask him twice. I wired him about what had happened, and within no time at all he was standing before me asking for the details. I think he cares a great deal for you, sister of mine."

Jordana turned to her brother. "That may well be, but his broken heart needs some healing first."

"Broken heart?" Brenton said. "How in the world did Rich O'Brian get a broken heart?"

"It was a stage accident," Jordana replied thoughtfully. "The stage overturned and

Rich's heart was inside. I'll tell you about it sometime, but first I want to get out of these horrible clothes and bathe."

"I can't believe how pretty you look in that gown," Brenton declared. "I even like your hair, and how it curls when it's short."

Jordana twirled around the room showing off the fit of the watered silk dress. "I don't know how you always manage to find such wonderful things, but for this I will kiss you and call you the best brother in the world."

She placed a kiss on his cheek and stepped away to admire herself in the mirror. It had been so long since she'd allowed herself the privilege of dressing as a woman, and now she would have her moment.

"That color does seem to suit you," Brenton said, watching her all the while, "but I would have liked to have found something brighter."

"Why, this is perfect. I love mauve," Jordana replied. She turned to see the back of the gown. "And this lace is exquisite." Gently she fingered the delicate weblike trimming.

"Well, I thought you might enjoy having a nice dinner after your ordeal."

"Too bad Rich can't join us," Jordana said. "It is he whom we should really be celebrating."

Rich had sent word that he was bound for Ogden to meet with Dodge. There was a train departing within the hour and thus he had to leave immediately without seeing them first.

Brenton gazed at his sister. "Yes, I owe Rich more than I can ever express. Ah, Jordana, I'm so glad you weren't hurt any worse than you were. I don't know how I could have lived with myself. I feel so guilty for what happened."

"Why must you men always think that way? Why do you take what happened so personally? You neither caused nor could predict the attack. Why does that make it your responsibility?"

"Because I should have been more astute. I should have been more cautious and alert. I became too casual in regard to our environment. And because I was in charge of our little party, I felt responsible for your safety."

Jordana shook her head. "Things happen without bothering to ask permission. People die, they are born, and as far as I know God never bothers to check it out with anyone before allowing His plan to move forward. You take too much upon yourself." She smiled and her tone softened. "But why should you be any different from the others of your gender? Now, don't get cross with me. I'm starved and ready to go show off this new outfit. Where's that sweet little bonnet you bought me?"

Later as they were seated at dinner in the finest restaurant Laramie could boast, Jordana was disappointed to be interrupted by a sugary-sweet greeting.

"Why, isn't it Brenton Baldwin?" Isabella Montego oozed, not recognizing Jordana. "We met in Wadsworth. You remember Mr. Baldwin, don't you, Father?"

Jordana looked up to find Isabella attired in one of her usual low-cut gowns. This gown, an exquisite shade of blue, trimmed in gold, was styled with a neckline that Jordana would have thought scandalous even for Isabella.

Baxter Montego stepped forward. "Mr. Baldwin, it is a pleasure. How are things in the photography world?"

"Slow right now. The winter weather makes it most difficult."

"Ah yes." Montego eyed Jordana with a look of curiosity. "And is this your lovely wife? I don't recall that she had such dark hair."

"No, of course it isn't his wife," Isabella purred as though she'd caught Brenton in some horrible act.

"This is my sister, Jordana," Brenton offered.

"Good evening," Jordana said before either Montego could speak.

Father and daughter exchanged a peculiar glance. Perhaps it was only that they noted her uncanny resemblance to Joe. She was sure of it when Isabella spoke.

"My, but you look like your other brother," Isabella replied. "What was his name? Joe?"

"Yes, people often have taken us for twins, but he is younger by two years," Jordana replied, thankful for the bonnet that covered her short hair.

"Won't you join us?" Brenton asked.

Jordana kicked him under the table for forcing her to endure an evening of Isabella Montego, but said nothing as the pair agreed and took the seats opposite Jordana and Brenton at the table.

"Twins, eh?" Baxter Montego said, his eyes narrowing slightly. "Must make it difficult for you."

"Not at all really. He is a wonderful brother." Jordana smiled sweetly.

"My sister has just been returned after being captured by Indians," Brenton said. "We are celebrating her safe escape."

"You were taken by the Indians? What a horrible ordeal that must have been," Montego said while Isabella leaned over to speak conspiratorially to Brenton. The ample display of bosom left Jordana feeling more and more at odds with the woman.

"They worked me like a beast but otherwise did me no harm, thank God," Jordana replied.

"But Rich O'Brian, ever devoted to my sister, rescued her," put in Brenton. "He would have been here tonight, but he had to go on ahead to Ogden. You do remember Mr. O'Brian, don't you?"

"Of course. He is a dear friend," Isabella said with a seductive emphasis on the words "dear" and "friend."

"It wasn't the first time Mr. O'Brian had to rescue Jordana," Brenton laughed. "And I don't imagine it'll be the last. They've been friends much too long to go separate ways for long."

"But perhaps Mr. O'Brian will marry another one day," Isabella said, her comment full of innuendo.

Her father laughed heartily. "He will if you have anything to say about it, my darling."

Jordana's skin tingled. And it was not merely at the idea that Rich might marry someone like Isabella. There was something else. That laugh.

That was the same laugh she had heard in the Indian camp!

With a shock that made her nearly drop her glass, she realized Baxter Montego was the man who had paid the Indians to take her away. She quickly averted her eyes, afraid to meet his gaze, but it was impossible. And then, upon considering it, she knew it would only give her away if she ignored the man. If he had read her journal, he must certainly know who she was. Of course, he could not reveal himself because that would indicate his guilt. But a sudden knot in her stomach made her certain he would not let the matter drop. Trying to pretend that nothing had happened, she looked at Montego and smiled.

He smiled in return, apparently none the wiser to her revelation.

TWENTY-TWO

"He must know it's me," Jordana told Brenton. "The thing is, I don't know if he realizes that I know it's him."

"Doesn't matter," Brenton said, falling over himself to get their things collected from the adjoining hotel rooms. "He'll be a threat to your well-being. We need to get to Ogden and tell Rich what's going on."

Jordana eyed her brother with a hint of amusement. "And where do you propose for us to get transportation at this hour? It's nearly midnight."

"I guess we'll rent a couple of horses. You still have that Indian pony down at the livery."

"It's the middle of winter," Jordana reminded him, nearly laughing out loud as Brenton tripped over the carpetbag he'd recently purchased for her.

Brenton paused and seemed to consider her words for a moment. "They'll try to kill you if we stay here. You can put Montego away for what he did to you. We can't stay, even if it means facing the elements. We'll just buy the bedding from the hotel, and you can wear some of my trousers — at least that won't be a departure for you. Anyway, the snow melted off pretty well this morning. It can't be that cold outside if the snow can't keep."

Jordana nodded dubiously, feeling just a bit odd trying to talk Brenton out of a harebrained scheme for a change. "I know it's warmed up some, but, Brenton, there's nothing out there. Short of the railroad, this is very desolate country. There are some farms and ranches, but they are few and far between."

"Then we'll stick to the railroad." He began shoving the remainder of his things into his own bag. "Wait a minute!" he declared, turning to Jordana. "There's probably going to be a supply freight heading out sometime soon. You know they keep the supplies moving at a steady pace down the line. We'll go to the depot."

"That might work," Jordana agreed. "But, Brenton, you're going to have to calm down. I've been through worse."

He took hold of her and hugged her tight. "I know, and I can hardly bear the thought."

"Don't feel bad about it." She said, reaching up to tenderly push back the sandy brown hair that had fallen into his face. "I'm no worse for the wear. It's the life I've chosen. The life I feel happy in. Think of the adventures I can someday tell my children."

"If you live that long," Brenton said, squeezing her hand. "I just couldn't bear to lose you, Sis. You're as stubborn as anyone I've ever met, and I know you're very capable. But you aren't indestructible."

"True, but none of us are," Jordana replied. "You know how I feel about it. I trust that God is watching over me every step of the way. I feel His presence in my life, and when I stray from Him, I feel that too. Don't fret over me. When my time comes, it will be God and God alone who leads me home."

Brenton hugged her close again. "I know. I admire your faith, your belief that no matter what happens to you, God has already directed the outcome. I wish I could be stronger in that. Caitlan is always telling me to be more optimistic, but I feel I fail so often."

"You are one of those people who takes life much too seriously," Jordana said with a grin. She pushed away from her brother and let him see her smile. "Sometimes life is just plain funny and you have to learn to know when to laugh at it."

Three hours later they sat sandwiched between crates of chickens inside a freight car. With their knees tucked under their chins and hardly any room to breathe, Brenton turned to Jordana with a grave expression.

"Is this one of those times we laugh?" he asked wryly.

This sent a ripple of mirth throughout Jordana's cramped frame. She began to giggle and then to laugh and soon was gasping for breath in hysterical peals. "Yes, brother dear," she barely managed to say, "this is definitely one of those times."

Baxter Montego frowned at the hotel clerk's announcement.

"I'm sorry, sir, but the Baldwins have already checked out."

Montego moved several coins across the top of the counter. "Can you tell me when they departed? Where they might be headed?"

"No, sir. I can't say that I know. My pa might know. He would have been the one to see to it. Hold on a minute."

Baxter waited while the young man went

in search of his father. Turning to Isabella, he grimaced. "These Baldwins have become quite a liability."

"Maybe she doesn't realize your part in the matter," Isabella said.

"Then why their hasty departure?"

"She mentioned at dinner that they both needed to get back to Sacramento. I believe their sister-in-law is about to have a baby. At least that was my understanding. It's probably nothing more than they decided to check out early and take seats on the first passenger train west."

"You were askin' about the Baldwins?" a rough-looking man questioned. He stroked his long beard and gazed up at the ceiling. "I'm not entirely sure I know which folks you're talkin' about. We get a lot of travelers in here."

Montego reached into his coat and pulled out his wallet. Counting off several bills onto the counter, he watched as the man's memory instantly came to life.

"Oh, yeah, I remember who you're talkin' about. Skinny feller and his sister. Purty little thing even if she did have her hair all cut short."

"Just tell me when they left," Montego insisted.

"Well, they came down here just after

midnight and said they needed to check out immediately. Didn't say where they were going in the dead of night like that, but we get lots of folks that have to run off quick-like. I'm just grateful they paid their bill."

Montego nodded. "Thank you." He extended his arm to Isabella. "Shall we go, my dear?"

"Of course," she replied, watching him carefully.

Once they were outside, Montego muttered, "They must be suspicious about something or they'd not have felt the need to steal away in the middle of the night. The only problem is, where did they steal away to?"

"Well, we could check with the station agent. Surely he'd know if they bought a ticket on the morning train."

Montego realized his daughter's words made sense, but his irritation at allowing the Baldwins to slip through his fingers was making him most disagreeable. "I don't suppose it will matter even if he does remember them. You know the man. He hasn't much sense for keeping track of anything more than what he's ordered to do. He may recall the Baldwins, but I doubt he'll know anything at all about their destination."

"It's worth a try, Father, and the station isn't that far."

"Very well. I suppose we must start somewhere."

"What kind of plan do you have once we find them?" Isabella asked. "Are we to simply kill them?"

"No, I don't suppose another attack on Jordana Baldwin would be tolerated. Their parents are important people back east. They would no doubt refuse to stop investigating until they saw their children's murderers behind bars."

"What about an accident?" Isabella arched her brow, an evil glint in her dark eyes. "A train accident."

Montego smiled at her. "You have a gift, my dear."

"I take after you, Papa."

"That you do," Montego said, studying her closely. "But we shall have to work quickly and cautiously. If anyone gets wind of this, it will ruin all our other plans."

TWENTY-THREE

Finding Rich in Ogden proved to be somewhat difficult, but after searching for nearly half the day, Jordana and Brenton finally located the man in one of the town's eating houses — actually, as he was leaving.

"Rich!" she exclaimed. "We've been looking for you everywhere."

Rich registered his surprise, but before he could say anything, Brenton jumped in. "There's real trouble afoot. I think we should go someplace off the street. Someplace where we can talk freely."

"I have a room," Rich suggested, recovering quickly from his surprise.

"That would be good," Brenton replied. "We need to keep out of sight."

Reaching over, Rich pulled a chicken feather out of Jordana's hair. "New fashion?"

She grinned. "If you only knew."

"Just don't stand downwind of us," Brenton said, trying to prove his humor in the matter. "We smell like chickens."

Rich looked first at Brenton and then Jordana and finally rolled his eyes heavenward. "If your sister was involved, then I won't even bother to hear the whole story. With her, you can never tell what's going to happen next."

"Yes, well," Jordana said with a smile, "this occasion of our getting together will surely not be a disappointment to you, then."

"Great," Rich said with a sigh. "I should have known."

They settled in Rich's room with Jordana explaining in detail what had happened, and Brenton joining in from time to time. Rich listened patiently, his expression growing more grave by the minute.

"I, too, had figured the Montegos were a problem," he said. "When we were in Wadsworth I learned that they had just bought up large parcels of land there and in Reno. Montego said it was for development, and he met constantly with the people he thought could populate these regions and bring about settlement and prosperity. He owns land all along the UP as well, but mostly in the newly established Wyoming Territory."

"I fail to see how he benefits from sabotaging the railroad," Jordana replied. "If he wants people to settle on his land —"

"But his attacks are usually well away from the cities. Now we can see that he's paying the Indians to do part of the dirty work, if not all of it. After all, the army will go after them and brook no explanation. Can you imagine any soldier worth his salt paying much heed to some painted war chief explaining that a white man paid him to destroy track?"

"No, Montego has been very smart about this. First he aligned himself with Durant and established a position of contractor for the UP. There are entire stretches of track he and his men have been hired to build. Those lines have continually met with one mishap or another. Of course, this jacks up Montego's price for the repairs and also encourages him to seek a sort of risk bonus, which Durant has been good enough to give over to him. The land he owns and encourages settlement of is always within the established towns along the way. He buys advertising back east — I only just learned this," Rich added as he thought through the information. "He promises great benefits to new settlers. He tells them nothing of the corruption of those towns or the lawlessness of the territory. Did you two know that shortly before Congress decided to map out the Wyoming Territory, the Dakota territorial governor revoked Laramie's charter to be a town? That's how bad the corruption has spread."

"With leaders like Montego, what do you expect?" Jordana mused.

"But that's just it," Rich replied. "He's really not that much of a leader. He's well-known and apparently has called to himself quite a following, but he never bothers to get involved in the politics of the town he's working in. It's almost like he plans to set things in motion, then take the money and run."

"Probably so," Brenton replied. "It would be more advantageous to make a nice profit from the land and leave than deal with the people's disappointment once they see what the real story is. I heard some lots in Laramie were going for ten times their fair market value. If Montego is lining his pockets in that manner, then he wouldn't be so foolish as to stick around and see what repercussions there are to face afterward."

"This is all coming so much clearer," Rich said. "I think now is the time for plans of our own."

"Such as?" Jordana questioned, going to where Rich stood.

"We need to draw them out. We need concrete evidence that the destruction on the railroad has been orchestrated by Montego."

"How do we do that?"

Rich eyed her suspiciously, then shook his head. "*We* don't. I must do this alone."

"But I'm the one who was kidnapped," Jordana protested.

"Yes, exactly my point. They know who you are now. You are more of a threat now than you were two months ago. If they had you kidnapped then, what do you suppose they would do to you this time, especially if they fear you can identify Montego?"

"But you can't do this by yourself," Jordana replied stubbornly.

"I have friends," Rich replied. "There are trustworthy men in my acquaintance. If I need someone else to help me, I'll solicit one of them. My suggestion to you, Brenton," he said, turning to the weary-looking young man, "is to get your sister back to Sacramento as quickly as possible. If she's there among your family and the management of the Central Pacific, she should be safe enough."

"I agree," Brenton replied.

"Well, I don't," Jordana said, stomping her foot. "I don't like knowing you are out there working alone."

Rich smiled and reached out to touch her arm. "Jordana, I thought we agreed that neither of us ever worked alone. We both agree that God is on the side of justice and righteousness, and that is all I am seeking to accomplish. I want justice. I won't work alone."

After wiring ahead to one of his trusted men to spy out Montego's whereabouts, Rich disembarked from the afternoon train in Laramie and immediately set off on his course. Sneaking around the depot and along the busy road, he tried to remain as inconspicuous as possible. At just the appointed moment, he saw a man with a large slouch hat headed his way. The man looked for all the world like one of the panhandling con men. His mismatched attire had been thrown together in a haphazard fashion, and the man positively reeked of rum.

"You certainly look the part," Rich intoned as the man approached him, asking if he wanted to play a game.

The man grinned. "Montego will be escorting his daughter to supper around six. They plan to eat at the Wellington."

"I thought Wellington had moved on and taken his business with him," Rich said.

"Heard Laramie was too rough for him."

"Well, apparently he had second thoughts. Now his plan is to stay on through winter."

Rich eyed the skies overhead and nodded. "Speaking of which, it looks like snow. Had heavy clouds threatening all the way from Utah. You'd do best to pull the men in from the line and settle them here in Laramie until we see how bad it gets."

"Aye, aye, Captain," the man replied, turning to go.

"Oh, and, Wes," Rich said to his former sergeant.

"Yeah?"

"You need a bath." Rich grinned.

Rich arranged a seemingly chance meeting with the Montegos. At six o'clock, he waited on the opposite side of the street from the Wellington. Sure enough, the Montego carriage arrived only moments later. Isabella, clad in a shimmering gold-colored gown, allowed her father to help her down. She stood impatiently as her father instructed the driver.

Well, it's now or never, Rich thought as he mustered up his courage and sauntered across the street. Funny. He would have rather dealt with Indians on his worst day than Isabella Montego on his best.

"Why, Mr. O'Brian," Isabella said as she

caught sight of Rich. "What a pleasant surprise! I do say you are a handsome sight on a cold winter's evening. Why, a lady could positively swoon at the sight of you."

Rich felt the heat rise up his neck at her syrupy praise, but he ignored it. "And you, Miss Montego, I must say you are quite an engaging vision as well."

Baxter Montego joined them. "O'Brian. You've certainly been scarce of late. Heard you were out and about on some rescue mission several weeks ago."

"That I was," Rich said, hardly desiring to allow the conversation to be controlled by Montego. "But now I'm on a mission to find a good meal. Wellington serves the best in that department."

"Oh, I heartily agree," Montego replied. "We were just about to go to supper. Would you care to join us?"

Rich smiled in great satisfaction. "I would be honored."

They were quickly seated at the best table, and after placing their orders with the waiter, Rich jumped right into conversation about the railroad. "I hope I won't bore you, Miss Montego, but I find the problems upon the Union Pacific tracks overwhelming my thinking these days. I wondered if you, Mr. Montego, might have some thoughts on what is happening."

"I'm not sure I understand," Baxter replied, clearly on edge by Rich's statement.

"Well, frankly, I'm sick to death of all the attacks suffered upon the UP. I figure the only party who is bound to benefit from such mayhem is the Central Pacific. No doubt they believe if they can keep the UP from building much farther, then they can take over and earn the government allotments for mileage. They have, after all, managed to get Congress to free up, to some degree at least, the restraints on how far east they could build. I believe if they can cause enough trouble on the UP line, they will be able to convince Congress that the eastern railroad is incompetent, thus allowing the CP to win the remaining mileage."

Montego nodded thoughtfully. "You know, O'Brian, I believe you may well be correct. You are a brilliant man."

Rich feigned pleasure at the man's flattery. All the while he wanted to slap Montego's confident face, and he wanted to put an end to Isabella's friendly hand upon his knee.

"I figure," Rich continued, "it's time to give the CP back some of its own."

Montego gasped. "Are you suggesting sabotage?"

Rich looked around the room cautiously. "If that's what it will take, why not? They apparently have no qualms about wounding us. You stand to benefit from the survival of the UP as well, Montego. What say you? Do you suppose we could find someone who might be willing to help us in this endeavor? Someone who wouldn't have a problem with a little bit of destruction."

"How little?" Montego questioned.

"I'm not sure I follow you."

"What my father is asking is how squeamish are you?" Isabella asked. Her hand softly kneaded Rich's knee, while she pretended for all purposes to simply have her hands folded in her lap.

Rich didn't wish to alienate the woman, but he was growing quite perturbed with her attention. "I'm not squeamish."

"So you wouldn't be adverse to a little bloodshed?" Montego leaned forward, brow arched.

A tingle crept up Rich's spine. Montego's icy expression was more than Rich had anticipated. The man had no remorse for the things he'd done, of this Rich was certain. "I'm sure the UP would want us to do whatever we had to do."

Montego nodded and eased back in his

chair. "I might know someone who could help."

It was nearly midnight and a light snow was falling when Rich ducked down the agreed-upon alleyway near the train depot. He waited and watched in the profound stillness of the night. Usually sounds of revelry and drunkenness could be heard throughout the night, but for some reason, perhaps the weather, things seemed much calmer on this night.

Pacing back and forth in the alley, Rich wondered if the man would show. Montego had said he was certain where he could find Rich help, but he also made it clear that he wanted no part in Rich's plan. Grimacing, Rich wondered if this idea would be at all productive. After all, if they couldn't fix the blame on Montego and make it stick, Jordana might continue to be in danger and the railroad would continue to suffer destruction.

He heard footsteps before he saw anyone. Crouching low behind some crates, Rich watched as a lone figure approached at the opposite end of the alley. It had to be his man. Standing to reveal himself, Rich waited as the shadowy form moved closer.

The man, slight of build, but just a couple

inches shorter than Rich, stopped two feet from Rich. "O'Brian?" he asked in a low, gravelly voice.

"Yes."

"I heard you wanted some help with a job."

"Yes, well, that's one way of putting it."

"Follow me," the man demanded.

They headed out and around the building, and before Rich knew it, they were going back toward the depot. "Where are we going?"

"Never mind," the man replied. He maneuvered around the platform and came to a stop not far from where several wagons of freight awaited the next train.

"Won't the guard see us?" Rich asked.

"I know his route. He's at the other end of the station."

"Why come here at all?" Rich tried to determine the man's game, praying he hadn't walked into some kind of trap.

"I have friends nearby," the man replied. "In case you decide to try anything. You and the guard are friends. I know that much. He won't worry if he finds us here, because you'll see to it that he doesn't."

The man's voice sounded almost familiar, but the way he kept his hat low across his face, Rich had no way of telling the man's identity. "Who are you?" Rich finally asked.

"That's not important."

"I figure it to be."

The man shifted. "It's not. I'm nobody. I'm just doing what I'm told. The boss sends me out."

"Who's your boss?" Rich asked earnestly.

"That's not important, I'm telling you. What's important is that you do what you're told."

"All right," Rich said, finally giving up. "What is it I'm supposed to do?"

Two days of snow left Jordana feeling rather discouraged. She hadn't heard from Rich, and she had no way of knowing if he were dead or alive. Likewise, she had to deal with Brenton's moodiness. Stuck in Ogden and unable to get west and home, Brenton's frustration mounted by the minute. What made it worse was to have to spend a lonely, dreary Christmas in that snowbound town. The holiday was now over, marked only by a dismal dinner of dried meat, stale bread, and a half-burned cake provided by the hotel dining room. Brenton and Jordana hadn't even bothered to exchange gifts.

Pacing in their tiny hotel room, Jordana went to the window for the tenth time in an hour as if hoping to see something that might indicate even a faint hint that the snow had stopped, or would soon.

"It's still out there," Brenton said gloomily.

"I beg your pardon?"

"The world is still out there. The snow is still out there."

"Yes, I know that very well. I'm just trying to busy myself with something other than listening to you complain."

"I'm not complaining!" Brenton lurched off the bed.

Jordana shook her head and sat down while Brenton took up the pacing. It was almost as if they'd agreed to take shifts. "I just wish we'd hear something from Rich."

Just then a knock came at the door. "Telegram for J. Baldwin!" came the voice.

"Rich!" Jordana declared. She jumped to her feet and rushed to the door. Two days ago they'd sent telegrams to half a dozen people explaining their whereabouts. But somehow Jordana was certain this telegram would be from Rich. It wasn't.

Charlie Crocker felt it necessary to expose himself and the Baldwins by risking a lengthy message. Jordana scanned the contents while Brenton tipped the messenger and sent the boy on his way.

"Who is it from?" Brenton asked as he attempted to look over her shoulder.

"Charlie," Jordana replied, completely taken in by the words on the page. "Rich is in grave danger. Apparently he must have put his plan into play, because Charlie has caught wind of rumors that Rich is a part of a plot to do harm to us and the Union Pacific."

"But I thought Rich was going to pretend to be plotting against the Central Pacific."

Jordana passed the telegram to her brother. "So did I. This doesn't look good at all." She grabbed her coat. "Brenton, we've got to telegram Charlie and explain. Better yet, maybe we should telegram someone else and let them get word to Charlie. Either way, we have to help Rich or he'll find himself swinging from the gallows."

Brenton quickly agreed. "Let's not worry about who sees it. Let's just send Charlie a telegram telling him he's wrong and we know all about it. We can word it so that it gives nothing away."

But when they arrived at the telegraph office they quickly learned that all lines were down. Heavy snows along the route from Cheyenne to Salt Lake had caused the wires to snap away from the poles.

"The only thing moving at all in any direction," the operator told them, "is the stage. They're loading up right now and due to head out in half an hour."

"Which direction?" Jordana asked.

"East. They're gonna try to make their way to Echo."

Jordana looked at Brenton. "You keep trying to get word to Charlie. You might even try to go to Salt Lake City. I think Leland Stanford is supposed to be there. Let Charlie know that Rich is not a threat and to say nothing more to anyone about it."

"What are you going to do?" Brenton asked suspiciously.

"I'm going to get a seat on the stage."

"No, you're not!" Brenton declared. "You are in enough trouble."

"I have to try," she stated flatly. "If I don't and it costs Rich his life, I'll never forgive myself. I owe him my life, Brenton."

Brenton nodded. "Then let me go. I owe him your life as well."

"Look, we have to split up in hopes of getting through to someone. We will both be taking equal risks. It only makes sense that you head west and nearer to Caitlan. She needs you, too, doesn't she?" Jordana said reasonably enough. "I have to do this and you have to let me."

Sighing, Brenton shrugged and gazed into

Jordana's eyes. "Yes, I see that now — that and so much more. It is wrong for me to hold you back. I am sorry I've tried." He smiled and gave her shoulder a pat.

Jordana nearly wept at his words, but she could only give him a quick embrace before turning her attention to the newest crisis.

"Stage is most likely full up," the operator told them, shaking his head.

"That's all right," Jordana said with a weak smile. "If I'm supposed to be on it, God will make a way."

Twenty-Four

The snows let up enough to let the stage through, and when Jordana was finally able to hook up with the Union Pacific Railroad, she was more than ready for a little bit of warmth and comfort. The temperature outside had to be near zero, if not lower, and the wind was not in the least bit disturbed by the barriers of mere wood and canvas offered by the stage.

Yet if she had hoped to find comfort on the train, Jordana was sorely mistaken. A passenger either roasted by sitting near the stove or froze if they passed more than a few rows back from the blazing heat. Unable to get comfortable and weary to the bone, Jordana wrapped herself in a wool blanket, which had been offered by the porter, and tried her best to go to sleep. When she awoke four hours later, she was discouraged to hear that the train had made very little progress.

"We're workin' at it, ma'am," the porter told her, "but the snows are makin' it hard."

Jordana knew the man did not deserve her anger, and so she bit back a retort and instead thanked him for the use of the blanket. Cuddling down in the wool cover, she felt her teeth chattering from the icy air. This was not her idea of traveling in comfort and style as advertised by the Union Pacific.

It was late in the afternoon of the next day before they finally reached Laramie. Jordana stepped from the train, praying that she might find Rich and, at the same time, avoid any entanglement with the Montegos. She was desperate to keep him safe. All night long she'd tossed and turned and fretted in her sleep. She kept imagining Charlie Crocker presiding over a hanging with Rich as the victim to be punished. Over and over she had tried to tell them of his innocence, but no one would listen to her. She was just a silly woman, they had said. A silly woman who was in love with a criminal.

She contemplated this thought now as she made her way from the railroad depot platform. Maybe she was in love with him, but there certainly were other good reasons — maybe better reasons — for saving Rich from harm. His innocence was right up there at the top. Rich hadn't committed any crime, and he didn't deserve Charlie's wrath, or anyone else's for that matter. Yes, she told herself, it had nothing to do with such emotions as love. Because she didn't really love Rich O'Brian — did she? But even this question paled in comparison to her worry over whether Rich would meet with harm because of Charlie's misunderstanding.

The images in her head were getting the best of her. Surely God wouldn't allow Rich to meet with such a horrible fate. She prayed silently, asking for Rich's safety and pleading for protection for both of them. She reminded God, as if He might somehow have forgotten, that they both put their trust in Him and that she knew He wouldn't let her down. Her faith had always been strong, unnaturally so, her mother and father had said. But she could not recall a time when that trust hadn't been fixed firmly in God. Some people thought her rather flippant in her faith. They confused her ability to believe God was in control with being smugly righteous or testing God with foolishness. But it was never like that. Never for even a minute. God's grace and mercy was just something she took at face value. Even when she had been kidnapped, she had known it was all just some part of a bigger picture. She didn't blame God for her situation. Yet even though God's hand had not caused her woes, she knew He was with her every step of the way. That's why she knew He was with her now. She hadn't been at all afraid for herself. Somehow she knew she wasn't destined to die in Laramie at the hands of the Montegos. She didn't know why she didn't have that same assurance for Rich.

Then, as if thinking of him had somehow drawn him to her, Jordana looked up to see him coming from the depot telegraph office. Without thought, she closed the distance at a run and threw herself into his arms.

"I'm so glad I found you!" she declared, burying her face against his wool coat.

"Jordana?" His disbelief was obvious, but nevertheless he wrapped his arms tightly around her.

They held each other for several moments until Jordana realized what she had done. Backing away, she began to stammer and stutter, trying desperately to sound nonchalant about her actions. "I . . . we . . . well, that is . . . Brenton and I learned something and I had to come. You're in danger. I'm sorry I attacked you like that, but I've . . . well . . . I've been afraid that I wouldn't get here in time."

Rich inclined his head, a slow smile spreading across his lips. "Well, I must say I was surprised. I don't get too many greetings like that, and since you didn't hurt me, I wasn't even sure it was you."

Jordana licked her dry, cold lips and laughed good-naturedly. "I'm glad I didn't hurt you, but I'm afraid someone is probably going to try to do just that."

"Well, let's get out of here," Rich suggested. "I have a room over at Nader's Boarding. They might have another available that we could secure for you."

"Sounds good. I need to tell you everything that's happening."

They arrived at the boardinghouse amidst a flurry of activities. It seemed Mr. Nader was just ridding the place of vermin. Two-legged vermin actually, a couple of seedy-looking men. Once the two men were sufficiently booted down the stairs to land in a heap at the bottom of the walkway, Mr. Nader put up a sign that read "Room for Rent."

Rich picked up the sign nearly as quickly as the man had turned to go. With the cursing and muttering of the two bruised and battered malcontents still ringing in their ears, Rich said, "My young friend here

363

needs a room."

Nader turned around and sized up Jordana. "We don't allow any nightly business, if that's what you have in mind."

Jordana laughed, not at all offended by the man. "The only business I do at night is sleeping, so we ought to get on just fine."

The man smiled. "We run a respectable house. Mrs. Nader wouldn't hardly stand for any problems. That's why I ran them two fellas out. They were gambling right here on my premises!"

"I shall endeavor to be more worthy of your trust," Jordana replied.

The man, apparently satisfied, took up the sign from Rich. "Come on in, then, and let's settle it."

After taking care of the room situation, Rich led Jordana to the front parlor to give her a chance to warm up before showing her upstairs to her room. It also made a more appropriate place for them to talk. "There's a fireplace in here, and it doesn't smoke as bad as the one in the back parlor."

Jordana smiled and began unwinding her warm woolen scarf. Rich watched her with a strange expression that seemed to be a mixture of awe and curiosity. Once she'd removed her bonnet and began unbuttoning her coat, she couldn't help but question him.

"You're looking at me oddly, Mr. O'Brian. Are you still afraid that I'll yet wound you?"

Rich laughed. "No, I guess I'm still so shocked to see you here. I'd resigned myself to not seeing you for months to come. I figured you to be safe and sound in Sacramento."

"We tried to get west," she explained, "but snow kept us in Ogden."

"Did you have a nice Christmas?" Rich asked.

Jordana shrugged. "As nice as we could. We both sat pining for our loved ones, wishing we could be anywhere but Ogden. Poor Brenton was half heartsick from wanting to be with Caitlan, and he grew more surly than I can begin to tell."

"Being away from the woman you love will do that," Rich murmured.

Instantly Jordana thought of Rich's dead wife. Poor man, she thought, but in the same moment she grieved for herself. He would always love another, and nothing Jordana did was going to change that.

All at once, Rich grew excited. "Wait here!" he told her and hurried out of the room.

Jordana removed her coat and had just

taken a seat on the well-worn sofa when he returned. She noticed he had a small package in his hands.

"I bought this for you. It's a Christmas present," he said, suddenly looking slightly embarrassed. "I suppose I was feeling rather sentimental, and when I saw it, I immediately thought of you."

Jordana took the package and opened it. "Why, it's lovely, Rich." Inside was a ladies' jacket pin in the shape of a bumblebee. There were tiny rhinestones of gold and black decorating the bee, and gold trim outlined the entire creation. She grinned up at him. "Might I ask how this reminded you of me?"

Rich smiled nervously. "I suppose because you're so flighty. Always rushing from one place to the next, never landing long on any one spot."

"I thought maybe it was because bees have a stinger and you were thinking of my inability to keep from wounding you."

Rich laughed. "Well, sure. That too."

Jordana took the pin out of its box and secured it to her traveling suit. "I love it. It was very thoughtful, and whenever I see it, I shall think of the fun we've had."

Rich's expression changed rather quickly. "You make it sound like that's all behind us now. Like there will never be any more fun."

Jordana swallowed hard. "It's just that I know we're both very busy and you have your duties and now things have gone wrong."

"You keep saying that. Tell me what it is."

Jordana explained as best she could. She started by telling him about the telegram and then adding her own thoughts on the matter. "If Charlie's had the chance, he's no doubt taken this to anyone he thinks will listen. He was apprehensive about you when you were in Wadsworth, and no doubt he feels this information will confirm that he was correct in assuming the danger in trusting you."

Rich paced back and forth in front of the fire. "Very well. I need to contact General Dodge and explain before word gets to him. The only trouble is, I'm not exactly sure where he is. He was stationed along the line trying to press forward the Echo Canyon work, but earlier in the month he was desperately trying to make his way to Washington. Last I heard, he was due to come back through here after the first of the new year, but who can tell for sure if that was just conjecture or truth?"

A man came into the parlor with Mr. Nader at just that moment. "O'Brian, this man needs to see you."

Rich recognized him as a UP man. He didn't know the man personally, but he had seen him with Dodge on many an occasion.

As Nader slipped out of the room the man asked, "Are you Richard O'Brian?"

The question seemed completely unwarranted, but Rich nevertheless answered, "I am."

"I have instructions to take you to Fort Sanders, where you're to be held until General Dodge makes his way back through."

"Might I ask why I'm to be taken there and held? Can I not just wait here? I mean, I want to see the general as much as I'm sure he wants to see me."

"No, sir. I have my orders. You're to come with me."

Rich nodded. "Very well." He looked at Jordana and shrugged. "I guess we'll be at the mercy of Dodge's schedule, but I'd appreciate it if you stuck close. I'll send word to you when he gets here and will no doubt need you to explain some of this."

Jordana experienced a terrible sense of loss. "Are you certain he can't remain here? We were just discussing our plans to find General Dodge. We want to talk to him. We need to talk to him," she pleaded with the stranger.

The man remained stern faced and unyielding. "I have my orders, ma'am," he repeated in the same monotone he'd used with Rich.

Jordana nodded. It would do little good to make a scene. She watched the man lead Rich away and quickly went to the window. Fingering the pin he'd just given her, Jordana observed the two as they marched down the street through the snow. Rich offered no resistance to his stern escort, and yet the man seemed to watch Rich as though he were the most hardened criminal in the world. With a sigh, she let the curtain fall back into place and took a seat by the fire. What was she to do now? Her worst fear seemed to have been realized. Although no one had used the word "arrest," it was fairly apparent that was the case. As astonishing as it looked, General Dodge had arrested Rich!

Rich had nearly lost his patience in waiting for Dodge. He knew this was a matter he could clear up once he actually had an audience with the man, but it was getting the man here first that stood in the way. Confined as he was to one of the furloughed officers' homes, Rich found himself growing bored and increasingly frustrated. No doubt Jordana was the same. He thought of how she'd risked her life for him. Of how her face had been filled with sheer relief at the sight of him coming out of the telegraph office. He had been so surprised by her actions there — the warm embrace, the desperate hold.

He knew without a doubt she cared for him, just as he cared for her. But to what degree, he had yet to discover. Thinking on this, Rich felt a sense of relief when a soldier appeared to announce that General Dodge had at last returned from Washington and would see him directly.

"Private, I need to get word to Miss Jordana Baldwin. She's staying at Nader's Boarding. That's on Fourth Street just south and west of the train station. I need someone to bring her here to the fort. Would you see to that?"

"That's a two-mile ride, sir," the private replied. "I can't leave my post."

"But surely you can get someone who can. Tell General Dodge that I said it was important. He should be willing."

The private reluctantly agreed and took his leave, while Rich waited to be summoned.

But instead of bringing Rich to his own quarters, Dodge came to him. The surly look on his face told Rich that the man had been inundated with doubts about his business for and against the railroad.

"Before you say anything," Rich said, holding up his hand as Dodge began to unfasten the buttons on his heavy coat, "I want to clarify a few things."

"I figured you would have plenty to say," Dodge replied dryly.

"First, I'd like to wait until Jordana Baldwin can be brought here. She knows a good deal more about some of this than I do."

"I spoke with the private and agreed to send him for her. She should arrive shortly. I fail to understand what part she plays in this, however."

"Jordana and Joe Baldwin are one and the same. Jordana donned male clothing in order to get stories for her New York newspaper. She found moving around as a man gave her a better reception than appearing as a woman."

"I can well imagine," Dodge said, his eyes boring into Rich with a steely look of displeasure.

"Please sit down and I'll tell you whatever I can," Rich continued. "But right up front you have to know that the things you've heard are only the reflection of my trying to get to the bottom of the Union Pacific's attacks. I figure you to have already considered that chance, and the fact is, it's true. I have done nothing to cause the line harm, and what I did do was merely to put myself into a position to learn who is causing our problems."

Dodge seemed to relax a bit and nodded. "I'm willing to see that as a possibility, but I'm going to need details and proof."

"I'll give you what I can."

An hour later Jordana arrived, and the trio sat down together. Rich explained to Dodge how Jordana had come to figure into the situation. He told his superior of the Montegos and their actions against Jordana when they saw her as a threat to their plans.

"Apparently they have something more in mind," Rich replied. "I feel confident of it, in fact."

Dodge had grown considerably more quiet as Rich explained about Baxter Montego's role in Jordana's kidnapping. By the time Jordana repeated what she'd heard Montego tell the Indians, Dodge began shaking his head.

"This is most serious," he murmured.

"Indeed it is," Rich replied.

Dodge met his expression. "More so than

you even know. Montego is the one who brought your activities to my attention. He wired Durant and Durant wired me. I have had direct contact with Montego via telegraph, at least up until yesterday. I figured I'd have a chance to see him face-to-face today, but so far no one has been able to find him or his daughter."

Rich looked at Jordana. "What do you suppose this means?"

"I think Montego wanted a scapegoat," she offered. "I think he figured to pin all of his deeds on you."

"Yes . . ." Rich drew out the word thoughtfully. "I should have realized that the meeting I had with his henchmen came too easily. Montego probably saw my game from the beginning and turned it around to set me up for the fall."

"The only thing is, he didn't plan on my being here to explain his part with the Indians," said Jordana.

"Has he given you any physical evidence of my participation?" Rich asked Dodge.

"He said he could furnish me with papers, correspondences that would implicate you in several activities where episodes of destruction occurred upon the line. This is most alarming. The man is a good friend of Durant's. He has been performing work for us all along the route. I hardly see an easy way to draw him out and call his hand."

Rich rubbed his mustache. "Well, I had thought by going to Montego and setting myself up as interested in creating sabotage against the Central Pacific that I would finally have the proof I needed to put Montego in jail. But now it's clear my cover is no good. Jordana's either. We're going to have to figure out another plan. But we will catch them."

Dodge looked from Rich to Jordana and back again. "So you two are working together now?"

"We've worked together many times and may yet figure a way to work this out while in each other's company." Rich glanced toward Jordana, his mustache twitching as he restrained the urge to grin. "Miss Baldwin has a great head on her shoulders, and I value her opinion. However, I do not wish to see harm come to her, and, therefore, it is my hope that her risk will be minimal."

"My risk will be whatever it takes to see this thing through!" Jordana declared unequivocally. "I'm sick to death of addlepated ninnies running the show. Crocker worries about what Dodge is doing, and Dodge worries about Stanford and Hopkins, and Durant worries about us all." Jordana rolled her eyes. "I swear it is worse than a bunch of jealous women sharing the only single man at the dance."

An obviously reluctant smile bent Dodge's stern expression, and though his mustache was now also quivering wildly, he managed to keep from laughing out loud. Rich didn't bother to conceal his amusement. He was used to hearing Jordana speak her mind. Might as well let Dodge get used to it too.

"There won't be any time to waste," Dodge said, growing serious once again. "We need to locate the Montegos, and we need to be at it immediately."

Rich and Jordana nodded. "We'll do what we can," they said practically in unison, as if they truly were a team.

TWENTY-FIVE

Before Jordana realized it, the end of January had come and she was nowhere nearer to figuring out how to bring the Montegos to justice than she had been when she and Rich had stood before General Dodge.

Laramie was suffering bitter cold, and Jordana had just about convinced herself to head back to California for the birth of her sister's baby. After all, Rich didn't seem to care whether she lived or died. He was seldom ever around to spend much time with her. And those times he managed to see her at the boardinghouse, Jordana found herself much too caught up in her own emotions to know exactly what to do with him. She wanted to confess her feelings, but how? Even if she told him that she'd changed her mind about marriage and children and that the thought of being more than friends with him was now appealing, who was to say he'd find this news favorable? After all, he'd made it clear that he had no desire to remarry. He carried an ever burning torch for his first wife, and Jordana was convinced she could never replace his Peggy.

"Do you want to come see my new horse?" Rich asked one icy afternoon as he stomped into the parlor, melted snow puddling around his boots.

Jordana looked up, surprised that he had bothered to include her. "What happened to Troublesome?"

Rich grimaced. "We had, shall we say, problems in the area of command. Troublesome thought he should be in command, and I thought that privilege belonged to me. Since I had the bill of sale in my name, it seemed only natural that I be the one to effect a change."

Jordana smiled. "And what have you hooked yourself up with this time? Indian pony? Grizzly bear?"

"A sweet-tempered gelding who was actually the mount of an army volunteer. The horse has been gun broke and trained to maneuver as silently as a horse is capable. He rides like a dream and yet has enough vim and vinegar that he rises to the occasion when the fight is on."

"What color is he?"

"Why don't you come out and see for yourself? I'm going to feed him some carrots. It will get you out of the house, and we can discuss our plans for the future."

Jordana reluctantly got up from her place by the fire. "Let me retrieve my things."

She was back within minutes doing up the buttons of her coat. She pulled on woolen mittens and wrapped a scarf around her head before nodding to Rich. "All right. Lead the way."

They walked across the backyard to the small stable. The only sound was that of the snow crunching under their feet. Jordana wondered if Rich had any new ideas in regard to the Montegos, or if he'd just used that as an excuse to get her out here alone. She had to admit his reasons were probably the latter. And what had he meant when he had said he wanted to discuss their future? The words left a knot in the pit of her stomach, but she forced herself to act nonchalant.

Rich opened the creaky barn door and ushered her into the dimly lit stable. The smell of sweet hay and horses immediately assaulted her senses. It wasn't at all unpleasant; in fact, Jordana had rather come to enjoy the smell. It took her back to days when she had been a child and they had visited her aunt Georgia's horse farm near Washington City.

"Here he is," Rich said, putting out a hand to run along the flank of a chestnut gelding.

"He's beautiful!" Jordana pulled off her mitten, reached out her hand to the horse's muzzle, and let him smell her scent. The white blaze on the horse's forehead beckoned her touch, and once the mount sensed she was no threat, Jordana put her hand there and petted him very gently. "You're right. His disposition is much better than Troublesome's. What are you calling him?"

"He came to me already named. My friend called him Scout."

"Sounds like an acceptable title," Jordana said, growing ever aware of Rich's presence as he moved to stand closer beside her. Hemmed in by the horse, the stall, and now Rich, Jordana had no means of escape. Why should that come to mind? she wondered. Why would I need a means of escape? Rich is no threat to me.

But in that instant he reached out and touched an errant curl. "You know," he said, his voice low and husky, "I think I've grown to like it short."

Jordana felt a thrill go up the back of her neck. Turning to face Rich, she forgot completely about the horse. "You've always teased me about it before now."

Rich's eyes darkened in hue as he allowed her hair to curl around his finger. Jordana was afraid to breathe. She felt overwhelmed by the moment. Would he kiss her? Would he declare himself in love with her? And if he did, would she counter with her own declaration?

Suddenly he stepped back. "I'm glad you are the woman you are, Jordana," he said, appearing almost shaken by the brief experience.

"You are?" Her voice squeaked over the question. She was both frightened and intrigued by his words. She watched as he reached up to touch the horse, his hand trembling quite obviously.

He turned away, as if unable to continue with his thoughts. He walked away from the horse and went to where a single window allowed a muted shaft of light to come in through the poor-quality panes of glass.

"You understand how it is for me." He was staring out the window as he spoke. "You know now about Peggy. You know about the past. Another woman might be upset by my lack of interest in marriage, but you understand."

His words were deflating, like having the air knocked out of her lungs by a sharp kick, but Jordana said nothing. Instead, she watched him as he struggled to continue.

"It's so nice to have a woman for a friend. I think of all we've been through, and I know we have a special bond that few men and women ever share, unless of course they are married." He turned to face her and shook his head. "But I shall never remarry. I can't ask any woman to share the kind of life I intend to lead. When I think of what happened to Peggy, and how if only we'd lived in a civilized part of the country — if only I'd never taken her from her family in the first place —"

"She'd still be dead," Jordana murmured.

Rich's face took on a curious expression. "What?"

Jordana gave the horse one final pat and went to where Rich stood. "I said, she'd still be dead. God chooses the timing, in spite of our locations. You can't tell me, Rich O'Brian, that you believe you somehow outdistanced or outsmarted God. Like Peggy's death somehow took God by surprise?"

"No, that's not what I'm saying," he protested.

"Then what? You have somehow convinced yourself that life on the plains is too difficult for women to endure. Therefore, it sounds to me as if you might be saying God is incapable of caring for His people if they happen to spend their lives upon the open plains."

"That's not it at all. Peggy's family didn't want her to go, and I took her anyway."

"Did Peggy choose to go or did you force her?"

"She wanted to go, of course. We had great plans for our new life," Rich admitted.

"So she went of her own free will," Jordana stated, "and even if you had forced her, do you suppose God would not have been able to keep her from harm? To watch over her tenderly as He always had? Rich, you take too much upon yourself." Jordana smiled. "I think it's why I get so frustrated with you and Brenton both. I am a woman of means and health. I desire nothing more than to live my life in the manner to which I feel called and comfortable. I trust God with the outcome, and I trust His guidance. I pray for it, in fact, but then I get up and about and do my business. And I trust that God is there all the time to lead me throughout my life."

"Some folks would call that foolishness," Rich said softly. "Some would call it testing God."

"Why? Why is it testing God to venture forth into a new world, trusting Him for the right path, putting all the tomorrows into His hands? The Bible says in Proverbs that 'a man's heart devises his way: but the Lord directs his steps.' I'm not ignoring God," Jordana defended. "I'm merely doing my part."

"And then some," Rich replied.

His expression suggested pride in her, and a pleased chuckle escaped her lips. "I can't help that I have a spirit for adventure. I am bold and courageous, and I believe I am that way because God made me that way. I am not afraid to step over the bounds of confining proprieties and set out for myself."

"I have the bruises to prove it, too." This time Rich let himself smile, lightening Jordana's worried heart.

She had hoped he might speak to her of love, and yet at the same time she held her own confused heart at bay. How could she speak of love when she had so much to accomplish? So many places were yet unexplored by her, and the world lay before her like a spread of presents on Christmas morning. She had only to decide which one to unwrap first.

"I'm glad we're friends," she finally said, eyeing Rich carefully. "I cherish what we have together. You have proven me wrong about men and women being incapable of stopping at friendship."

Rich opened his mouth as if to say something, then closed it rather abruptly. "Come on. It's getting cold out here. We should get you inside."

"I thought we were going to discuss the Montegos," she said as he swung open the door.

"I'm still not any closer to figuring out what to do with them than I was before. Dodge has put the word out that if anyone wants to turn in evidence regarding what Montego has been doing, that they would have instant pardon for their own actions, but no one's come to claim such a prize. I'm hampered, too, by the fact that I can't let myself be seen as the one trying to take the Montegos to task. I have figured that if and when I meet up with Baxter Montego, I shall make it sound as though I've had a close call. That someone in his organization is leaking information and that this person's carelessness got me thrown into house arrest."

"What if he wants to know what you did to convince your captors otherwise?"

Rich secured the door while Jordana pulled back on her mitten. "I shall tell them that I convinced Dodge that I was set up. I'll tell him that Dodge and I go way back and that being soldiers we had a certain respect for each other's word. It's the truth, so it shouldn't be hard to sound convincing."

"Then what?"

"Then, hopefully, he'll take the bait and realize that he can do more with me on his side than by trying to see to my defeat."

"And Isabella?" Jordana asked, trying hard not to sound jealous.

Rich grinned. "I already told you that I wasn't the marrying type."

Jordana looked away as her face grew hot. He'd very nearly read her mind. She was certain that Isabella would stop at no means to snag Rich into matrimony once her father was convinced that he wasn't a threat to their plans.

Rich must have sensed Jordana's feelings, however, because he took hold of her arm and drew her back to face him. "If I were the marrying type, it certainly wouldn't be to someone like Isabella Montego."

Jordana glanced up at him and smiled. "I would imagine she could do you more harm than I ever could."

Rich touched her cold cheek. "You might be surprised. There is more than one way to hurt a man."

Jordana could no longer bear his touch.

She needed to put some distance between herself and Rich O'Brian or she was going to make a fool of herself. "I need to get back," she said abruptly.

Rich did nothing to stop her, which only made Jordana feel worse. Somehow she had to come to terms with the way she felt. If she didn't, she was going to be very sorry. Of this, she had no doubt.

TWENTY-SIX

As the winter dragged on, the Laramie town council declared a winter ball to liven things up. Jordana allowed herself to get caught up in the spirit of the event, despite the fact that Rich appeared uninterested in inviting her to the dance.

"They've closed the line between here and Rawlins," Rich announced as they made their way to do a bit of shopping.

Jordana had begged Rich to help her get to Sacramento, knowing that Victoria would be due to have her child very soon now; at least she had given that as her reason. But she knew it was more than this. Jordana had to get away from Rich. She couldn't bear the way she felt when she saw him each morning. She wanted to run and throw herself into his arms, shower his face with kisses, and pledge her undying devotion. She tried to chalk it up to the approaching celebration, as everyone seemed to be in a mood for love — with exception to the good Captain O'Brian.

Nevertheless, her desire to leave Laramie was constantly being thwarted, as now evidenced by snow beginning to fall on Rich and her, causing a thick white blanket to coat the now muddied offering from the week before. Snow made Laramie a much prettier town, but it also wreaked havoc with the railroad. But perhaps that was merely the hand of God keeping her here. But to what purpose? What was He about, anyway? Surely He knew how hard it was for her to be trapped in this place with Rich.

"What will happen now?" she asked uneasily. She kept her focus on the passageway.

"Well, until they get the tracks opened again, everyone is stuck here. All the westbound traffic has been held up here, and folks are overflowing the hotels and boardinghouses."

"Are there really that many people stranded here?" She had seen the crowds for herself, but she was still hoping it was merely her imagination.

"I've heard tell that there are easily two hundred already and that more are pouring in by the minute."

"Hey, O'Brian!" a familiar voice called out.

Jordana glanced up to catch sight of Patrick Worth making his way through the drifted snow to speak to Rich. She saw Rich visibly tense, his hand moving toward his pistol.

"I just got into town," Worth said. "Can you suggest a place to stay, I mean rather permanent-like?"

"Permanent? You mean you've moved to Laramie?" Rich asked.

Patrick nodded at Rich's question, then turned to Jordana and tipped his hat. "My pardon, Miss Baldwin. May I say you look to be in particularly good health." He smiled warmly at her.

"Better than the last time you saw me," she replied.

"Many things are better since then," Patrick said. Then he eyed Rich. "You can relax your gun hand, Rich. I mean you no harm." He glanced around at their icy surroundings as if gauging its appropriateness for a discussion, then shrugged. "I've had quite a time of soul-searching since I last saw you. I talked to my ma and I read Peggy's letters. I especially read those letters. I finally see the truth in all you tried to tell me before."

Rich did seem to relax. "I'm glad to hear that."

"I don't know if we could ever be friends again, Rich, though I'd welcome it, but I want you to know you don't have to watch your back from me anymore. Peggy's death was a tragic accident. I see that now. There just ain't no one to blame, and I could tell from her letters that the last thing she would have wanted was there to be hate and discord in the family."

"I think so, too, Patrick." Rich thrust out his hand, and Patrick grasped it firmly. "Now, what's this about a move to Laramie?"

"I've got me a new job," he answered. "So, what is the living situation?"

"You sure know when to pick a time to show up. The whole town is overflowing as it is. Can't you come back in a few weeks?"

"Nope. I've been hired on by the Union Pacific. I'm gonna be a railroad guard here in Laramie." He made the announcement so proudly that Jordana couldn't help but praise him.

"That sounds like a wonderful job, Mr. Worth. My congratulations," she said enthusiastically.

Patrick reddened a bit at the ears, but Jordana couldn't be sure if it was from the cold or her compliment.

"Well, that is good news," Rich replied.

"But things are filling up fast. Why don't you come with me over to Nader's Boarding House? That's where Miss Baldwin and I are staying."

Worth eyed them suspiciously until Rich added, "We each have our own rooms, of course, and there might be yet another opening for you." Again Jordana wasn't certain, but it did appear as if Rich had also reddened a bit.

Worth openly relaxed. "Sounds good. Lead the way."

But when approached, Nader shook his head. "I was going to ask the two of you if you were of a mind to share your rooms with other folks. I could cut down on your rent and pick up the balance from the others."

"No, thanks," Rich replied for both of them. "I don't think that is of any interest."

"Well, then your rent is going up," Nader replied. "You might as well know that here and now."

"Going up?" Jordana questioned in clear dismay. "But I've paid up for the rest of the week."

"Well, things change," Nader replied. "Either you want the room or you don't. If you don't, there's plenty of folks who do, and I'll not have any trouble at all in renting it out to someone else."

Jordana and Rich exchanged a glance that suggested they knew he'd do exactly that. "Very well," Jordana replied, "but don't expect me to recommend you to anyone else once this crisis has passed."

"Worth, you want to room with me?" Rich asked. "You'll probably not be able to find anything else anyway. Come on. You can pay this old cheat later," he added with a glare at the innkeeper. "I'll show you what's what."

Worth smiled. "I'd like that." He turned to leave, then seemed to remember something. "Say, I hear talk about a dance going on day after tomorrow. You wouldn't want to go with me, would you?" he asked Jordana.

Jordana felt a sense of deflation but refused to show it.

"She's not interested in those things," Rich replied before she could speak.

"Rich O'Brian, you have no right to answer for me. I'd love to go to the dance with you, Mr. Worth. I appreciate that you would bother to ask me."

Pat smiled. "No bother at all. We can talk about the particulars later."

"That would be fine," she replied with as sweet a smile as she could muster. She noted the scowl on Rich's face and rather enjoyed it. She didn't care if she'd embarrassed him by contradicting him. He shouldn't have answered for her.

By Friday the dance had been canceled, much to Jordana's disappointment. Over six hundred people had crowded into Laramie, taking up every conceivable bed or open floor space. The dance committee deemed it necessary to use the party space for victims of the snow, and even Fort Sanders had opened its quarters to help as best they could. Lawlessness set in immediately, and it soon became evident that martial law was needed. The Union Pacific found passengers at near stages of rioting, and so with instructions from General Dodge, army soldiers were dispatched to guard the depot and were stationed elsewhere in town to help keep law and order.

Of course, this didn't necessarily meet with the approval of the townspeople, who were still reeling over their town losing its charter and being deemed a hopeless pit of scum and depravation.

Jordana moped around after getting the news. She didn't really care about the dance, but she had hoped for the diversion. Rich had been in a foul mood all week, but once the dance was canceled, he appeared in much better spirits. It seemed their attitudes had simply reversed.

Unhappy with the crowds of people who streamed from one room to another inside Nader's Boarding House, Jordana wrapped up in her warmest clothes and made her way to the stable, which seemed her only sanctuary as she had finally relented and allowed Mr. Nader to put three elderly sisters in her room with her. It was either that or watch him kick them back out into the snow, and Jordana couldn't bear that idea. It was almost comical how all three slept in the double bed together, while Jordana slept on a pallet on the floor. At first the sisters wanted no part of that and insisted she share their bed, but one look at that situation and Jordana clearly thought it best and more comfortable to stay where she was.

Jordana actually enjoyed the brisk breeze on her face as she made her way across the yard to the stable, but the dark, heavy clouds overhead did nothing for her mood. Everyone was certain it was set to snow again, and that could only mean further delay on getting Laramie emptied of its thronging crowds. And especially for her desire to also leave the town.

Inside the stable, Jordana quickly re-secured the door and pushed back the woolen scarf she'd wrapped around her head and face. The barn was cold, but it felt tolerable and certainly bore more hope for clear thinking than the house.

"I thought that was you," Rich said, coming from out of Scout's stall. "What in the world are you doing out here? The temperature must be below zero."

"I couldn't stand it anymore. There are three little old ladies in my room who don't understand why, when I have such a sweet little figure and charming smile, I'm not already married with a brood of children. They, of course, never married, but that was because their mother needed them at home. Now that Mama has passed on to her reward, they are going west, where they are sure to find husbands." Pausing, she gave an exasperated toss of her head. "But that aside, I came out here to give Scout some sugar."

"Sugar? For Scout?" Despite his surprise, Rich grinned broadly. "What about me? I've had to suffer with black coffee, cold biscuits, and canned meat. Something sweet would be a treat for me as well. Where in the world did you get sugar for Scout?"

"I bribed Mrs. Nader," Jordana admitted. "I promised her that once the trains were running again, I'd see to it that she got a whole bolt of that blue calico print she so admired."

"Why wait? Surely you have enough funds that you could get it now," Rich commented.

"Yes, if I wanted to pay three or four times what it's worth. Anyway, I got an extra blanket out of the deal, this sugar, and" — she paused, giving a conspiratorial glance around the barn — "this." She pulled out a small bundle from her coat pocket. Inside she revealed four sugar cookies.

"Oh, you are a crafty one!" Rich eyed the cookies with as much desire as Jordana had seen him show for anything.

"I had thought to come and enjoy at least one of these, hopefully where no one would find me, but since you are here, I suppose it would only be fair to share."

"I think so," Rich replied.

She handed him a cookie and nibbled on one for herself after shoving the others back into her pocket. Reaching into her other pocket, she brought out a little handkerchief knotted and tied to protect the sugar inside. She put her cookie down on the edge of the stall, carefully watching that neither Scout nor Rich made a run for it while she untied the cloth. As if sensing that Jordana had brought him a treat, Scout stirred in his stall and quickly swung his head over the rail to greet her, nuzzling eagerly at the offering.

"You're spoiling him," Rich said with cookie crumbs still dusting the front of his coat.

Jordana shook her head and offered him a smile. "Like master, like horse."

Rich noticed where her glance had fallen and quickly cleaned off the crumbs. "At least I made you smile. I began to fear you were going to be moping about for the next week to come. You know there will be other dances, and you can rest assured that when they take place, yours truly will dance with you. I know you missed out on that at the party they had at Fort Sanders. Of course, you did get to dance with Isabella and you handled that so nicely. You led rather well." His eyes glinted with merriment.

Jordana grabbed up her cookie and threw it at Rich. Unfortunately, his reflexes were lightning swift and he caught the treat easily.

"Ah, more good fortune. Pull out the other two. I'm sure I can figure a way to further insult your respectability."

"You haven't insulted my respectability, and why would I want to dance with you anyway? You said you'd given up on women.

You weren't going to ever marry again, as I recall," she said betraying her irritation with his smugness.

"I don't recall it ever being said that I had to marry a woman if I danced with her. Is that some strange Baldwin rule?" He popped the cookie into his mouth just as Jordana charged him with raised fists.

She didn't really intend to hurt him, but her toe caught the edge of Scout's saddle, which was propped up against the stall door, propelling her forward with more force than intended. Her fisted hands crashed into Rich's midsection. The shock of her attack left him standing unguarded, and when her fists met his stomach she heard the wind go out from him. Though not in a way to really incapacitate him, it did cause his carefully constructed guard to drop. And it left them both standing only inches apart, staring nearly nose to nose as he bent over to regain his breath.

"I didn't mean to . . . it's just that . . ." Guilt assailed her as she tried to steady herself. Why couldn't she just act like a lady and treat Rich with the distanced respect that society expected of her? Hadn't her mother and finishing-school teachers taught her that ladies simply did not go about touching men for any reason? She was certain this especially applied to beating them up or charging after them with fists flailing.

Rich recovered, but as he did, he reached out and took hold of her arms. "I suppose I shall have to restrain you in order to have a civil conversation with you," he taunted.

"I'm sorry, Rich. I really didn't mean to hurt you." She was trembling at his nearness. Her knees grew weak as her eyes fixed upon his lips. She wanted so badly for him to kiss her.

"Jordana?" She heard him murmur her name, but the pounding of her own heart refused to allow her to hear anything more.

He reached out to touch her cheek, his thumb tenderly caressing her face. Somehow, she had brought her hands up to his neck, and rather than her usual desire to strangle him, Jordana gently toyed with the black curls touching the collar of his coat.

An instant later, he had pulled her closer, bending her back ever so slightly so that she could still see his face, though blurry and ill defined from only an inch away. She heard a low moan but wasn't sure if it had come from Rich or from herself. She only knew that she wanted very much for the moment to go on forever. When he lowered his lips to hers, Jordana was certain she could hear the angels singing in heaven. She clung tightly to his neck, pulling him closer, wanting this kiss — needing this man.

He tasted sweet, like sugar cookies, and the thought made her smile as the sensation of his warm lips against hers sent shivering tingles throughout her body. Rich's kiss was all she had ever hoped it would be. Rich's kiss was perfect.

Then as if both had realized her thoughts, Rich and Jordana jumped away from each other, standing panting and staring as though they weren't entirely sure what had happened, what had truly taken place.

"I don't know what to say," Rich muttered.

"I . . . I suppose," Jordana struggled to think of what words might make sense as an explanation. "It's just that everything is getting to me. The crowds and the snow. I can't get home to my family." She began to ramble, because at least this made her feel more in control. "I should never have burdened you with my troubles and I shouldn't have gotten angry."

He nodded. "That's all it was. Just a case of the world getting you down — just nerves. No harm done." He acted just as shook up as Jordana felt.

She nodded. "I'd better get back to the

house." She picked up her skirts and made for the door. Just a case of nerves, he had called it, but in her heart she knew better. In her heart, she had come to the stable hoping to find him. And in her heart, she had wanted his kiss for nearly as long as she had known him.

■ ■ ■ ■

PART V
FEBRUARY–MAY 1869

■ ■ ■ ■

TWENTY-SEVEN

After weeks of putting distance between herself and Rich, Jordana finally forced herself to approach him on another matter. It was rumored the snows were being cleared and folks might expect to be able to travel as early as two days hence. If the rumors were true, it would indeed be answered prayer for more reasons than one. Travelers in Laramie who had been cooped up for weeks were becoming a problem as tempers grew ugly from the scarcity of food and the close quarters. Frankly, Jordana was sick of the entire lot. It seemed few people had any conscience whatsoever and were making money off anyone and everyone in whatever manner they could. Why, a single slice of bread dipped in watered-down molasses was selling for a dollar fifty! And most palatable foods, such as beef, potatoes, ham, beans, and even coffee, had long since run out. Jordana would be happy to leave

Laramie and not look back. Well, she would be happy to be rid of the chaos. She couldn't promise that her heart wouldn't look back.

As soon as the snow had been cleared from the track and train travel was once again possible, Jordana asked Rich to pull some strings and see her onto the first westbound train. Rich seemed to understand. Although he said very little when she explained that she had to get to Sacramento, she wondered if he was as eager to be rid of her as she was to be leaving him. The awkwardness between them had grown as huge and chilly as a snowdrift. Did that kiss haunt him as it did her? Or did he simply regret it? Were they both fools for courting such futile entanglements, or were they just fools for avoiding them? She had no ready answers. Thus, she merely let him believe it was the urgency of seeing Victoria's baby born, of being there where she was definitely needed. He came through, as he always had, with a ticket as far west as the train could take her, and then he'd even managed to arrange a stage that would take her to the nearest CP depot where she might continue her trip home to Sacramento.

Leaving Laramie had been both a relief and a sorrow. Jordana could hardly refuse him when Rich offered to see her to the train, but the painful awareness of his presence was almost more than Jordana could deal with. There was a moment of revelation when Jordana realized that everything had changed between them — and all because of one little kiss.

Only it hadn't been a little kiss. That kiss had held all the passion and fervor that Jordana had been missing. That kiss made her feel alive and excited in a way that nothing else ever had. But it was obvious that the kiss meant nothing to Rich. Or had it? He stood so very calmly, almost formally, as she waved down from the train window. He waved back and gave her a casual salute as the train lurched forward and started her toward Rawlins.

He doesn't care about me the way I care about him, she thought, tears misting her vision. Now I know how G.W. felt when I didn't return his love. How very awful to feel this kind of love and know it isn't reciprocated.

She dabbed at her eyes and tried to fortify her spirit with the reasoning that leaving was for the best. Rich could be free to go about his business for the UP, and Jordana could claim a quiet respite with her family. It felt good to know they would welcome her with open arms and, hopefully, no questions. Oh, there would be a few questions, but nothing so out of line that Jordana would deny them answers. Of course, if they asked about Rich, she would just have to be very careful with how she answered. No sense in working everyone up with a hope that she and Rich might settle down and marry. No sense at all.

Sacramento proved to be a blessing for Jordana. Coming back to Victoria and Kiernan, as well as Caitlan and Brenton, offered her a kind of comfort she hadn't even realized she'd been missing. Victoria, due to deliver her baby any day now, waddled proudly around her new home that Kiernan had helped to build for her.

"He thought of everything," Victoria said, pointing out special built-in shelves in the pantry. "Look here, this table folds down from the wall for times when I need extra counter space. Kiernan suggested it might be useful for making him fresh fruit pies."

Jordana laughed. "I'm sure he did. What a wonderful husband."

Caitlan smiled as well. "Brenton is naggin' Kiernan to help him build us a house as well. He has a hankerin' to settle down and stay a spell in one spot."

"I thought you were both considering the

idea of living back east near our parents," Jordana replied.

Caitlan, pushing back several errant strands of cinnamon hair, patted her own rounding abdomen. "He'd like to be havin' us in a place of our own before the baby comes. I told him I didn't mind the idea of goin' east, but he's come to really enjoy the mild climate here. He hates bein' separated from yar folks, but maybe once the railroad is actually in place, it won't be that much of a concern."

"The transcontinental railroad will change lives from coast to coast," Jordana said, sounding like those prophetic men who wrote handbills. "Do you realize that a person will be able to cross the continent in just a matter of days? Remember when mother talked of Uncle Maine going west to be a missionary just north of here? He was months getting out here, and the hardships were so numerous he couldn't even write of them all. And they all accepted the fact that they would never see one another again. It's hard enough to fathom the telegraph and getting word to family in New York and hearing back from them almost always within hours of each other. I can't even begin to imagine what new inventions they'll come up with to top these."

"But no doubt they'll be comin' up with somethin'," Caitlan replied.

Victoria led the way back to the front room and motioned them all to sit. "I want to show you both something very special."

Jordana looked at Caitlan, who only shrugged her shoulders in ignorance. Apparently she had no better idea of what Victoria had planned than Jordana did.

Victoria returned with a cloth bundle. It looked like some sort of blanket, but Jordana couldn't be sure. Spreading it out on the rug in front of the sofa, Victoria awkwardly straightened up. "It's the baby quilt I've been working on for over ten years."

"Oh my!" Jordana exclaimed, kneeling down on the floor to better see it. "Why, Victoria, this is lovely."

"Oh, and for sure it is," Caitlan said in near reverence. "Why, look here, there's a block that deals with the potato famine in Ireland. Look, she's made the outline of me homeland."

"All of the blocks have something to do with important times in our lives. Kiernan's coming to America and his accident, our travels to the goldfields, the building of the railroad, it's all there."

"I'm notably impressed," Jordana said, grinning up at her sister. "You are a wonder with a needle, Mrs. O'Connor. I just hope that when I get married and have a family, you'll be kind enough to stitch a few of these together for me."

"Oh, and so now you'll be gettin' married and havin' children?" Caitlan teased. "I thought for sure ya'd keep yarself to bein' an old maid. I think since I'm already married and with child, there should only be stitchin' done on account of meself."

The trio of sisters laughed. "I'll happily make quilts and baby blankets for each of you," Victoria said, her hand rubbing at the small of her back. "But first, I think it's time for me to think about this baby. I didn't want to cause either one of you to fret, but I've been having pains since daybreak, and I think the baby will be born today."

"What!" Jordana nearly screamed while jumping to her feet. "Why didn't you say something? You should be in bed. For goodness' sake, we'd better send for the doctor."

"Aren't we the silly pair, fussin' over a quilt while ya stand there in labor," Caitlan said, quickly drawing up the quilt from the floor. "Let's get ya to bed."

"I suppose if I must," Victoria said, this time clutching at her swollen stomach. "The pains are much stronger of late, and more frequent."

"Of course they are, you ninny!" Jordana took hold of Victoria's arm. "That's the way they're supposed to be."

"Oh, and where did you get so knowledgeable about such things?" Victoria asked.

"I've read up on it and listened to plenty of talk about it," Jordana replied, quite pleased to be able to boast this much. "Of course, I realize that dealing with actually delivering a baby or expecting one is entirely different. Nevertheless, I feel confident that I can make myself useful in this case."

By this time Caitlan had tucked the quilt under her arm and had come up alongside Victoria. "Let's be gettin' ya upstairs and changed. Jordana, I can get her upstairs if you'll fetch Brenton and Kiernan. Oh, and the doctor, of course."

Excitement surged through Jordana. "I'll be back before you can have her into bed." She raced for the front door, then realized she had no idea where the men had taken themselves off to.

Hurrying back to the staircase, Jordana called up to Caitlan and Victoria, who were already halfway up the stairs. "Where are the men? Who is your doctor and where can he be found?"

Victoria laughed, then moaned painfully and doubled over. Unable to speak, Caitlan replied for her. "The men are lookin' at some property just three blocks from here. Ya go straightaway up two blocks, turn left a block, and then up one more. Ya'll see the carriage. Kiernan knows where to find the doctor."

Jordana ran from the house, not even bothering to worry about a mount or a carriage of her own. She ran the entire two blocks before stopping to remember what Caitlan had said. Then turning left, she once again hiked up her skirts and proceeded at a most unladylike trot. Along the way, she thought of the time she had taken the dare of her school friends and climbed up the four-story brick building that had housed her school. The fear and exhilaration she felt then was nothing compared to what she felt now.

She could make out her brother's carriage just ahead. "Brenton! Kiernan!" she called, not seeing the men. Where could they be?

The property was a pleasant little piece, several acres wide with double the distance in length. There were large, towering oaks reminding her of her grandfather's plantation back in Virginia. They had called it Oakbridge because of a large bridge created from the oak trees that populated the plantation.

"Brenton!" she called again, pausing near the middle of the clearing. She looked around, knowing that they had to be there. Within a moment, she caught sight of a lone figure and then another coming up through the trees from the far side of the property.

"Kiernan! Brenton!"

Both men seemed to hear her at once, and Jordana thought that they must have had some idea of why she'd come, because they raced toward her as if they'd planned the competition. Kiernan reached her first, with Brenton only steps behind.

"Is it Victoria?" he asked, panting heavily. He still wore a black eye patch, which had caused his Chinese employees to call him "One-Eyed Bossy Man." The name amused the family to no end.

"Yes," Jordana replied. "It's time. The baby's coming."

"Get in the carriage," he said. "We'll make for home."

"We must get the doctor first," Jordana said, following Kiernan up into the buggy.

Brenton was right behind her, sandwiching Jordana tightly between the two men. "I didn't know where the doctor lived, or I would have gone for him first. The pains have been coming since morning."

Kiernan shook his head. "She's a stub-

414

born woman, me wife. I asked her before I left if she was feelin' all right."

"Apparently she thought she had plenty of time," Jordana replied. "First babies can take forever."

"Or they can come quickly," Kiernan replied. "I was there when me siblings came, and for many of the neighbors' babes as well. Every birth was different." He released the brake, then flicked the reins on the horses' backs. "Come along, boys, step lively."

Jordana had no idea what to expect when they returned to the house. For all her book learning and such, she knew there was very little she could do to help. Dr. Benson had not been in his office when they stopped there, but his wife said she expected him back soon and would send him directly. Kiernan jumped from the carriage, scarcely giving it a chance to come to a full stop in front of his house. He raced into the house with Brenton and Jordana only a few paces behind.

"I hope everything is all right," Brenton murmured. "I hope Caitlan is all right. I wouldn't want Victoria's ordeal to worry her about our own baby."

"I'm sure she's fine," Jordana replied, patting her brother's arm tenderly. "Don't fret so. I'm sure all is well."

They entered the house to hear a baby's cry. Startled, they looked at each other in dumfounded surprise. Kiernan was bounding up the stairs two at a time.

"Victoria!" he cried as he reached the bedroom, flung open the door, and disappeared inside.

A few moments later Caitlan, fairly dancing as much as her girth would allow, appeared and started down the stairs, meeting Jordana and Brenton halfway. "It's a boy!" she declared. "Me brother has a son!"

Jordana laughed out loud. "What wonderful news!"

Brenton embraced his wife and held her tight. "Did you deliver the baby?"

"I did," Caitlan answered, pulling away. "It wasn't the first to be brought in by me hand, but it was one of the most precious. I can't tell ya the look on Kiernan's face when he came boundin' into the room and saw me holdin' his son. I said, 'Brother, ya have a fine boy.' And ya know what he did?"

"What?"

Caitlan began to laugh. "He fainted dead on the floor!"

Jordana joined Caitlan in laughing while Brenton chuckled in a more reserved manner. His pallor indicated he might well be thinking of his own turn to become a father.

"I promise, we won't laugh nearly as much if you faint, Brenton," Jordana said.

Caitlan composed herself and nodded. "That's right. I promise I'll not laugh at all when I present ya with our son."

Brenton reached up and touched her cheek. "Oh, my darling wife, you may laugh all you like, for I know my heart shall be singing with laughter and joy just to have you safely delivered of our child."

Jordana felt awkwardly out of place. The tenderness that passed between her brother and sister-in-law was private and intimate. She felt like an intruder. Turning away, she thought of Rich and their kiss and how she had in those few moments foreseen an entire future with this man. She could only imagine in her mind what it would be like to be happily married to Rich and feel his child growing within her.

"I suppose me sister told ya it's a boy," Kiernan announced, stepping from the bedroom. He was still looking a bit pale faced behind his black eye patch.

Jordana nodded. "She did and then some."

Kiernan frowned. "Oh, so ya told them about me fallin' away dead to the world. Well, thank ya very much!" But his lips, twitching with mirth, proved he could not be upset by anything, even his own embarrassment.

"Oh, go on with ya," Caitlan said, smiling. "I thought it rather sweet. So how is that fine strappin' boy of yars? Did ya give him a name?"

Kiernan nodded and proudly hitched back his shoulders. "Aye, we did. James Kiernan O'Connor."

Moisture sprang to Jordana's eyes. "Our father will be very proud."

"Indeed. We should go wire them immediately," Brenton declared. "Would you like to come along with me to the telegraph office, Mrs. Baldwin?"

"Aye, I'd like that very much," Caitlan replied. "Watching a new life come into the world puts yar head a bit in the clouds. I might as well be outdoors."

Jordana watched them go, then turned to Kiernan. "Congratulations! I can't imagine any parents more deserving."

Kiernan smiled. "No one deserves a baby more than yar sister. She has patiently endured this life with me, and now at last, she has a worthy reward."

Just then the doctor arrived, apparently having been let in by Brenton and Caitlan as they left. As Jordana and Kiernan waited in the hall, he gave the new mother and child a careful appraisal. "She looks to be in perfect health," he announced to them several minutes later. "Your son, too. I'll be back to check on the both of them tomorrow."

"I can't wait another minute!" Jordana told Kiernan. "I have to see them." Knocking lightly on her sister's bedroom door, Jordana peeked her head inside. "May I come in?"

Victoria looked radiant as she sat propped up in her bed, baby James tucked snug in the crook of her arm. "Oh, please do."

Jordana came to the bed and, at Victoria's insistence, sat on the edge beside her sister. "How proud you must be," she said, leaning close to kiss Victoria's forehead. "May I hold him?"

Victoria nodded and handed the wrapped bundle to Jordana. "He has my coloring, but I think he looks like Kiernan."

Jordana pushed back the blanket to reveal a dark matting of hair. The baby yawned and opened his eyes for only a moment before closing them again. He dozed back to sleep as if completely unconcerned with Jordana's presence.

Jordana marveled over his little button nose and tiny lips. "Oh my, but he's sweet," she said, an aching ever growing in her heart. How perfect he felt in her arms. What a joyous feeling. What a wonder.

Quickly she handed him back to Victoria. Tears coursed down her cheeks. "I cannot be happier for you. You, who above all other women, deserve a baby to love. I thank God for this miracle."

She left before Victoria could say a word and passed Kiernan as he returned in a boisterous spirit from seeing the doctor off. "What a fine day it is for the O'Connor house!" he declared.

Jordana nodded, wiping at her tears with the back of her hand. "That it is!" But she could not shake her gnawing sense of being torn between two worlds.

She wanted to be a part of the things she saw here in this household. She wanted them more than she could say. For years the settled existence of home, hearth, and family had been completely unimportant, but now, as she neared her twenty-third birthday, Jordana had given birth to a change of heart. And at the center of that change was the one man whom she could not have. The only man she would ever love. Richard O'Brian.

Twenty-Eight

Rich found Ogden to be a muddy, frozen mess when he rode into town on the first train to travel into the city. March eighth would go down in the town's history with nearly all fifteen hundred of its inhabitants turning out to be a part of the celebration. The trip was actually rather impromptu and very understated for this celebratory accomplishment. But while it might have been understated by the officials of the UP, the citizens of Ogden quickly organized. Captain Pugh's band rapidly assembled and began to blast out marches and hymns to accompany the continued laying of additional track. For, in spite of their accomplishments in reaching Ogden, the work had to go on. The Union Pacific could not yet rest.

Captain Pugh was followed up by Captain Wadsworth's artillery. They fired salutes of honor amidst the cheering of the growing crowds. By the time the clock struck five that afternoon, a complete civic ceremony had somehow been orchestrated, and those of importance to either Ogden or the Union Pacific were assembled for official speeches.

Rich found their enthusiasm a precursor for the days to come. Whenever Congress finally decided on where the Central Pacific and Union Pacific would be joined together, a party of grand proportions could then be planned. No doubt someone was already detailing the way it would be and was just waiting to hear where it would be. Rich marveled that the railroad was so close to completion and this momentous decision had yet to be made.

Leaving the well-wishers and speechmakers, Rich made his way to the hotel. He wasn't more than ten feet from the door, however, when he tripped over someone's forgotten baggage and stumbled headlong into another man, causing a satchel of papers to scatter everywhere.

"I do apologize, sir," he said, righting himself quickly. He glanced up to assure himself no harm had been done to the other gentleman and found himself face-to-face with Baxter Montego.

"Mr. O'Brian!" Montego declared with obvious surprise.

"Mr. Montego," Rich said, then glancing around, he lowered his voice. "I've been looking all over for you. I fear you are in grave danger."

Rich had already decided the course of his game should he ever actually find himself with Montego. And now the situation had presented itself to him, and although he was shocked to find the man here, Rich quickly recovered.

Montego rapidly covered his own surprise, then bent down to pick up the papers and things he had dropped upon encountering Rich. Rich, too, bent down to assist, much to Montego's immediate agitation.

"There's no need for you to worry yourself with this." Montego attempted to brush aside Rich's eager hands. "I do want to hear more about the danger you believe me to be in, however."

"Nonsense," Rich said, picking up a leather-bound book. The initials "J.B." were clearly evident on the cover. Handing it to Montego as though he had no clue what the book might contain, Rich had to force himself to remain calm. The book proved that Montego had had something to do with Jordana's capture by the Indians. After all, it had been the Indians who had taken the book away from her. Montego would have had to have been among the Indians in order to put his hands on it.

"Thank you," Montego said rather harshly as he snatched the book from Rich. "I can manage."

Rich decided not to push the man. He waited as Montego gathered up his other papers. They appeared to be a variety of things — some were clearly correspondences, while others might have been lists of figures and other detailed information. If only he could get a closer look.

"We have to talk," Rich said, again glancing around at the people on the street. "I believe you have a traitor working among your people."

Montego eyed him curiously. "Why would you say that?"

"Well, I sent a message just as you suggested back in Laramie. A man came and met me at the appointed time. We talked at the depot and arranged what I thought would be a good case of sabotage against the Central Pacific. But the next thing I knew, someone from the Union Pacific had picked me up as a spy and traitor to the UP."

"Do tell," Montego said, acting surprised. "However did you manage to escape?"

Rich played the moment for all he was

worth. He ran his thumb and finger along the edges of his mustache as if to smooth it down. "I'm good friends with General Dodge. We go way back. I told him I was obviously being set up and he believed me. I was never really worried for myself, but I was terribly concerned for you and Isabella. She is all right, isn't she?" Rich thought he masterfully feigned deep concern.

"She's fine. She's here in the hotel. I know she'll be glad to see you," Montego replied. "I still don't understand why you feel I am in any danger."

"Well, I discussed business with the man you put me in touch with. He only knew about me because of my involvement with you. I'm afraid he might well betray you as he did me. He is probably a man of little means — or integrity for that matter."

"So what do you propose to do now?"

Rich glanced around. "Is there someplace we could talk more privately?"

"Well, not right now. My daughter and I are to attend a special dinner to celebrate the UP reaching Ogden. I wouldn't want to disappoint her. After all, she's been upstairs primping and fussing over her costume now for nearly an hour."

"What time is your dinner?"

"Six o'clock. We could arrange to meet

here in the hotel afterward," Montego said, finally replacing his papers and Jordana's journal back into his leather satchel, snapping it securely shut.

"That would be good," Rich agreed. "I plan to have a room here myself. I could meet you in the lobby, say around eight o'clock?"

"I would imagine the celebration will continue until nine or ten."

Rich nodded. "Ten, it is."

Rich waited until he was certain Isabella and her father had left their hotel room before going downstairs to inquire as to their room number. If he could only get a look inside Montego's room, maybe he would find that Montego had left the precious satchel behind and Rich would be able to sort through the papers.

"I'm to meet Baxter Montego at his room, but I don't remember the number. I believe it's on the second floor," Rich told the desk clerk.

The man nodded. "The Montegos are in rooms 203 and 204. I'm uncertain as to which room Mr. Montego has taken."

"That's all right," Rich stated with a smile. "I'm friends with both Montegos. I'm sure it won't matter all that much if I knock on the wrong door."

Finding his way to the rooms, Rich eyed their locations for a moment before deciding that Montego was most likely in 203. The situation of the room was better, but, from gauging the positions of the doors, it appeared 204 was the larger of the two rooms. Isabella Montego would not only require more room for her luggage and finery, but, unconcerned with her father's comfort, would no doubt insist on the larger of the rooms.

With a cautious glance down the hall, Rich pulled out a ring containing several skeleton keys, which he had obtained from the cleaning lady for the mere cost of two gold dollars. As he slipped a key into the lock, he prayed his money had been well spent. It seemed strange to pray that God aid him in breaking into another man's room, but Rich figured this was a matter of heart. God knew his heart wasn't set on wrong but rather was seeking to do right. Rich felt that the crusade he'd found himself caught up in was a fight between good and evil. To Rich it was quite clear. There were evil men attempting evil deeds, and there were good men attempting good deeds. Of course, between these, there were plain folks who cared very little either one way or the other, but simply wanted to be left alone to live their lives and make their way. He didn't know what to think of them. In a way he envied them and longed for a more mediocre life. But for the most part, he felt sorry for them. They seemed to lack any real interest or vigor for life. Unlike a certain young woman whose kiss he still could not put from his mind.

Jordana Baldwin's presence haunted him like nothing he had ever known. Even Peggy's death and the love he'd lost with her were being quickly swallowed up in the wake of that one kiss, that one woman so vibrant and full of verve. He had been the worst sort of fool to let her leave him. Who could say when they'd meet again? And even if they managed to meet, how could he possibly get her to change her mind about marriage?

The third key worked and the door quietly opened. Replacing the keys in his pocket, Rich brushed the handle of his revolver. Something inside him had caused Rich to strap it on. Under normal circumstances he would never have given the weapon a second thought, but tonight he had an ominous feeling about what he would find.

He quickly glanced around the room before closing the door. There was a lamp beside the door and a box of lighters next to this. Rich took up one of the pieces and stepped back into the hall to light the wood from one of the hall lamps.

With the room properly illuminated, Rich could easily see that this was Montego's room. He closed the door and wondered what to do first. He would have to work quickly in order to put out the light before anyone could notice from the street that someone was messing about inside.

Moving around the room, Rich looked at the clothes Montego had laid out on the bed, then went through the bags that sat nearby. Finding nothing, he was about to admit defeat when he spied something sticking out from beneath the bed. Lifting the quilt covering, he found the satchel.

Silently thanking God, Rich shuffled quickly through the papers, stunned by the things he read. There were not only correspondences here that clearly linked Montego to various disasters along the Union Pacific tracks, but there was also some strange plan Montego was putting together to kidnap Thomas Durant. Shaking his head, Rich put off finishing the reading of that particular missive to find Jordana's journal. Pulling it out of the satchel, he smiled. The book was simple, nondescript, except for the initials emblazoned on the cover. Though he told himself he needed to read the pages so as to be informed about the kind of information they might have revealed to Montego, he nevertheless felt like an interloper. Still, he scanned through the pages, both mesmerized and amazed at the detailed accounts that had been kept. Jordana had even drawn little pictures, sketches that were really quite good. He knew exactly what she was trying to portray by each one. Here was a clear depiction of a trestle bridge, then several pages of script followed by a rough drawing of snow sheds in the mountains of the Central Pacific. He could easily ascertain this, not because the UP had no use for snow sheds, but because the CPRR initials had been included on the side of the locomotive engine Jordana had included. Her artistic talent was really quite something.

Continuing to flip through the book, Rich found a sketch of what could only be Brenton and Caitlan at work with their photography. Why, Jordana even had a flair for sketching people. They stood beneath a large shade tree, camera between them and a bevy of equipment at their feet. But Rich's eye was quickly drawn away from the scene upon which Jordana had intended the focus to be and instead rested on the trunk of the tree where a tiny heart had been sketched as if carved into the bark and the initials "R.O." had been set inside. R.O.?

"Why, that's me," Rich said, the realization suddenly dawning on him. "That little ninny. She *does* have feelings for me. It isn't one-sided. And from the looks of this, she's been having them for some time." He snapped the book shut and grinned broadly. "Well, I'll be. Just wait until I get ahold of her."

He fell silent at the sound of voices in the hallway. Without thought, he quickly pulled his gun and dropped the journal. Moving toward the door, he reached it just as it opened.

"I promise I'll only be a moment. I just need to get —"

Baxter Montego fell silent as he entered the room with a genuine look of amazement, first at the well-lit room, then at the man with the drawn pistol. Rich stepped forward in time to see Isabella, apparently alerted to a problem, flee down the hall. Montego looked around as if he were going to do the same, but Rich shook his head.

"Don't even think about it," Rich said, pointing the gun at the man's chest. "I'd just as soon blow a hole in you for what you've caused me and my friends as to look at you."

Montego gave a strained smile. "Are you certain we can't come to some mutual understanding?"

"I have a great mutual understanding about you already," Rich replied. "You're going to jail. I understand that much, and so do you. That makes it mutual."

After gathering up the evidence and seeing to Montego's incarceration, Rich wired General Dodge to let him know what had happened. He explained in brief about the plans to kidnap Durant and figured they should count themselves lucky that much of what Montego had planned would now be thwarted. His only real concern was that Isabella Montego had managed to escape.

And because she had escaped, Rich felt compelled, for reasons that went beyond his immediate understanding, to wire Jordana in Sacramento. Isabella was a threat, but to what degree, Rich couldn't say. He felt that he should warn Jordana, even though he knew Isabella would be foolish to remain anywhere near either railroad. She would have to presume that Rich would put the word out about her activities.

Wiring Jordana also served another purpose. It allowed Rich some much desired contact. Perhaps he could even pin her down as to when she might once again be coming his way. Or maybe he could suggest that he would be free to come to California once the railroad was actually completed. One way or another, he was going to find that little woman and teach her about toying with people's emotions and feelings. And the lessons he had in mind were quite grand. He'd start with another kiss and then . . . well, who knew?

The last thing Jordana expected that afternoon was a telegram. She immediately feared some calamity had befallen Rich or her parents and sat down in Victoria's front room, staring at the paper for several moments, before allowing herself to scan the message.

"Hope this finds you well. Your sister too," Jordana read aloud. "Caught B. Montego, but Isabella escaped. Be careful. The frontier has grown rather boring without you. Yours fondly, Rich." She reread the last sentence. "Yours fondly? Since when?" She mused over this so thoroughly that she didn't hear Kiernan come into the room.

"I heard someone at the door," he said.

"Yes. I had a telegram from Rich O'Brian.

You remember him, don't you?"

"Aye, that I do," Kiernan said, readjusting the black eye patch. "I'm rememberin' that the two of ya looked mighty fine together."

Jordana's cheeks burned suddenly. "Well . . . ah . . . we're good friends."

"That's the best way to be startin' out."

"Starting what out?" she asked innocently.

Kiernan grinned and gave her a wink with his good eye. "Ya go on and play those games with somebody else. I'm no fool. I can see how ya feel about the man. Mebbe it's time ya saw for yarself how ya feel about him and do somethin' about it."

Jordana smiled. "Well, I just might at that. Charlie wants me to report about the progress of the Central Pacific, and the *Tribune* demands I be on hand at the joining of the rails. Are you certain you won't be going back on the line? I could travel with you."

"No, I'll not be going back. Charlie and I agreed it's best for me to do what's important to me. I've a hankerin' to make furniture. I'm good at it, if I do say so meself."

"Yes, you are," Jordana quickly agreed. "And a fine house builder as well."

"Well, now, there I did have me fair share of help, but furniture is me true love. Second only to me wife and our son."

Jordana stood. "I kind of figured that would be your answer, and I can't say I don't admire you immensely for it. You're a fine man, Kiernan. I've always thought so. And now, you're a father and rightly so, for I cannot imagine a man who could possibly love a child more than you do."

"God go with ya, little sister!" Kiernan leaned over to kiss her cheek.

"God go with her where?" Victoria inquired, gliding into the room with little James in her arms.

"I'm heading back up the line," Jordana announced, realizing that her heart had already set her plans in motion. "First, however, I need to find me a pair of trousers, a couple of work shirts, and a good sturdy hat. I'm not going to cut my hair again, not now when it's finally reaching my shoulders, but I'll need to hide it."

Victoria laughed. "Oh, Jordana! You'll be the end of proper society and fashion as we know it."

"Maybe that will be for the better," Jordana declared. "Trousers are quite comfortable and certainly nowhere near as confining. Maybe you should get yourself a pair."

"And for sure she'd better not," Kiernan replied. "I wear the pants in this house."

Jordana laughed and shook her head. "Which is precisely why I am leaving."

TWENTY-NINE

Jordana was happy to be back among the track layers and graders. It made her wonder about her longings about home and family while in Sacramento. She felt more conflicted than ever.

The men exhibited an infectious eagerness as the tracks moved ever closer to completion. Competitions and wagers were constantly going on to see who could do the most work, lay the most track, grade the most road. Often the men challenged each other in teams, and always Jordana watched and wrote and dreamed of the day when the railroad would actually connect the East to the West in one long, continuous iron ribbon. The wounded country would be bound together. Now with General Grant as president of the United States, Jordana felt confident that the progress could move forward. The War Between the States would fade from memory and the settling of the western territories would take precedence in conversations and plans. An old age would pass away and a new one would take its place.

She wondered about the future as she watched the railroad workers expend their energies on a line some might not even live to see to completion. Workers led a hard life. There were dangers from the explosives used, dangers from the elements. There was even the toll the work itself took on the body. Men had to be sturdy and capable, healthy and well-muscled, in order to swing those hammers from sunup to sunset, not to mention carrying rails that easily weighed six hundred pounds apiece. And while the latter task was done as a team, there were still duties that taxed the body nigh onto death. Lesser men grew weak and sick; some even died from heart attacks, passing away in such horrible pain and misery that it left everyone lethargically transfixed for hours afterward. Snakebites had claimed the lives of several men while Jordana had been along the route, and while laying track in the Sierra Nevada, two men had met their death from a mountain lion attack, and another half dozen had died in rockslides. The life of a railroad man was simply not an easy one; neither was it always a happy one.

Jordana had picked up with her routine of interviewing the men about their jobs and asking questions about their homelife and families. Many of the men were lonely and far from home. Some had families; others had no one in the entire world who even knew if they lived or died.

Jordana often sorrowed at the stories she heard. Some of the men seemed so hopeless. They had no idea where they would go after the railroad was completed. They'd come west in hope of making their fortune, but now they felt that hope was gone. Even the Chinese suffered this fate.

Jordana had reestablished her nickname of Preacher and had also taken up giving Bible readings on Sunday mornings. At first only a few men showed up to listen, but usually within the hour there were nearly fifty men gathered round. Some of the men looked as if they were hungry for the Scriptures, while others just looked bored and indifferent. Either way, Jordana felt good about sharing this part of her faith with the men.

Meeting up with some of the Chinese who had befriended her, Jordana found her skills rekindled in the art of self-defense as well as her meager ability to speak their language. She even managed to get a long, detailed account of China and the trip many had endured to come to America. It would make a great story in the future, and perhaps after the railroad was completed, she could suggest an entire series on the Chinese in America.

But through it all, Jordana continued to think of Rich. She often took out the telegram he had sent and reread the words "Yours fondly." Was he really hers? Could she ever hope this to be the case between them?

Nearly a week before, the final point of joining the Union Pacific and Central Pacific had been agreed upon. Promontory Summit would be the place where the building would finally come to an end. Jordana knew very little of the area, with exception to what she could dig out of Charlie. But of late, he was so preoccupied with seeing the thing completed that he had little patience for her or her stories. He was often to be found with sleeves rolled up and working right alongside his men. He told Jordana, "I believe if it becomes necessary to jump off the dock in the service of the company, instead of saying, 'Go boys,' one must pull off his coat and say, *'Come* boys.' " He followed his own words.

There came to be a general frenzy of activities along the railroad, and emotions and tempers flared through misunderstandings more than once. It was the best of times to be alive, Jordana decided. Glancing around at all that she had witnessed, she knew without doubt she could not have been happy any place else on earth. Unless, of course, that place was with Rich.

In an effort to locate Charlie farther up the line, Jordana left one camp for another. She caught the train as it headed up to the front of the tracks, hauling with it a good portion of supplies. There was still much to do, but the most difficult portions of the Central Pacific were already built. They had conquered the Sierra, and now the path to Promontory seemed like an easy accomplishment.

Sighing, Jordana got up from her seat and walked to the end of the passenger car where a tank of water and a tin cup were kept for thirsty passengers. Satisfying her thirst, she returned down the aisle, barely sidestepping in time as a willowy-looking man strode past her in the opposite direction. The fellow, a young man, looked vaguely familiar, but for the life of her, Jordana couldn't place him. Curiosity got the better of her, and seeing the man take down a bundle from one of the racks overhead, Jordana watched as he moved to the end of the car and opened the door to the outside platform.

How very strange, she thought. And before she knew what was happening, Jordana had followed the man outside. Evening was coming on rather quickly in spite of the balmy spring day. The sun faded against the western horizon, catching Jordana's eye for just a moment before she heard the unmistakable sound of a gun being cocked.

"What are you doing out here?" came a low voice from the shadows of the platform.

Jordana jerked around, only to find herself staring into the eyes of the last person she had expected. "Isabella Montego?"

"Do you think you're the only one who can dress in pants and disguise your identity?" Isabella asked smugly. "You didn't invent the idea, you know."

"I didn't think I had," Jordana replied, shaken but regaining her composure. "I just find it surprising that someone who appeared as particular as you did about your fashions and hair would run about in knee boots and trousers. What are you doing out here?"

"I asked you that first," Isabella said, her voice clearly angry. "Besides, I have the gun, so why don't you just go ahead and answer before I lose my patience."

"I thought I recognized you, so I followed. I didn't expect it to be you," Jordana admitted. Then, with a steady gaze, added, "Now that I've told you why I came, why don't you tell me why you have a gun on me?"

"You're the enemy. I always take care of my enemies," she replied coolly.

"I see, and why is it that I'm the enemy?" Jordana thought it was best to feign ignorance about Rich and his capture of Baxter Montego.

"You know very well," Isabella sneered. "You and O'Brian have caused my father's plans to take a bit of a turn. But never fear — I'll find a way to free my father, and with you both out of the way, we should be able to accomplish whatever we set our minds to. I nearly had O'Brian taken care of back in Laramie. He never even knew it was me he'd met that night after arranging with my father to have someone help him plot against the Central Pacific." She laughed harshly. "As you well know, a pair of pants and a hat worn low over your face are most effective. No one gives you much consideration, at least. I don't know how he ever managed to get out of that situation, but sooner or later he'll make a mistake and I'll be there to take advantage of it."

"If you try to hurt him, I'll —"

Isabella grimaced scornfully. "You'll what? Dead men, or women for that matter, are hardly any threat to me. And believe me, you will soon be quite dead." She leveled the gun at Jordana's heart. "Pity you couldn't have been on the right side."

Without warning, Jordana leaped into the air, taking hold of the platform rail. With one swift kick she sent the gun flying from Isabella's hands. It clattered for a moment against the platform before slipping over the side to be forever lost along the Central Pacific route. Her practice of Chinese self-defense had paid off.

Isabella seemed undaunted, however. She was a cool number. And even as Jordana was recovering from her own action, Isabella had grabbed up the bundle at her feet and swiftly vaulted over the railing. Jordana stared in surprise as Isabella jumped the short distance between cars and took hold of the ladder on the end of the opposite car. In a flash, Isabella was up the ladder and on top of the baggage car. Jordana spent only a moment wondering what she should do. Clearly the woman was up to no good, and there was nothing else to do but pursue the culprit up to the top of the car.

Not letting another moment pass, Jordana went to the platform railing and climbed over. She held tightly to the rail, her feet narrowly fixed on the platform overhang. Nervously, she watched the landscape fly past beneath her feet. This was a very stupid thing to do, she told herself, even as she reached to close the distance and take hold of the iron rungs of the ladder.

Just as she managed to get a good grip on the ladder with her left hand, the train shifted rather hard to the left. Losing her footing, she sailed out over the opening between the joined cars. Holding on for dear life with only one hand, Jordana felt as though she were a flag flying in the wind. For a split second, it was both perilous and wonderful and then she was slammed back up against the car, her right hand searching madly for a hold on the rungs.

Panting for breath, Jordana struggled to climb up the ladder and pull herself up on top of the car. She would never have given it a second thought to climb topside at any other time, and in fact had done it a few times before, but with the train in motion, it clearly raised the stakes. Scanning down the car, Jordana couldn't catch any sign of Isabella. Licking her dry lips and trying to swallow the lump of fear in her throat, Jordana crawled along the top of the car on her hands and knees. She'd seen grown men walk the top of the car while it was moving, but she wasn't about to give this a try for herself. She supposed she was becoming more cautious in her old age, but the risk of this type of adventure simply seemed foolhardy.

From time to time she'd feel the train hit a rough spot, and at those times she'd flatten herself against the top and grab on to anything that presented itself as a handhold. Her heart pounded wildly, and all she could do was pray for strength and help. *This has to be the dumbest thing I've ever attempted,* she told her heavenly Father, *but I have to stop Isabella before she can hurt anyone else. Please help me.*

She had no sooner breathed the silent prayer than she came to the end of the car. There was nowhere to go but over the side or across to the next car. Which way had Isabella chosen? Where had she gone? It was then that Jordana heard a moaning sound. It seemed to come from over the side of the car. Moving closer to the edge, Jordana was horrified to find Isabella clinging to the top by her fingers.

"Here, let me help you," Jordana said, flattening against the roof.

"Get away from me," Isabella managed to say between clenched teeth.

"I only want to help. I'll grab hold of your wrist and —"

"I don't need your help." And then as if to prove her point, Isabella somehow managed to hook her foot into the ladder and regain control.

Jordana breathed a sigh of relief, feeling the knots in her stomach push her close to losing her supper. She watched Isabella struggle to reach the bundle, which she had apparently dropped as she'd lost her hold going over the side. The bundle rode precariously between the two cars, fixed atop the coupling piece.

"Isabella, it's too far to reach," Jordana called down. "Don't be a fool."

"I told you," Isabella said, glancing up only for a moment, and even then, there was no fear in the woman's eyes, but only cold determination. "I don't need your help. I have enough dynamite here to blow you and this entire line to kingdom come."

Jordana had heard of this new explosive from Charlie. He found it only marginally more stable than nitroglycerin. "You'll never reach it," Jordana yelled.

"If I wanted your opinion, I would have asked for it." And Isabella stretched out away from the ladder, still not close enough to snag the bundle.

Jordana held her breath and watched in terror. "Please, Isabella. I won't say anything about what you planned to do tonight until you're well away. You'll have a good head start before I get a chance to tell the authorities of your whereabouts. Just please, forget the dynamite and climb down. You can get off at the first stop —"

Isabella only laughed. She was still laughing when she lost her grip and fell onto the bundle. Only then did terror flicker in her eyes. But somehow, with her grace and agility, she managed to keep from slipping from her new perch on the coupling piece. But this amazing luck only lasted until the train hit another rough spot and then without warning, Isabella fell between the cars and was gone. Without so much as time to scream, she was crushed beneath the wheels of the train she had hoped to destroy.

Jordana stared at the place she'd last seen Isabella, finding it impossible to believe what she'd just witnessed. One moment the young woman had been there and the next minute — nothing. A wave of nausea and dizziness hit her. Isabella Montego was dead.

Jordana couldn't say how long she lay on

top of that train car frozen in stunned horror. The skies passed from a soft muted lavender to navy and then black before Jordana regained her senses. Realizing that she had to get down, Jordana couldn't bring herself to go over the same side that Isabella had taken. Yet, the dynamite had to be retrieved before the rough movement of the train caused it to finish what Isabella had intended. She forced her rubbery legs and arms into motion, and only by sheer grit, and much silent prayer, did she descend the ladder. She ducked back into the car, found the poker for the stove, and with this, managed to grasp the satchel of dynamite, which she flung as hard as she could into the prairie grass. The explosion shook the tracks and the moving train, and Jordana had to grip the platform rail to keep her feet, but there was no rail damage that day.

Still sickened at the thought of what she'd witnessed, Jordana made her way to her seat. She would find Charlie at the next stop and let him know what had happened. And then she would wire Rich with the news that Isabella Montego was no longer a threat.

THIRTY

"And then she fell between the cars," Jordana told Charlie Crocker, still in a state of shock.

"I'll send someone back down the line," Charlie told her, then added, "Jordana you couldn't have done anything more. You tried to help her even though she was trying to kill you."

Jordana shook her head. "I just can't believe it really happened."

Charlie watched her for a moment. "I wish I could tell you to just go take it easy for a few days, but in truth, I don't think that would be good for you. So, instead, I'm going to insist you come with me tomorrow. We've set up a little competition about fourteen miles west of Promontory Summit."

"Competition?" Jordana asked, still unable to really focus her attention on Charlie's words, but grateful nonetheless for the prospect of a distraction.

"That's right. The UP boys believe they can lay more track than the CP crews. We've shown them once before that we could lay a fair piece of track, but then they turned around and bested it. Now we're going to prove once and for all that the Central Pacific is clearly the superior railroad."

"I don't understand," Jordana replied. She toyed with her felt hat, turning it over and over while she waited for Charlie to explain.

"We're going to lay more track in a single day than has ever been laid before. The UP is sending their big brass out to watch us beat their record of laying eight miles in a day. Of course, their men had to start at three in the morning and work by lamplight to accomplish that much, but it has been done and they'll not let us hear the end of it."

"I see. And what do you propose to do in order to top it?"

Charlie grinned. "The UP has little more than twelve miles left to reach the summit. They've had to slow way down, however, because their graders aren't as fast. Besides that, there are still some bridges and tunnels to finish out and their supplies are running thin. Still, I told our men we have to make a distance that will leave no room for challenge. We're going to lay at least ten miles in a day, even if it kills us all."

Jordana shook her head. "Men are the silliest of all God's creatures."

Charlie cocked a brow at this. "Those are fightin' words, missy. You want to explain?" He spoke good-naturedly, but Jordana still frowned.

"The competition will push everyone to their limits and could very well kill several good men. And for what? A race? A competition between two bickering railroad companies?"

"But think of the good it will do the men's morale. This line is nearly complete in spite of the eastern populace acting as though the Central Pacific was a no-account line that would have to be entirely reworked after the completion of the transcontinental line. They've pushed government inspectors on us and spies —"

"Yes, and you've always managed to come out smelling like lilacs and lavender," Jordana replied drolly.

"I've never known you to back down from a challenge or wish to see anyone else back down either. Where's your spirit of adventure, Jordana?"

"I think I lost it on the tracks between Wadsworth and Elko," she replied flatly.

After several moments of trying to pull her emotions together, Jordana nodded. "I'll go with you, Charlie. I need the diversion. When do we leave?"

"We'll take my private car and leave in a couple of hours. You can sleep on the way. There are several compartments for just that and no one will bother you."

Jordana sighed. "Very well. I'm sure the *Tribune* would want the competition covered for their readership. I'll meet you back here in an hour. I need some time alone, and I need to send Rich O'Brian a telegram."

"Say, about that whole situation with O'Brian. I want to apologize," Charlie said as Jordana got to her feet. "I jumped to all the wrong conclusions, when it was the Montegos who were giving me grief all along. I hope neither one of you will hold that against me."

"I can't see either of us as the type to hold a grudge, Charlie. If I ever see Rich again, I'll tell him what you've said."

The competition got off to a false start on the twenty-seventh of April. Charlie ducked his head in sheer embarrassment when a locomotive went off the track and forced the delay of the race. Even more embarrass- ing for him was the fact that Jordana wasn't the only one to be reporting the event. There were other newspaper correspondents there and even a photographer or two.

But within moments, Charlie stuck a cigar in his mouth and challenged some of his guests to a shooting match. Soon they had set up the cigar box in the sand some one hundred yards away, and the men were quickly occupied with meeting Charlie's dare. Jordana busied herself with gaining information. She heard from two other reporters that the delay was actually the best thing that could have happened, because the UP was bringing in Dodge, Durant, Reed, the Casement brothers, and many other officials for this impromptu time test of endurance and wills.

Jordana wondered if Rich would also be accompanying the Union Pacific visitors. She hoped he might, and even uttered a couple of prayers to that effect, but she tried not to dwell on it. She didn't want to think too much about Rich, because it just made her more miserable than she already felt. There might well be a future for them one day — perhaps. After all, it was evident that Rich cared for her. But even so, could he understand her heart on the matter? Could he find a way to let her go on being herself, not expecting her to do the expected?

April twenty-eighth dawned bright and clear, and by seven o'clock that morning the officials from both sides had arrived on the scene and were ready to watch the competition. Charlie had challenged that not only could his men start at a reasonable time and complete their desired ten miles of track, but they would also end at a reasonable time as well. They would accomplish their goal in no more than twelve hours.

Jordana noted this, as well as the laughter and guffaws that followed from the Union Pacific officials. Thomas Durant was especially snide about the entire matter. There was no way he believed it possible for Crocker's Pets and a score of Irishmen to accomplish such a feat.

Jordana, less dazed from her ordeal with Isabella, worked hard to get into the spirit of things. After a time, she put away her journal, which had come to her in the post while she had still been in Sacramento, and began to simply observe the setting. She paid close attention to the sights and sounds, the smells and feel of the day. A definite charge of energy ran through the crowd as she maneuvered down the line. This would truly be a day to remember.

The signal was given at exactly seven

o'clock with a long, loud blast from the train engine. Charlie's men went to work like a well-organized machine. They had long ago learned an effective pattern for laying track, and now that strategy went into play.

The first of five trains with sixteen flatcars was positioned at the front of the line. A group of horse-drawn wagons were moved alongside, while the other four trains waited farther down the main track on sidings. The idea was to distribute enough goods to construct the entire ten miles of track.

When the whistle sounded, Jordana watched with fascination as the Chinese rushed the cars, bounding quickly on top to throw down kegs of bolts and spikes, along with bundles of fish plates and the heavy iron rails to be used. Within eight minutes they had cleared sixteen cars of equipment. The noise was deafening and stirred the crowds into enthusiastic cheers.

Jordana watched raptly as the first train was moved down the track to the siding and another train was brought forward. Six-man teams lifted open flatcars onto the existing track and began to hoist each of these with sixteen rails. These little iron cars, as they were called, had rows of rollers along the edges that assisted the men in sliding the rails forward and off the car when they were needed. Atop the rails, the men added kegs of the hardware needed to join the rails together and spikes to fix them to the ties. These cars were then hitched by a rope to two horses, positioned single file with riders on their backs.

The next line of duty required a three-man team. These men carried shovels and formed a sort of advanced alignment guard. Nicknamed "Pioneers" for the fact that they went ahead of the line of other workers, their job was to follow the grade and align the ties. This happened by butting the ties to a rope that had been stretched out parallel to a row of stakes the surveyors had previously marked down the center of the track. Jordana had seen this done a million and one times, but she never failed to be amazed at the great number of details that went into forming up the line.

Cheers of encouragement continued to be raised from the Central Pacific supporters, while the Union Pacific observers either remained silent or threw out discouraging comments of how they would call Crocker's challenge "Crocker's Bluff."

After the pioneers did their work, eight strong men stood ready at the rails. As the Chinese unloaded the iron cars and distributed the rails, they would also crack open the kegs of spikes and pour them out atop the stack of rails. This way the spikes were ready at hand to use when the rails were affixed to the ties. As the team worked the rail into place, a portable track gauge ensured that the rails were laid exactly four feet, eight and a half inches apart. This gauge moved ahead of the track layers all day long, forever keeping the measurements precise.

"Well, they're certainly going at it," Charlie said, coming up beside Jordana. "Now, aren't you glad you came?"

"I am, Charlie. I truly am!" Jordana replied. "I must admit, men and their competitions are a fascination for sure."

"I thought we were all ninnies," he commented in between puffs of his cigar.

Jordana smiled. "Oh, that you are, but your competitions are nevertheless of interest." At this Charlie laughed heartily and moved off to be with his men.

The whistle blew for the midday meal, and Jordana overheard Charlie offer to bring in the second reserve team of workers. The men protested loudly. They were proud of their accomplishments. The teams had already advanced the rails six miles, and they weren't about to let another group of men take over at this point.

Jordana helped to distribute water and boiled beef to the workers, while Charlie chided the UP officials for ever having doubted their abilities. After all, they'd already laid six miles of track. What possible trouble would it be to lay another four?

After lunch the progress slowed considerably, however. Rails needed to be bent, for the remaining miles consisted of a steady climb and a great many curves. Jordana jotted notes to herself as she watched the men very crudely place each rail between blocks and hammer a bend into it at the appropriate place. By the time the curved rails were ready, the teams of men were also better rested and eager to continue.

It soon became evident that unless something happened to interfere, Charlie's challenge was going to be met and then some. Jordana listened to the comments of others and smiled.

"Crocker's men are no fools. They've found themselves a style that works, and now they've proven themselves to the world," one newspaper reporter said to another.

"The Central Pacific is a force to be reckoned with, that's for sure," the man responded.

While the rails went in at roughly an average of a mile of track per hour, the telegraph lines followed right along behind. The telegraph already ran coast to coast, but it was easy to install them along the railroad and proved necessary as well. Often messages were sent out from the trains themselves and the telegraph had made easy work of passing information along the line. Jordana had heard it said that there were plans to have telegraphs crisscrossing to every single city in the country before the end of the century, and the wonder of it all fascinated her greatly.

As the sun set in the west and twilight painted the sky in soft shades of dusty blue and tinged the clouds in pink and purple, Jordana rubbed her tired shoulders. Taking out her handkerchief, she tried to wipe the grime and dust from her face. With evening coming on, the night air was growing chilly and she was grateful to have already put up her tent for the night. As soon as the competition finished at seven o'clock, she had only one plan and that was to get back to her tent and curl up in her blankets and go to sleep. Warmth and rest. That was truly all she desired.

A train engine had been continually backed along the new track, and when the appointed time was signaled, the engineer blew the whistle. The competition ended with a ring of dropped hammers and moaning men. The final measurement was taken and everyone seemed to collectively hold their breaths as the man walked to Charlie Crocker and whispered in his ear.

"Ten miles and fifty-six feet in twelve hours!" Charlie declared.

Cheers went up from all sides. The UP men knew a feat of wonder when they saw it. The workers lifted each other in the air and danced jigs in the firelight, as though they hadn't just spent the day exhausting themselves on the track. Jordana laughed to see the celebration. No doubt they would party long into the night. There were barely another four miles to Promontory Summit.

"I've arranged for Jim Campbell," Charlie announced as he tried to quiet the crowds, "to prove the craftsmanship of this track. Jim is going to take this engine now and run it over the new track at some forty miles per hour. I'll not have any man here going back to their papers or their governors or the Congress of the United States of America to suggest this line is anything but sound."

Jordana could hear a hint of amusement in Charlie's tone, but there was also a clear and decided tone that suggested he'd brook no nonsense from the likes of Durant and Dodge on whether his line was faulty and haphazardly constructed.

The train and the track performed perfectly, and Jordana watched with great pride as the supervisor for the Central Pacific shook hands with Jack Casement.

"I suppose I should own up to be being beaten," Casement told Crocker. "You've done a wondrous thing here."

"Well, I'll not own up to it," said Dan Casement. "Mr. Durant, what say we have our own competition. My men can do twice this much."

Durant shook his head. "There isn't twice that much track left to be laid."

This still did not deter Casement. "Then let me tear up several miles. I know we can vindicate ourselves."

Durant actually appeared to be considering this for a moment, then shook his head. "No. They won fair and square. The point now is that we put the rest of this railroad together. Let us go back to Ogden and see to the work at hand."

Jordana enjoyed the banter of the men, then decided she'd had enough. She paused long enough to congratulate Charlie, then made her way down the track to where the tents had been assembled for those who needed housing for the night. Most of the other newspapermen were interviewing the workers who had laid the track that day, but Jordana already had plenty of information on them. Most were old friends by now.

Yawning and giving a wide stretch of her arms, Jordana relished the growing silence. Moonlight glinted dimly on the iron rails, giving an illuminated path for Jordana to follow back to the tents. She found herself wishing that Rich could have been there to see the competition. She wished, too, that her mother and father might have seen it as well. Going over the details in her mind, she didn't hear the man sneaking up beside her until he had already reached out to take hold of her arm.

With lightning-quick reflexes, she called upon her self-defense lessons and quickly flipped the man over her hip, dumping him on the ground in front of her.

THIRTY-ONE

"Good to see you again, Jordana," Rich O'Brian called from where he'd landed. "Nice technique you have. You're really going to have to teach it to me sometime."

"Rich?" She looked down at him with such an expression of shock that Rich couldn't help but laugh.

"When am I going to learn not to try to surprise you?" he asked wryly.

"At least you know I can take care of myself," she said rather impishly.

Grinning, he extended his hand. "Help me up, old friend."

She reached down and Rich took hold of her hand. Getting to his feet, he continued to hold on to her. "I wasn't at all sure it was you for nearly half the day. You were running from one end of the line to the other, and every time I tried to get close enough to talk to you, someone eyed me like I was there to thwart the competition."

"I looked for you, too," she said softly.

He rubbed her hand with his thumb. "You did?" He could feel her tremble and it made him smile. Reaching up, he pulled off her hat. "Oh, I'm so glad you didn't cut it all off again."

"You are?" she asked, seeming almost mesmerized. "I thought you liked it short."

"Short like this is okay," he replied, feeling less and less certain how to tell her why he'd really come.

They stood silent for several minutes until finally Jordana pointed toward the tents. "That's where I'm sleeping . . . uh . . . we could . . . I mean," she paused, seeming to realize what she'd implied. "We could sit outside and talk," she added quickly. "That is . . . if you . . . if you want to."

"All right, but you should know one thing."

She looked up at him, her eyes wide in anticipation. "What?"

"I'm in a very serious mood."

"Oh." She looked at him oddly for a moment. "Serious good or serious bad?"

"That all depends," he replied.

"On what?"

"You."

She said nothing more, but turned and walked toward the tents. Rich had no other choice but to follow after her. He only hoped that he hadn't frightened her too much with his words and tone of voice.

"Hey, Preacher," a man called out from a nearby group of men, "looks like you need a haircut. You just come on over when you're ready and I'll do it up for ya."

"Thanks," Jordana replied. "I'll think about it."

"No, you won't," Rich muttered softly.

Jordana turned around and met his smiling face. "Rich, you'll completely give away my cover."

"Jordana Baldwin, if you don't think that a good half of these men haven't already figured out that you're a woman, then you've got another think coming. They tolerate you because . . ." He fell silent because she was looking at him in such a way that his heart was near to overflowing with love for her. She seemed so small all of a sudden. So fragile and lovely, like a delicate desert flower, and yet only moments ago she'd landed him on his backside without any warning at all.

She tucked her hair back under her hat and walked over to a tent that had been pitched away from most of the others. "You were saying?" she questioned as she plopped down on the ground.

Rich joined her before attempting to answer. "They tolerate you because you're a nice person to be around."

"A nice person, eh?"

"Exactly," Rich said, watching her carefully. "I mean, that's what I figured a long time ago. Despite your penchant for wounding me, I've grown rather accustomed to having you around."

She chuckled and the tension eased a bit. "Rather like the bumblebee with its stinger, eh?"

Rich remembered the pin he'd given her and nodded. "Sort of like that."

"So what's this serious matter you have to discuss with me?" she asked him bluntly.

Rich was taken aback for a moment. He hadn't figured she'd just jump in like that, though he should have known better. Now he was hard pressed to remember how he'd planned it all out. "Well, to begin with, I . . . well . . . I missed your company once you'd left."

"That doesn't seem too serious."

Rich swallowed hard and looked at the ground. "It's more serious than you could imagine."

"Oh, I don't know. I can imagine quite a bit. I'm a writer, you know."

"And quite the artist," Rich added.

"How'd you know that?" she asked, eyeing him suspiciously.

"I found your journal with Montego. It was I who sent it to you. I saw your sketches there. I especially liked the one with Brenton and Caitlan working together. Looked so cozy and romantic."

Jordana shifted uncomfortably and looked up at the moon. "Oh, really? I don't suppose I remember that one as well as some of the others."

"Well, it certainly caught my attention," Rich replied. He watched her for a moment, not at all sure how to continue. Why should it be so hard to speak the truth? What was keeping him from just declaring how he felt? His promise to her, that's what. He'd promised he wouldn't be more than a friend and now he had to either deny himself or break that promise. "It's a lost cause," he muttered.

"What is?"

"Fighting this."

"Fighting what?" Jordana countered, causing Rich to lift his gaze to her face.

"You know very well what I'm talking about. I knew it was a lost cause to fight this, especially when after seeing you in breeches looking for all the world like some grubby railroad worker, you still made my heart race. You cut your hair off and dance with women, you flail knives at me and flip me onto the ground, and still I'm consumed with my thoughts and desires."

Jordana's face took on an expression that bordered on horror. At least that's what Rich was afraid it was. "What are you talking about?" she asked very slowly.

Rich got to his feet and began to pace. Glancing at a group of men playing cards not twenty feet away, he motioned to Jordana. "Come with me."

She followed him away from the tents and off to a distant outcropping of rock and sage. When he finally deemed them to have enough privacy, Rich tried again to explain. "That kiss back in Laramie . . . well . . . it's just that —"

"It's just that what?" she prompted, suddenly seeming to take great interest in his words.

Rich pushed his hand back through his hair in frustration. "Well, it changed things." He could feel his chest grow tight. How in the world was he ever going to say all he was thinking — all that he felt?

"I thought we decided it was just a case of nerves," Jordana replied, her voice not sounding at all sure.

"Well, it wasn't just that," Rich answered

and shook his head. "Look, I don't know what to say. I want to be with you, Jordana, not just part of the time, but all of the time. I want to protect you, but you obviously don't need protecting. I want to be a friend to you, but then we end up kissing. I want to make you happy, but I don't know how to do that either, except to avoid any kind of matrimonial entanglements." She was looking at him very oddly, and finally Rich gave up and began pacing. "I just can't go on like this," he added. "I know I made you a promise about just being friends, but I feel like everything changed with that kiss."

Jordana nodded. "I know. It changed for me as well, and now I don't want to be friends with you anymore."

The words so startled Rich that he stopped pacing. "What? What are you saying?" He thought his heart would break if she told him good-bye, and yet he felt certain that this was exactly what she would say.

"I'm saying that I agree with you. The kiss changed my mind on us being just friends," Jordana replied.

"But . . . I mean . . ."

She lifted her slim hand to push back the hair that had fallen across his forehead. Just then the wind caught the brim of her hat and sent it flying off her head. She went after the hat, but rather than put it on her head, she simply held it at her side. Her own hair fell down around her face and with a mischievous grin, she shook it out and said, "I might as well look a little bit like a young lady. That way maybe it will help with what I have to say to you." She moved toward him and Rich backed up a step. "Better yet, maybe it will help you with your response."

"I don't understand," Rich said. He longed only to hold her, to touch her, and she was driving him mad. Why couldn't she see that her nearness was making a fool out of him? He was babbling one minute and stammering the next. What kind of hold did she have on him that she could evoke such a response?

"I don't want to be friends," she reiterated, again moving toward him. "I want more. I want to be your wife and your friend. I want to wake up with you in the morning and go to sleep with you at night. And I want to spend all the time in between with you . . . well, maybe just most of the time in between," she said with a grin. "Do you understand what I'm saying?"

Rich felt the wind go out from him. Had he heard her correctly? His mouth dropped open in amazement. Finally he found his voice. "Miss Baldwin, are you proposing marriage to me?" She was only inches away.

She bit at her lip and stepped back as though he'd somehow slapped her with his words. Uncertainty crossed her expression. "I . . . well . . . like we said, the kiss," she stammered, then seemed to compose herself. "Look, you may never want to marry me. You may never want to marry anyone, but things have changed. I've fallen in love with you, and I know that was probably foolish, but I couldn't help it," she babbled uncontrollably. She looked up at him with a helpless kind of shrug. "I always go after what I want. And, while I know our agreement, I also know I was the one to set it in place. I only wanted friendship. I wanted you to prove to me that men and women could just be friends, and now I've gone and messed it all up. But . . . well . . . it's your own fault. You kissed me and —"

"And I'm gonna kiss you again," Rich said, pulling her into his arms. Without waiting for further comment, he bent down and touched his lips gently to hers. She sighed against him and wrapped her arms around his neck, leaving him little doubt of her pleasure in his actions.

Rich lost himself in the moment, and all he knew was his love for this woman. This sweet, overwhelming sensation of being washed away in a flood of passion and happiness. "I love you," he whispered as he let his lips trail along her cheek. She was grubby and dirty, but he'd never wanted her more than he did just now. No matter what happened, he couldn't let her get away from him again.

"Oh, Rich, I love you," she said, gazing up with such longing that Rich thought they'd both be better off to return to camp. He let go of her rather abruptly, then reached back out to take hold of her hand. "Come on. I know if I hang around here any longer, you're going to put me in danger again."

Her look of confusion was quickly replaced with a grin of understanding. "You'd just better watch yourself, Mr. O'Brian. I believe you've met your match."

"Oh, I'm quite certain of that," he replied. "And just so you know it, the answer is yes. I'll marry you. God knows there's probably not another man around who could handle the job. Besides, you've already got me halfway broken in."

She giggled out loud. "I know. I know. And you have the scars to prove it."

THIRTY-TWO

"But you can't mean it, Charlie!" Jordana declared. "You have to be there when they drive the last spike in at Promontory."

Charlie smiled and shook his head. "I'm going to help Mark Hopkins run the ceremonies in Sacramento. We mustn't disappoint our own people, those who helped us to get this thing started in the first place. We have to include them. We would never have made it without their support, and they deserve to have some fun as well."

"But, Charlie, you've worked so hard to make this happen," Jordana replied. "I feel like we've been friends forever, and yet I know it's just because of all that we've been through together. I can't imagine your not being there. Why, even my parents have wired and they will be there. In fact, I believe my mother would have hired her own private coach if she could not have found a seat on the Union Pacific train.

She's so excited about this railroad, my father can hardly control her."

"Sounds like you and your mother favor each other considerably," Charlie chuckled, and the warmth in his eyes showed he meant the words fondly. The train whistle sounded outside and Charlie instantly put away his books. "I have a bit of a surprise for you on the train. Why don't you come along with me and see what it is?"

Jordana rose and smoothed the lines of her simple calico gown. She had styled her rather unruly hair by simply using a ribbon as a band to hold it back away from her face.

"You looked decent as a young man," Charlie said, pulling on his coat, "but you look even better as a young woman."

Jordana gave her shawl a coy flourish. "Well, I must say, dressing this way gets me a great deal more attention."

"I'll just bet it does!" Charlie opened the door for her. "But what about that Mr. O'Brian? I doubt he'd want you getting too much attention in his absence."

"Well, he won't be absent for long. He just has a few loose ends to tie up with General Dodge and then he'll be back to share in the celebration with my folks and me."

Jordana stepped down from Charlie's private railcar, which was parked on a siding at the Ogden station, and allowed him to help her across the tracks to where the afternoon train was coming in from the West. She had no idea what Charlie had in mind but hoped it wouldn't involve too much on her part.

Glancing up, Jordana saw Brenton step down from one of the passenger cars. Caitlan was right behind him, her pregnancy quite evident.

"Brenton! Caitlan!" she squealed in delight, hurrying to cross the remaining distance, and was soon embraced by her brother. "Charlie said he had a surprise and this is just grand."

"Oh, but we're not the only part of it," Caitlan offered.

Jordana turned from Brenton's embrace just in time to see Kiernan step down from the train holding baby James. Victoria, in a lovely gown of mauve and gold, waited for Kiernan to offer his hand before also stepping onto the depot platform.

"Oh, Charlie! This is wonderful! Now we shall all be together," Jordana said with great joy.

"And you can share your news with them." Charlie gave her a wink.

Jordana shook her head and poked Charlie in the ribs. "It's a surprise, Charlie."

They all laughed at her unladylike response.

"So when do Mother and Father arrive? And where will we meet them?" Brenton asked anxiously.

"They're coming out immediately," Jordana replied. "And they're bringing Amelia and Nicholas. Although how they ever managed to pull Amelia away from her beau is beyond me."

"I can arrange for your folks to be picked up and brought here," Charlie stated with a broad smile. "I don't want them celebrating on the wrong side, after all."

"That would be grand, Charlie. But just remember, there won't be a wrong side after the eighth of May." Jordana still couldn't believe that soon she'd be seeing all of her family in one place. "The whole idea of this railroad is to be a binding tie to pull the country together. We're celebrating unity, after all."

"It should definitely be a celebration to end them all," said Brenton.

"Yes, and Charlie refuses to be there. He feels he owes the people of Sacramento some sort of party." Jordana assumed a mock pout. She quickly grinned, however, and gave Charlie a wink. "But I guess I can forgive him. After all, he's brought you all here to me, and nothing could have been nicer."

When they tired of chatting on the platform and Caitlan appeared to need a rest, Charlie escorted them all to his private car. "I'm not taking this one back. I'll leave it here so that you and your family can enjoy it. There are plenty of beds and a nice sitting room and office. You should have it much better here than in the makeshift hotels they're putting together."

"Oh, Charlie, how thoughtful." Jordana leaned up and kissed the older man's cheek.

"Now you'd best not do too much of that," Charlie told her. "Mrs. Crocker is a mighty jealous woman."

"And with good cause," Jordana replied. "Men like you don't come along every day."

"And for that, the railroad and half the population of California are most grateful," Kiernan added.

After the laughter had died down and the party made their way inside to the comfort of Charlie's private car, the family was able to sit and share all the news.

"The baby is to come sometime in June," Caitlan replied when Jordana inquired of her condition. "I'm supposin' there are those who will question me bein' seen in public in my condition, but I had to come."

"Of course you did," Jordana assured her sister-in-law. "Expectant mothers can't just hole up in some hiding place until they deliver. What a convoluted notion! Now, tell me all about your plans for building a big house in Sacramento."

"Our plans have changed," Brenton replied before Caitlan could answer. "We're going back to New York with Mother and Father. Caitlan would like to see something of our home in Baltimore, and we thought it might be nice if she had the baby where Mother could be nearby."

"Aye, especially since she missed out on seein' little Jimmy when he was born," Caitlan offered.

"New York can be painfully hot in the summer and freezing cold in the winter," Jordana reminded. "You'd best prepare yourself for almost anything."

"I'll keep that in mind," Caitlan replied.

"I might as well tell you that Kiernan and I are going to accompany them as well," Victoria said, smiling with pure admiration at her husband. "Kiernan feels we deserve the visit, and besides, he wants to check out some supply houses that might be able to offer him the goods he needs for his new furniture business."

Jordana felt rather deflated. It wasn't that

479

anything had really changed for her, but suddenly everyone had plans that didn't include her at all. But wasn't that how she wanted it? But then she reminded herself that she *did* have plans. Very special ones!

"Well, I suppose I should tell you my news as well . . . although I had thought to wait until Mother and Father arrived," Jordana said hesitantly.

"What is it?" Brenton asked first.

"Yes, tell us now," Victoria pressed.

Jordana drew a deep breath. "I plan to stay out here — somewhere. I'm not entirely sure where I'll be or for how long." She saw their expressions take on a worried look. "However, you'll be happy to know that I do not plan to remain alone. I've considered all the counsel everyone has given me, and I believe I would be better off having someone with me all the time. Someone who could afford me a little extra protection. Someone who could help me not to feel quite so lonely."

"What are you saying?" Brenton questioned.

Caitlan laughed. "She's saying she's finally going to marry Captain O'Brian."

Jordana grinned. "You are always so intuitive, Caitlan."

"That's your news?" Brenton asked. "Is it

480

really true?"

"You and Mr. O'Brian are marrying?" Victoria half questioned, half exclaimed.

Kiernan looked at her with a knowing nod, and Jordana was extremely gratified by the obvious approval in their eyes.

"Yes," she finally replied. "That's my news. Rich and I are going to be married right away. Hopefully before everyone goes east."

"Oh, but won't you come back to New York with us?" Victoria asked. "Just think of it. Mother could have such a grand time giving you a proper wedding."

"Aye, and ya could be there for the baby's comin'," Caitlan added.

"Mother and Father would probably enjoy that a great deal," Brenton encouraged.

Only Kiernan remained silent and Jordana was glad for that. She had no heart for telling them how much she despised the East and all its conventions. Not that the West wasn't setting up its own rules for society, but there were still places out here where she could get away from it all and be herself.

Realizing she'd hardly heard the continuation of the conversation around her, Jordana interjected, "I promise to think about what you've said. I know it would please Mother greatly if I were to let her plan a wedding for me." Suddenly she felt as though convention had settled upon her shoulders. Oh, why aren't you here, Rich, to make me feel better?

"They're here! They're here!" Victoria declared, peering out from Charlie's office window. "Mother and Father are coming this way, and look who's with them!"

Jordana's pen stopped its scratching, but she didn't look up from Charlie's desk. She had been writing out the details for the railroad ceremony that would take place the following day. There would be reporters galore and photographers, and she wanted to have her story ready for the post as soon as the deed was actually done.

Her parents were finally here, but she now experienced a sudden shyness. What would they think about her engagement? What would they think about Rich? All at once her heart started pounding and her legs couldn't move. This was quite silly. It was only her parents, after all. But she had changed so much since last seeing them.

"I'll be there in a minute," she told Victoria, trying to calm herself. She just didn't want to go to pieces the instant she laid eyes on them.

"Well, all right, suit yourself," Jordana

barely heard her sister reply. "But I'm certain you'll be sorry."

"Don't be a fussbudget," Jordana said. "It'll only take a second, and the rest of you won't even be through with saying hello and showing off the baby. I'll be right there."

She heard Victoria leave the room, then felt a surge of annoyance when someone knocked on the office door. "I'll be right there," she said, the irritation in her voice evident.

"So that's how it's to be," Rich answered instead of Victoria.

Jordana looked up in disbelief and found him leaning casually against the doorframe. "I didn't know you were coming!" she exclaimed. She jumped up and crossed the room, meeting him in the middle as he joined her. He appeared as eager to be in her arms as she was to be in his. "Oh, I've missed you!" Was it possible that he was actually better looking than before? She felt her heart skip a beat. This was the passion and desire her mother had always talked of finding in the man you loved. Her mother had told her many times that marrying for comfort was all well and fine, but marrying a man who could light the fires of your heart and keep the blaze burning throughout the ages was better than all the silver and gold in the world.

He grinned. "You're looking at me rather queerly, Miss Baldwin. You seem surprised. I hope you haven't changed your mind about our plans for the future."

"Not a chance, Captain O'Brian. You'll not rid yourself of me that easily. I just wondered how in the world you'd come to be here. It's almost as if I conjured you from my lonely dreams."

Rich tightened his hold on her, his expression betraying his pleasure at her words. "Charlie wired me about your folks, and so I met them en route and accompanied them here. I even had the opportunity to ask your father for your hand."

"You what?" Jordana questioned in surprise. "You know that he doesn't hold with that old-fashioned notion. He wants his children to marry for love and not for —"

Rich put a finger to her lips. "He said it would be fine by him."

Jordana leaned against him and kissed his finger. "Well then, I suppose it's all right." She relaxed considerably, realizing she no longer had to worry about her parents' approval. Rich had taken care of it for her!

"Give me a quick kiss and then I shall let you go greet your folks," Rich commanded.

Jordana thought about resisting his demand, but then decided against it. It would simply break her heart if she refused him. Besides, he gave into her and let her have her way so often it wouldn't hurt for her to do the same for a change. She lifted her face to his and welcomed his kiss. After several moments of breathless bliss, she murmured, "I don't think that would qualify as quick."

He chuckled low and gave her a roguish grin. "In O'Brian time, as far as kisses are concerned, that was quick."

"Where's Jordana!" they heard Carolina Baldwin call from the other room.

"I'm in here, Mother!" Jordana replied. "Come on, let's join them."

"Oh, there is some serious business we need to attend to as soon as possible," Rich told Jordana as they walked to the door.

"What?"

"It would appear from news given me by General Dodge that Thomas Durant has been kidnapped en route to Promontory."

It was hard to sit through the reunion with her family, even though it had been some time since Jordana had last seen everyone. Amelia had grown into a ravishing beauty, and Nicholas was all talk of college in England and his plans for the future.

"You simply must come back to New

York," Amelia told Jordana. "There are so many people I want to introduce you to and so much fun to be had. Why, there are parties nearly every night during the season and my debut will be this summer. You have to be there."

"Surely you can't be preparing to celebrate your sixteenth birthday," Jordana replied with a glance at Rich. He was deep in conversation with Brenton and their father and seemed totally at ease. How could he just dump the news of Durant's kidnapping on her like that and then seemingly forget all about it?

"It would be rather nice to have you back with us," Carolina said softly, hesitantly. "And Amelia's party will come in June on her birthday, and you could help me with the arrangements. Why, you haven't even seen the house in New York."

"No, I haven't," Jordana agreed.

"And now that you're getting married — well, we could have quite the party for you both."

"Not just a party, Mother. We should have a grand wedding for Jordana."

Jordana saw so much of Victoria in Amelia, though they were not related at all by blood.

"That's exactly what I told her," Victoria

said, as if privy to Jordana's silent observation. She handed the baby to Carolina. "Here, he's all dry and happy now."

Carolina cooed at her grandson and cuddled him close. "I'm sure you don't have to decide such a thing right now. After all, I know you have a great deal on your mind for tomorrow's celebration."

Jordana nodded, but the feeling of being trapped continued to grow. What if they all forced her back to New York and then demanded she stay? What if something happened and she found it impossible to leave? What if Rich loved it there and wanted to stay? How would she ever return to her own life and regain her freedom? She'd be trapped and hopelessly given over to the conformity of genteel society. And marriage.

Suddenly the room grew unaccountably hot. "I think I need a little air." Jordana fanned her hand before her face. "I'm going to step outside."

"Don't go too far," Carolina said. "It might be dangerous."

Jordana grinned but said nothing. She didn't have to. Caitlan was already filling Carolina in on some of her exploits, and Jordana thought it the perfect opportunity to escape. Bless Caitlan anyway, she always seemed to know just the right thing to do.

The May evening was warm but breezy. Jordana walked away from the siding track where Charlie's car continued to rest. She felt a growing urgency to don breeches and a work shirt and make her way to the nearest livery. What would they all think if she simply disappeared?

"Running away?" Rich asked softly as he came up behind her.

"Yes," she replied. "Yes, I am."

He turned her tenderly and gave her a doleful look. "From me too?"

"You don't want to be with me right now," Jordana said, shaking her head. "I'm not fit company."

He smiled and gently rubbed her cheek with the back of his fingers. "I think you're marvelous company."

"Not now. I'm afraid I probably rank somewhere down below Troublesome."

Rich laughed out loud. "That is impossible. Now, why don't you come over here and tell me what's going on?" He pulled her along to where a freight wagon sat empty and waiting for the next train. Lifting her up, he placed her on the wagon bed and leaned over to kiss her lightly on the nose. "Now tell me everything."

Jordana felt herself close to tears. Why was this happening to her? "It's just that I feel so trapped."

"By me?" he asked solemnly, his expression quickly showing her words had hurt him.

"No, not you," she replied. "By them. My family. They all want me to go with them after the celebration and visit in New York for the summer. In fact, I believe Mother would love nothing better than to throw us a wedding of grand proportion."

"And you wouldn't like that?" Rich asked gently.

"I don't know what I would like," Jordana admitted. "But I do know what I despise and that's the conventions of proper society. Oh, Rich, I can't be the dainty lady serving tea that everyone is going to expect me to be."

"I don't expect that."

"Oh, but you might. Then you might change your mind and decide you'd like a more conventional wife. Then you might decide we needed to live there and be prim and proper like the rest of New York."

Rich let out a roar of laughter. "Oh, Jordana, you can't mean it."

She frowned and tears welled in her eyes. "I do mean it. What if things change? I love traveling and doing new things. I want to explore the country and live in an unconventional way. Even if we marry and have children, I want the liberty to just strap them on my back like the Indians do and continue on my way."

"What do you mean 'if'?" Rich asked. "Are you having second thoughts about marrying me?"

"Never!" Jordana declared. Then she gave a sheepish shrug. "Perhaps just about marriage in general. It's so scary."

"Yes, it is. For me too. But I have a feeling that is exactly why God put us together. Only two independent souls like us could truly understand each other. I don't expect the road will be entirely smooth, but like this railroad, the benefits to the binding will far outweigh the difficulties."

Her lips twitched as she tried to smile. "Do you think so?"

"I am confident of it."

"I suppose an analogy to the railroad is apropos. I rather like it."

Rich placed his arm firmly around her shoulders. "Now, will you stop fretting about all of this? No one says you have to go east. Simply tell your family thank you for the invitation, and we'll get married right after the train ceremony as planned. Why, there's bound to be a preacher somewhere in the crowd." He reached into his pocket and pulled out a cloth.

"Oh, Rich, I'm so sorry for acting this way." She wiped at her lingering tears with the back of her hand.

"It's all right, sweetheart," he whispered and pushed her hands away. He dried her tears with his handkerchief.

Then another thought came to Jordana. "What about your own fears, Rich? What about having a wife out in the wilds where something bad might happen?"

Rich shrugged. "I figure that's the kind of thing I have to entrust to God. I believe with His help and your Chinese fighting skills, we ought to get along just fine."

Jordana laughed and opened her arms to embrace him. "Thank you for loving me — and, oh, for tolerating me, too."

"Yes, you are a real chore," he said with a dramatic sigh. "But it's a chore I think I can come to live with."

"You'd better. I plan to be around for a long, long time."

"I'm holding you to that," he whispered before kissing her.

Jordana's peace returned, and she knew one way or another it would all work out just fine. Laying her head on Rich's shoulder, she believed she could finally put her issues and worries to rest. With Rich at her side, there wasn't much she couldn't face.

"It might actually be fun to see New York with you. I'd even get dressed up — maybe even dance with you," Rich commented.

Jordana pushed him away. "I'm not sure I want to dance with you, Rich O'Brian. You are not very discriminating with your dance partners."

"If you're referring to Miss Montego, just remember you danced with her, too."

Jordana's smile quickly faded. "I wish I could have kept her from dying."

"You can't live in regrets, Jordana. Only God can give or take a life, remember?"

"Yes, I know that's true. It's just that . . ." She was on the verge of becoming despondent again.

"Now, I believe we were talking about New York," he said, pushing aside her gloomy thoughts. He seemed to understand her better than she understood herself. "A wedding, I believe, was mentioned."

"Well, Mother's eyes did light up when we talked of letting her plan a wedding," Jordana said thoughtfully. "I suppose we could give it a try, but if you start acting all conventional and rotten, then I'm catching the first westbound train, no matter whose line I have to get a ticket on."

Rich laughed. "It's a deal."

It was then that Jordana remembered Thomas Durant. "Oh, goodness, what in the world is going on with Mr. Durant? You said he'd been kidnapped."

Now Rich grew sober. "Well, it seems Montego has many, many friends and that Durant owed all of them a great deal of money. The kidnapping took place with several men storming the train he was on. They separated his car from the rest of the passengers coming to the celebration and demanded that Durant pay up over two hundred thousand dollars or they wouldn't release him."

"But the celebration is tomorrow."

"Not anymore," Rich told her. "They've had to postpone it until this is settled. I'm heading back into Ogden tonight to see if I can help Dodge get the matter resolved."

"I'm going with you." Jordana jumped down from the wagon.

"No, you stay here with your family. There's nothing you can do," Rich responded.

Putting her hands to her hips, Jordana eyed him sternly. "I beg your pardon?"

Rich shook his head. "No, Jordana. There's no need for you to go."

For a brief moment it seemed a battle of wills was impending. Then Jordana realized brute force was out of the question and allowed her demeanor to change. She recalled moments observing her sister when Victoria would get her way with Kiernan by turning on her feminine charm. It was worth a try. After all, she certainly had never used it on Rich before. Maybe the shock of it alone would push him into acquiescence. Slowly she lowered her arms and joined her hands together. Hoping that she looked horribly disappointed and completely subservient, she lowered her face and raised her eyes just enough to catch Rich's expression.

"Please, Rich?"

"No."

She stepped forward and ran her hand up his arm bringing it to rest alongside his neck. Toying with his hair, then letting her fingers trail designs around his ear, she pouted. "Please?"

He studied her for a moment and sighed. Eyes lifted toward the night skies, he said, "Dear Lord, what have I gotten myself into here? You send me a woman who can melt my heart in a single glance and at the same time irritate me until I want to throw her over my knee."

Jordana stretched up on tiptoes as she drew closer. "I promise to be good," she murmured against his mouth.

Lowering his head, Rich held her tight. "Maybe you can convince me," he said in a voice that clearly betrayed surrender.

She kissed him lightly and smiled. "I'm figuring that I can."

She kissed him again, this time longer. "In fact, I'm certain of it."

She wasn't entirely sure, but she would have sworn she heard him murmur, "Just don't hurt me," right before his mouth covered her own. Perhaps feminine powers of persuasion held merit after all. She would have to practice them more often.

THIRTY-THREE

"If it were up to me," Dodge said gruffly, "I'd leave Durant to his fate. Considering all the times he changed the route on me, pulling his weight and rewriting the plans and refusing to hear me out, I'd say he's getting what he deserves."

"I thought you appeared to be enjoying this entirely too much." Rich grinned, leaning back in his chair in the office Dodge had commandeered in Ogden to coordinate the final railroad details.

"Still, there is the celebration to consider," Jordana said. "How will it look to the public if a man with Durant's prestige can't even ride the rails west without fear of being taken hostage?"

"Miss Baldwin has a good point, and it's the same conclusion I already came to hours ago. That's why I requested the army at Fort Bridger to dispatch some three hundred soldiers to where they are holding Durant.

We've told the people it's because of the heavy rains in the Wasatch Mountains and western Wyoming. And that much is true. The downpours have caused all manner of trouble. It will buy us some time."

"But how much?" Rich asked.

Dodge shook his head. "Hopefully, enough. The bad thing is, those men have a valid argument. Durant has not been paying his debts. He has little trouble spending UP dividend money whether earned or not, but he is quite behind in paying the contractors and other workers for the UP."

"That's why I work for you instead of him," Rich replied, smiling. "Still, we have to find a way to put this to an end. The plans for this were written up by Montego. You have the proof you need to see him put away for a long time."

"True enough." Dodge looked past Rich and Jordana as if studying the wall behind them. "I hate to admit this, but I almost wonder if Durant isn't in on this."

"How so?" Rich questioned.

"Well, it's just the kind of stunt he would pull in cooperation with someone like Montego. Knowing he couldn't really get hurt, he might arrange for this kind of action in order to rally up enough funds to help out his friends. I know it sounds scandalous to suggest such a thing, but I really wouldn't put it past him."

A knock at the door drew their immediate attention. "Excuse me, sir," a young man in civilian clothes interrupted. "I have a telegram here that you need to see immediately."

"Very well," Dodge replied. He took up the message and read it silently. Jordana watched his expression change from concern to anger. "It seems our original request to Fort Bridger was intercepted by the same group holding Durant. They tell me here they will create a general strike from Ogden to Omaha if I don't find a way to force Durant to meet their demands immediately."

"Do you have that kind of power — that kind of money?" Rich asked.

"No, but the president of this company does and so do other board members. Send this wire to Boston," Dodge told the messenger. He began writing furiously on a piece of paper and thrust it into the man's hands. "Do it quickly."

Word rapidly spread that the celebration at Promontory was to be delayed until May the tenth. Leland Stanford, one of many officials representing the Central Pacific at Promontory, quickly wired Charlie to hold off on the Sacramento celebration. Word came back, however, that Charlie could hardly stave off the festivities when they were due to occur that very day. The citizens of Sacramento and San Francisco had amassed for a party, and Charlie would not refuse them. Stanford understood but realized it would hardly be official until the last spike was actually driven into the line.

The conclusion of Durant's kidnapping was rather anticlimactic, and considering that someone might actually have been hurt, Rich and Jordana were glad for this result. As soon as they heard that UP President Ames had supplied the money to free Durant, and that the man was actually on his way to Promontory once again, Jordana and Rich made their way back to just west of the Promontory celebration point. Here, Charlie's private car had been moved up and positioned nearby to allow Jordana's family to enjoy the festivities in luxury. Of course, Leland Stanford had his own private car behind theirs, along with a couple of other luxury cars. It was like a rolling hotel positioned on the side track of what was to become the country's most famous railroad. Nearby and running for some distance down the UP side of the track, fourteen saloon tents had been erected to sell all manner of libations and ease the boredom of waiting for the Durant party to finally show up. Otherwise, in spite of the growing crowd, the land was harsh and desolate. In the distance, patches of snow hung on the Promontory Mountains and lent a rather scenic backdrop to the barren land, but beyond this to commend it, it seemed a poor location for such a festive occasion.

Jordana and Rich took the opportunity afforded by the delay to enjoy quiet moments of conversation with Carolina and James. Brenton and Caitlan had dismissed themselves from breakfast to move from camp to camp taking photographs of important members of the celebration. And seeing that Rich and Jordana could use the time alone with Carolina and James, Kiernan and Victoria took Nicholas and Amelia and baby James and went off to visit old friends along the line.

"We've decided to let you throw us a wedding," Jordana told her mother after everyone else had gone. She glanced nervously at Rich, who simply squeezed her hand reassuringly. "We can stay through the summer, but no longer than that. We have other plans for exploring, and we'll need to be on our way before the winter weather sets in."

Carolina smiled and looked at James with

such obvious joy that Jordana was glad for the decision she'd made. "We will have a fine time of it," she told her daughter. "June will make the perfect time for a wedding."

"June?" Jordana looked at Rich. "I don't think we want to wait that long."

"But it's already the ninth of May. By the time we return home and get the plans together —"

"Your mother's probably right," Rich stated, glancing at Jordana with sympathy but also with a resigned shrug. "June is just a few weeks away."

"We could have the wedding the day after Amelia's coming out," Carolina suggested. "That way, those who have traveled to attend will still be on hand to celebrate with you as well."

Jordana sighed. It seemed a small concession. "June the fifth?"

"That sounds like a good date," James said, winking at his daughter. "It's a Saturday and that will allow for an all-day celebration. You'll see. The time will fairly fly. Especially with your mother involved. Why, she'll have you all over town getting a gown made and arranging for flowers and such."

"Your father is right, Jordana. The time will fly and then we'll have the rest of our lives together."

Jordana knew without a doubt that he spoke the truth. He would keep this promise to her if nothing else. He knew her heart in the matter and knew how desperately important it was for her to feel secure in their plans. God had known exactly the right person to send into her life. Not a G. W. Vanderbilt, who would expect her to keep a proper house and raise children in a proper society, and not a Damon Chittenden, who would parade her about as though she had been a prize to be won. No, Rich would lead the way through the wilderness, then step aside and let her have a go at it. But mostly he would walk at her side, needing and wanting for her to be his partner in everything.

"June fifth sounds just right," she finally said, bestowing a smile upon her parents. "And I know it will be perfect, because you will all be there."

But Monday, May 10, was the first celebration to concern themselves with. The closing of the line at Promontory Point was clearly heralded as the event of the decade. Gone were the images of a wartorn country, which only a brief five years earlier had seen some of its bloodiest and fiercest battles. Gone were the concerns and prejudices, at least for the moment, as to whether Irish or black, Chinese or red man, had contributed more to see this project put through. Now all that mattered was that the country was united.

The morning dawned bright and chilly. There was even a thin layer of ice on the puddles near the track, and almost everyone went about in their coats and wraps. An American flag was quickly hoisted up the top of the nearest telegraph pole, and the day's celebration was put into motion. Workmen quickly assembled to put the finishing touches on the line.

The last two rails lay ready beside the grading. All of the ties were in place with the exception of one space, which had been left for the eight-foot length of polished laurel wood that would be used for the ceremony. The anxiety and excitement of the crowd built as everyone collected together to watch history being made.

Jordana stood nearby with Rich and her parents. Amelia and Nicholas chatted amiably about their adventures in the western wilderness, but Jordana barely heard any of the conversation. She felt as though this railroad was as much a part of her life as it was for any other person in attendance. She had been connected to it since the early years, sitting in privileged conversations among men of power, riding with the survey teams, and interviewing the workers. She'd accompanied her brother to photograph the various accomplishments along the line, and she'd attended the funerals of men who had given their lives to bridge the country together.

UP locomotive No. 119, a brand-new coal-burning engine with a long, slender smokestack, approached very closely, pulling the two passenger cars that housed the UP officials.

Rich glanced at his pocket watch. "Ten o'clock," he said as though Jordana had asked him.

Jordana watched as the engine slowed to a stop, and Durant, the source of all their latest delays, emerged in velvet coat and gaily-colored necktie. General Dodge followed him, looking much as he always did, sophisticated and gentlemanly. Other men emerged, some whom Jordana recognized, others who were strangers. They all looked rather like a wedding party awaiting the bride.

Then to everyone's amazement an argument broke out. It seemed no one had planned out how the ceremony should go. Jordana and Rich left their family and moved to where Dodge and Stanford stood amidst a bevy of arguing officials.

Mindless of her gender, Jordana demanded Stanford tell her what was happening. "Everyone is waiting and watching for something to be done," she said. "What is the delay?"

"Dodge believes Durant should be allowed to drive the final spike because the Union Pacific is a longer line," Stanford answered.

Rich looked at Dodge and then Jordana. "That makes sense. After all, the Central Pacific started laying track first. They might as well let the UP end it."

"It makes no sense at all," Jordana declared, standing up for Stanford's position. "They started first, and thus, logically, they should end it. And the only reason the UP has more track is because they refused to let the CP build at will."

"Well, you can have your ceremony without us!" one UP official huffed, glaring at Jordana contemptuously.

"Maybe we should," Jordana countered.

The audience continued to grow, and Jordana felt a growing frustration that she and Rich should be separated on the issue. It seemed a silly thing to argue, yet it was an important moment in the history of both railroads.

As they spoke, another UP train arrived, bringing with it three companies of the Twenty-First U.S. Infantry and a few men from the Thirty-Second Regiment who had been camping near Devil's Gate the night before. They had a band with them, as well as some of the officers' wives, and this seemed to liven up the occasion considerably. Jordana could only hope it would take the attention off the immediate crisis and let clear heads prevail.

Dodge was in deep discussion with Rich, who pointed toward the track and then to the ceremonial gold spikes and silver hammers.

Crossing her arms, she leaned over to Stanford and whispered, "I should have worn breeches for the occasion and then they would have listened to me as well."

He laughed out loud and put an arm around her shoulder. "My dear, when you speak, people listen despite your attire. You really should consider a future in business or politics."

Now it was Jordana's turn to laugh. "No, thank you," she said, shaking her head. "There are too many rules and regulations to abide by."

Just then Rich and Dodge came back with the other UP men. Rich pulled Jordana aside, while Dodge took Stanford in hand. The two men put their heads together as Rich leaned down to whisper in Jordana's ear.

"I don't know how we managed to put ourselves at odds again, but I think I've hit upon a solution."

"Oh, really?" She wasn't at all sure that his solution would meet her idea of a fair arrangement.

"There are two golden spikes and two hammers. There are two sides of the tie and holes have been drilled in each. Why not have them both drive the final spikes together?"

Jordana saw Leland Stanford shake Dodge's hand and nod enthusiastically. She grinned at her husband-to-be. "Ever the diplomat, my dear!"

He smiled. "I just did it to impress you."

She looped her arm through his. "Well, you already managed to do that some time ago."

With the issue settled, the ceremony proceeded. The Union Pacific's best Irish track layers moved the west rail into place and spiked it down, with exception to the last tie. Next it was the Central Pacific's turn. Using a gang of Chinese, clad in blue jackets and full-legged pants, the east rail was brought to the line.

"Now's the time! Take a shot!" someone yelled. The words were the signal for Brenton to take a picture, but the Chinese apparently knew only one meaning for the word "shot" and dropped the rail immediately. Fleeing into the crowd to escape danger, the men were stopped by the nearly hysterical crowd and brought back with the reassurance that they were in no danger. Finally the rail was in place.

By noon, the entire country was standing by via telegraph. Western Union had arranged to wire directly from Promontory to let those in the East know when the deed was done. And to everyone's amazement, they had even wired the tie and hammer so that when Leland Stanford drove his spike into the hole, a circuit would be closed and the signal would go out as far as Halifax, Nova Scotia, announcing the completion of America's transcontinental railroad.

At 12:27, Dr. John Todd, a Congregational pastor of great renown, stepped forward to offer a prayer. Jordana recognized the name, if not the man. He had authored over twenty moralistic, best-selling books, many of which had been translated into several languages. A good friend of Thomas Durant, he seemed quite inspired by the entire situation.

"What a place in which to pray!" he exclaimed.

The anxious crowd bowed for the two-minute prayer, but Jordana wondered if anyone truly had praying on their mind. She had thanked God already for the wonder and ingenuity that had brought them to this place, and she had no doubt that He must surely be sitting in heaven smiling down on them now, for the day was perfect and the moment pure exhilaration. Had they not been blessed by the hand of God, Jordana had no doubt they would never have made it this far.

Stanford and Durant each said a short piece, but Durant looked tired and clearly less than enthusiastic. Jordana wondered if he were still considering the money that had been given over in order to bring him to this place.

With a telegraph wire coiled around his silver hammer, Stanford poised over the spike. Durant too stood ready. Jordana reached for Rich's hand. The moment had come and her own excitement caused her to want to run up to the place and drive in the spike herself.

With nothing more needed than a simple tap on the spikes, Stanford and Durant joined the two railroads together. The transcontinental railroad was complete.

Cheers went up and the engine whistles blasted. The band kicked in amidst the wild celebration, and without warning, Rich gathered Jordana in his arms and silenced her joyous cries with a kiss. It was the best possible way to celebrate as far as Jordana was concerned.

Days later on the eastbound train to New York City, Jordana felt a strange sense of privilege and honor. She rode in complete luxury in the private train car that belonged to her father and mother. She had her family all around her and the man she loved at her side. There seemed no better place on earth to be, and yet as the train ate up the landscape and the wilderness passed into civilization and cities, Jordana felt a tugging in her heart.

Standing at the window, she pondered her choices and the life that awaited her. Soon she would be a married woman. She turned and studied Rich sitting across the car, a book resting idly in his lap as he also watched her. She smiled, and he set the book aside and came to stand beside her.

"You're awfully quiet tonight, Miss Baldwin. Plotting against me?"

Her smile broadened. "But of course. What else would I be about? From that first entanglement with Missouri bushwhackers and your famous blue bottle of painful medication, I have desired for nothing but revenge."

"You got me to marry you. Isn't that enough?" he teased.

She jabbed him hard in the ribs, startling Rich and causing him to let out a surprising howl of protest. The entire car of passengers looked up to see what the problem was.

"Is he all right?" Carolina questioned in concern.

Jordana nodded innocently at her mother's worried expression. "It's just a little something that bothers him from time to time. Something he picked up in his army days."

Everyone looked gravely concerned, except for Brenton, who immediately caught on to Jordana's meaning and gently nudged Caitlan and winked. Both began to laugh, and the more they laughed, the bigger Jordana's smile grew. Shaking their heads, Carolina and James went back to their conversations with the other children. Jordana leaned against the wall and smiled sweetly at her husband-to-be.

"You really should do something about

that affliction," Brenton called out between his chuckles.

Rich rubbed his sore ribs. "Oh, I intend to," he said, his look of pain quickly passing into a devilish grin. "You just wait. I have plans for you, Miss Baldwin."

"And I have plans for you, Captain O'Brian," she replied. "The most interesting and adventurous plans a man could ever hope for."

He reached out and touched her tenderly. His index finger traced her cheek gently as he stepped close. "I only hope God can keep up with us."

"Oh, but of course He will," she replied. "He'll be in the lead, remember?"

"Indeed He will!" Rich smiled. "Of course."

ABOUT THE AUTHORS

Judith Pella is the author of several historical fiction series, both on her own and in collaboration with Michael Phillips and Tracie Peterson. The extraordinary seven-book series, THE RUSSIANS, the first three written with Phillips, showcases her creativity and skill as a historian as well as a fiction writer. A Bachelor of Arts degree in social studies, along with a career in nursing and teaching, lend depth to her storytelling abilities, providing readers with memorable novels in a variety of genres. She and her family make their home in northern California.

Visit Judith's Web site at: http://members.aol.com/Pellabooks.

Tracie Peterson is a full-time writer who has authored over thirty-five books, both historical and contemporary fiction, including *Entangled* and *Framed,* contemporary love stories in the PORTRAITS series. She spent three years as a columnist for the *Kansas Christian* newspaper and is also a speaker/teacher for writers' conferences. She and her family make their home in Kansas.

Visit Tracie's Web site at: http://members.aol.com/tjpbooks.

The employees of Thorndike Press hope you have enjoyed this Large Print book. All our Thorndike and Wheeler Large Print titles are designed for easy reading, and all our books are made to last. Other Thorndike Press Large Print books are available at your library, through selected bookstores, or directly from us.

For information about titles, please call:

(800) 223-1244

or visit our Web site at:

www.gale.com/thorndike
www.gale.com/wheeler

To share your comments, please write:

Publisher
Thorndike Press
295 Kennedy Memorial Drive
Waterville, ME 04901